Janie Crouch h
This *USA TOD*
Mills & Boon R
on to a passion for romantic suspense as an adult. Janie
lives with her husband and four children overseas. She
enjoys travelling, long-distance running, movie watching,
knitting and adventure/obstacle racing. You can find out
more about her at janiecrouch.com

R. Barri Flowers is an award-winning author of crime,
thriller, mystery and romance fiction featuring
three-dimensional protagonists, riveting plots, unexpected
twists and turns, and heart-pounding climaxes. With an
expertise in true crime, serial killers, and characterising
dangerous offenders, he is perfectly suited for Mills &
Boon Heroes. Chemistry and conflict between the hero
and heroine, attention to detail, and incorporating the
very latest advances in criminal investigations are the
cornerstones of his romantic suspense fiction. Discover
more on popular social networks and Wikipedia.

Also by Janie Crouch

Calculated Risk
Security Risk
Constant Risk
Risk Everything
Daddy Defender
Protector's Instinct
Cease Fire

Also by R. Barri Flowers

The Big Island Killer
Captured on Kauai
Honolulu Cold Homicide
Chasing the Violet Killer

Discover more at millsandboon.co.uk

TEXAS BODYGUARD: LUKE

JANIE CROUCH

DANGER ON MAUI

R. BARRI FLOWERS

MILLS & BOON

First Published in Great Britain 2023
by Mills & Boon, an imprint of HarperCollins*Publishers* Ltd
1 London Bridge Street, London, SE1 9GF

www.harpercollins.co.uk

HarperCollins*Publishers*
Macken House, 39/40 Mayor Street Upper,
Dublin 1, D01 C9W8, Ireland

Texas Bodyguard: Luke © 2023 Janie Crouch
Danger on Maui © 2023 R. Barri Flowers

ISBN: 978-0-263-30713-9

0223

TEXAS BODYGUARD: LUKE

JANIE CROUCH

Since this book is about family, it's dedicated to Kiddo #1. What a talented, beautiful and resourceful woman you've become—you amaze me constantly. Thanks for making me a mom.

Prologue

Everything in this house was clean.

The kitchen had been recently mopped and wiped down to almost sparkling. The bedsheets were freshly laundered; soft, not scratchy like what he was used to. The shower was clean, his clothes were clean, the walls were clean. *Everything* was clean.

But Luke was dirty.

He'd been at the Pattersons' house for a month. Hadn't been hit or kicked by adults or the other three boys who lived here. Kids could sometimes be the most vicious, especially ones feeling like they needed to defend their territory. But not these guys.

Luke had his own room in this giant old house. He definitely hadn't had his own room at the group home. Or on the streets when he'd run away.

And his door locked. Clinton Patterson, the guy here with his wife, had shown Luke how to use the lock.

That was all great, but Luke still put the wooden desk chair under the doorknob every night. It wouldn't keep someone out, but it would at least warn him if someone was trying to get in.

The three other boys living here seemed okay. They were all foster kids, and all close to fourteen like Luke. Luke had seen one of them, Brax—*what a stupid name*—

last year for a few days at Skyline Park group home, before Luke had sneaked out again as soon as possible. By
the time the cops had caught him and brought him back,
Brax was gone.

The other two boys were okay, too. Weston was the
quiet Black kid. He hardly ever said anything, but always
let Luke play video games with him. The Hispanic kid,
Chance, was supersmart. Luke didn't mind him, either.

This place was way better than Skyline Park. It was
probably temporary—great foster parents like Clinton
and Sheila didn't keep kids like Luke long-term. They
adopted babies or sweet blonde angels who floated into
group homes for a few months and needed someone to
look out for them.

At least that was one good thing Luke had done.
Maybe a few months in the Patterson house was his reward for helping out the little girl.

He sat up in his bed and swung his legs over the side.
He was hungry. It was late and Clinton and Sheila were
old as dirt—like forty or something—and had probably
gone to bed. He could sneak some stuff like he'd been
doing every night.

Because if being here was a reward, he might as well
take advantage of it as long as he could. There were no
locks on the pantry or fridge here. There was so much,
no one even noticed that Luke was stealing food.

Going to bed *not* hungry had been nice, he wasn't
going to lie.

He got up, still fully dressed in sweatpants and a T-
shirt, and moved the chair from the doorknob. He padded down the stairs but stopped when he heard Clinton's
and Sheila's voices in the kitchen. He was about to turn
around and go back to his room when he realized they
were talking about him.

He sat on the stairs so he could listen. If they were going to kick him out, it was better if he knew ahead of time.

"I just don't feel like we're reaching him, Clint. Even Weston, with his abuse, didn't take this long for any sort of breakthrough."

"Give him time." Clinton's voice was much deeper. "He's been alone. On the streets and in that group home. We'll get it shut down, don't you worry. Now that social services knows exactly what's going on, they'll make changes."

Sheila gave a shuddery sigh. "I'm just glad he's here where we can keep him safe."

A few seconds later, Luke heard chopping.

"Nothing else bad is going to happen to him. Not while he's in our care." More chopping. "What are you doing?"

"I'm cutting some carrots and celery sticks."

Clinton let out a sigh. "It's after ten thirty at night. Why?"

The chopping resumed. "He comes in every night and gets food. I thought I'd at least make him something nutritious. These vegetables, and I made a sandwich, too. Maybe he'll eat that. I just want him to know he can have all the food he wants."

"I love you, Sheila Patterson." Clinton's chuckle was muffled, like he was saying it with his lips pressed against something. "Luke is going to love you, too. Give him time."

The chopping stopped. "He's been so hurt. He's been on his own too long. He tries to carry too much. He thinks we're going to dump him at the first opportunity. I don't know how—"

"Hey." He cut her off. "Luke is strong. With the right

guidance and nurturing, that strength will grow and flourish. He's a protector."

"But he's also just a boy. I want to hug him… I wish he would let me."

Luke couldn't even think of the last time an adult had hugged him. He had no idea what he would do if Sheila tried.

"He will. Someday. When he's ready. Now put that stuff away and let's go to bed."

Luke climbed the rest of the way down the stairs and hid in the dining room until Clinton and Sheila left the kitchen and went up the stairs to their bedroom. Then he slowly walked into the kitchen.

He opened the fridge and grabbed the plate with the sandwich and veggie sticks.

And it was the most delicious food he'd ever eaten.

Chapter One

Claire Wallace wasn't a hero. No one, by any stretch of the imagination, would ever call her one.

Heroes were outgoing and good-looking and quick to take action.

She, on the other hand, was a relatively slow-moving, rather plain, introverted loner who rarely talked to others unless that "person" happened to be her cat, Khan. Khan didn't tend to answer back, but that didn't bother Claire much. She still preferred his company over almost anyone else's.

Right now, she was sitting where she had sat almost every weekday for the past five years since she graduated from college—at her desk at Passage Digital, a software and phone app development company. Most of the people hired five years ago had moved up the corporate ladder at least a little bit. Claire still worked on the third floor with mostly newbs, fresh out of school with their first career-oriented job.

Not being promoted didn't bother her much, either. Getting promoted generally required regularly interacting with other people and getting noticed.

Did she have crippling social anxiety? Yep.

Did she plan to tackle that any time soon? Nope.

A hero she was not. So when her coworker/partial

boss, Julia Lindsey, emailed her an hour ago to be at her terminal at 10:00 a.m. and that it would make Claire a hero, Claire had been less than enthused. But here she was.

Maybe she wanted to offer Claire a promotion?

But promotions came with more responsibility, and more responsibility came with increased human interaction, and increased human interaction came with...

Claire pressed a hand to her suddenly tight chest. *Had someone turned up the office's heat?*

Taking a deep breath, she did her best to shake off the bad feelings.

The clock kept ticking. It was only 10:02, but Julia had always been early to meetings; her punctuality was one of the things Claire had appreciated the most while they were working on the camera phone filter app Julia had conceived.

"Hey." Claire reached a hand out toward the guy walking by her cubicle, not quite touching him.

Tom? Trent? Terrance?

Who knew? He'd been working there a couple of years, but the two of them had never spoken.

His eyebrows shot up in surprise. "Uh...yeah?"

Claire cleared her throat, swallowing past the lump. "Have you seen Julia?"

Tom-Trent-Terrance shook his head. "No. Sorry."

Claire nodded and slumped back into her chair. That had been hard enough. She wasn't asking anybody else.

Julia probably wanted to talk about their cell phone filter app, Gouda. The first version of the app had been hugely popular. The new version they'd been working on—with a much more complex facial recognition matrix—would be able to do so much more.

Teenagers all over the country would be beside themselves with excitement as they were able to morph their faces into all sorts of animals, celebrities and objects.

Or would've, until Julia halted all work on Gouda last week. There'd been no explanation given for the project's sudden stop, which was probably weird.

But, of course, Claire hadn't asked for reasons. She never did.

Today's meeting probably wasn't about the app, anyway. That was over. It was probably related to doughnuts or something. Passing treats out would make anyone an office hero.

Claire's phone beeped with a text from Julia.

Bring a portable drive to my office ASAP. Get on video chat.

Snatching up a portable drive, Claire did as instructed. Julia's office was at the other end of the open work space, nice and private, with windows and its own door—exactly the kind of isolated area Claire dreamed of having.

The office was empty, but the computer screen wasn't. Julia was already on the video chatting app the two of them had used regularly when working on their filter software. Her dark hair hung limp and tangled while bags underlined her eyes.

Taking a seat at the computer, Claire frowned. Julia was usually so polished.

"Are...are you okay?" Claire hated the way her voice shook.

"Listen, we don't have much time." Julia leaned closer to the screen. It was then that Claire recognized the board table in the background. Julia was in one of Passage Digital's executive offices.

Did that mean she'd been called in for a meeting with

CEO Vance Ballard? Was Gouda being green-lighted after all?

Julia licked her lips, seeming to not notice the hair falling in her face. "I don't know who I can trust, but I believe you're out of this entire mess. It's gotten more dangerous than I thought."

Claire's stomach hardened. "What are you talking about?"

"Gouda. Ballard is using it to steal identification and money…from kids. He's creating a database to utilize once these preteens become adults. He'll be able to access their phones and bank accounts."

They'd known this was a possibility with the camera software. Which was why they'd changed it—spent dozens of hours specifically designing it so the pictures that were taken weren't stored.

Claire let out a shaky, disbelieving laugh. "No. We took all those sensitive fields out—"

Julia shot a look over her shoulder at the door behind her. "And Ballard put them back in. Hook up the drive. I'm sending you everything that proves Ballard has knowledge about what the camera filters do."

Claire's hands shook so much that she wasn't sure if it was physically possible to connect the drive to the USB port.

"I don't think this is a good idea. We don't know what—"

"Claire, we don't have time. Do it. Hurry."

Gulping, Claire did as she was told. Oh yeah, she definitely wasn't hero material.

"We're going to have to go to law enforcement. Ballard doesn't know that I know, so we should be able to—" Julia sucked in a breath and glanced over her shoulder again.

The box with Julia's face went small on Claire's computer. This meant Julia had turned off the picture on her screen—Claire could see Julia, but nobody on the other end could see Claire.

Vance Ballard strode in with two big security guys behind him. "Trespassing in my office, Julia? That's a shame...it truly is."

The Passage Digital CEO's voice was smooth and calm—making it even more frightening. He patted his graying hair as he strolled closer to Julia and the camera. Claire had only spoken to the older man once, muttering an apology when she bumped into him in the hall.

"I just left some papers I needed to pick up. But you're right, I shouldn't have come in here without permission. I'm sorry." Julia sounded nervous and high-pitched—the opposite of Ballard.

"You left papers on my laptop?" Ballard raised an eyebrow. "*Convenient.*"

Claire looked over at the drive. Whatever Julia was sending was still transferring.

It didn't take long for Ballard to realize it, either.

"Oh, Julia, what have you done?" He shook his head and reached for his laptop.

The transfer to the drive stopped. Now Ballard's face took up most of the screen as he typed. At the very edge of what the camera captured, Claire could see Julia backing up until one of the large guards stopped her, holding her arm.

"Looks like you were transferring some pretty important data to your office," he tsked as he turned to glance at Julia.

"I'm not going to let you steal all these people's identities." Julia tried to jerk herself away from the guard, but he held her tight. "And these filters are mostly for children. There are even more laws against that."

Ballard shook his head. "You should've just minded your own business. I gave you the perfect out. Told you I'd take care of it. You should've looked the other way."

He nodded at the man holding Julia and almost before Claire could process what was happening, the man grabbed Julia by the head and snapped her neck.

Claire clapped her hand over her mouth as she watched Julia's body hit the ground, her eyes still open staring toward the laptop.

"Take care of this." Ballard gestured toward Julia. "Make sure the body is found far away from this building and that it looks like an accident."

Claire pressed a hand to her chest, her heart thumping uncontrollably against her shaking fingers.

Julia was dead.

Ballard had just had her killed.

"Go down to her office and get the drive she was sending the data to. Bring it back up here so I can look through it before destroying it."

Claire had to get out of here. She pressed the key on Julia's computer that downloaded the recorded interactions they'd had on each other's screens.

Including, in this case, Julia's murder.

It went straight onto the Passage Digital hard drive where Claire would be able to access it later.

But something happened on Ballard's end, tipping him off.

"What the hell? That bitch was recording this whole thing?" Claire jumped back as Ballard's face jerked right up to the camera. He couldn't see her, but it sure felt like he could.

"We need to get to her office right away. Damage control."

The monitor went blank.

Claire sat there, eyes wide, trying to draw enough air into her lungs. What should she do?

She could leave the drive, leave the footage of Julia's death on the system, and nobody would know Claire had been here at all. But as soon as Ballard got hold of the drive and footage, he would wipe them both completely clean—and all proof of his wrongdoing would be gone.

Claire only had two or three minutes tops before Ballard's men got here. If she was going to do something, she had to do it now.

Almost without conscious thought, her fingers were flying over the keyboard. She buried the footage of Julia's murder deep inside the Passage Digital system. When Ballard tried to access it, it would look like a corrupted file—damaged beyond utilization. No link to Claire.

But if she took the hard drive, Ballard would know someone had been here. He wouldn't know it was her, but how long would it take to figure it out? She stared at the drive, about twice the size and weight of a smartphone, still plugged into Julia's computer.

She couldn't let Ballard get away with this. With any of it.

She yanked the cord from the computer and grabbed the drive, then walked to the door. When she opened it, she expected to find the entire third floor staring at her, but no one so much as glanced in her direction.

Keeping her head down, she walked toward her desk. Nobody tried to engage her in any sort of conversation, as usual. Thank goodness.

She wasn't sure what to do. Should she stay at her desk? Wait stuff out? Should she move? Get out of the building?

A voice from her group foster home days floated back into her mind. A voice she trusted. *Luke.* He'd never let her down, always protected her.

If you can walk away rather than fight, then do that. Especially you, kitten.

He'd never walked away from a fight. But for her, his advice had been true then and was true now. She grabbed her purse from her desk drawer, tossed the drive inside it, and walked down the corridor between rows of cubicles.

All she could hear was the thrashing of her own heartbeat in her ears when she saw Ballard's men rush toward her. She couldn't let them take her. She knew what would happen if they did.

But they didn't even so much as glance at her, just brushed right by her, beelining for Julia's office.

Claire didn't look back, just kept a steady pace until she'd made it to the elevator. The doors couldn't open fast enough, and she rushed inside the moment there was sufficient space, pounding the garage-level button with more force than necessary. Once the elevator had begun its descent to the lowest level, she began to shake.

"Come on, come on," she murmured.

Just as Claire stepped out of the elevator, an announcement boomed over the loudspeaker that the building was being locked down due to a possible outside security threat.

She pushed through the elevator doors to the garage before they had a chance to seal her inside, racing toward her car. Once inside, Claire forced herself to drive at a reasonable speed out of the garage and onto the street.

Only after she'd made it onto the interstate did she finally feel like she could afford to breathe.

She'd made it out.

But she knew she was far from safe.

Chapter Two

Luke Patterson rubbed his face and stared at the tall stack of paperwork covering most of his desk. Closing his eyes, he took a long sip of coffee.

Unfortunately, when he cracked his lids, all the papers were still there.

He sighed. "Damn it."

San Antonio Security, the company he'd started with his brothers five years ago here in their hometown of San Antonio, really needed to hire an office manager. The business—everything from bodyguard-type work to situational awareness and weapons training to private investigation—had grown exponentially over the past few years. And rightfully so. Among the four of them, the Pattersons had years of background in both the military and law enforcement.

And they had all learned early on in their lives how the world really worked. How to reads situations and people, how to use people's weaknesses against them when needed.

Having to turn away clients was a good place for a business to be. Buried under paperwork...not so much. But if it meant Luke could work with the three people he trusted most in the world—his brothers—then he'd take it.

He grabbed the top sheet from the most offensively large pile, ignoring the chiming from the bell on the office's front door. Even if he wasn't in paperwork purgatory, no one would expect Luke to meet a client entering the office. Brax liked talking to people, which was why his office was near the front.

Luke was the opposite. He was too gruff, too impatient with people to deal with them on a regular basis. Even Weston, quiet as he was, or Chance, always inside his own head, was better suited to talking with clients than Luke was.

A tap on Luke's open office door a few moments later made him glance up. Brax stood there, a smile playing on the edges of his lips.

"Please tell me that's the fire marshal and we're all being ordered to abandon the building, saving me from this." Luke gestured to his desk.

Brax only smiled wider. Despite the fact that the two of them could be as different as night and day, they were closer than Luke had ever believed possible. Their time together in the army probably had a lot to do with it.

Then again, Luke was equally tight with Weston and Chance, who had skipped the military in favor of careers in law enforcement.

"Someone's here to see you." Brax tilted his head toward the front of the office. "She asked for you by name."

Luke sat straighter. "Who?"

No one ever asked for Luke, especially not women. He couldn't remember the last time he'd been on a date. He blamed it on the business growth, but the truth was he hadn't found a woman he'd felt like he could open up to—one who could even understand his past, much less accept it.

Brax glanced over his shoulder at someone down the short hall. "He said come on in."

"I didn't—"

The rest of the sentence died in Luke's throat as a delicate blonde woman walked into the office, her big blue eyes pinned on him.

He knew her immediately. "Claire."

"Luke." Only one word, but her voice trembled as if she barely had the strength to say his name.

Scratches covered her arms, and she held a big gray cat close to her chest.

The scene was painfully familiar. As a kid, she'd been scratched and bruised way too often, and she'd never gone anywhere without her stuffed cat.

"Looks like you got yourself a real cat." The words were out before Luke gave himself the chance to think them over.

He started to wince, but she smiled. "Yeah."

What now? A handshake? A hug?

Nothing seemed right for the girl who'd never been far from his mind, even though he hadn't seen her in fifteen years.

She loosened her hold on the giant cat, who jumped from her arms and landed gracefully on the chair in front of Luke's desk.

Stepping forward, Claire offered her hand. Her palm trembled against his, her skin cold. Dark circles hung under her eyes, revealing exhaustion and fear.

"What are you doing here?" He forced himself to let go of her hand after briefly shaking it.

Claire withdrew her palm and hugged herself. "I saw you on TV a few months ago."

Behind her, Brax snickered.

"Right." Luke's jaw tightened. "I remember that."

It had been following the successful resolution of a kidnapping case. After a heated custody battle, a preteen girl had been taken by her father, who'd then proceeded to barricade the two of them in an abandoned house. As the Pattersons had been hired by the girl's mom to help locate her, they'd assisted the police in recovery.

A news crew had shown up and stuck the microphone in Luke's face before he'd gotten a chance to duck away. His brothers still made fun of how awkward and stiff he'd been on camera. But it had brought in even more business for San Antonio Security.

"Hey, did we hear the front door chime?" Weston's head popped around the doorway, Chance close behind him.

Claire turned and took a rapid step away from them. The cat jumped into her arms and she clutched it to her, discomfort clear on her face.

Luke cleared his throat. "Claire, these are my brothers, Weston, Chance and—"

"Brax." Brax stepped forward and offered Claire his hand. "I'm the mutt of the bunch."

Most people did a double take when it was revealed the four were brothers. Since Luke was white, Chance was Hispanic, Weston was Black, and Brax was biracial, they looked nothing alike. Brothers, just not by blood.

Claire seemed to take it all in stride. But she wasn't most people. She knew Luke hadn't come from a traditional home.

Brax shook Claire's hand against the cat for an unnecessarily long time. Luke had to swallow a growl in his throat.

Brax never had a problem finding a woman to date. His charm and wit made him pretty irresistible, not to mention his looks.

It was Chance who read the potential disaster of the situation and hooked a hand over Brax's shoulder, pulling him back. "We, uh...have the storage closet to clean out."

Brax's nose wrinkled. "Since when?"

"Since now." Weston tugged on Brax's other arm. "It's nice to meet you, Claire."

Luke could hear his brothers whisper and the whoosh of air as either Chance or Weston no doubt hit Brax in the stomach.

And then he was alone with Claire.

With the others gone, the cat jumped to the floor and sat in front of Claire like he was her guard, his hard gaze locked on Luke.

"That thing looks like a watchdog."

"Khan thinks he's a dog. He's protective." Claire rubbed him with her foot. The cat looked at Claire, somehow knowing she was talking about him.

"Maine coon, right?"

Those cobalt blue eyes lit up with surprise. "Yeah."

Back when they were kids in their group home, Luke gave Claire the nickname Kitten because she dragged around a stuffed animal cat. Half of what that little girl with braids made of sunshine and eyes cut from the sky talked about was getting a cat one day.

Looked like her biggest dream had finally come true. Despite the exhaustion apparent on her face and the scrapes and bruises, he was glad at least that much had happened for her.

"I'm glad you have someone looking out for you. I always wondered what happened to you." Luke's heart squeezed tight. He'd probably never admit to anyone just how much he'd thought about her.

"After I left the group home, I went into two long-term foster families." Claire shrugged. "It worked out okay."

It didn't have to be added—she never got adopted.

"You?" Her pale eyebrows lifted.

Luke's mouth went dry. He'd only stayed at the group home a handful of days following her departure. She was the only reason he hadn't run away earlier. Claire had a way of always being the kid who got picked on, and she'd needed someone to watch out for her.

"Not long after you left, I was adopted by the Pattersons." He chose to leave the few months on the streets, before he was found and dragged back to the group home, out of the story.

"Oh wow."

"They adopted all four of us. Gave us the chance to take their name if we wanted, and all four of us did." His voice swelled with pride. "Those two gave me a direction. Stability. I owe them my life."

The look in her eyes said it was an experience she couldn't relate to. He pointed to the chair across from his desk and she took a seat. Khan immediately jumped into her lap. Damn thing was nearly half the size she was.

"What about you? What do you do now?" He sat behind his desk, hoping that if he got her talking it would help her to relax. And eventually get her to admit to whatever had brought her through San Antonio Security's doors.

"Software design and programming." She shrugged like it was no big deal, but she was stiff.

"That's great. You always did love computers."

She fell into silence, not saying anything else about her work. But the hand that stroked Khan was unsteady.

He shifted some papers over so he could lean toward her. "Claire, I'm real glad you're here, and you're always welcome to visit… But I get the feeling you're not here to catch up on old times."

She slowly lifted her head, her throat rolling with a swallow. He wanted to leap over the desk and pull her into his arms. Promise her that everything would be okay, that he would help now like he'd tried to help then.

But she looked so fragile, like the slightest touch might break her.

He kept his tone gentle. "You have scratches. A bruise on your cheek."

"I-I was mugged."

"Do you know who did it?" He grabbed a pad of paper so he could write down details, ignoring the fury pooling in his gut at the thought of someone hurting her.

"No, I…" Avoiding his gaze, she licked her lips. "It's been rough lately. I-I kind of started hanging out with the wrong people. I think it has something to do with them. And the guys who mugged me know where I live."

He waited, knowing this wasn't the whole story, but she didn't say anything else. Claire was hiding something, the truth buried in details she wasn't telling.

Not that he needed the full story. Not yet, anyway. She needed assistance, and hell if he wouldn't do anything he could.

"How can I help, Kitten?"

He hadn't meant to call her by that old nickname—didn't even know if she would remember it—but its escape from his lips had been natural.

Claire wrapped her arms around Khan, peering out at Luke from over the protective creature's head. Her voice cracked as she spoke. "I can't go home. The men who mugged me took all my credit cards and some of my cash."

Luke kept his features carefully blank. Muggers stealing credit cards and leaving cash behind was highly unusual. It was yet another sign that Claire hid something, but he wouldn't press for more. Not yet.

Not when she looked like she was going to shatter at any moment.

"When was the last time you got some sleep?"

"I'm not sure." Her voice dropped to a whisper. "A few nights… I didn't know where to go."

Still not the whole truth.

"I'm going to get you a hotel room," Luke said. "I'll pay for it."

She parted her lips like she might protest, but in the end, she nodded. "Okay. Thank you. But I don't want you to think that's why I came here. I'm not trying to use you."

"You're not using me. I'm glad to help out an old friend. Once you get some sleep, we can figure out what to do next."

She smiled, though it wasn't without uncertainty. "Okay. Thank you."

A few minutes later, he had her and Khan bundled into her car and she was following him to a motel a few miles away. He would've liked to put her up somewhere nicer—and closer—but she'd explained that Khan liked to go outside to use the bathroom so it would be more convenient not to stay at a traditional hotel.

Damn cat really did think he was a dog.

He took her to a motor lodge where she could let Khan in and out easily and could park right in front of her room. She waited in her car while he checked her in at the front desk, not wanting the clerk to know she was staying alone.

When he came back out, Claire was staring out her windshield, almost glossy-eyed with exhaustion. He'd planned to take her out to a restaurant to eat and talk some more, but instead, he settled for driving her to a nearby fast-food joint where he made her eat. Greasy calories were better than none at all.

Back at the motor lodge he carried her small bag of belongings as he walked her to the door and placed the bag on the dresser inside. She looked like she was about to fall over. "Get some sleep. Everything will feel better after a night of rest, I promise."

"Thank you," she whispered, sitting down on the bed.

He didn't want to leave her here alone, but sleep was the best thing for her right now. And he'd be much more useful back at the office digging into her situation more thoroughly.

"I'll be back first thing tomorrow morning. We'll talk more then. Lock the door behind me when I leave."

She nodded. "Luke, I—" She stopped whatever she was going to say. "Thank you for helping me."

Unable to stop himself, he softly touched her cheek. "Get some rest, Kitten. You're not in this alone anymore."

Chapter Three

Luke's gaze was stuck to his rearview mirror as he drove away from the motel. Leaving Claire alone went against everything in his gut, but he had to do it.

He needed answers, and at that moment, they weren't coming from her.

At the first stoplight, he put in a call to his friend over at the San Antonio PD, Rick Gavett.

"Gavett." The background sounds of a busy police department undercut Rick's voice.

"Rick, it's Luke Patterson."

"Luke! I usually get a call from Weston, not you. Who do you need found today?"

They'd all known Rick for years, although Weston was closest with him. He'd been on the force with Rick before a bullet during an undercover assignment gone wrong had ended Weston's law enforcement career and almost his life. Rick had always been willing to help out San Antonio Security whenever he could.

"Not trying to find anyone today, believe it or not." Luke looked in the rearview again, even though he couldn't see the motor lodge any longer.

"No one? What, are you guys shutting down San Antonio Security or something?"

"Not while I'm alive and kicking." The light turned green. "I need a different kind of favor from you today."

"Do tell."

"I have an old friend I need to check up on. Name's Claire Wallace." The name tasted achingly sweet on Luke's tongue, like he'd gotten one bite of the best dessert in the world and now wanted more.

"A lady friend?"

"A childhood friend. She's in some kind of trouble and needs my help, but the details are slow coming."

"Claire Wallace. Got it. I'll see what I can dig up later this afternoon when things aren't so crazy. I'll call you soon."

"Thanks. And hey, Rick?"

"Yeah."

"I'd appreciate if you keep this on the down-low." Luke cleared his throat. "Claire isn't the kind to get involved in trouble. Whatever's going on, I don't think it's her fault."

At least, he hoped it wasn't.

He ended the call with Rick and drove the rest of the way back to the office, waiting a second in his truck before getting out.

Everything outside looked normal. No cars with tinted windows cruising by slowly. No one watching from the bus stop bench across the street. But that was because the people waiting to pounce on Luke were already inside.

His brothers were going to have questions, a lot of them. He got out with a sigh and walked to the door.

Sure enough, Luke wasn't inside two seconds before his brothers were all over him.

"Who was that?" Weston, serious as always, frowned in concern. "Why have we never heard you mention Claire Wallace before?"

Chance fired out his question before Weston was even

done. "You didn't buy that whole 'stole my cards but not my cash' story. No mugger in the history of the world has ever done that."

Brax held out his hands to calm everyone down. "Guys. Let's start with the most important question… Can I be the flower girl at your and Claire's wedding? Because seriously, I've never seen you be so sweet and soft-spoken with anyone, even Mom."

Chance and Weston chuckled, and Luke rolled his eyes, brushing past them and walking toward his office. "She's a potential client. Can a guy get some space?"

They followed. He knew they would. Ignoring them, Luke sat at his desk and powered on his computer.

"We're concerned." Chance took the seat across from him, the same one Claire had sat in.

"She's an old friend. I knew her when we were at the group home together in Skyline Park before it was shut down."

"Right." Brax leaned against the doorjamb. "The group home. You were there much longer than me, but never talk much about it."

Luke shrugged. He didn't talk about his past because none of it was worth repeating. He'd never known his biological father, and his mother had lost custody of him when he was seven because of the drug problem that eventually led to her death. He'd bounced around foster homes until he ended up at the hellhole Skyline Park at thirteen, and tried to get out of there as often as possible. Living on the streets had been preferable. He'd probably be dead or in prison if the Pattersons hadn't taken him in.

What was there to talk about?

"Why did Claire come here?" Chance asked after it became obvious Luke wasn't going to say anything else. "Have you been in touch with her since the group home?"

"No. I haven't seen her since she was placed with a family when she was eleven. Obviously, she's in some kind of trouble," Luke said. "She won't tell me what. We're supposed to talk more tomorrow."

Chance nodded. "But she specifically sought *you* out after all these years. You must've made some kind of impression on her."

Luke looked up at his most quiet and thoughtful brother and nodded. Had he impacted Claire that deeply? It would certainly be nice to think so. "We sort of looked out for each other at the group home."

"You mean, you looked out for her," Brax inserted. "It looks like a door slamming too loudly could scare that girl."

"Yeah, I guess." Luke nodded thoughtfully, his eyes on the wall. "Claire was younger than me. I was thirteen when she showed up at the home at ten years old. I'd been about to run away again, actually. Had my bag packed and everything."

It had been a plastic shopping bag. The backpack he'd shown up with long gone—stolen by another kid before he'd aged out of the group home.

Luke hadn't had a plan; he just knew staying there wasn't going to work.

A lot of foster homes weren't great, but the group home was terrible. Kids were cruel to each other, stole and fought all the time, and the adults barely paid any attention to what was going on. You had to sleep with one eye open, if you got any sleep at all in the dormitory-style bedrooms.

"But you didn't leave?" Brax went to the window and surveyed the parking lot.

A distant memory tugged on Luke's heart. Little Claire. She'd been so delicate. Ten, but more the size of an eight-or nine-year-old. She'd pulled on every protective instinct Luke hadn't even known he'd had.

"Kids there were the worst of the bunch—most of them unplaceable. Older ones were always looking for someone to pick on, and it didn't take long for Claire to be cast in that role. Her head was always in a book or on a computer. So quiet and shy. A bully's dream."

Only a couple of days after she arrived at the group home, Claire showed up at the breakfast table with bruises and scratches.

Not unlike how she showed up at the office this morning.

A girl always known for starting trouble had been picking on little Claire—bullying her in ways just short of overt.

Luke wasn't the oldest or biggest kid at Skyline Park, but he knew how to take care of himself and had long since proven no one should mess with him. And for a reason he still couldn't identify, he'd stepped in and helped Claire.

"I helped her out." He shrugged like it wasn't a big deal. But it had been a big deal for them. "She was scared all the time. Boys and girls slept on separate ends of the house, which meant I could only protect her during the day. So I stole some walkie-talkies from the dollar store so we could talk at night."

He looked up from his computer to find all three of his brothers staring at him thoughtfully. He'd never talked about his past this much.

"We checked in every night until she was placed with a family when she was eleven."

Luke's throat constricted. He hadn't realized just how important Claire was to him until she wasn't there anymore. With her gone, the bag came out again. He was living on the streets not even a week later before he was caught and brought back.

Not long after, the Pattersons had found him and offered him a place in their home.

"She meant something to you," Weston said in his quiet way.

Luke scrubbed a hand over his short brown hair. "Yeah, I guess. In a kid way. If she's in trouble now, I'd like to help, too."

Chance stood from his chair. "Then that's what we'll all do."

Luke turned to Weston. "I've already got Rick Gavett running her to see if anything comes up. I'm going to dig into her, too, so I know what we're up against when I see her tomorrow. I'll keep you posted."

He spent the rest of the morning and a big chunk of the afternoon alternating between the paperwork still overwhelming his desk and seeking info about Claire.

The basics were easy to get. Claire had stayed close to home for college, then she started developing software and apps for Passage Digital right out of school. She'd never been married—he refused to even acknowledge whatever feeling it was that zinged through his chest at that info—and had committed no crimes.

Nothing stuck out as particularly notable or questionable.

So, what then? How had Claire accidentally gotten involved in some bad news? Hopefully, Rick would be able to shine more light on that subject because Luke was having no luck, meaning he had no choice but to face the paperwork piles.

The doorbell ringing made Luke look up a couple of hours later, before glancing at his watch. Already nearly five o'clock.

"Can we help you?" he heard Brax ask.

"Are you Luke Patterson?"

"No, I'm his brother, Brax. We're partners in San Antonio Security. Are you looking to hire us?"

"I'm Officer Arellano." He pointed to the shorter man next to him, who was also in a suit, pulling out a badge and showing it was real. "And this is Officer Fisher. We have a few questions about Claire Wallace."

At the sound of Claire's name, Luke dropped the papers he was filing and zoomed into the waiting area, forcing himself to slow as he walked in. "Afternoon, officers. I'm Luke Patterson."

Arellano's eyes narrowed as Weston and Chance also entered the reception area. "I thought you guys were brothers."

Luke didn't have time for a cultural sensitivity lesson right now. "Did Rick send you over with info?"

Fisher crossed his arms over his chest, ignoring the question. "We're looking for Claire Wallace. Is she here?"

Luke shook his head. "Nobody is here but us right now. Is there a reason you're looking for her?"

"Why don't you let us ask the questions," Arellano bit out.

Luke forced himself to keep a relaxed posture against the doorframe. Something about these guys was off, and he wasn't going to give them any info about Claire until he knew more.

"We know you've been in contact with Claire Wallace today. We need to ask her some important questions."

"She wanted for something?" Brax asked with his friendly smile.

Fisher and Arellano glanced at each other. "We're not at liberty to say. It's in your best interest to let us know where she is."

Like hell it was. If Rick hadn't sent them, then how did they even know Claire had been in contact?

Luke took a step forward. "She was only here for a few minutes."

"What did she want?" Fisher asked. "What did she talk about? You need to tell us everything she said."

Luke shrugged. "She wasn't here very long. Was asking if we had any protection agency contacts for Toledo. It was Toledo, right, guys? Wasn't that where she was going?"

His brothers backed him up with affirmative responses immediately. Luke hadn't had any doubt they would.

"Toledo, *Ohio*?" The tall cop's face folded in annoyance.

Chance perched himself on the edge of the couch. "I know, right? Why would anyone leave Texas to go to Ohio? Sadly, we didn't have any contacts there to offer her."

Arellano's eyes narrowed. "Why'd she come here in the first place?"

Brax hooked a thumb in Luke's direction. "McDreamy over here was on the news a month ago. Now we're overwhelmed with clients of the female persuasion. Not that we're complaining."

"Sorry we're not more help," Luke said, not at all sorry. He wanted them out of here so he could talk to Rick and find out exactly what the hell was going on. "If you want to leave your card, we can let you know if Ms. Wallace contacts us from Toledo."

The officers glanced at each other again like they weren't exactly sure what to do with that offer. Just another clue that something was off.

"We'll be in touch if we need you," Fisher said, and they walked out the door without another word.

"What the hell was that all about?" Brax asked.

Luke wasn't sure if his brother meant the fact that there was something completely off about those cops or the fact that they'd just lied to them.

He was saved from answering by his ringing cell phone. Pulling it from his pocket, he saw it was just the man he wanted to talk to.

"Rick. Talk to me."

"Who the hell is Claire Wallace, Patterson?"

The words were so loud, Luke knew all his brothers could hear.

"What did you find?"

"It's crazy. I've haven't seen such red flags in my whole fifteen years of law enforcement. It's like she's a fugitive and there's a statewide manhunt going on for her—all inquiries are sent straight up to the top of the law enforcement food chain to the Criminal Investigations Department in Dallas."

Luke's heart sank. "So she's wanted for something pretty bad."

"You would think so. But that's where it gets really weird. There's not even an official APB on her. She's got no record, and she wasn't even in the Texas Department of Public Safety system until a few days ago."

"I don't understand what you're saying, Rick. Is Claire a wanted criminal or not?"

"I'm saying something really weird is going on, and it's way above my pay grade."

Luke ran a hand through his hair, looking at his brothers. "We just had a visit from a couple of officers. Fisher and Arellano. They legit?"

He could hear Rick type into his computer. "Yeah," he whispered a minute later. "They're Criminal Investigations Division in Dallas. My inquiry must have led them to you. There's something not right about all this, Luke. It doesn't make sense to send someone from Dallas when they could've just sent someone from our office to talk to you."

"Yeah. That doesn't seem right."

"Look, I'll send you what I have on Wallace, although it's not mu—" Rick muttered a curse under his breath.

"What?"

"File on Claire Wallace had been locked. I can't get into it anymore."

Luke had no idea what to say about that.

"Look," Rick finally said. "Someone way high up is looking for this woman and not through normal channels. I'll see if I can find anything else, but it looks like they're closing it down on my end. They'll probably say it's an Internal Affairs issue."

"Thanks for trying, Rick."

"Listen, Luke. This whole thing stinks to high heaven, and now you're right in the middle of it. Until we know what's going on, you guys be careful."

"We will."

Luke hung up and looked around at his brothers, who all wore matching grim expressions. They'd heard enough to know this had just gotten ugly.

Luke needed answers. They all did.

The quickly falling night drew his attention outside. He wasn't supposed to talk to Claire until tomorrow morning, but this couldn't wait. She was the only one who really knew what was going on.

And it was time for her to start talking.

Chapter Four

"No!"

Claire threw her hand out toward Julia, but it was no use. The other woman slumped against the floor, her eyes open but lifeless.

A force on her waist pulled Claire backward. She screamed and thrashed but it did no good. She couldn't get away from what was dragging her down.

"Mee…rrow."

Claire froze. *Meow*?

In an instant, Julia was gone. Claire opened her eyes. The pressure on her waist was Khan, pawing at her in concern, nothing more. She was in the bed of the motel room Luke had left her in hours ago.

Pressing her palm to her forehead, she found her skin slicked with sweat. Another nightmare. It had happened every time she'd closed her eyes. Sleeping shouldn't be this hard when she was this exhausted.

She'd barely slept since the moment Julia's lifeless eyes had looked out at her from where she'd hit the floor.

Three days since Julia's death, and the terror eating Claire from the inside was only getting worse.

She dragged herself out of bed and into the shower, washing off the last of the nightmare.

The water, as hot as she could stand, washed over her. She was alive, and that was the most important thing.

She had rushed home after fleeing Passage Digital. She knew it wouldn't take them long to figure out she was the one Julia had been communicating with.

She'd parked down the street and sneaked into her house. She needed to run, but there was no way she was leaving without Khan.

She'd thrown what she could in a bag and grabbed any cash she'd had squirreled around the house. She'd been just about to slip out the back door when two of Ballard's men broke in through the front.

"Remember, no guns. When she comes in here, we've got to make it look like an accident."

"Mr. Ballard said the best plan will be to put her with the other body and run a car off a ravine. Won't raise many red flags."

Claire had stuffed her fist up to her lips, so frozen with fear it had taken all her strength to move. *They were really going to kill her.* Somehow, she got herself and Khan back out through the side kitchen door and down the block to her car, although not without bumping into a neighbor's fence and taking a spill that resulted in a bruised face.

From there, she hadn't known what to do other than drive around aimlessly. Nightfall found her outside of Austin, a couple of hours from San Antonio. Wanting to see if Ballard was tracking her, she paid for a room with a credit card, then hid behind the fast-food joint across the street and watched.

Sure enough, it hadn't taken long before the same men who'd broken into her house appeared. They'd gone inside the hotel and Claire had no doubt they knew what room she'd been given—it would be easy for Ballard to hack a computer system.

Claire had gotten back into her car, once again parked down the road, and left. Her little experiment had proven just what she thought it would. Ballard would trace her any time she used a credit or debit card.

She'd slept in her car at a rest area that night—as much as she could sleep, which wasn't much at all.

Not knowing who to trust and being down to her last few dollars, she'd gone to her last foster family's house. The Romeros had cared for Claire through the tail end of high school and still checked in with Claire every once in a while to see how she was doing.

She was running out of money and soon wouldn't be able to feed herself or Khan. Popping into the Romeros' and getting a meal—and maybe a bed that wasn't her car—had seemed like the perfect plan. They'd definitely take her in for a day or two. Give her a chance to rest and figure out a plan.

She'd parked down at the end of the block and had been walking toward their house, rehearsing her story in her head, when she'd realized there was a car at the curb across from the Romeros' house.

They were being watched.

She'd immediately turned to make it look like she was going to a neighbor's house, then as soon as she was out of sight of the car, had jumped a fence—leading to more scratches and bruises—and run to her car in a panic.

Her entire body had been shaking. Ballard had figured out where she would go before she had. He had resources she hadn't even dreamed about.

He was going to hunt her down wherever she went. There was nowhere she could go where he wouldn't find her. And going to the police without evidence was just going to make it her word against Ballard's.

He was a millionaire businessman with huge ties to the community. He had friends everywhere and was highly influential.

She was...nobody. No friends. No family.

She'd spent another night in her car, in a random apartment complex parking lot, nearly out of gas and hope. When she'd watched the sun come up, trying to keep from having a complete breakdown, a last-ditch plan had come to her.

Luke.

It had been his voice in her mind telling her to get out of Passage Digital.

She'd never forgotten him. Had wondered what had happened to him.

Then she'd seen him on the news a few weeks back, stoic and handsome. The same Luke, but all grown up. Obviously successful and...

No longer Luke Baldwin, like when she'd known him. He was Luke Patterson now.

Of San Antonio Security.

Protection was definitely what she needed, and she prayed maybe he could help her. Protect her like he had when they were kids.

That was, if he even remembered her.

But she hadn't had any other options, so she'd looked up San Antonio Security's office and driven there. She sat in the parking lot across the street for three hours before finally going inside.

He'd remembered her.

He'd helped her.

He'd somehow heated the female parts of her she wasn't even sure worked correctly. Despite her fear and exhaustion, a few minutes in Luke's presence had her more wound up than any of the guys she'd had relationships with during college—all two of them.

She turned off the water and towel-dried her body, getting dressed in one of the two sets of clothes she had left to her name. Then she lay down on the bed, rubbing Khan's gray fur, stretching as she thought of Luke.

No matter how uncharacteristically revved up he'd gotten her, she still hadn't been able to tell him the truth. What if he didn't believe her?

Even if he did buy her story, he couldn't protect her from Ballard. No one could. But he'd bought her a little time.

Khan meowed again and climbed up next to her head on the pillow.

"It's okay, buddy." She scratched the magic spot behind his ears.

A loud purr filled the room.

"You like it here?"

After Luke left, she'd taken Khan outside to do his business and seen the sliding glass door in the adjacent room. With that, Khan would be able to go in and out as he pleased.

All it took was telling the guy at the front desk that her room had a musty smell. He'd traded her key, barely looking away from the TV.

After three days trapped in a car, her precious dog-cat was thrilled to have space and freedom.

"We won't be able to stay long. Sorry. But we'll find a safe place. Somewhere." She didn't know how, but they would.

Claire nestled deeper into the pillows and Khan was finally feeling comfortable. Her eyelids grew heavy, and before she knew it, they couldn't stay open.

Bang!

Gasping, Claire sat straight up in bed. Khan hissed, his fluffy tail swishing against her face.

Had that been a gunshot?

"Police." More banging. "Open the door."

Not a gunshot, the cops knocking on her door. She felt like all the oxygen had been sucked from the planet.

More banging.

But wait… The voice had been too muffled. The police weren't at her motel room; they were at the one next door.

The *first* room she'd checked into.

That wasn't good, either. These "police officers" hadn't gone to the front desk like real ones would. If they had, they'd have known she switched rooms.

That meant they'd gotten her room info via a computer search—the *Vance Ballard* way.

Unless Luke had turned her in.

No, she couldn't think like that. Not if she wanted to keep it together and not get arrested.

"Ma'am, we're going to need you to open the door."

Claire threw the blankets off her legs. She needed to get out of there.

Grabbing Khan, she slipped on her shoes and grabbed her small purse with the computer drive. The bit of money she still had was in it, along with her car keys.

Not that she could make it to her car, which sat in the front parking lot.

As quietly as possible, Claire opened the sliding door. Thick woods separated the motel and the interstate. She could hide there.

The loud crack of wood made her cringe. They'd broken the door to the room next door. Muffled male voices barked at each other.

It wouldn't be long before they figured out that they had the wrong room.

Holding Khan for dear life, Claire bolted for the woods at an angle away from her predators, in case they looked out the window and spotted her.

She ran as fast as she could, not daring to look back. Cursing at how much time she spent at a computer instead of getting exercise, she was gasping for breath before she even hit the tree line.

Were they behind her? She didn't know. She couldn't hear anything anymore and it was getting dark. The dark would work in her favor.

She had to keep going, just keep putting one foot in front of the other.

Khan was so damn heavy in her arms, but she didn't dare let him down. If he decided to go after some critter, she might not have time to find him again. That was an unacceptable option.

She tucked the squirmy cat up against her and she stepped around a big tree, almost sobbing in relief at the sight of a bridge visible through the woods. If she could get to that, it would take her over the interstate.

She heard sounds behind her. Men talking. They'd figured out she'd come this way. She gulped in a couple of deep breaths, then forced herself to run again.

She'd only gone a few steps before she was stopped mid-stride. Terror engulfed her as an arm wrapped around her waist from behind, lifting her up. A hand pressed hard against her mouth, muffling her scream.

It was just like in her dream earlier, except this nightmare was a reality.

There would be no waking up from this.

Chapter Five

"Kitten, it's me," Luke whispered into Claire's hair, ignoring the sting from that giant cat's scratch. He hadn't wanted to scare her, but he was afraid she'd scream if he just stepped out in front of her.

Her squirming subsided and he loosened his hold so she could turn around.

"Luke?"

"Shh." He put a finger to his lips.

She nodded at his forearm. "Khan scratched you."

"I'll be fine."

"I almost let Khan loose on you." Claire's voice shook.

It sounded like a joke, but the vicious feline could no doubt do some real damage.

"There are men at the motel," she continued. "They said they're the police, but I don't think they are."

"I know." Luke stole a glance around the tree. They were in a good hiding spot for the moment, but they couldn't stay long. Someone had tailed him from the office, and it had taken him a while to lose them without seeming like he was losing them. He'd parked around the corner and walked over. "Cops don't have MAC-10 semi-automatic machine pistols. Those are what bad guys use."

They were close enough that he could feel the shiver come off her.

She had every right to be afraid. Whoever it was breaking into her room had meant business.

"How did you get out of your room?" He took her hand and they walked quickly toward the bridge. He didn't run; right now, stealth was more important than speed.

"I traded rooms so Khan could use a sliding glass door to get in and out."

He picked up speed when they heard shouting not far behind them. They must have figured out what had happened.

"There's something a lot more serious going on than mugging and falling in with the wrong crowd, isn't there?"

She deflated and buried her nose in Khan's fur. "Yes. I'm sorry."

He squeezed her hand. "There'll be time for explanations later. Right now, we need to get out of here. Stay close to me and keep as low as possible."

He moved them forward at a rapid pace, keeping her in front so he was between her and the MAC-10s.

They broke from the trees to the roar of traffic. Cars whizzed by, nothing more than blurs of color. Luke glanced over his shoulder but didn't see anyone.

"When I say run, get to the divide." Luke studied Claire to make sure she'd heard him.

"O-okay."

"Now!" Taking advantage of a break in traffic, they ran for it.

Claire kept up, despite her heavy load with the cat. They made it to the divide, then successfully across the other side of the interstate.

Climbing over the low railing between the road and a Laundromat, Luke checked over his shoulder. Still no sign of the attackers.

Which almost felt worse than seeing them would.

If they weren't in sight, Luke didn't know where they were, and he liked to always have a target on his enemies.

"Where did you park?" Claire adjusted Khan in her arms as they continued.

"Right up here. Half a block." Luke pointed. "Let me carry him for a minute."

She pulled the cat closer. "I don't think he'll let you. He's very protective."

Luke nodded. Now wasn't the time to find out. He quickly moved again, keeping her hand tucked in his.

They crossed behind the Laundromat not far from where he'd parked when a gruff male voice from around the corner made them freeze. Luke yanked Claire down with him behind the side of a dumpster.

"Jennings swears he saw two people cross the highway."

"Jennings also told us she would be in the motel room where she obviously wasn't," another man barked back. "Just because we found her car and stuff in the next room doesn't mean she hadn't run a long time before we got there."

Claire let out a low whimper and shrank into herself. Luke put a hand on her arm and pulled her to his side. Their shoulder blades pressed against the hard brick of the Laundromat. The voices had sounded close, real close.

Khan decided he'd had enough of being held. He struggled in Claire's arms before slipping through her crooked elbow. As Claire gasped, Khan jumped onto a nearby trash can. He didn't quite make the landing, though, and the can toppled over with a loud crash.

"What was that?" one of the men asked.

Claire reached out for Khan, but Luke wrapped his

arm around her shoulders and held her back. She loved that cat, but he wasn't letting her get killed for it. He slid them both farther behind the dumpster, peeking through the crack.

Spooked by the trash can, Khan skirted farther into the parking lot, his tail fluffed out in surprise.

A man laughed and hit the chest of the guy who'd pulled at his gun. "It's a damn cat. Come on, there's no-body around here. Let's check out the parking lot and see if anyone is around."

Luke stayed flush against the wall with Claire pressed up against him as the men made their way toward the parking lot. With every breath, Claire heaved against him. She'd buried her face in his chest at some point, and one of her hands fisted his shirt.

Heat rushed through Luke and his heart sped up.

Neither physiological response could be completely blamed on the danger they'd just dodged.

"You okay?" he whispered against her hair.

She nodded, then took a step away from him. "Khan. Come here."

The cat leaped right into her arms, and Luke swore the thing looked sheepish and Claire looked like she was about to lecture the cat about proper behavior.

"Save it," he whispered, taking her hand once again. "You'll have to give the cat a time-out after we're not about to get shot."

Making it safely to his truck a few minutes later only slightly lessened the adrenaline coursing through Luke's veins. He gripped the steering wheel tight as they drove out of the city, his gaze raking the road ahead and behind them for any signs of being followed.

Next to him, Claire looked out the window. Her tangled hair fell in front of her face and her shoulders curved forward like she wanted to disappear.

Luke's chest constricted. He almost didn't want to say anything or ask details about what was going on. She looked so fragile, like the wrong word might break her into a thousand pieces.

But silence wouldn't do, either.

"Were you able to get any sleep this afternoon?" he asked as gently as he could.

"A little."

He turned onto a side road leading out of San Antonio. He wasn't sure where they were headed yet; he just knew that they needed to get the hell out of Dodge.

"Want to tell me what's going on?"

She continued staring out the window for a long minute before she finally spoke.

"I work—well, *worked*, past tense now, I guess—for Passage Digital."

"The software and apps company. Yes, I did a little research on you this afternoon."

She glanced over at him but didn't look surprised. "I developed this business-to-customer mobile application with someone at work. Julia." Her voice cracked on the name.

"Three days ago, Julia told me that our boss, Vance Ballard, had removed certain safety restrictions from our coding. Basically, he made it so that Gouda would illegally collect data from users. That data could eventually be used for financial and identity theft—bank account information, Social Security numbers…pretty much everything."

Luke shook his head. "Hold on. Business-to-customer? And what was that about cheese? The only word I understood was *illegally*."

She gave him the tiniest smile. "Sorry. The program is called Gouda. It's the app Julia and I developed."

"Gouda. Catchy. Okay, keep going. What happened?" He wanted to understand the details more, but that wasn't what was important here. What was important was that she was finally talking.

"Julia transferred Ballard's files to me while we were at work. Evidence we would need to prove what he did. And then…" She lowered her face, nearly burying her nose in Khan's fur. "And then they killed Julia right in front of me, while we were on video chat. They didn't know I was at the other end or that I was watching. Vance Ballard ordered one of his guys to kill her and the guy just snapped her neck."

He wanted to pull over and stop the truck. Haul Claire into his arms and just hold her.

He muttered a curse under his breath. He had witnessed death in the army, and it had been scarring enough. He couldn't imagine what witnessing the brutal murder of a colleague would do to a person.

He reached over and took Claire's hand where it was balled in Khan's fur. It wasn't enough, but it was all the comfort he could offer for now.

"I was lucky to get out of the building before they realized it was me. I've been on the run ever since. I can't use my credit cards and I'm almost out of cash. Ballard seems to have people watching anywhere I might go to get help or rest."

"Well, he doesn't have anyone watching us now. You're safe, and I'm not leaving you alone again."

Claire nodded, then turned to stare blankly out the windshield. He didn't press her for more info. Her blue eyes had such deep shadows under them that they looked like bruises. The latest adrenaline spike from being chased and almost caught was gone now, and she was bottoming out.

Her physical and emotional reserves were on empty. He'd seen it before in soldiers, and it was never pretty. He needed to get her somewhere immediately so she could rest before she completely broke down.

Going back to the office wasn't an option, and neither was his house—both were probably being monitored.

Luke pulled out his phone and sent a quick text. He shouldn't have been doing it while driving, but the current situation made stopping the vehicle for even a minute seem riskier.

Couldn't find Claire, she ditched the hotel. I'm taking a few days and going fishing on Calaveras Lake.

"I'm texting my brothers. Telling them I'm off on a fishing trip for a few days." He pocketed his phone. "They'll know it means I'll be off-grid and can't contact them. I hate fishing."

It would also have the people who were undoubtedly monitoring his phone going way out of town to search for him on a huge lake. Luke immediately powered his phone off and took out the battery so there was no way he could be traced.

"Okay," she whispered.

They drove north, in the opposite direction of Calaveras Lake, in the dark. With every rotation of the truck's tires, Luke's mind turned over their predicament.

Where could they go and not be found? Ballard was a powerful man.

Outside of town, he stopped for gas and paid with cash. In case they had to make a quick run for it, having anything less than a full tank would be a dumb move. He grabbed a couple of candy bars while he was in there.

Claire was visibly shaking when he got back in his truck. He peeled open the chocolate bar.

"Here, eat this. Your blood sugar is bottoming out after the chase earlier."

When she didn't so much as move, he gently pressed the candy to her mouth, offering encouraging murmurs as she took tiny bites at a time.

Across the street from the gas station, the lights of a three-story hotel beckoned. Luke wanted to get farther out of town, but Claire was done. She needed to rest.

After paying cash for a room on the bottom floor, he made sure to park the truck where he could see it from the hotel window.

Claire dragged her feet as she walked down the hotel hall. His arms itched to pick her up and carry her, just like she did Khan. Instead, he kept a hand on her arm and slowly led her to their room.

He parked her just inside the door while he checked every inch of the hotel room before he let Claire climb into the bed.

Khan immediately jumped up beside her and curled up against her stomach. When Luke looked back up at Claire's face, she was already asleep, her hand resting in Khan's fur.

Luke scrubbed his face with his palm. The intense day had also left him tired, but sleep wouldn't be easy coming.

Grabbing the armchair from the table, he hauled it over to the space between the bed and the door. If trouble were coming for her, it would have to get through him first.

He ate his candy bar, wincing as she whimpered in her sleep. Bad dreams. If he could wipe them all from her mind, he would, along with everything else that had happened over the last few days.

But he couldn't. All he could do was guard over her, like he had when they were kids. She may be all grown up, but she was still fragile, still needed a protector.

He couldn't stand to think about what might have happened to her if she hadn't escaped Passage Digital. And then all those risky moments between then and now…

His hands fisted. Claire was with him now, and no one was going to hurt her.

Not on his watch.

Chapter Six

Ballard leaned back in his chair, closing his eyes for a moment. When was the last time he'd enjoyed a solid, uninterrupted night's sleep?

It was definitely before certain treacherous employees, who didn't know the value of keeping their mouths shut, decided to poke around in matters that did not concern them.

When his eyes opened, his gaze immediately fell on the spot on the floor where Julia's body had fallen. No blood. Brooks was good that way—a professional, efficient, somebody who did what needed doing without asking questions or allowing personal feelings to muddy the waters.

If only all his associates shared that professionalism.

He should've known Julia wasn't the only weak link. And she was clever, too. He had to give her credit for that. A shame to lose such a brilliant mind, all because her brilliance hadn't lent itself to self-preservation.

In the end, she hadn't even come up with a solid reason for lurking in his office. Julia had not been a practiced liar since her excuse had been almost juvenile.

It was Claire who interested him these days. Having evaded him, Claire seemed to be somewhat better at lying, at least for now. She couldn't run forever, not with so many eyes on her every move.

The knock at his office door didn't come as a surprise. "Enter." He sat up and straightened his tie while the door swung open and the pair he'd expected joined him. They stood before him, knowing better than to take a seat unless offered one.

He looked from one to the other, noting—not for the first time—how similar the men were in build and mannerisms, right down to their crew-cut hair. Both were men of few words, too, which suited Ballard. "Talk to me."

Brooks and Masters exchanged a look that didn't go far toward granting confidence. "There's not that much to tell, sir," Brooks said in his deep growl.

"Not that much to tell?" He blinked, looking from one to the other. Waiting for one of them to crack. People always cracked when pressed hard enough in just the right place. "How can that be?"

"She got away." Masters remained with his hands clasped behind his back, but beads of sweat at his temple told a story of nerves...of cracking under them.

His blood pressure began to rise. He knew it from the telltale roaring in his ears. "How?"

"We don't know." Brooks lifted his thick shoulders. "I'm sorry, sir, but those are the facts. When the men entered the room, she was gone. She left her things behind, too."

"The drive?"

"No, I'm sorry. They turned the place upside down." As if that made it better.

Control. He took several deep breaths. His men waited, silent, probably wondering if and when he would explode in rage. How was the girl a step ahead of them? She was nothing! One single girl who all but faded into the background. He hadn't recognized her face upon examining her ID badge and the photos compiled by his team after her escape. She might as well be no one, a nonentity.

Yet she'd managed to escape. Again.

"Why did she go to San Antonio Security?"

"I spoke to Arellano after the visit to their office but he didn't have anything concrete about that." Brooks exchanged another shrug with Masters. "They're either good liars or they were telling the truth."

"The truth being…?"

"That they didn't know her."

"It was probably a last-ditch effort on her part," Masters added, eager to sound insightful and useful after delivering bad news. Ballard was not a man who took bad news easily. "One of the guys from the agency was on TV recently and it upped their visibility. Otherwise, they were all firm on not knowing her or anything about why she came in."

"There's no connection between her and the firm's partners?"

"None that Arellano could find, and you know how thorough he is."

Motivation would do that to a man. Find the right pressure point, and the impossible suddenly became commonplace. Ballard doubted the detective would leave a single stone unturned.

Though that certainty did little to help at the moment. There was still the problem of the girl, where she'd gone and whether she was receiving help. She had to be.

If ever there'd been a poster child for solitude, it was that girl. A lifelong loner. For her to reach out to anyone meant she was desperate. She knew the stakes. Her awareness, her watchfulness spoke of understanding as well.

There had to be an end to her resourcefulness.

Brooks cleared his throat. "What direction do you want Arellano and Fisher to take?"

"I want eyes on their office, these Pattersons. Ears on their phones, as well. Whether there's any connection or not, now that she knows we're able to find her, she'll look for any port in a storm." Masters nodded and left the office, presumably to pass the word to the detectives overseeing the police aspect of this unfortunate dustup.

"What next?" Brooks asked, standing at the ready. Ballard knew through experience that his right-hand associate was up for anything. No request was too large, nothing too far outside the realm of what he was willing to do—like for instance, the Julia problem.

Ballard tented his fingers beneath his chin, staring at the wall over the man's shoulder, seeing the entire situation laid out before him. Like a chessboard, the pieces were already in play. He saw the various parts of Claire's small, uneventful life. The people from her past whom his men were already watching in case she ran to them.

It wasn't enough to wait for her to make a move.

She had to be forced into one.

Yes, it was all so clear. Put his pieces in place, wait for her to make one move after another. No matter what she decided, he would be ready.

A smile spread slowly as everything fell into place. "It's time to turn up the heat under our target," he decided. "Make it so she has nowhere to turn without being noticed. Remove whatever sense of security she still possesses."

"And how do we do that?"

His smile widened. "Oh, that won't be difficult."

IT ONLY TOOK a second for Claire to remember where she was when she woke up the next morning. It took longer when a glance at the clock told her she'd been asleep for nearly thirteen hours.

Even before Julia's murder, she hadn't slept this soundly. One look at the man sleeping upright in the chair next to the bed told her why. Her subconscious had trusted Luke to protect her.

The way he'd always protected her.

She sat up, the bed frame groaning as she moved. In an instant, Luke was awake, his brown eyes trained on her.

"Sorry," Claire whispered. "I didn't mean to wake you."

It couldn't have been comfortable sleeping in that chair, but he stood with no stiffness and with two steps, was at the side of her bed. Claire's breath hitched in her throat. His eyes were serious, face drawn tight, but when he touched the back of her hand, the gentleness there made her head spin.

"Feeling better?" Luke drew his fingers back way too soon.

"Yes." Her voice sounded funny. Did she always talk like she couldn't pronounce words right?

"I'll take Khan out and look for any problems. How about you take a shower?"

"Okay. Thank you."

The hot water had her feeling somewhat human again. She didn't linger, unsure of how long Luke would be gone.

She made a face as she put back on yesterday's clothes. She'd gotten out with the computer drive and Khan.

And her life. She'd just have to be thankful enough for that.

She came out of the bathroom and found Luke standing at the window, peeking at the parking lot through the curtains.

Khan meowed at the sight of Claire, except he didn't come to her. He rubbed against Luke's legs.

"Wow." Claire stared. "I've never seen him do that to anyone but me."

"I got him some beef jerky from the gas station." Luke's smile made her stomach do a flip, despite her traitorous cat.

Claire kept on rubbing her hair with the towel, even though it had never been thick enough to take long to dry. Her hands just needed something to do.

"What now?" she asked.

The smile disappeared, his lips drawing into a thin line. "We keep moving. First, we'll need to make a stop to buy some stuff."

"Yeah, I'm going to need another change of clothes, if possible."

"Me, too. And some other stuff. We can stop at a superstore. I have some cash."

She grimaced. "I'm going to keep a list of what I owe you."

"That's really not necessary."

"It is to me."

He was already doing so much for her that she'd never be able to pay him for. Case in point, sleeping in a chair and watching over her so she could get the rest she needed. What was the price tag on that?

She would damn well pay back what she could. The idea that he possibly thought she was using him crushed her.

"Okay." He nodded, his brown eyes still somber. "If it's important to you, you can keep track and pay me back."

"Thank you."

He respected her feelings. That meant more to her than he could know.

He led her back out to his truck, opening the door for her. Khan jumped in and she climbed in behind him.

"Where are we going to go?"

Luke started the truck and pulled out of the parking lot. "I spent a lot of time thinking last night."

While he was guarding her. "Thank you for letting me rest."

He glanced at her briefly before turning his eyes back to the road. "You needed it."

Her hopes sank. That wasn't anywhere close to a romantic declaration, not that she'd been expecting one. But she needed to face the facts that maybe this attraction was completely one-sided.

"What were you thinking about last night?"

"Your best bet now is to go to the police."

She flinched and turned toward the window. Would the cops even believe her?

She was about to argue her point when her stomach growled loudly, the sound filling the cab.

"Hungry?" He looked over at her again, one eyebrow raised. "Let's get something to eat and we can talk about this more."

A few minutes later, he slowed the truck and turned into the parking lot of an old-timey diner.

The place, full of shiny countertops and red vinyl booths, felt warm and inviting. Khan had to stay out in the truck, but the weather was mild, so they left the windows cracked and the cat sleeping on the floor.

"Over there." Luke headed for the booth in the far corner, by the kitchen.

He waited until Claire slid in, then took the booth facing the door.

"Going to the police makes sense…" He trailed off as a waitress approached.

"What can I get you two today?" The older woman smiled at them both.

Luke didn't even look at the menu. "Whatever your most popular dish is. And coffee."

"Same," Claire said. "Please."

"All righty." The waitress collected the menus. "Eating the same dish. What a cute couple."

Claire could feel the heat crawl up her cheeks, but Luke didn't even seem to notice the comment. The second the waitress was gone, he rested his arms on the table and leaned into them.

"The police can help. You witnessed a murder." He kept his voice low. "That means there's a body somewhere."

Claire choked on her breath. "But what if they don't believe me? I don't have the footage of Julia's death with me; I had to hide it on Passage Digital's servers. It's possible Ballard found it and deleted it."

She dropped her gaze to the table. Talking about this was so hard.

He reached over and grabbed her hand. "I'll be honest, that could be true, and if it is, Ballard might not be convicted. But if you go to the police, show them what you have about the Gouda app and tell them Julia was killed…it throws a lot of suspicion in Ballard's direction."

"But what if they don't believe me?"

They were interrupted by the waitress bringing their coffee, and Claire was glad to have the distraction. She wasn't sure if going to the police was the best plan or not.

Luke took a sip of his steaming brew. "Why didn't you go to the cops as soon as you got out of the building once Julia was killed?"

She stirred creamer into her coffee, then brought it up to her lips. "My head wasn't on straight. All I could think about was getting to Khan and getting him out before they got to him. Plus, the police were always the enemy when we were kids."

His eyes narrowed behind his cup. "You had run-ins with the police?"

"No, not me."

Awareness dawned. He leaned back in the seat. "I had run-ins and filled your little head with stories about the big bad officers of the law."

She shrugged. "I guess it tainted my opinion. I've never trusted cops."

"You know that was just me talking fourteen-year-old smack, right?" He shook his head. "Not a single police officer who picked me up when I ran away ever did anything to harm me. Most of them got me some food and tried to talk to my sullen ass, not that it helped. Two of my brothers went into law enforcement for a while. I have the highest respect for them and the people they worked with."

She sighed. "I should've gone to them first thing. It's too late now."

They were stopped again by the delivery of their breakfast platter, though Claire had lost her appetite.

He bit into his scrambled eggs, then pointed to her plate with a piece of toast in the other hand. "Don't even think about not eating that."

He was right. She had to eat. She took a bite of her eggs, then continued to eat as he watched her like a hawk while wolfing down his own food.

He was completely finished before she'd even made it halfway through her meal—except for the piece of bacon he'd put in his napkin. She knew it was for Khan and tried to ignore the things it did to her heart that he was thinking about the well-being of her cat.

"The most important thing is to keep you alive. The people after you—they have instructions to make sure you're not alive to talk to anyone."

She handed him a piece of bacon to add to the collection for Khan.

"Going to the cops and raising as much ruckus about this as possible will make it harder for Ballard's men to take you out without causing suspicion," he continued. "Ballard is powerful, but he's not God."

She lifted her fork to her mouth but then set it back down without eating. There was no way she could keep it down. She wanted so badly to believe what Luke was saying.

"I'll stay with you through it all. I'm here to help you." He reached over and grabbed her hand, running his fingers across her knuckles.

Tears filled Claire's eyes. "Thank you. I'll do it. But are you sure? This is so dangerous."

"It's nothing I'm not used to," he said with zero hesitation.

Claire's laugh was ragged. She seriously doubted his workday involved running from men with assault weapons.

"You came to me for help. This is my job. And besides, it's you."

She didn't have the nerve to ask what that last part meant.

She looked at what was left on her plate. "I wonder if Khan would eat the eggs. He's not very picky. We could get a to-go box."

Luke smiled. "Khan's a very lucky cat-dog."

"He's my family. My only friend." She cringed at

her pathetic words, immediately wishing she could take them back.

"That's not true." Luke's brown eyes softened, but they turned to steel a second later. His thick brows knit together, his attention on something behind her.

Turning in the booth, Claire found the TV screen mounted on the diner's wall. It was on mute, captions scrolling the bottom of the screen while a reporter talked.

She gasped when she saw the picture in the upper corner of the screen.

It was *her*.

The shot was from a Passage Digital picnic a few months earlier. She wouldn't have gone at all if it hadn't been basically required.

Wanted for the murder of coworker...

She couldn't stop reading the caption running under her photo.

Authorities are asking for anyone with information on Claire Wallace to contact them immediately...

Claire's mouth filled with chalk, the food she'd eaten threatening to come back up.

"Come on," Luke gritted out in a low voice. "We need to get out of here."

Nobody in the diner was paying much attention to the TV or them, but all it would take was a second and they might.

"I-I…" Oh no. She was going to lose it right there in this booth.

"Look at me, Kitten."

His words, his brown eyes, brought her back. Grounded her. "We're going to make it through this. Keep your head down and stay close to me."

They stood and he wrapped an arm around her, pulling her close. He handed her the bacon in the napkin.

Each step to the exit was a nightmare. Several people glanced at the TV between bites. Had they noticed her? Had anyone called the police?

She leaned into his chest, breathing in his scent.

"That's right. Just act like there's nowhere else you'd rather be than cuddled close to me."

No acting necessary.

She felt his lips against her hair. "We're going to make it through this," he repeated before paying and ushering her out the door.

She felt frozen, even though the fall air was mild.

Making it through this seemed impossible now.

Chapter Seven

Luke didn't waste time getting them out of the parking lot once they were in the truck, but it was all a blur for Claire.

Khan immediately jumped into her lap to get the bacon he could smell through the napkin. She unwrapped it and began to break it into pieces, barely aware of what she was doing.

She watched while he gobbled it up. Hot tears stung her eyes. The days where she and Khan could count on regular meals and the safety of their home were long gone. It could be that they'd never return to their little cottage with the cozy window seat and sunny back porch.

She was well and truly a fugitive now.

"What am I going to do?" she whispered.

Luke's knuckles were white against the steering wheel. "It was a smart play on Ballard's part. Make it so you can't go to the police. It puts you on the defensive, not to mention legitimizes the reason he's had police looking for you."

None of that made her feel any better.

Luke drove, keeping to side roads, his gaze constantly sliding to the rear and side mirrors to check for people following them. He reached into his jacket pocket and pulled out an older-model cell phone.

"Here. I need you to dial a number for me."

"Whose phone is this?"

"I borrowed it from someone in the diner… When I saw one that didn't require a pass code, I couldn't resist. We can't take a chance on using either of our phones. It could lead Ballard right to us. I'll make sure it gets returned."

She shrugged. "You're probably doing the person a favor so he or she can upgrade."

She dialed the number he gave her and then pressed the speaker button, handing it back to him. Luke laid the phone on his leg as it rang.

"Gavett." The voice on the other end was hurried and gruff.

"Officer Gavett. We spoke earlier about a locked computer file? I was wondering if we could talk again." She noticed Luke was careful not to use either of their names.

There was silence on the other end for a few long moments. She started to worry the officer didn't know who it was or maybe didn't care now that she was a fugitive.

"Yes," Gavett finally said. "I need a few minutes. I'll call you back on this number."

He hung up and she looked over at Luke. "Was that a bad sign?"

"Do you mean is he going to try to trace our location? I don't think so. My brother Weston saved his life when he was on the force."

The cell phone rang a few minutes later. Luke once again put it on speaker. "Rick?"

"Patterson. I had to leave the office to make this call. Had to find an honest-to-God pay phone, and let me tell you, not many exist anymore."

Luke's jaw flexed. "That doesn't sound like good news. I'm not trying to get you in trouble."

"After what Weston did for me, whatever you need is worth it. You in a private space?"

Luke glanced over at her. "Claire is here. We're on the road."

Rick was silent for a moment. "You sure we shouldn't talk alone for a few minutes?"

Claire caught his eye. "It's okay," she whispered.

How could she possibly blame Luke if he felt like he needed to talk to his police officer friend without her listening in?

Luke shook his head. "She didn't do it, Rick. She didn't kill Julia Lindsey. Her boss, Vance Ballard, did. Claire is a witness."

Rick let out a loud sigh. "Well, the mandate to find her is coming all the way from the top of the Texas law enforcement chain. Through the same office of the guys who paid you a visit yesterday—Arellano and Fisher."

Claire caught her bottom lip between her teeth. Cops had questioned Luke yesterday?

"What's that mean?" Luke asked. "Are they dirty?"

"I don't think so. But this whole thing feels wrong. It's got a political flavor to it, like someone is using Texas law enforcement for their own personal vendetta—especially if you're assuring me Ms. Wallace didn't have anything to do with the murder."

Claire stopped chewing her lip long enough to speak up. "Vance Ballard is powerful. He would probably have friends very high up the chain. They may not be corrupt, but they would be more willing to listen to what he says about me because they know him."

"Right," Rick agreed. "The problem is, I'm the only one who was looking into you before all this went down. I'm the only one who knew your file had been locked and that there was something not right about this entire situation."

"How bad is the evidence?" Luke asked.

"Bad. And there's nothing I can do for you from my level. Even if I started to shout that something smells fishy, I don't have any proof of any wrongdoing. Bottom line is, watch your back because there's a giant target on it."

Claire caught Luke's eye. He offered what was probably an attempt at a reassuring smile, except it looked more like a grimace.

"Roger that, Rick."

"I've got to go." There was the sound of muffled voices on Rick's end. "I'll email you the files I have on the evidence in about ten minutes. But it won't make you happy."

Luke nodded even though Rick couldn't see him. "Thanks for everything. Take care of yourself."

Hanging up, Luke passed the phone to Claire. Mute, she took it.

Fifteen minutes later, they stopped at a higher-end hotel—one that had a business center where he could access his email and print the files Rick had sent.

Claire knew by the look on his face as he came back out that it wasn't good. Like Rick had said, he wasn't happy.

He handed the printouts to her as he pulled back onto the street.

Reading the printouts soon had everything she'd eaten at the diner curdling in her belly. Ballard had created a fake email chain that made it look like Claire was jealous of Julia because of her position at Passage.

Her tongue had become impossibly heavy. "It's all false."

Tears blurred her vision. It was a good fabrication. It looked like Julia and Claire had messaged back and forth multiple times, with Claire accusing Julia of stealing her ideas. Claire came across as bitter and ugly—warning Julia to "watch her back," and that she would make sure the emails would never be found by anyone.

Then Ballard had swooped in like the hero and dug them up.

The papers shook in her hand as she read it all again. "It makes me look unstable. But the chain is reasonable with just enough detail without going overboard. He probably took real emails between me and Julia and just changed the content."

Ballard had manipulated it to make it look like the communication started weeks ago and then escalated.

"That can be done?"

"Not by most people." She closed her eyes, wishing it would all go away. "But by Ballard, yes."

He had to be applauded. He'd done a fantastic job making it seem Claire had reason to kill Julia. If Claire read this, she'd believe it, too.

Luke continued to drive them farther out of town. "It gives proof of motive. That's all Ballard needed right now."

"There's no going to the cops now." Hot tears pressed against her closed eyelids. "No one will believe me. I don't even understand why you do… You don't really know me."

Luke's silence just added to her fear.

Maybe he thought she'd lied to him. Could she really blame him?

Abruptly, the truck slowed down.

Claire opened her eyes to find they were entering a

wooded area. The sign read Government Canyon State Natural Area.

She tensed, papers crumpling in her hands. Was he planning to leave her here?

Again, she couldn't really blame him. Like Rick had said, she had a target on her back and staying with her would put one on Luke's back, too. Not to mention anything he did to help her was illegal.

She couldn't bring herself to ask what he was going to do.

By the time he pulled into the nearly empty parking lot and turned to her, she wasn't sure she was going to be able to keep it together.

"Luke, I—" She wasn't sure what she was going to say, just knew she needed to say something.

"Let's go for a walk—let Khan get some fresh air and exercise."

They walked along one of the many paths, stopping when they got to a picnic table.

"Luke," she started again. "I know it looks bad. I know you must wonder if I'm lying to you, and rightfully so."

He turned and climbed up onto the picnic table, sitting on the table itself. "Do you know what I remember most about you from Skyline Park?"

She shook her head.

"Well, I mean, besides those big blue eyes that were always studying everyone from afar. You never liked to talk to anyone. And you always tried to get on the computer—not that the bigger kids gave you much of a chance."

She shrugged. "I was too young to do much computer-wise then anyway. That's what you remember? Me on the computer?"

"No, what I remember is you sneaking your snack money into Amelia Whalen's backpack."

Claire felt her face burn. "She needed it. She stayed after school and always got hungry. Her stomach used to growl at night. I was never hungry, so I didn't need the money."

The side of his mouth pulled up in a smile. "Even though you never liked talking to anyone, you were always aware of what was going on around you, even as a little kid. And you did something about it."

She swallowed hard, her throat burning. "Anyone would've done it."

He reached out and snagged her hand, pulling her over until she was standing between his knees where his feet rested on the picnic bench.

"No." His voice was firm. "They wouldn't. I've been around a lot of people, both when I was a kid bouncing from place to place before the Pattersons, and in the army. I've learned how to read them. How to judge intentions and purposes. Little Claire had no reason to help Amelia Whalen, especially not secretly."

"I'm not little Claire anymore."

She stared down at where Khan had come to rub against her legs, sensing her distress. She shifted her gaze back up to his when his finger tilted her head gently under her chin.

"No, you're definitely not little Claire anymore...but your heart is still the same. Still generous. I've learned to trust my instincts, and they're telling me you're one of the good guys."

She parted her lips, unsure of how to respond. Luke had helped her so much already. Him putting his faith in her now wasn't something she took lightly.

"Thank you," she whispered. "I want to prove it wasn't me who killed Julia."

He leaned his forehead against hers. "We will."

His lips touched hers, softly, briefly, before pulling away. All she could do was stare at him.

He actually growled at her. "Staring at me with those big, beautiful eyes is just going to get you kissed again, Kitten."

Was that supposed to scare her off? She tilted her head and raised an eyebrow at him.

He chuckled. "So, the kitten has little claws."

He slipped his arm around her waist and yanked her closer. She laughed breathlessly as her body fell against his.

Then he kissed her for real.

His lips were gentle but firm, commanding but careful. So perfectly Luke.

Claire scooted up onto her knees on the bench between his legs, wrapping her arms around his neck as one of his hands gripped her waist firmly and the other trailed along her spine.

She'd dreamed about this kiss for years. Even when she hadn't been old enough to really know what kisses were supposed to be, she'd known that she'd wanted her kisses to be with Luke.

This one didn't disappoint.

He kissed her with shattering absorption, as if he couldn't get enough of her. His tongue invited hers to play, to dance. His teeth nipped at her full bottom lip gently before soothing the sweet hurt with a gentle lick.

They were both breathing heavily by the time they

broke apart. This wasn't the time or place to get lost in each other.

But now she had even more reason to clear her name. *More kisses with Luke.*

Chapter Eight

The feel of Claire's lips and that sexy little breathless moan she made as he kissed her were still in the forefront of Luke's mind two hours later as he paid for his purchases at a local superstore.

The cashier popped her gum as she scanned his items. Some food for both them and Khan, a change of clothes for the both of them, a brunette wig for Claire, and a prepaid cell phone he could use without worrying about tracing.

Burner phone.

Luke scrubbed a hand over his face. He definitely hadn't been expecting to need burner phones when this week had started.

If the cashier found his collection unusual in any way, her popping gum never let on to the fact. She looked more bored than anything as she placed each item into the bag after scanning it.

Good. Bored meant she wasn't paying attention and made him much more forgettable.

She told him his amount. "Card or cash?"

"Cash." Luke pulled out his wallet and handed her some bills.

This stuff wasn't cheap. He had enough to cover it,

but between paying for last night's second hotel, gas and all this with cash, he was now officially running low.

Turning away from the cashier as she counted the money and put it in the drawer, he looked out the store's window. His truck sat close to the front where he could access it easily, Claire's blonde head tucked low in the window.

He hadn't wanted to leave her out there with just Khan as protection, but that was a better option than taking a chance on her being recognized in the store. Plus, she was already coming up with some ideas on how to fight back against Ballard.

A smile tugged at Luke's lips. That big brain of hers. He had no doubt she would figure out how to access the data she needed to prove her innocence.

And he was going to provide her with whatever help she needed.

Taking the bags, he hurried out of the store. Claire sat up straighter when she caught him approaching and gave him a little wave. He smiled but couldn't stop staring at her lips.

He wanted another kiss. Forget the fact that his arms were full of items that were supposed to help hide them from a law enforcement hunt.

Focus, Patterson.

His focus was something he was usually known for. But something about Claire Wallace blew his focus to hell.

He opened the door and tossed the bags in beside him. "Are you okay? Any problems?"

He reached over and squeezed her hand before starting the engine. "You're the one who has her picture all over the news, and you're worried about *me*?"

She shrugged. "I can't stand the thought of anything happening to you."

He leaned over and stole a kiss. Just a brief one, afraid that if he let his lips linger, they might start a show right here in the parking lot that would get them arrested for nothing having to do with her fugitive status. He kissed her forehead before he moved back into place and started the truck.

"Did you get everything we need?" Claire asked, putting the plastic bags on the floor near her feet.

He drove out of the parking lot, careful not to draw any attention to them. "Yes. I think you'll look good as a brunette."

She made a face. "I guess so. Did you get cat food?"

"Are you kidding? I'm not taking any chances on that cat-dog chasing me down a back alley because I forgot."

"Good. He can't keep living on bacon and beef jerky."

She looked through the bag. "You didn't use a credit card, right? I should've mentioned that before. Ballard is definitely watching for movement on mine. He's probably watching yours, too."

"No, I used cash. I always carry a pretty good amount with me—a by-product of growing up so long without any money at all."

For years he'd tried not to carry so much, refusing to let the past dictate his present. It was his dad who'd finally sat him down and told him that not everything about his past needed to be fought. If carrying cash helped his subconscious be at ease, then carry the damn money.

Fight the real wars, not the cosmetic ones.

She tried on the brown wig. "How do I look?"

He glanced over. "Good. I like your natural look better, but this helps you blend in a little more."

He didn't even say anything when his truck smelled

like cat food a few minutes later when she cracked open a can for Khan.

But they were going to have to come up with a plan. Driving around increased their chances of being pulled over.

"I think I know what I need to do," she said after Khan finished eating. "I have the drive with the info that proves Ballard planned to use Gouda for illegal purposes…" She looked out the window, her fingers twisting in Khan's fur as he settled on her lap. Luke knew that meant she was thinking, so he gave her time.

"Thing is," she started up again suddenly, "the data can't be read outside of Passage Digital because of the proprietary coding we use."

"Can you find a way around that?"

She nodded. "I think I can build a shell program robust enough to extract the information. It won't be perfect, but it will be proof enough to get the police looking into Ballard and Passage Digital."

"Okay. That's good news. What do you need?" Luke bypassed the turn onto the highway in case they needed to stay in town. "Special equipment?"

"No, it's all coding based. I need a computer that's on public Wi-Fi, so I can make it more difficult to find where I'm located, with uninterrupted time and nobody else around."

"How much time?"

She grimaced. "It's hard to say exactly, but it won't be short. A few hours."

"We'll be too noticeable at a coffeehouse or hotel lobby for that long. We'll have to break in somewhere."

"That might bring the cops straight to us."

It wasn't a perfect plan. Hell, it wasn't even a *good* plan. He would much rather have a few days to scope somewhere out to see if they had alarms or security. Or go somewhere he was familiar with and could protect her more easily.

A location came to mind. One where he'd watched out for her when they were kids.

"How about the Wars Hill library?" He watched for her reaction.

A little smile lit her face. "That would be perfect."

Of the limited time they'd had together when they were young, a lot of it had been spent there. She'd stayed at the library until closing just about every evening. Book time. Computer time. Avoid the group home time.

Once Luke had discovered where she was disappearing to, he'd begun joining her. At first, he was only looking out for her.

But Claire, who'd read way above her grade level, started recommending books to him. That library, waiting for her to finish on the computer so he could walk her home each day, was where he'd developed a love for reading.

The next time Brax wanted to tease him about staying in with a book on a Friday night instead of going out and having fun, Luke would tell him to blame Claire.

At the next red light, he turned south in the direction of the library. He drove by it often enough to know the building hadn't changed much. But more importantly, he was familiar with it and would be better able to keep watch there.

"It's a plan," he said. "We'll park a pretty good distance away, get there before it closes, and hide. That's better than trying to break in."

He glanced over at her and she smiled at him, her brown hair not right, but still beautiful. "Maybe by this time tomorrow, this can all be over."

Chapter Nine

The library hadn't changed much in the past fifteen years. The puffy blue couches in the children's section had been reupholstered but were the same. The glass study rooms in the back hadn't changed much, either.

They'd parked the truck a quarter mile away—he hadn't wanted to take any chances on it being spotted near the library. Claire hadn't wanted to leave Khan behind. A backpack Luke had forgotten about and found stuffed under one of the truck's seats did the trick. Nestled in there, with the top unzipped a bit for air, the cat only meowed occasionally.

It was impressive, really, the amount of trust that animal had in his human. Then again, she'd no doubt worshipped the little furball from the start.

Kitten.

Luke smiled to himself. Claire was definitely more of a kitten than Khan was.

They slipped in separately about an hour before closing, long enough ahead of time so the librarian wouldn't be paying attention. Claire headed back to the fiction section and Luke ended up in poetry.

He was the least poetry-reading guy he'd ever known but forced himself to crack open a book anyway. Walt Whitman wasn't so bad.

A mom with three young kids came in about twenty minutes before closing and couldn't have provided a better cover if Luke had been designing it himself. The librarian's attention was immediately homed in on them, undoubtedly because the older man didn't want to have to clean up whatever the kids dug out right before closing.

Still, finding a place to hide where he wouldn't find them wouldn't be easy. Luke started scoping it out. He was back in the nonfiction section when Claire found him and motioned for him to follow.

"I can't believe it's still here," she whispered.

"What?"

She didn't answer, just gestured for him to keep following as they took a back aisle toward the children and teens section. The librarian was busy checking out the books for the mom and kids.

"Here." She walked over to a display that took up the entire back corner of the room. Worldwide scenes lit up the front, telling kids that reading could take them wherever they wanted to go.

"It's really nice." Luke didn't know what more to say. He vaguely remembered the display from their time here.

She walked over to the side of the display. "It's also still got a false back…"

"What?"

Claire pulled the back of the display from the side it should've been attached to. Sure enough, it created an opening big enough to slip into.

An announcement came over the speaker that the library was closing in five minutes.

"Is it big enough for both of us?" he asked.

She nodded. "As long as you're not claustrophobic."

"Closed-in spaces aren't my favorite, but I'll manage."

He followed her as she slipped inside, then pulled the back panel into its rightful place.

It was definitely tight between the two of them and Khan's backpack. But claustrophobia was the last thing Luke was thinking about.

How could he when Claire's body was pressed up against him from head to toe?

"Hi," he whispered.

Her head dropped against his chest. "Fancy meeting you here. This space seemed a lot bigger when I hid here as a kid."

He put his hands on her hips. "You doing okay?"

He pulled her closer when she slid her arms around her waist. "Yeah."

They fell quiet, both smiling as they heard the librarian sing Broadway show tunes as he went about his closing duties. A few minutes later, when they heard everything switch off, Luke knew they were probably in the clear.

"Do you think it's safe to leave?" she whispered.

"I think we better stay in here a few more minutes."

A plan that had nothing to do with the librarian and everything to do with him tilting up her face and bringing his lips down to hers.

He kept the kiss gentle and lazy, giving her plenty of opportunity to pull away if she wanted, and it wasn't long before he could feel her fingertips pushing against his back, bringing him *closer*, not away.

She wanted him, but it couldn't possibly be as much as he wanted her. He could stay here for hours and worship the generous curves of her mouth.

And that was nothing compared to what he'd like to do to the rest of her body.

But he forced himself to ease back. This wasn't the

time or place for all the things he wanted to do to her, wanted them to do to each other.

He tilted his forehead against hers. They were both breathing heavily. "As much as I want to continue, we should save this for another time…"

"Yeah, you're right."

Khan meowed softly as if to offer his agreement, too. They both chuckled.

"Do you think it's safe to come out now?" she whispered.

"Yes." Luke turned so he could edge the back of the display open again. It was dim in the library. "Stay here while I double-check."

It didn't take long to confirm the building was empty. He returned to Claire and helped her out from the display.

She immediately set the backpack down so she could let the cat, literally, out of the bag. Khan stretched and walked around as if he owned the place.

"Okay, what do you need?" he asked.

"The computer lab. I'll hack into the statewide system so it hides where we are, then I will need to backdoor into Passage Digital." She began walking toward the lab.

"Stay away from the windows." It was dim in here, but not completely dark. They couldn't take a chance on being spotted by someone out walking their dog.

"Okay."

She chose the computer station in the back corner of the lab, fired it up, and started typing right away. There was no hesitation whatsoever.

"First, I have to bypass their password system."

He watched from over her shoulder. "How long will that take?"

"Already done it." Pleasure filled her voice. She was in her happy place.

"Already?" It took him longer than that to remember his own password most days.

She seemed not to hear him. With Khan at her feet, she was completely focused on the task at hand. He respected that kind of concentration and left her to it.

He moved back out of the computer lab and into the main section of the library, walking over to the side of a window and peeking out. Nothing out of the ordinary was happening in the empty parking lot. A glance out a window on the other side of the building, looking out into a playground and other buildings, resulted in the same.

This place brought back some good feelings for him. There weren't a lot in his earlier years. His life hadn't been too traumatic—nothing like what his brothers Chance or Brax went through—just a lot of hunger, combined with kicks and hits and well-placed bruises.

Life with the Pattersons had changed all that. Which reminded him that he needed to call his brothers.

He used his burner phone to dial Brax's cell number.

"Brax Patterson." Brax's voice was tense.

"It's me."

His brother let out a long exhale. "You all right? We saw the news."

"Yeah. We're both still alive." Luke leaned around a shelf to check on Claire. She typed away with laser focus, though her brown wig was askew.

"We've been waiting for you to call. The cops came by looking for you."

Even though it was news he'd expected, it still made Luke tense. "What did you say?"

"Exactly what you did. That you were away on a fishing trip. We even showed them the text."

"Did it throw them off?"

"They were still suspicious. Weston had a tail on him when he went out today. Where are you?"

"Somewhere that Claire can get the info she needs to clear her name." He lowered his voice. "She witnessed the murder of a coworker at Passage Digital. Now the CEO is trying to frame her for it. He's using all his political connections to bring her down hard."

Brax cursed sharply.

"Yeah, my feelings exactly."

"How can she prove her innocence?"

"Ballard isn't only guilty of murder. He's trying to use some app to illegally collect data on minors to be stored and used later—think access to bank accounts and private identity when the kids come of age."

Brax cursed again.

"She has proof of that on a drive," Luke continued. "But it's only readable through some proprietary software at Passage, so she's trying to hack her way into that. Once she can prove Ballard is guilty of identity theft, she'll be able to go to the police and show that he was using her as a scapegoat."

"What about the murder?"

"She's got video footage of it stuffed into the Passage Digital intraweb. She can't access it from outside, but if they arrest Ballard and let her into Passage, she'll be able to access it."

"Sounds like she's some sort of computer genius."

Pride filled Luke. "Exactly."

"How long will that take for her to get what she needs?"

"A few hours maybe. Hard to say." He rubbed the back of his neck. He didn't like the thought of being in one spot for so long, but there was no way around it. "Listen, once she gets what she needs, I need you to get Weston to meet Rick and arrange for us to come in tomorrow."

"Okay."

"Go see him face-to-face. Calling is too dangerous," Luke warned. "Rick left his office to use a pay phone earlier to call me. He thinks this whole search for Claire smells rotten."

"That's because it is. We'll take care of it. You worry about everything on your end. I'll contact you in a few hours."

"Thanks, Brax." Some of the tension left his shoulders. He could always count on his family to come through.

Hanging up, Luke pulled one of the granola bars he'd picked up at the supermarket from his pocket and went back to the computer lab.

Claire was hunched forward, her face inches from the screen. "Dumb general user interface... So unprofessional..."

"Hey." He leaned against the wall next to the computer. "Time to eat something."

Her gaze remained fixed on the computer. "I'm not hungry."

"You need to keep your energy up. It's a stressful situation. You're burning more calories than you realize."

She extended a hand in his general direction but missed the granola bar by about a foot.

Chuckling, he slipped the bar into her palm. She promptly slapped it on the table next to the keyboard.

"You need to put it in your mouth for the eating thing to work." He crouched beside her and opened the wrapper. He took her hand off the keyboard and put the granola bar in it.

He stood back up when she gnawed on the snack with one hand still typing. Khan stretched out under the desk, waving a paw in the air. They were both in their zones, with only Luke left with nothing to do.

But he could do what he'd done for Claire even when they were kids—he would look out for her.

Leaving them at the desk, he walked to the other end of the library and back. He constantly kept diligent watch out various windows in between checking on her.

An hour went by.

Then another.

Then another.

By the time five had passed, and it was closer to dawn than sunset, he was starting to feel itchy. They'd been here too long. His instincts were starting to holler at him.

He wanted to give her as much time as possible, but time was running out.

"That's right…" she mumbled, as wide-awake as she'd been when they stepped into the library. "What do you think of that, Khan?"

He smirked from his perch near the periodicals. She'd been talking to the cat all night, and it made her even cuter.

But then she stiffened and stopped typing, the first time he'd seen her do that all night. "Uh-oh. That's not good."

He straightened and in a handful of strides, reached her chair. "What?" The coding stuff on her screen was all but a foreign language to him.

"I had to access the Passage Digital system remotely to be able to do what I need to."

He nodded, although he wasn't exactly certain what that meant.

"I knew they would see my intrusion into the system. I set it up so it looked like it was coming from one of the remote offices in Canada—nothing they'd deem too suspicious, just someone working late."

"What was the *uh-oh* about?"

"A few minutes ago, I thought maybe they'd caught me. An extra firewall went up."

"And that's bad?"

"Yeah, but expected. I was about to work my way around it, but then it dropped on its own."

"Why would it do that?"

She looked at him. "I'd like to say it's because the system doesn't see what I'm doing as a threat. But—"

"But it's more likely they're trying to keep you on-line," he finished for her.

She nodded. "Yes."

"How much more time do you need?"

"An hour. Maybe two. This is the most critical time."

"That's too long. Can you get any info at all in a shorter amount of time?"

"Maybe. It'll be a smash-and-grab, but it might work." She immediately started typing again; if possible, her fingers flew faster than they had been before.

He went back to the windows.

If they wanted to keep Claire online, it was because they were trying to track her.

He'd give her twenty more minutes, tops. After that, they had to go. It would no longer be safe here.

But less than a minute went by before one of the shadows out near the parking lot caught his attention. It was different than it had been before. Three hours of watching out these windows had ingrained the specifics of these shadows into his brain.

Sure enough, a few moments later, someone darted across the edge of the parking lot, moving from shadow to shadow to the side of the library. The only gleam that gave him away was when the moonlight reflected for a split second off the gun in his hand.

They didn't have twenty minutes.

"Claire," he said, raising his voice, "pack it up. We've got to go right now."

Chapter Ten

She didn't look up from her screen. "I'm almost done. Maybe thirty minutes."

They barely had thirty seconds, forget thirty minutes. "Now, Kitten."

She still didn't stop typing. "Really, I only need—"

Her protest morphed into a yelp as he wrapped an arm around her waist and lifted her from the seat.

"Ballard has been keeping you online to give his men time to get here. They're outside. We've got to go."

He set her down and she spun to face him. "What?"

"Ballard's men. Outside. I think that's what the firewall reversing was all about. They traced you here, and they're probably going to kill you."

He pulled open the backpack and shoved it into her hands. Khan bristled at the sight of the bag but allowed himself to be put inside. Luke zipped it almost the entire way, then loosened the straps and put it on his shoulders. He'd be able to run faster with it.

"We need to go out the employee exit." Taking Claire's hand, he rushed with her along the back wall.

At the door, they kept to the side as he looked out the window.

Damn it. Luke spotted two men before pulling his

head back. Ballard's men had the library surrounded and it wouldn't be long before they breached the building.

He cursed under his breath. There would be no quick getaway.

"What?" she whispered.

"They've got us surrounded. They're covering both doors."

"What are we going to do?"

His mind raced. They needed a distraction. Calling the police wasn't an option, but…

He pulled the burner out of his pocket and dialed.

"9-1-1," the dispatcher answered, "what's your emergency?"

Luke took a couple of shallow breaths to make himself sound more panicked. "The Wars Hill library is on fire. Oh my gosh, it's spreading so fast. Please hurry." He hung up before the dispatcher could ask any further questions.

Claire's eyes widened. "Are we going to start a fire?"

"No, but the fire trucks and paramedics will be here soon. Hopefully, that'll chase off Ballard's men and we'll get away in the confusion."

She looked skeptical, and he couldn't blame her. He fought back a tiny smile at the sight of her. Her brown wig had gotten pretty twisted and wisps of blond hair kissed the corners of her face. Once again, she looked like the little girl he'd known.

Little girl or grown woman, there was no way in hell he was letting Ballard's men get her.

The sound of a lock breaking and the emergency alarm being smashed to eliminate the noise echoed through the library. Luke grabbed her hand and pulled her back to the display in the children's section.

They barely made it inside before they heard voices.

"Check every aisle," a man called. "They're in here somewhere."

Luke pulled Claire's stiff form against him. He cocked his head, trying to figure out exactly how many men there were as they talked. Three? Four?

He was a good shot, but he wouldn't have much chance at getting them all before they got shots off themselves.

A ringing phone only a few feet away from the display made Claire jerk. Luke tugged her closer to him, wrapping his fingers around her nape, massaging gently. It was over for them if she had some sort of panic attack now.

"Hello?" one of the men answered. Brief silence followed. "Damn it. We haven't found them. Maybe they got out before we got here, but there's not going to be enough time for a thorough search." More silence. "Yes, sir."

The man yelled louder, "Fire department is en route thanks to a 9-1-1 call. ETA less than five."

"Bathrooms and employee rooms are clear," another voice responded from farther away. "No sign of them."

"We don't have enough time to search thoroughly. But we'll give the fire department a real fire to fight and cover the exits. There's a gas canister in the van. Have Brickman bring it in. Hurry."

Damn it, Luke had handed the bad guys exactly what they needed by placing that emergency call.

The best bet was still to stay put. Getting out in the chaos of the fire would give them a better chance of survival than facing their guns.

The smell of gas a minute later had Luke reconsidering that notion. Then the pungent smell of smoke.

"Make sure we've got both doors covered. We'll get them running out or when the fire department brings out their charred bodies." The voices faded as the smell of smoke grew stronger.

"What do we do?" Claire's pitch was high and her breathing was way too rapid.

"It's okay," he whispered. "Just wait a minute." They had to make sure no one was still inside the building.

Their best bet was to stay alive until the firefighters arrived, and then they could get out with them. More witnesses equaled more protection.

But that was easier said than done. The smoke invading the air caused all his survival instincts to kick into overdrive. His feet ached to run.

"Luke?"

"They have to be gone by now. We're going to keep low and crawl out." He pushed aside the display so he could crawl out.

They moved on their hands and knees, Khan meowing pathetically from the bag slung over his back.

"Which door are we using?" She coughed into her hand.

"We have to stay here and wait for the fire department."

He had to give her credit; she didn't give in to hysteria. "Will we make it that long?"

"We have to. If we go out either door now," he said, "they'll shoot us on sight."

She was right, the fire was spreading too fast for them to be able to breathe by the time the fire department arrived, even if it was just a couple of minutes. This place was an arsonist's dream.

They both had pulled their shirts to cover their mouths, but even low to the ground, the smoke was getting thicker. The heat from the burning books surrounded them from all directions.

They were going to have to exit. Take their chances.

"We're going to go out the front door." He put his lips

right next to her ear so she could hear him. "You stay behind me and then run for the nearest emergency worker."

Her whole body was shaking. "They'll shoot. They'll shoot you first to get to me."

"It's a chance we'll have to take. They're covering the doors, but we can't stay in here."

Her eyes grew larger. "Wait. I have an idea. Follow me."

She scurried off toward the back of the building. He almost stopped her—going out the front where there were potentially more people was probably a better plan. But then she turned toward the western end of the building.

The bathrooms. That might buy them a little bit of time, but it might trap them.

He grabbed her ankle where she crawled in front of him. She turned. "The bathrooms might trap us," he yelled to be heard over the fire.

She yelled something back, but he could only make out one word, but it was the most important one.

Window.

They made it inside, the thinner smoke allowing them to stand and breathe a little easier. Luke unzipped the backpack and let Khan out, grabbing the clothing that had lined the bottom and stuffing it in the crack at the door. It would buy them a little more time.

"There's a window in the storage closet." She pointed at a closed door. "I used it once when I was maxed out on my book checkouts but had another story I really wanted to read. But I returned it."

Even in the middle of all this, she actually looked embarrassed that she'd stolen a book.

Luke didn't waste any time; he moved to the door and when he found it locked, he kicked it near the knob.

One look at the window had him swallowing a curse.

He was sure eleven-year-old Claire had made it through with her stolen book. Adult Claire was going to be a tighter fit, but she would make it. *Him?*

Claire chewed her bottom lip. "Wow. That's a lot smaller than I remember…"

"You'll fit."

"What about you?"

"I'll fit, too."

He grabbed the large flashlight in the corner of the closet and wrapped it in a shirt, using it to break the window as quietly as possible. Ballard's men probably wouldn't be looking for them in this direction, but there was no point in drawing their attention.

It broke with the second hit and he cleared the glass out as much as possible. "You need to go first. I'll hoist you up. Watch the edges."

When he whirled around, she was holding Khan out to him.

Of course she was.

"Come on, cat." Khan knew what to do and scurried through the window to safety. There were no sounds from the outside, a good sign.

He turned back to Claire, linking his hands together so she could step into them. It took barely any effort to hoist her up, and she slid through the opening without difficulty.

His turn.

Grabbing hold of the window's bottom frame, he pulled himself up. Little bits of glass pricked his palms, but he ignored the pain and wiggled into the window until his shoulders got stuck.

Damn it.

He had to ease himself back into the closet to come at the window from another angle. The smoke was getting bad. If he couldn't make it through, he might not be getting out of this building at all.

He pulled himself up again, twisting to make himself as narrow as possible through the shoulders. He bit back a curse at the sharp pain ripping through his shirt and into his flesh—a piece of glass that had shifted. There was nowhere to get away from it, so he pulled his shoulders the rest of the way through, gritting his teeth at the burn.

Once his shoulders were out, the rest was slightly easier. Twisting again, he used the wall to give himself leverage. By the time he was all the way out, he could feel the blood soaking his shirt and was barely able to keep from coughing from the smoke inhalation.

He sucked in a deep breath. There would be time later to rest and worry about his wound. Right now, he needed to get them out of here. "Let's head for the bushes, Kitten."

When there was no response, he looked in both directions but didn't see any sign of Claire. Ignoring his screaming shoulder, he moved to rise.

And stopped at a voice that definitely wasn't Claire's.

"Don't move and keep your hands where I can see them."

Chapter Eleven

Luke's gun was tucked in the back waistband of his jeans. This guy would definitely get a shot off if he went for it, especially slowed down by his shoulder.

He raised his hands. "Easy."

"Where's the woman?" The man took a step closer.

Luke fought not to let his relief be seen. If they were still looking for Claire, then that meant they didn't have her. Yet.

"What woman?" Maybe feigning innocence would buy him some time.

The guy stepped closer. "You know who I'm talking about."

"I don't know who you're talking about. I just fell asleep in the library. The place is on fire, man."

He tried to check his peripheral vision for any sign of Claire. Was she safe? She wouldn't have just left him there. Maybe she'd run off after Khan.

The guy's eyes narrowed. "I don't know who you are or how you got involved with her, but she's guilty of murder. If you tell me where she is, we'll make sure she's brought to justice before she hurts anyone else. You don't have to get hurt. Nobody else needs to get hurt."

The guy kept his weapon steady and trained on Luke. He was definitely a professional.

"I don't know who or what you're talking about." Luke continued his charade, spoke slowly and kept his hands up. "I just want to get away from this burning building."

"If you don't know who or where she is, then you're not of any use to us. Might as well get rid of you now."

So much for them being the good guys.

The man kept his gun trained on Luke as he brought his walkie-talkie up with his other hand. "This is Brickman. Tell Kenneth I've got—"

With a sickening thud, Brickman crumpled. His gun hit the ground, followed by his face.

Right behind where he'd just been standing, Claire stood, holding up the wooden skateboard she'd just used to clobber the guy. "Is he dead?" Poking his head around Claire's legs, Khan meowed.

Luke hauled himself to his feet, pain shooting through his shoulder. "No. You knocked him out." He nudged Brickman with his foot just to make sure. The jerk groaned incoherently.

"Are you okay?" She dropped the skateboard. "I heard him coming around the corner and had to hide. I didn't just leave you."

He forced a smile. "I never thought that. You did the smart thing. Now we need to get out of here before they come looking for Brickman."

He grabbed her hand and began to pull her toward the bushes. She immediately yanked her hand free. "Luke. Oh my gosh. You're covered in blood!"

He grimaced. "I cut my shoulder going through the window. I'm okay. We've got to go."

A blue light flashed across Claire's face from a police car. One vehicle was just pulling into the library's front parking lot, but the sirens screaming through the night promised that more first responders were on their way.

She was still staring at his shoulder. "You're hurt bad," she whispered.

He would have to suck it up—Ballard's men were everywhere. "Survive now. Tend to the wounds later."

She nodded. Taking her hand with his good one, they darted for the few trees near the playground on the side of the blazing building. Khan stayed right with them.

They needed to get away from here.

"I don't think we can get directly to the truck," he muttered with a curse. There were too many of Ballard's men and now too many first responders.

"We should go that way." She pointed toward the back parking lot. "That leads farther into town, which means more places to hide."

He glanced back at the line of tall, manicured bushes behind the library's back lot. It would provide a perfect escape, but he was less familiar with that area and it was in the opposite direction of the truck. "Are you sure?"

She nodded. "Yes. I came back to this area for my last foster family in high school. We can hide until it's clear, then circle back."

More lights, both red and blue, flashed against the greenery. The fire department had arrived out front.

But another cop car had pulled up in the back lot. Damn it. They'd have to be doubly careful now—avoiding Ballard's men and the police.

They crept along, staying in the shadows. Organized chaos was evident in the front with the fire department concentrating on the burning building. Hopefully nobody would be paying much attention back here.

He nudged Claire forward through a break in the

bushes. Turning sideways to fit, he scooted through, wincing when the sharp leaves scraped his shoulder.

Claire's gasp turned his blood cold.

One of Ballard's men was there waiting, his weapon drawn.

The man gave them a cocky smile. "I knew you two were still around here somewhere. Count yourself lucky. Bullet is a better way to die than fire."

A helpless rage swallowed Luke. He wouldn't even be able to get in front of Claire to shield her.

"Freeze!"

The command came from the parking lot a few yards to the side of Ballard's man. He kept his gun trained on Claire as he tilted his head to the side to talk to the cop.

"Officer— Thank goodness! I've got that fugitive that's been on the TV. She has a gun, be careful!"

Then, without hesitation, Ballard's man spun and shot the cop.

Luke leaped for the guy, pushing Claire out of the way. The man had shot that cop and there was no doubt that Luke and Claire were next on his list.

The sharp edge of his palm came down hard on the inside of the man's elbow. The stranger's hold slackened and the gun fell to the ground.

He was quick, though. Trained. A fist came flying toward Luke's face.

A swift block and ignoring the screaming pain from his shoulder, Luke nailed his opponent with an upper-cut. The man staggered back. Luke followed, hitting him with a right hook.

The punches had the intended effect—Ballard's man hit the ground, knocked out cold.

But the fight had taken a toll on Luke, too. Hot, sticky blood dripped down his hand. It had been a bad idea to strike with that arm. He drew a deep breath, trying to stop his head from spinning. A tug on his hand brought him back to his senses.

Claire.

"Are you okay?"

"Yeah." No. He needed to sit down. Needed to get this bleeding under control. Needed to take a moment and regroup.

And maybe he would've if it was just him on his own. But he couldn't. He had to get Claire to safety.

"Is that policeman…?"

"Dead? I don't know. But we can't wait and help him, not if we want to get away."

He took out his burner phone. It wouldn't be much use any longer anyway, now that he'd used it to call Brax. He dialed 9-1-1 again. As soon as the responder picked up, he spoke.

"Officer down behind the Wars Hill library. He's been shot."

He ended the call immediately before the dispatcher could ask questions and grabbed Claire's hand. It would be only moments before the 9-1-1 dispatch notified the police already on the scene here. Calling might have been a mistake, but if there was anything that could be done to save that cop, Luke had to take that chance. Hopefully, it would be enough.

But he and Claire had to get out *now*.

They moved slower along the bushes toward the street on the east side of the building. Luke didn't want to take a chance on stumbling into another one of Ballard's men. The odds of him winning a second fight in his shape were slim.

And Claire would be unprotected.

But if they kept moving this slowly, they might get

caught anyway. Luke was slowing them down. Running was not an option. The way the night was spinning, fast *walking* was barely an option.

He squeezed her hand as they passed by the alleyway. They just needed to make it a few more blocks.

But he wasn't sure he was going to be able to.

"You need to run. Leave me behind. Get farther into the main section of town. You know your way around, you can hide."

"No. I'm not leaving you."

"You have to. I don't think I'm going to make it much farther."

They only needed to go another mile or so, but that seemed impossible. Ten more steps seemed impossible.

She slipped her arm around his waist, tucking herself under his good shoulder. "Lean on me. Just take it one step at a time."

"Go without me."

"You're wasting time and energy arguing, Patterson. I'm not leaving you, so we either both stay here or we both go."

He almost smiled at her bossy tone and took a step forward. And another.

Praying none of Ballard's men would find them, he kept moving forward. Left down a dark block. Right down a second alleyway. His legs weakened. His arm burned like hell. He couldn't stop, though. Wouldn't let anything happen to Claire. *Kitten*.

Were they far enough? He had no idea where they were—walking along some empty street. Had no idea how much time had passed since they left the library. Five minutes? An hour? Ten years?

He had to stop. He leaned heavily with his good shoulder against a parked semitruck that shielded them from anyone on the street.

"You keep going." The words sounded raspy, breathless, not like his voice at all.

She ignored his statement, tentatively touched his shoulder, making him wince. "It looks bad."

"It's okay." A lie, but what else could he say?

All he needed was a few minutes. A place to rest until he regained his strength.

He couldn't contact his brothers—he'd had to dump the burner phone. They couldn't make it back to the truck.

Think, Luke. Think.

He couldn't. He slid to the ground.

It felt so damn good to sit. He closed his eyes. One second of rest. Maybe two…

Something fluffy brushed against his chest. Khan's tail.

Good doggy.

"Bandage it… Shirt is dirty…"

Claire's voice went in and out, impossible to follow.

"We need to go." Planting his palm against the cold metal of the truck, he pushed himself to standing.

And promptly collapsed toward the concrete, the world spinning uncontrollably around him.

Chapter Twelve

"Luke!" Claire caught him before he hit the ground.

His weight bowed her over. Using all her strength, she got him back to sitting, his back propped against the truck.

The streetlight at the end of the block shone on his shoulder. The cut gleamed, shiny and dark.

She'd thought about putting her shirt on the wound, but it had gotten so dirty from crawling out the window, it would probably cause infection.

His head lolled to the side. "Kitten."

Khan spun in a circle, his dance move when anxious. He could tell something was wrong.

A ball formed in Claire's throat. She had to get Luke somewhere safe. She hadn't seen any sign of Ballard's men in the last thirty minutes, but that didn't mean they weren't still searching for them.

She was going to have to take Luke to the hospital, and hope nobody would come looking for them.

She trailed her fingers through his hair, then cupped his cheeks. "Luke. I need you to listen to me, okay?"

His brown eyes blinked open at her. They were glazed with pain, but he was still with her.

"We need to get you to a hospital."

"No. Find us too easy."

"We have to. You need stitches."

He grabbed her wrist where she cupped his face. "No. Too dangerous. Promise."

Damn it. He was probably right, but she had to do something. Get him somewhere they were inside and safe. They didn't have enough money left for another hotel—and Ballard would undoubtedly be searching any nearby establishments for check-ins anyway.

All right, no hospital. No doc-in-a-box, either. They would want names, insurance info, stuff that went into a computer and would enable Ballard to find them.

Khan rubbed up against her. "Where would you want to go if you were hurt, Khan?"

A vet. Of course. That's it!

"You're a genius, Khan."

The cat continued to prance around like he was well aware of the fact that he was amazing.

She'd spent a lot of time in the neighborhood they were in. After leaving Skyline Park, the first foster family she'd gone to had lived only a couple miles from here. And then, the summer after high school, she'd worked at the independent vet just up the block. It had been one of the happiest times of her life—waking up early and spending her days with animals.

The first time she'd seen a Maine coon in person was when someone brought theirs in with a hurt paw. She'd fallen in love with the breed right away and started saving that night in order to buy her own one day.

"Luke. Listen." She bowed her head so they were eye to eye again. "There's a vet's office near here. It has an apartment garage we might be able to get into. It's only a couple of blocks away. Can you walk that far?"

For a second she thought he was unconscious again, but finally, he nodded gingerly. "Yeah."

"Great." Scooping a hand under his good arm, she helped him stand.

Years had passed and she didn't even know if Dr. Mc-Graw's practice was still open. Back when she worked there, he'd converted the space above the detached garage into a studio apartment. On nights when he worked overtime and was too tired to commute home, he stayed there. But that had rarely happened on weekends. He'd wanted to be home with his wife because the grandkids came over.

They walked slowly in the correct direction, her carrying as much of his weight as possible.

This plan had a lot of unknown variables. She prayed it would work, because otherwise, she didn't know what she was going to do.

Khan circled them as they walked, darting ahead and coming back to check on their progress. It was slow going, and every time headlights appeared, they ducked behind the nearest vehicle or trash can.

They turned a corner and she glanced behind her and saw the orange of the fire in the distance. The sight made Claire's chest ache. Her beloved childhood safe haven was gone.

Ballard's men may have been the ones who'd started the fire, but Claire had been the one who led them to that building. And now Luke had been hurt because of her.

She pushed the feelings down. Right now she had to focus on getting them somewhere safe. Luke's wound seemed to have stopped bleeding. He was conscious but still so very weak. He'd always taken care of her, and now it was time for her to do the same for him.

It was dark in the veterinary clinic. It sat next to a house that had been renovated into a beauty salon, across the street from a local hardware store. Luke was on the last of his reserves as they made it down the narrow drive between the salon and the clinic to the garage in the back.

She let out a sigh of relief when there were no lights on in the garage or the studio apartment that rested above it.

She set Luke at the bottom of the wooden steps that went up the side of the garage.

"I'll be right back," she whispered to Luke as he slumped on the stairs. Khan sat down at his feet.

"I'm coming with." Luke grabbed hold of the weathered railing and started to pull himself up. "Not…leaving you."

"No, you're staying." She put a hand on his chest, and he stilled. "I'll be right back. I can move faster without you."

A quick kiss to his lips revealed they were cold. Not good. They had to get him inside pronto. The fact that he didn't argue further just proved that point.

She took the steps two at a time. Cupping her hands around her eyes, she pressed against the window on the door and peered into the apartment.

The vague shapes of furniture rose from the dark room. She didn't see any people—just a lot more boxes than had been around when she worked there.

She reached over to the light fixture and ran her fingers under the edge, letting out a shuddery sigh of relief when she found the key in the same place Dr. McGraw had always kept it.

With shaking hands, she unlocked the door and let it swing open, listening for any sounds before stepping inside.

"Hello?" Nothing. She went in and looked around. It was empty. Thank God. She turned and hurried back down the steps.

Khan was still standing guard over Luke. She wrapped

her arm around his torso while he held on to her shoulder. "Come on, it's empty." They slowly made their way up the stairs. "And tomorrow is Sunday. If Dr. McGraw didn't spend tonight here, he won't come in tomorrow."

At least, she hoped that was still true. If not, the police would just have to add breaking and entering to their list of reasons to arrest her.

The studio apartment wasn't much. Boxes and supplies took up one entire wall. There was a small full bed in one corner and a love seat in front of the TV in the middle. She helped Luke sit on the carpet, leaning his good side against the couch so he wouldn't get blood on it. Khan started his rounds, sniffing the corners of the room, while Claire closed all the blinds.

Once she was confident no light would escape the apartment and give away their presence, she switched on a standing lamp. The paleness of Luke's face was striking, made even more prominent by the dark circles under his eyes.

"We need to get your shirt off so I can see the cut." Sitting on her knees next to him, she helped remove it. He winced when he had to move his hurt arm but didn't make a peep.

His shirt was completely ruined and most of his back was covered in blood. She gasped when she saw the cut. It wasn't very deep, but it was long and had to be painful. "Luke, you need stitches."

"No." His voice was thin, weak. "They'd put my name in a computer. Ballard would have us in thirty minutes."

"Luke…" An invisible weight pressed against her throat and chest. He was too big for her to force to a medical facility.

She gritted her teeth, hating that it was her situation

that was causing him literal physical pain right now. Her situation that meant he couldn't get the help he needed.

"Let me see what I can find."

Rooting around in the cabinet under the sink, she found a fully stocked first aid kit, as well as some protein bars and nutrition drinks. Those would help his body begin to replenish everything it had expended.

When she returned, Khan had stopped his exploring and sat next to Luke, licking his hand.

She opened a drink and handed it to him before settling cross-legged behind him. She pressed a clean piece of gauze to the cut but fresh blood quickly seeped through.

She changed out the gauze and applied pressure the best she could as he finished one nutrition drink and she handed him another one.

"How's it looking back there?"

He finally sounded like Luke again, like he wasn't about to keel over. But she still had to tell him.

"It looks like this gauze isn't enough. You need stitches. Really, Luke."

"Okay."

"We can go to the hospital?"

"No, you're going to use that suture kit over there and do it yourself."

She looked over to where he was pointing, and sure enough, resting on one of the boxes of supplies was a sealed suture kit for the clinic.

She shook her head frantically and scooted back from him. "No, I can't do that. I don't know how to give someone stitches." She was glad for the nutrition drinks and that a chance to rest had him feeling better, but this was crazy.

"When you worked here at the vet clinic, did you ever see them stitch up an animal?"

"Sure, a lot."

"It's the same concept. Basically, just sewing. I had to do it once in the army when our medic got injured while we are on a mission. He talked me through it. I can talk you through this."

"If you're Hannibal Lecter," she muttered.

He chuckled. "That was the other guy. Hannibal just ate them." He turned so he was facing her more fully. "I know this is gross, but it's our best bet."

"It's not that it's gross…" she whispered. "It's going to hurt you."

He leaned over and kissed her tenderly, his full lips soft against hers. "I'll be okay, I promise."

"I don't know if I can do this."

"You can, Kitten. I trust you."

Chapter Thirteen

Her hands shook as she got the kit and cleaned out his wound. She knew it had to hurt every time the needle pierced his skin—it hurt her just to see it—but he never gave her any indication of distress.

"How did you end up working here?" he asked when she let out a distressed breath at the start of the third stitch.

"It was the summer after my freshman year in college. The Romeros, my last foster family, were nice enough to let me come back and live with them after my first year at school. They didn't live too far from here, so it was a fun and convenient summer job."

She winced as the needle pierced his skin again and she pulled the string to pull the edges of skin together, then tied it up with a knot.

"That's good. My parents, Sheila and Clinton Patterson, are big fighters for older-age adoption and foster. One of their biggest causes was that kids needed a family, even after they aged out of the system. They still need somewhere to go when they're young adults… The need for a support network doesn't change just because you turn eighteen."

"Yeah. The Romeros were good. I haven't talked to them in the while. I probably should."

She started another stitch.

"So, you liked working here?"

"Absolutely. The first time I ever saw a Maine coon was here. I even thought I might want to be a vet for a while, but I knew that would take a lot of schooling. Plus, I was already really good at computers."

"Chance and I both went into the army straight out of high school. Brax and Weston went on to college."

"No college for you?"

"I finished my associate's degree in business, but I'm not a huge fan of sitting in classrooms. I'd rather be out crawling through burning buildings and dodging bullets."

She laughed as she finished another stitch.

"The army gave me a purpose. I was always pretty physically strong and had good hand-eye coordination and spatial awareness. I was good at reading people and recognizing threats. It would've made a good skill set for working for someone like Ballard, or the equivalent. Being in the service helped me hone a sense of honor. Clarified the path that Clinton and Sheila started me on. I got out with the skills and purpose I needed to start San Antonio Security with my brothers."

"And you like it? It's done well?"

"Being in business with family always has its pros and cons. For example, none of us like to do paperwork and this month it's my turn. I'd honestly rather sit here and let you do this to me for the rest of the month than have to do all the filing that's waiting for me at my desk. So if we get this murder charge cleared up, we might have to rob a bank or something just so I don't have to go back to the office." She laughed again and finished another stitch.

"Maybe that's how I'll have to pay you back for helping me—paperwork."

"I wouldn't wish that on my worst enemy. Well, maybe

I'd wish it on Ballard. Except for what has happened over the last few days, have you liked working at Passage Digital?"

He was helping her, she realized. In the only way he could.

"Thank you."

"For what?" he asked. "Asking about your job?"

"I know what you're doing…you're distracting me. Given the circumstances, it should be the other way around. So, thank you."

"I do want to know about your job. About you. I thought about you all the time, Kitten. I can't tell you how many times I thought about using San Antonio Security's resources to find you, check up on you, but I didn't want to invade your privacy like that."

"I've had a pretty uneventful life up until a couple of weeks ago. I liked working at Passage. Mostly because people there left me alone, as pathetic as that sounds."

He chuckled. "You've never been a people person."

"Nope, that didn't change about me. My job was…a job. I went in, I did it, and I was good at it. I understand computers and they don't exhaust me. My team leader, Julia—" Claire had to swallow back tears. "She and I weren't really friends, but she was nice to me. She knew I worked best alone, so she rarely put me on group projects."

"I'm sorry, Kitten. Friendships come in all different shapes and sizes. Yours may not have been a traditional one, but she was still your friend."

"Yeah." She never thought of it that way, but it was true.

"We're going to make sure Ballard pays for what he has done."

Claire wasn't so sure. Ballard seemed to have the

upper hand and now he was going to be looking any time she tried to access Digital Passage remotely.

She finished another stitch. She had to focus on what was in front of her; looking at the big picture was just going to overwhelm her. That was how she worked a computer problem, and it was how she needed to work this situation.

"How about your personal life? Ever been…married or anything?"

"No. A couple of boyfriends in college, but nothing serious. Trust issues, people issues, you know the deal. You?"

Her heart clenched as he waited so long, she was afraid he wasn't going to answer.

"You and I are a lot alike in terms of people. I don't necessarily avoid all contact with people, but my brothers all know not to send me in with clients. I'm way too gruff."

"You're not too gruff with me."

"You're the exception, Kitten. You always have been. And no, there hasn't been anyone very serious for me, either."

She finished the last two stitches.

"You vaguely resemble Frankenstein's monster, but I think this will at least help it heal more quickly and keep out infection."

"Thank you."

She began cleaning up all her supplies on the table and put them in a trash bag. They'd have to take that out with them when they left in the morning.

"You got that because of me, so no thanks is necessary."

He moved in front of her and cupped her cheeks.

"I got that because Ballard is a lying murderous bastard, not because of you. Because of your bravery and grit, I'm safe here in this apartment. I'm stitched up and better able to help protect us if we need it. That is because of you. Not the other stuff." She didn't know if she believed that, but at least for the moment, they were safe.

He chugged down a third nutrition shake and helped her finish cleaning. They found a couple of cans of soup and some crackers and Luke made a meal of it. Now that Luke was looking much steadier on his feet and strong enough to take on the world again, she found it difficult to stop staring at his very well-developed and muscular chest. Eventually they would have to find a shirt for him to put on, but for now she would enjoy the view. Fortunately, he didn't seem to notice her embarrassed fascination, or if he did, he was too polite to tease her about it.

As a matter of fact, he may claim to be gruff, but he was charming and friendly to her despite her having tortured him for the past hour.

"I'm going to take a shower," she announced after they cleared away the few dishes they had used. They were trying to clean up any messes as they went, just in case they had to leave in a hurry.

"Good idea. I'll wash off the best I can after you."

He flipped on the TV as she headed for the bathroom, but she stopped, turning in horror when she heard her name on the news.

"Local police this evening are asking for special assistance to find Claire Wallace."

A picture of Claire filled the screen.

"Wallace was already wanted for questioning by the police for the murder of Julia Lindsey, a colleague and employee at Passage Digital. Now Wallace is wanted for the fire that destroyed Wars Hill library earlier this evening and for the shooting of a police officer. There is a reward for any information that leads to the capture of Wallace." A phone number and email address floated across her picture on the screen.

Claire couldn't stop the sob that escaped her. Luke was at her side in an instant. He reached out with the remote control and flipped the TV off.

"Hey." He reached out to pull her into his arms, but she stepped back.

"Hey," he said again. "This doesn't change anything. We're still going to figure out a way to clear your name."

She nodded blankly. But how? How were they going to clear her name? Ballard had all the advantages, especially now that the cops thought she was the one who had shot that officer.

"I'm going to take a shower."

She wasn't sure if she was relieved or disappointed when Luke let her go. Once in the bathroom, she pulled her clothes off but brought them with her into the shower.

She used the body wash to try to get rid of some of the smoky smell on her clothes, then rinsed them thoroughly. Then she scrubbed her body from head to toe until she was almost raw.

That got rid of the smoky smell, but it didn't change the fact that the situation had gotten even more dire. Who was she kidding? What were her real chances of being able to beat someone like Ballard? All she was doing now was dragging Luke into danger. He'd already been hurt because of it.

The towel was her only option while her clothes dried. She wrapped it around herself, thankful for once of her small stature since it covered enough of her to keep her decent.

Luke watched as she came out and sat on the bed, studying her with concern.

Certainly, he was not as distracted by the sight of some of her skin as she had been by his bare chest.

But what did she expect? Just because he'd been nice to her and had kissed her a couple of times didn't mean he thought of her as anything more than just someone he used to know and was helping for old times' sake. Given the circumstances, she should be glad he was even willing to do that.

"At least I don't smell like a furnace anymore." She tried for a lighthearted laugh, but it came out sounding stilted at best.

He nodded. "I'm going to wash off as best I can without getting my stitches wet. Then we should probably try to catch a few hours of sleep before figuring out our next plan." She nodded and lay back. It was well after midnight and they could both use the rest.

Given everything, she should've been exhausted, but sleep wouldn't come. Still wrapped in the towel, she got under the covers hoping that would help, but it didn't. She just kept seeing the fire and Luke's wound and that guy with the gun.

It was a nightmare she couldn't wake up from.

"Whoa. Hey, Kitten, you're shaking."

Claire hadn't even been aware that Luke had gotten out of the shower or sat down on the bed next to her.

"I'm… I'm okay."

She wasn't okay. She very definitely wasn't okay.

"Hey. Hey, come here."

She didn't even think about resisting when he pulled her into his arms. He held her so close to him, his body absorbed her tremors until they finally stopped.

"I'm sorry. I'm acting like an idiot."

He kissed along her forehead, keeping her wrapped

up against him. She couldn't remember ever feeling so secure.

"Don't say that. I've known guys in the Special Forces who would have crumbled much harder under the pressure you've been through. You're doing amazing."

"I just don't see how anything is ever going to be right again."

She felt his fingers stroke along the bare skin of her shoulder blades as he laid them back. The shiver that ran through her this time had nothing to do with despondency.

"We're going to figure this out. I know it seems hopeless right now, but I promise you, we are going to figure out a way to clear your name and make sure Ballard goes down."

He said it with such deep, gruff authority, it was impossible not to believe him. She lifted her head off his chest so she could see his eyes. He was so sexy.

"Thank you. For everything."

She leaned forward to give him a friendly kiss, but the moment she did, everything changed.

The kiss started soft but grew passionate and heated. This was what she wanted. She wanted to have this passion with him, even if it was only for tonight. She might have to make some hard choices to protect him in the morning, but for tonight, she wanted whatever she could get.

When she felt his hand tangle in her still-damp hair, pulling her closer, she knew Luke felt the same. She gave herself over to the kiss, almost scrambling on top of him in an effort to get closer.

But then he stopped.

She was so wound up, she didn't even realize that he wasn't kissing her with the same abandon that she was kissing him. It wasn't until the hand that had been fisted in her hair loosened and he slid back that she became aware of it.

"Luke?"

"Kitten. You've been through so much. I'm not sure this is a good idea."

Claire felt like her insides were being turned to pieces of ice. "You don't want me? You don't think of me that way?"

"Are you kidding?" He slid his hand down and yanked her hips against his. "Believe me, I want you. But you've been through enough. I don't want you to feel pressured. I don't want this to be something you'll regret."

The ice inside her began to fall. He did want her. He was just so protective, always had been.

She reached up and scraped her fingers gently down his jaw, loving the feel of the stubble growing there.

"I want you. There may end up being a lot of things I regret, but this is definitely not one of them."

His brown eyes bored into hers. "Are you sure? I don't expect anything. You don't owe me any—"

She shut him up with a kiss. He probably still had another twenty minutes' worth of protective alpha male speech to give her.

But she knew that she wanted him.

He took the hint and stopped trying to talk her out of what they both desperately wanted. Their lips fused together in a duel, a battle in which both of them won.

Then, as he kissed down her body, moving away the towel as he went, it chased away all the thoughts of Ballard and death and the inescapable mess she was in.

All she could feel was Luke.

Chapter Fourteen

Luke woke up the next morning groggy, which was unusual for him. His life had never been one where deep sleep and waking up disoriented were leisures he could afford.

But clarity came when he realized Claire was not in the bed beside him. A quick glance at the bathroom and around this small studio space confirmed his worst fears.

She was gone.

Damn it. His body was tired from yesterday's trauma and then the three rounds of lovemaking with her last night. He hadn't been able to keep his hands off her. And he wouldn't trade a single second of it, except that it meant he hadn't woken up when she decided to sneak off.

Khan.

He saw the note on the small table at the same time he saw Khan stretch out by the door.

His heart sank as he read her words.

Dear Luke,
I couldn't stay. This was too dangerous for me to have involved you in—and now you've gotten hurt. I'm going to go to the police, tell them everything I know, and hope for the best. Maybe I can make them listen and give me a chance to prove my in-

nocence. This lets me protect you for once. Please take care of Khan. I know you know how important he is to me. Thank you for last night. Thank you for everything, now and when we were kids.

Love,
Claire

Luke was already getting dressed, having to use one of the vet clinic polo shirts lying in a box since his was way too bloodied and he did not want to draw attention to himself. He grabbed Khan, knowing she'd never forgive him if something happened to the cat, and rushed out the door, praying he wasn't too late to stop her.

There might come a time when her only option was to go to the police and hope they could find one who was on the up-and-up and would listen to her, but that wasn't until they ran out of all their other options.

And it damn well wasn't going to be because she wanted to protect him.

The closest precinct was about a mile away. Luke didn't even bother trying to blend in with any sort of walk. There was no way he could blend in when carrying this giant cat anyway. He ran full out, ignoring the pain in his shoulder and the occasional cat claw hooked into his biceps. At least the cat wasn't fighting him and trying to get away.

"Good boy."

This thing really was more like a dog. Maybe he sensed his mistress was in trouble. "Not on my watch, buddy." It was early enough on a Sunday morning that there weren't many people out. All things considered, Luke made pretty good time. When he turned around the last corner that put the precinct in his sights, he let out a silent prayer.

Claire was standing just down the block from the station, pacing and talking to herself. *Thank God.*

Luke slowed to a walk; he definitely couldn't draw attention to himself now. He kept his eyes trained on Claire. There was no way he was going to let her go in there.

He had just found her again after all these years, and he couldn't lose her now.

He kept on the other side of the street from the precinct. She was so busy arguing with herself, preparing her statement or whatever she was doing, that she didn't even see them.

Even in this dire situation, Luke couldn't help but smile. This woman… She'd amazed him when they were kids, and she continued to do so now. Last night had just solidified that.

He crossed the street a little farther down from her so he was coming up behind her. Khan began to get a little restless in his arms as he saw Claire.

"I know, buddy. We're going to get her out of here."

Luke moved quietly up behind her and was able to see the two cops who walked out of the precinct and headed in her direction at the same time she did. She stiffened, and he knew she was about to make her move.

He dropped Khan and quickly stepped in front of her, blocking Claire from the cops' view.

He pulled her in for a hug. "Hi, honey," he said just loudly enough that the cops would be able to hear him but not so loud that it seemed unnatural. "Ready to go get our coffee?"

The officers never even slowed down, caught in their own conversation as they continued down the block.

Luke kept one arm around her and turned them to

cross the street in the opposite direction of both the cops and the precinct.

"Did you get my note? I want to turn myself in."

He didn't stop walking and Khan stayed right at their feet. "That's exactly what Ballard is hoping you'll do. He's prepared for that. You can bet he has some sort of plan. You turning yourself in without proof in hand will be a death sentence."

She was still resisting. "You got hurt. You could've been killed. I meant what I said in the note."

He stopped walking so he could turn and face her eye-to-eye. He brought both hands up to cup her cheeks and ran his thumbs over her delicate cheekbones. "Kitten, you have no idea what it means to me that you want to protect me, but this is not the way to do it. We find the proof and we get it into the right hands."

"But—"

"You're not in this alone anymore. We'll figure it out together, okay?"

He thought she might argue, but she nodded. "Together."

He slipped his arm back around her shoulder and they began walking again. They needed to get as far from here as possible.

THEY USED THE last of the cash to take a taxi across town. Luke needed to talk to his brothers and couldn't take a chance on anything being bugged.

Claire donned the brown wig, and they walked a couple of miles before calling a cab at a hotel. If Ballard was smart, he would have the media put a picture of Khan all over the TV. He was much more noticeable than either Luke or Claire was. People would be recording them left and right if they needed to look for the giant cat.

Luke and Claire talked as little as possible in the cab. He didn't want the driver to have any reason to remember them. He had the driver take them to a small mall a couple of miles away from the San Antonio Security office. He hated to make her walk more, but it was better this way.

He knew she was surprised when he led her into an underground parking garage a couple of blocks from his office. They took the elevator back up to the ground-level floor, then walked down the hallway and out the back door.

It led out to the alley that led between the two buildings. It gave him and the guys a second hidden entrance into their office. It was one of the primary reasons they chose this particular space to rent.

If someone were watching their building, they would still never know Luke and Claire were inside.

The relief on his brothers' faces was apparent as soon as they came in through the back door.

"Thank God," Brax murmured.

Weston and Chance immediately closed the blinds on the front window. The glass was tinted, but this gave them an extra measure of privacy.

Brax sat down and switched on the signal blocker. That would block anyone attempting to use audio surveillance equipment to listen in on their conversations.

"Are you guys all right?" Brax asked. "When we heard about the Wars Hill library fire, we immediately got over there but we couldn't find any sign of you."

Luke led Claire so she could sit on the small couch in the corner of the waiting room. Khan immediately jumped up into her lap.

He gave Weston a look, who immediately nodded, knowing what they needed. Weston headed toward the small kitchen and dug up something for them to eat and drink.

"We hid, then sneaked out a bathroom window. I got quite a few stitches for my trouble."

Claire winced and he reached over and grabbed her hand, rubbing his thumb across her knuckles.

"If you thought everyone was looking for you before, it's definitely worse now that they think you shot a cop."

Both Luke and Brax shot Chance a look when Claire let out a shuddered breath. Chance didn't mean any harm by his words; he just didn't pull any punches. Luke was gruff in the same way, and actually prided himself on it.

But not when it came to Claire. He didn't want anyone to do or say anything to upset her. She'd been through enough.

"Sorry," Chance muttered.

"No, you're right," Claire whispered. "Did he die?"

Brax shook his head. "Weston put in a call to see what he could find out. It's still touch-and-go, but there's a chance he'll pull through."

"Any chance he would be able to identify who shot him if he makes it?" Luke asked. It wouldn't solve all their problems, but at least they wouldn't be after Claire as a cop killer.

Chance shook his head. "It seems unlikely given the trajectory of the bullet that hit him, and we only know that because of what Weston was able to get from his cop friends."

"My vote is for you to turn yourself in." Weston walked back in the room and handed a plate of sandwiches and a couple of water bottles to Luke, who nodded his thanks. "There are good cops in the San Antonio PD. You two can back up each other's statements. Otherwise, they are going to be after you in full force after what happened at the library."

"That's what I wanted to do." Claire sat up straighter on the couch. "Luke has already gotten hurt—"

All three of his brothers stiffened.

"How bad?"

"Do we need a doctor?"

"Status."

It was impossible to tell who was saying what with them talking all over one another.

"I'm fine. Nothing that couldn't be fixed by breaking in at a local vet's clinic. It wasn't a big deal."

"And if I hadn't been there to hit that guy in the head with the skateboard? He would've shot you."

Luke picked up half of a sandwich from the plate on his lap and stuck it in Claire's mouth.

"Yes, Ballard and his men are dangerous. Deadly, even. And that's why you can't go to the cops." He turned to his brothers. "Ballard would've already thought of that. He has to have a plan in place if she goes running to the cops and claims her innocence."

"I should've done that from the beginning. I should've walked out of Passage Digital and gone straight to the police. I don't trust cops. I don't like people. I'm so stupid." Luke took the sandwich back out of her hands.

"Hey." He cupped her cheeks with his hands. "Maybe… Maybe you might've been able to catch Ballard before he could get any stopgap measures in place, but probably not. He's too wealthy and too well-connected to not have been able to handle that. The most likely thing that would've happened is that you'd be dead right now and my whole world would be crushed without me even knowing it."

"I just don't want you to get hurt. I don't want anyone else to get hurt."

Luke could never have been much of a poet. No one had ever accused him of being in touch with his sensitive side. But suddenly, he had a very clear understanding of what drowning in someone's eyes meant. He couldn't have escaped the hypnotic pull of Claire's baby blues even if he had wanted to.

And he very definitely didn't want to. What he definitely did want to do was kiss her, but he couldn't with his brothers staring at them.

"So, we need a plan that involves Claire not going to the police," Brax said. "Anybody got one of those?"

"Not yet." Luke forced himself to look away from Claire. "We're going to go to ground until we figure out a way to get the proof we need."

Weston leaned back against the wall and crossed his arms over his chest. "That works as a temporary measure, but unless you plan to be on the run for the rest of your lives, it can't be permanent. They'll be after you, too, soon, Luke. Right now, there's no ties between the two of you but once there is, you could be arrested for aiding and abetting."

"That could affect...things," Brax said, his usual charming smile nowhere to be found.

Luke nodded. He knew exactly what his brother meant.

"What things?" Claire asked, feeding a piece of chicken to Khan. "Bad things?"

Luke didn't want to tell her.

"In this together, remember?" she whispered.

He scrubbed a hand over his face. "If I'm charged with aiding and abetting, or any crime really, it could affect a lot of things with our business. The licenses we're able to hold, our relationship with law enforcement..."

"Oh."

He wanted to tell her it was worth it to him, all of it…even if it meant losing everything. But it wasn't just him this affected. San Antonio Security was part of all of them. And he loved his brothers.

"I think you do need to go to ground. Get out of Dodge," Chance said.

Luke turned to him. "What about the business?"

"Go to the cops first. Clear your name and distance yourself from this."

Luke could almost see Chance's strategic mind working.

"Tell the cops the truth, but the selective truth. Tell them that Claire came to you, a pretty lady all big eyes and sad story. You two knew each other as kids. She was broke, but you put her up at a hotel and were supposed to meet the next morning but evidently, she took off in the middle of the night. Next thing you knew, her photo was all over the news."

Luke caught Claire's flinch out of the corner of his eye. He grabbed her hand. "None of that is true."

"All of it is true," she scoffed.

"Hey." Brax smiled at her. "Those statement may be true but they're not all the facts. We know all the facts, and that's what matters.

Claire didn't look very relieved.

They all turned to Weston. "Would this work?" Luke asked. "You have the most experience with law enforcement."

"Maybe. Probably. You keep it as general as possible, giving the cops what they already know. We have a good reputation—you have a good reputation—so there's no reason for them not to believe you."

"We'll get your truck out of the vicinity of the library so nothing is traced back to you," Brax said.

"Is it possible that they'll arrest me? Maybe I shouldn't go at all."

Because he damn well wouldn't be able to protect her behind bars. She'd be on her own.

"Think about your life, Luke. This company. You can't ruin your reputation."

"San Antonio Security is not more important than your life, Claire. I don't want to leave you alone unprotected."

"We'll keep her safe if something happens to you," Brax said, and both Weston and Chance were beside him, nodding their agreement. "You'll probably only be with the police for a few hours, tops. But however long it is, we've got your back."

"Both of your backs," Weston said.

Chapter Fifteen

Luke glanced to his right in time for amber light to wash over Claire's face. She was sleeping, which brought him a small measure of peace after a long day.

Weighing everything now as he headed out of town on the last leg of their journey, he knew he should be glad they'd made it out. And he was. But it hadn't been anything he'd want to do again.

Like the seven hours he'd spent with Detectives Arellano and Fisher.

He had a hard time believing neither of them was dirty, or at least being pushed from behind by the large, firm hand of one Vance Ballard. Weston still couldn't offer insight into the two of them, which meant he had no way of smoothing things over or asking them to pull back a little. They weren't his former colleagues, unlike the local San Antonio cops.

Luke had known that going in.

But seven hours of constant questions had worn his nerves to their breaking point. No amount of preparation could keep his frustration at bay, though he'd fought against it until the end. He repeated the story he and his brothers had come up with, right down to the smallest detail, giving neither detective so much as an inch they could slide a wedge into.

If he'd been frustrated, they'd been near the end of their ropes by the time the questioning wrapped up. It was clear they had an end in mind, a goal—drawing connections between him and Claire, figuring out what role he played in this. Whether they could use him to get to her or not.

They'd had no idea who they were dealing with going into the questioning. He figured they had a pretty good idea by the time they'd finished, though.

"Do you really want to protect a murderer?" Fisher had asked more than once.

"You know she shot that cop, too, right?" Arellano had demanded. Luke still wondered, hours later, how much the two of them knew. Whether they believed Claire had been behind it or if they were aware of Ballard's henchmen.

Better to stick to the prepared answers Weston had helped coach him through before the interrogation. Claire was appealing, big-eyed and in need of protection. He hadn't asked too many questions because he couldn't have imagined she'd be wrapped up in something this big. She'd asked for help, had made him feel like the only one who could provide it—she'd played on his protective instincts.

Even as the words had soured in his mouth, he'd watched understanding dawn on the faces of the men in front of him. Probably identifying with the sentiment. He was surprised his teeth were still intact after grinding them so hard.

In the end, there'd been no way to prove he wasn't telling the full truth, and no way to connect him and Claire. Even if they knew about her time in the Skyline Park group home, his name hadn't been Patterson then.

His release had come as a relief, but not a total win because they'd still be watching.

Which meant doing something he couldn't have imagined being capable of at this particular time—going into the office like it was an ordinary day and pretending to work for hours. All that had kept him in place was knowing Claire was safe. Brax had taken her someplace and was guarding her while Luke and the rest kept up the charade of everything being status quo.

One memory of those long, tense hours made him smile—the fact that two weeks' worth of filing had been done for him by Maci Ford, the new office manager his brothers had hired. His office was much easier to kill time in without those files staring at him. It would be nice to meet the person responsible for that.

Once this was over. Once life felt like life again.

For the afternoon, all he could do was look forward to being with Claire. He trusted Brax with his life, but there was nothing that could touch the certainty of having her in his arms. Seeing as how Brax couldn't tell him where he'd planned to take Claire for the sake of keeping Luke honest when he claimed he had no idea where she was, his anxiety had been through the roof.

Even Luke was impressed with what his brother had come up with. Chance always was the tactical mastermind. He'd found four cars of the same make and model, and working together, they'd crisscrossed all over town. Trading cars in parking lots, beneath overpasses. Talking on the phone all the while, just in case anyone was listening, comparing notes on their favorite teams and player stats the way any group of brothers would. Like there was nothing out of the ordinary going on.

That was what outsiders didn't understand, and it was the Pattersons' most powerful weapon—the fact that they were brothers, not simply business associates. They'd go out of their way to have one another's backs, would spend hours leading anyone on their trail on a wild-goose chase. All for the sake of protecting one of them.

And what mattered most in the world to him.

After two hours, Luke had finally landed in the car holding Claire and Khan in the back seat, the two of them lying low to avoid notice. That was when he'd finally been able to breathe without a weight on his chest. Chance had continued the game with the tail following his car, thinking Luke was the driver.

Luke, meanwhile, was on his way out of town with his woman and her cat-dog safe and secure.

He was only a few miles away from his destination. Nobody knew about this place. It wasn't even on the grid, using a generator and solar panels to keep it powered up. The perfect hiding spot.

Though that wasn't what his parents had intended, obviously. Back in the day, it was a getaway. Somewhere to disconnect from the pressures of the world, somewhere for their dad to teach them to fish, where they could breathe fresh air outside the city.

In other words, an ideal location for him and Claire to spend a few days. She needed the rest, needed to feel secure for a little while. They could come up with a plan for moving forward once they had the time to reset.

He was still thinking along those lines as he turned off the main road onto the rocky trail leading up to the cabin. The change in terrain left the car swaying a little, which stirred Claire into wakefulness. "Is this Lake Conroe?" she mumbled, still sleepy.

Even now, she struck him as hopelessly adorable, rubbing sleep from her eyes before immediately looking to check on Khan. "Almost. Just a few minutes more."

"I can't wait to stretch my legs."

"I'll bet. Cramped up in a car for hours." But she'd held on, going with the flow. She might've been the strongest woman he knew, except for maybe his mom.

That thought lingered in his mind as he pulled closer to the cabin.

And found the lights on inside.

"Oh," Claire breathed. "For some reason, I thought the cabin would be empty."

"It should be…" He brought them to a stop, staring at the familiar structure with his mouth open.

She went stiff. "Are we in trouble?"

It was almost laughable. And he would've laughed if this latest twist didn't complicate things even further. "No, we're not in trouble. It's just that this is happening earlier than I thought it would." He got out of the car, shaking his head.

"What's that mean?" Claire followed him, a note of fear in her voice even after he'd told her it was okay. She'd pulled Khan out of the car with her and held him to her chest, protective and a little scared.

"It means you're about to meet my parents." He put an arm around her waist and pulled her toward the house before she could ask any more questions or, even more likely, plant her feet and refuse to take another step.

Timing had never been his parents' strong suit, but how were they supposed to know?

"Well, what's this?" Clinton bolted up from his chair at the opening of the door, and a huge smile threatened to crack his face wide open. "What a great surprise!"

Sheila came in from the kitchen, wiping her hands on her apron. "Luke! How terrific! I was just thinking about you!"

He'd only just been thinking about her, but there

wasn't time to explain that without explaining a great deal more about Claire than he was comfortable with just then. Besides, there were more important things to talk about.

Such as, who Claire was, for starters.

"Claire, these are my parents, Clinton and Sheila Patterson." Not the way he'd hoped to introduce her one day, but these were strange times. "Mom and Dad, this is Claire."

He didn't know what else to say. Certainly, he couldn't go into detail. He didn't even want to use her last name since they might've heard it on the news.

The two of them jumped into action, with Clinton directing Claire to the chair he'd just vacated. "You two look half-starved," Sheila decided. "I was just putting supper on. And look at that gorgeous cat! I'm sure I can dig up a little something for you, too."

Either Khan understood English or his instincts were sharp enough to know who he needed to become best friends with. He took his leave from Claire and trotted into the kitchen on Sheila's heels. Clinton added wood to the fire. "The cabin's been closed up for a while now, and you'll find the nights get fairly cool this time of year."

Neither of them asked questions, either because they knew better than to delve into their sons' lives—no telling where their work led them or how much they could share—or because they had enough tact not to make things awkward.

That was one thing the two of them had to spare, tact. It was what had made them ideal foster parents to four wounded, scared boys. They knew when to ask questions and when to leave well enough alone.

Before he knew it, the four of them were seated around the kitchen table, and Sheila was piling pasta on Claire's plate. "One thing you learn as a mother to four boys is how to quickly double a meal. I swear, I don't know how I managed to keep the kitchen stocked in those days." She added vegetables to the plate before handing it over. Ever a parent.

"It must've been…interesting." Claire's gaze darted over to Luke, a tiny smile tugging at the corners of her mouth.

"Oh, sweetheart, it was a real challenge sometimes. Well, it was!" Sheila laughed when Luke rolled his eyes. "The four of you were so spirited and stubborn. Remember the one trip we took up here, where you almost drowned yourself in the lake? Convinced you'd caught a big one."

"It was a tire." Clinton laughed. "And I warned him, I did, but he insisted he'd caught something legendary. Lost his balance and ended up in water over his head."

"This was before he learned to swim, mind you." Sheila shook her head, laughing. "Life wasn't boring, I'll tell you that much."

Luke couldn't help but marvel at his mother's ability to draw Claire out of her shell. They weren't more than a few minutes into the meal before she was laughing, not to mention the way she tore into her supper like she hadn't eaten in ages. It did him good to see her with an appetite.

It was just like being a kid again, when he'd first arrived at the Patterson home. How scared and wounded and untrusting he'd been. How Sheila had worked her way into his trust, how she hadn't pushed but instead pulled him into the warmth of her love with food and laughter, letting him come around in his own good time.

He could almost forget what was happening around them, the cloud hanging over their heads. It all felt so right, being there with her, sitting down with his parents...like Claire was already part of the family.

There was no more awkwardness until it came time to turn in. Naturally, his parents expected to take the master bedroom with its king-size bed.

Leaving the second bedroom to Luke and Claire.

"Bunk beds." Claire's amusement was evident, no matter how she tried to hide it.

"Two sets." He leaned against one set with a sigh as memories bumped against each other, almost too many for him to handle.

"This is where you boys slept?"

"Mm-hmm."

"Which bed was yours?"

He jerked a thumb toward the top bunk just behind him and Claire nodded. "I want that one."

"You're serious?"

"I am. What?" she asked when he chuckled. "I want to sleep in the bed you slept in. Is that funny?"

Funny? No. In fact, it was sort of sexy in a weird way. He kept that thought to himself in favor of sliding his arms around her waist. "Not much room for more than one person in these beds."

"Good thing I'm too wiped out to think about anything but sleep right now." But she was smiling, and for a moment, it was almost possible to forget there was anything more important happening in their lives than an unforeseen meeting with his parents.

"I'm glad you got to meet them, even if this wasn't what I had planned." He pressed a kiss against her forehead while her arms linked around his neck.

"They're wonderful people."

"They are. I had no doubt you'd get along with them."

"And they love you. That much is obvious." She stood

on her tiptoes to kiss him softly, almost playfully. "I mean, not that I blame them or anything. You're pretty wonderful, too."

"Mom's superpower is loving," he murmured, careful to keep his voice low, the way they used to when they were kids pretending to be asleep. "They're perfect for each other, those two. They are both very special people."

Claire changed into pajamas and climbed into her bunk while Khan took the bottom bunk across from her. Watchful, but comfortable in his own right. "Keep an eye on her," Luke whispered to the cat once Claire was sound asleep.

THE CABIN WAS DARK, quiet, though Luke knew better than to accept things at face value. His father would want to talk. They'd only exchanged a single long look before retiring to their respective bedrooms, but that look had carried a lot of weight.

He was waiting on the small porch overlooking the lake. The water was still and smooth under a cloudless sky, giving the illusion of there being two moons thanks to a motionless reflection. "Beautiful," Luke whispered. There was nothing like being out here, away from the rest of the world.

Clinton nodded, staring off in the same direction. "I recognize your friend from TV."

"It's not what you think."

"I figured as much."

"We only need to lie low for a few days. It'll give us time to regroup and come up with a plan. The people after her are dangerous and connected enough to use law enforcement as a personal tool to catch her."

"Your brothers are helping?"

"As much as they can."

"Who is this girl that she's important enough for you to go to all this trouble?"

"I knew her back at Skyline Park. She was important to me then. She still is."

Clinton sighed, finally turning his face toward his son. "You know your mom won't want to leave now, not with another baby bird to take care of. But I can't put her in a situation where she might be in danger, either. Not with her blood pressure."

"I wouldn't want to put her in danger, believe me."

"That being said, if you think it's okay, we'll stay tomorrow. Give her a chance to mother you both for a while. It'll do her good."

"I think it'll do Claire good, too." He didn't bother mentioning himself, as his needs were fairly far down on the priority list. But he suspected it would do him good, just the same.

They fell into an easy silence while nature's sounds filled the air. Even at night, there was never real, true quiet. An owl's cry pierced the air. Leaves rustled. There were sounds of scurrying as some small animal foraged for its supper.

At least they had a natural alarm system all around them. If intruders decided to approach, the animals would sound an alert.

Luke's heart swelled when he looked over at his dad, whose profile stood out against the moonlit sky. They didn't share blood, but Clinton had taught him everything he knew about being a man and about what mattered in life. He'd set Luke's feet on the path they currently trod.

"I know that whatever you do, it'll be the right thing," Clinton decided. "I don't know a lot of things, but that much I know for sure."

Luke hoped his father was right.

Chapter Sixteen

Claire woke the next morning and found herself trapped in a family sitcom out of the 1950s.

The mom wore an apron and bustled around the kitchen, laughing and rolling her eyes at her husband's terrible jokes. Their pride in their son shone through every time he was in the room, as did the love and respect they had for each other.

Definitely something out of a '50s sitcom, except the dad was Black, the mom was Puerto Rican, their son was white, and their guest was a wanted fugitive.

It was all a little surreal, especially when she had never fit in at her foster homes. Most of them hadn't been bad; nobody had been mean to her, except for the people at Skyline Park.

Even so, she'd been the quiet kid. The one who wasn't good with people, who slipped through the cracks. Foster families tended to be full and busy, the parents already stretched thin by trying to provide for all the kids in their care.

None of them had set out to ignore her. It had been easy to do since she was the kid who basically wanted nothing more than to be left alone. The squeaky wheel got the oil, the quiet wheel ended up alone with a cat.

That wasn't the case with Sheila Patterson. Nobody was left out when she was around.

She'd coddled Luke ever since finding out about his wound, looking after it, making him his favorite foods.

More surprising? Luke had let her do it.

He loved her and she loved him. Nothing could be more evident. And the more evident it became, the more Claire found herself withdrawing. Not on purpose. It was what she did whenever she was on the outside looking in.

But Sheila was having none of it.

She'd included Claire in every conversation. Every game of spades. Cooking, washing dishes—Sheila included her in that, too. She didn't treat Claire like a guest; she treated her like family.

It was amazing and alarming, like nothing Claire had ever known. Yet every time she started to withdraw and shut down, some member of the Patterson family pulled her back in.

"Mom." Luke found Claire and Sheila in the kitchen, and he didn't look happy. "Dad is dragging me down to the lake so he can show me his new rod and reel. Please tell me you have something I can do here so I don't have to go. Like scrubbing toilets."

He sounded like a whiny little kid and Claire couldn't help but smile.

Sheila sighed with a shrug. "I'm afraid you're going to have to go fishing with your father. I'm going to teach Claire how to make apple turnovers."

That was news to Claire, though the fact that the mere mention of turnovers made Luke's eyes literally light up told her this was a good way to spend the time. "You are?"

"That way she has something to lord over you when

you're not behaving the way you should." Sheila dropped a knowing wink Claire's way.

Luke shook his head. "You're a cruel woman, Sheila Patterson. Equipping the younger generation to operate in that way."

Sheila raised one dark eyebrow. "We women have to stick together."

Luke was still grumbling good-naturedly as he and Clinton walked down to the creek that fed into the lake. Meanwhile, Claire had the feeling this situation was a setup to give Sheila a chance for them to talk privately.

She tried to keep a positive expression on her face, but she couldn't help but worry. Sheila might not have been related to Luke by blood, but she thought of herself as his mother.

And undoubtedly, thought of Claire as a threat to her son.

The irony of the situation didn't escape her as Sheila took her through the process, step-by-step. There was nothing Claire wanted more than to know how to make Luke's favorite dessert, though ideally, she'd make it when he wasn't in danger because of her. She was only learning the recipe because they'd come here to hide out for a while.

There was also a sense of waiting for the other shoe to drop—for Sheila's tone to change as she took Claire through the steps. When was she going to get around to it?

As it turned out, Sheila got around to it while Claire was busy folding the homemade pastry dough around apple slices. "Luke is important to me. All of my sons are." She didn't stop working as she spoke, so Claire didn't, either.

"I could see that. He loves you and Clinton, and you

both love him. I'm so happy he found a family who appreciates him."

Sheila glanced over at her. "And you? Do you appreciate Luke the way he is?"

"Luke was my hero when we were kids. He looked after me when we were in the group home together. I guess he's still my hero."

Sheila smiled a mother's knowing smile. "He's always been very protective. It's his nature. It's easy to see he's protective toward you, even more than normal. He cares about you."

"I care about him, too," Claire whispered.

"He doesn't talk much about his life before us. We know about Skyline Park, of course, and what a terrible place it was before it got shut down. I'm sorry you were there. I hope it wasn't too bad."

"It would've been much worse if it hadn't been for Luke." She forced herself to look Sheila in the eye in spite of her nervousness and the sense of being judged by a protective mother. "I don't want to complicate his life. I want him to be safe and happy. I don't know how much you know about how we ended up in each other's lives again, but the last thing I want is to complicate things for him."

"I believe you." Sheila pointed to the turnover Claire was working on. "Make sure that seal is tight or the juice will run out."

And that was that. Sheila seemed satisfied, and Claire had the sense of having passed a test—maybe the most critical test she'd ever taken.

By EVENING, it was just the two of them. Clinton and Sheila had gone home, but not before Sheila made sure they had plenty of food for a few days and a clean cabin to stay in. "Take care of each other," she'd whispered in Claire's ear as they hugged goodbye.

Luke certainly looked and sounded like he was well taken care of as he finished his third turnover. "She taught you well," he groaned, patting his belly. "Too well. I might end up popping the button off my pants after this dessert."

"Your parents are amazing. It's easy to see how you boys turned out so well. You got so lucky."

"We did." He took her hand and slid his thumb over the knuckles. "I wish you had, too. I want you to know that. I've been wondering ever since we got here and found my parents if you were thinking about how our lives diverged."

"If you're asking whether I'm jealous or not, the answer is no." She meant it with all her heart. She would have never held Luke's good luck against him. "I want the best for you. That's what it's all about, right? And you got the best, no doubt."

He pulled her in for a kiss. "I sure did."

If her first full day at the cabin had been something out of a sitcom, the next two days were a happy dream—an idyllic, perfect little dream full of nature's beauty and peace. The joy of being together, of making love all through the night and sleeping in each other's arms.

There was fun, too. Like when Luke took her fishing, knowing she didn't have the first clue about it. "Wait. You mean I have to stick the hook through the worm?"

"How did you think this went? I'm genuinely curious."

"I thought I went to the store and whoops, there was fish in the case. Can we not, I don't know…drag a net through the water and see what we pick up?"

"I mean, we could," he offered as he hooked a worm, "but that would take a lot of time. And, you know, a boat.

We can fish from the banks. But hey, at least we'll have the fun of cleaning the fish we catch. Aren't you looking forward to that?"

Only the fact that she caught twice as many trout as he did made the day salvageable. That, and the company—the stories he told and the way his entire demeanor changed as he relaxed. She had no doubt he was still on guard, that his skilled gaze took in everything around them and processed it for signs of trouble, but he did his best to be in the moment with her.

She couldn't have loved him more if she tried.

This might be their life one day. She reflected on that while they sat together on the porch, side by side in rocking chairs. There was peace and quiet, the sort of quiet that settled on a person's heart and spread all through them, making everything a little sweeter. A little better.

And he might be hers. For always. If he wanted to be.

She had the feeling he did, and it made her heart swell with pride and hope. If they could only think about that right now…if only there wasn't so much in the way.

"What are you thinking about?" He turned to her with a smile, amber light all around his head cast from the setting sun. He looked like the angel he'd always been to her.

"How sweet this is. How I needed this." She let out a long sigh, gazing out over the lake. "How I would love to come back here someday…when I'm not afraid anymore."

His hand closed over hers, giving her strength. "You don't have to be afraid."

"Luke…"

"I know it's easy for me to say, but I'm in this for the long haul. Whatever it takes. You have me, and you have my brothers. You have Sheila and Clinton Patterson at your back. In case you couldn't tell, they're a force to be reckoned with."

"You don't need to tell me that." She laughed. "Anybody who could keep you boys in order has my full confidence."

"They like you. I could tell."

"That is a massive compliment." She winked with a smile. "I liked them, too. A lot. They didn't have to be so nice to me, so welcoming. Here I am, a random person they'd never met before, walking into their special cabin."

"Love is what they do. It's who they are."

"I see a lot of them in you." He snickered a little and she continued, "No, I do. You're the same person you always were, don't get me wrong—you're still kind and brave. But you're not as afraid to show it now as you used to be when we were kids."

"You bring it out in me, too, Kitten. It's not all my parents. It's you." He stood, pulling her to her feet and wrapping her in one of his all-encompassing hugs. "It's always been you."

She hadn't made a ton of good decisions in her life, and she knew it.

And while she regretted dragging Luke into the insanity, she couldn't help but think that walking into his office was one of the best decisions she'd ever made.

"I wish we could stay here forever," she admitted in a soft, shaky whisper, wrapped up tight in his arms.

"Me too, Kitten," he whispered, stroking her hair. "Me, too."

Chapter Seventeen

"Let me get this straight."

Vance Ballard leaned forward, his hands folded atop his desk. Could the pair of useless idiots standing before him see how tightly he'd clenched his fingers? His joints ached, yet the discomfort kept him sharp, focused.

And as long as his hands were folded, he couldn't reach for the paperweight sitting on one corner of the desk and throw it at them.

Brooks and Masters did what they could to conceal their growing discomfort. He gave them at least a bit of credit for delivering yet more bad news to his face. Surely even a pair of idiots had to know how their update would be received.

He spoke slowly, with care. "A nothing. A nobody with no family, no friends and hardly any past has managed to elude you. *Again*."

Brooks cleared his throat. "Sir, there's nothing any of us can come up with to explain it. We're missing something."

"So are those detectives," Masters blurted it out, bringing to mind a child tattling on their sibling. "They've been following those Patterson guys around; they questioned the one she went to but they didn't find anything to connect her to them."

More discomfort, this time resulting from Ballard gritting his teeth to hold back a string of bitter profanity. "And we're certain she doesn't have a bank account or credit card we haven't discovered?"

"If she had anything, we would know. No one can get past our monitoring," Brooks insisted in a far steadier voice than that of his partner.

Ballard knew this was true, though the truth of it only infuriated him further. She couldn't access her money. She had nowhere to run. Yet she'd run and continued to elude capture.

How was she doing it? He could've turned the office upside down, but that wouldn't have brought Claire Wallace to him. How could she get past him? *No one got past him.*

"The library fire… We know she had help." He looked at his men, who were increasingly useless. "She couldn't have pulled that off on her own. And Hopkins was clear on there being a man with her." There had been thick smoke at the time, and Hopkins had sustained a head injury moments after seeing the man, but no amount of questioning could shake his certainty.

Claire had the help of a man that night.

"Hopkins didn't see the man," Masters mumbled. "Or, rather, he doesn't remember what he looked like. The smoke was too thick and his memory's hazy. But there was—"

"I know. There was definitely a man. Don't tell me what I already know." A lot of good it did them, knowing about the presence of someone who surely had to exist. No way would Claire be able to manage that escape on her own. The presence of another person came as no surprise.

There was a ticking noise in the back of his mind, the

sound of precious seconds slipping away. Was she enjoying this? That useless, pathetic—

After slowly releasing a deep breath, Ballard asked, "And reports from the detectives confirm she wasn't with that Patterson man after they questioned him?"

"He went to the office, stayed there all day, ran a couple of errands." Masters looked to Brooks, who offered a slight nod in agreement.

"They missed something…they must have. The police are not looking in the right places." Ballard clenched his fists beneath the desk, out of sight. He barely flinched when discomfort slid into pain. It kept him focused. Kept displeasure from turning into fury.

"We'll keep looking," Brooks offered, though there was uncertainty in his voice. He doubted the usefulness of this course of action because he wasn't a complete moron.

"No, there are other ways. More efficient ways. Perhaps a bit messier, but in the end, they'll serve our purpose more effectively than searching for a needle in a haystack. I want that girl's world to dwindle to the size of a pinprick. I want her terrified. I want her to scurry for cover, because that's when she'll make a mistake that will allow us to ensnare her. When she's most unsettled."

"And then?"

For the first time in days, Ballard smiled. "And then we'll kill her."

"Give me the rundown."

Claire paused in the middle of drying the last of the dinner dishes. She'd known Luke was on the phone with his brothers—the only people who'd know how to get in contact with him on his burner phone.

It was the tone in his voice that stopped her and made

her listen. She held her breath, though that didn't do much to quiet the pounding in her ears.

Luke muttered a curse that made her flinch. "You're sure about that? What's their status?" Another curse, delivered with the sort of bitterness that nearly curdled her blood.

She was still holding a plate. Best to put it down before she dropped it. There was no way Luke was about to deliver good news, and for some reason, in the middle of the fluttery panic threatening to take control of her mind, she felt it extremely important to take care of Sheila and Clinton's things. They had been good to her, and she didn't want them to regret even a broken plate.

He was in the living room, standing with his back to her as she tiptoed out of the kitchen. He might as well have been made of stone—so still, so tense. He'd been still for so long that it almost came as a surprise when he ended the call and slid the phone into his pocket.

"What is it?" she choked out. "What's happened? And don't tell me it's nothing because I know something bad's going on."

"I wasn't going to tell you it's nothing." He turned his head, giving her a look at his profile. "I was trying to figure out how to tell you, is all."

"Maybe you should come out with it and get it over with. I can handle it."

He let out a deep breath as his shoulders fell. "There've been problems. That was Weston on the phone, giving me reports from the police department. A truck was run off the road into a ravine overnight. The driver didn't make it."

He might as well have broken out in Greek for all the sense he was making. "If the driver didn't make it, then how do the police know they were run off the road?"

"There were skid marks on the road, along with damage to the rear of the truck. Like another vehicle pushed it." A ghost of a smile played over his lips. "You would think to ask that, even now."

"I still don't understand what this has to do with anything."

"We might not have made a connection if it wasn't for the fire."

She was more lost than ever. "Fire?"

He crossed the small room in three strides and took her by the arms. "I'm sorry, but the Romero house went up last night… It burned to the ground. There were at least two people inside when it did. The bodies haven't been identified yet, but it seems likely your foster parents were home. When Weston got word, something clicked. He checked on the identity of the truck's driver… It was Glen Parker. I'm so sorry."

"Another foster parent." They'd killed her foster parents, people she hadn't seen in ages. The Romeros had always kept her in mind, even after she'd left them. The Parkers had always been kind.

The world started to gray at the edges. Luke's voice started to fade.

"Claire. Stay with me." His hands tightened, squeezing her biceps a little.

It had the intended effect. The world sharpened again, no matter how she wished it wouldn't.

People were dead because of her, good people. She'd been only one of many kids taken in by them. Life might not have been perfect or even fun all the time, but it had been better than living on the street and eating out of trash cans. They had spared so many kids so much danger and pain.

And now? The thought of them dying in terror and

pain threatened to crush her. If it wasn't for Luke, she might've crumpled to the floor and never gotten up.

"You didn't do this." He took her in his arms and held her close. "This isn't your fault. You need to know that."

"In my head, I know it." She closed her eyes as she buried her face in his chest.

"But it's another story once we reach your heart. Right?"

"Right."

"I understand. I do." He stroked her hair, soothing her at least a little. "You couldn't know what he would do. Only a truly sick, twisted person could dream up something like this. A means of smoking you out."

"I can't have him hurt anybody else. I can't let that happen." She pulled back enough to look up into his eyes. There were as many questions there as she had running through her head...doubts, too. Was he wondering if they'd make it out of this the way she did?

One thing she knew—even if he did have doubts, he would never voice those doubts in front of her. He would try to be strong the way he always did.

She could be strong, too.

"I'll turn myself in. Listen," she insisted when he grimaced, "it's the only way. I should've done it in the first place. I could've gotten ahead of this somehow, ahead of him. I was too busy trying to be clever."

"You did the only thing you could do given the circumstances."

"And look where it got me. Look where it got them. This is the only way to stop the bleeding, you know what I mean? Put an end to it, go in and tell the police everything."

"I need you to listen to me." He leaned in until his face was the only thing in her field of vision. There were no more questions or doubts in his eyes. "You go in and there's no protection for you. Those detectives—the ones who questioned me—can't be the only ones under his influence. There are more, so many more, and one or more of them will get to you. They'll find a split second when you're outside the range of a security camera and that'll be that. He will have you killed. Do you understand?"

Funny how speaking became impossible with the threat of her murder dangling in front of her. She could only nod.

"I don't want to scare you, but that's just the way it is." His eyes darted over her face. "Do you understand?"

"I do." She struggled to say the words.

"The only way to get through this is to work together. We have to come up with a plan. We've outsmarted him so far. We just have to keep outsmarting him until he's beat. Do you believe we can do this together?"

There were moments in Claire's life when she'd known nothing but doubt, but this wasn't one of those moments. "I believe you."

"Good." His eyes shone. "That's as good a place to start as any, I guess."

Chapter Eighteen

Trying to sleep was a waste of time.

What was not a waste, however, was lying in bed with Claire in his arms.

She was asleep, her breathing soft and even. She whimpered every once in a while but would relax when his arms tightened. Like she knew she could trust him even when sleeping.

Now he had to earn that trust.

Which was probably why he couldn't sleep to save his life.

So many factors, so many possibilities. A man like Ballard had a lot of connections, a lot of ties. Like a weed-strewn lawn. Pulling up everything they saw would only get them so far, since weeds spread underground, too. Tomorrow morning there'd be more, and more after that.

How to put an end to it once and for all?

He had to be smarter. Think clearer.

How was he supposed to think clearly when the only woman in the world who'd ever mattered was asleep in his arms, trusting him, needing him? It had never been as important as it was just then to rise above it all, look down at it, see it. Plan a way out.

It had never been more impossible.

She stirred and he went still, careful not to wake her. At least one of them should be well-rested.

But it was no use. She lifted her head from his chest, blinking away sleep. "Mmm?"

"Mmm?" Even now, he couldn't help but grin at how cute she was.

"Did you say something?" Her voice was thick but still sweet.

"No. You might've been dreaming. Go back to sleep."

"Not if you're awake."

"I'll go to sleep, too," he offered.

She touched his cheek with tender fingertips. "Something tells me you haven't been asleep at all."

"You're sharp, Kitten." He bent one arm, propping his head up on his forearm with a groan. "I've been too busy thinking to sleep. But one of us should, if we can."

"I kept having bad dreams, anyway," she admitted. "It's easier to be awake, when my subconscious doesn't make things seem so real."

"I'm sorry." He stroked her silky hair, letting it run between his fingers like a golden waterfall. When this was over, he would take a solid day and devote it to nothing but this—the simple pleasure of touching her.

"What are we going to do?" He knew it wasn't a question she expected him to answer, at least not right away.

"We've spent all this time on the defensive, right? Running away, hiding, barely escaping. He hasn't backed down an inch—if anything, it's made him more determined than ever. He's getting desperate. Going after the people who were once a part of your life, at least the ones he can trace. He figures he has to cut out anybody who could be helping you until you have nowhere left to turn."

"Until I figure the only way out is to turn myself in,"

she whispered, cringing. "Which is exactly the impulse I almost followed."

"It's not your fault. He knows you're a decent person with a soul and a conscience. He might not have either for himself, but he knows they exist in other people. He wanted to prey on that. We're still smarter than he is. We won't fall into his trap."

"So what will we do?"

"We'll go on the attack. We'll turn the tables on him."

"How? He'll know in a heartbeat if I try to hack him again. He'll be waiting for that."

"I know. I'm not talking about hacking."

"What are you talking about?" She pushed herself up on one arm and looked down at him. "What are you thinking?"

"I'm thinking we use his weaknesses against him."

"How do you know he has any?"

"Everybody has a weakness, Kitten. One of the things I've had to learn in my business was how to figure out what those weaknesses are. They're a way inside." His breath caught when he realized what he was saying.

She knew it, too. "The way Ballard's been using my weaknesses to flush me out."

"I'm sorry."

Chewing on her lip, she lifted a shoulder. "Okay. So, we'll use my skills to find his weaknesses. You know by now that I can hack my way into anything. There's got to be information about him somewhere—though knowing him, he's done everything he can to hide it so nobody can find it."

"We don't have to find his personal weaknesses, per se." He sat up, scrubbing his hands through his hair as the closest thing to a plan he'd come up with all night started to reveal itself.

"What does that mean?" In the early-morning light, he could clearly see the skepticism written all over her face.

"Think about it. A man like Ballard surrounds himself with a lot of people to do his dirty work. He thinks it keeps him safe, but what it does is leave him vulnerable. Because those people have weaknesses, and they're more likely to leave their weaknesses where a person with your skills can find them. They don't have the resources he does."

"So we look them up, instead." A smile began to dawn. "Of course."

"I knew you'd understand." He got out of bed, eager to get started. That was always the way. Once a path showed itself, he couldn't wait to move.

Claire wasn't so eager. "Where would we start?"

"Personally, I'd like to know more about those detectives who made it their mission to trail me and my brothers, Fisher and Arellano. One or both of them have to be in bed with Ballard, which means he's either holding something over their heads or giving them money— again, because he'd know they need it for some reason. Which means you'd be able to find what he found. I know you can."

"I'm glad you have that much confidence in me," she said. "What if he has people monitoring their accounts or whatever, in case I go looking around?"

"What if he does?" Luke knelt beside the bed, taking her hands in his.

She drew a deep breath. "Right. Of course. I know how to be careful."

"I know you do."

Her shoulders squared and her jawline hardened. When she spoke, her voice was firm. "I can't be afraid of what might happen. I only need to be prepared for it."

He couldn't have loved her more. "Exactly." He kissed the backs of her hands before standing. "I know you can do it. You have what it takes. And once you've dug up all that information, you can give it to me and the boys. We'll know what to do from that point."

His brothers needed to know about this. He padded down to the kitchen to fix coffee—if ever there was a morning when he'd needed it—and once the aroma began to fill the air, he pulled out the burner phone he'd been using to keep in touch with them.

"I was just going to call you." Brax's voice was like a snarl. That, paired with the early time of the day, made Luke's palms go slick with nervous sweat.

"What's up?" He looked up the stairs, wondering if he should let Claire overhear this.

"We're not sure… Keep that in mind. We don't have proof."

"Talk to me," Luke barked as quietly as he could. "Stop dancing around it."

A heavy sigh. "Dad called. Mom had trouble with her brakes."

Luke gripped the counter as hard as he could, forcing himself to process this without giving in to emotion. Emotion was the enemy at a time like this. "And what happened? How is she?"

"She's fine. She was smart enough to pull off the road and call for help the second she felt something was wrong."

Luke exhaled. "But no proof."

"No proof. Still, it seems—"

"A little too convenient? Yeah, it does." He muttered a string of profanity under his breath. If he had Ballard in front of him just then, what he wouldn't do to that snake.

"Chance is going to stay with them for the time being, just as a precaution."

"Good," Luke agreed. "I know it'll make me feel better knowing they have protection. And Mom will love the opportunity to stuff Chance full of her cooking, so it's sort of a win-win."

Brax chuckled. "Yeah, it's just a shame about the circumstances. What are we going do about this guy? He's smart. He knows there has to be a connection between us and Claire, even if he can't find it. He's starting to get desperate with these so-called accidents."

"It just so happens that's why I was calling you. I have an idea that has the possibility of becoming a plan."

"I'm all ears."

Claire started down the stairs, locking eyes with him. She must have seen his troubled look for what it was, because her smile faded.

"I have a better idea," he offered. "Why don't I catch you up on it in person?"

Her chin trembled only once, enough to remind him how scared she was in spite of everything. Then she nodded. Stronger. The way he needed them to be for both their sakes.

It was time to go home.

Chapter Nineteen

Luke Patterson had done a lot of difficult things in his life.

His time in the service hadn't exactly been a cakewalk.

Even before then, when he was a kid, he'd survived a lot of situations that might have broken somebody without his strength or determination. He hadn't exactly seen it that way at the time—adulthood had a way of casting things in a different light. All he'd known back then was survival.

Yet as he drove away from the safe house where he'd stashed Claire with Weston keeping watch, he was sure he'd never done anything harder. Not even close.

"You know she's in safe hands with me," Weston had reminded him, only partly kidding around. He understood what Claire meant, how Luke felt, and what it did to him to leave her behind. Safe hands or not.

None of them would ever be satisfied with letting others protect the ones they loved, no matter who those others were.

If it wasn't for the need to put in face time around the office, he would never have considered leaving her side, no matter how remote her location. It wasn't like the cabin, in that the cabin hadn't been deliberately rigged to keep it off the grid.

This safe house was. Luke and his brothers used the cabin's generator and solar panels as inspiration to keep clients as protected as possible by making them as invisible as possible.

Even having set up the safe house himself wasn't enough to make leaving any easier. But facts were facts, and Ballard wouldn't be satisfied without confirmation of Luke being in the area and following his normal routine.

Which was why he drove to the office with his hands gripping the wheel tight enough that he could've sworn he heard the thing creak from the strain. It was why he stopped off for coffee and a bagel, making sure to take his time getting in and out of the car so anybody driving past could see him easily.

Brax was waiting at the office. "No bagel for me?"

"Here. You can have this one. I'm not hungry." He handed the bag to his brother before heading to his desk. The absence of files was still a minor miracle and enough to make him smile for a second.

"You've got to take care of yourself if you plan to take care of her." Brax leaned against the doorjamb, picking at the cinnamon raisin bagel but watching Luke all the while.

"I realize that. But I couldn't swallow a bite right now if you paid me, not since we talked this morning." He couldn't shake the mental image of his mother realizing there was something wrong when her foot pressed down on the brake pedal and nothing happened. If she had been on the freeway—

He shook himself free of this. It was enough that she was safe. He'd drive himself insane if he kept asking "what if."

"You think Claire will be able to find what we're looking for without being noticed?"

That much he was sure of. "Absolutely. She knows what she's doing. It's one thing to not get around safeguards placed specifically to keep her out of Passage Digital's network without raising a red flag, but Ballard's people can't put up blocks to other sites not under their control. So as long as she uses her tricks to mask who she is and where she's accessing the information from, she'll be fine."

"You sound pretty confident."

"I am. She's the best. And it isn't like she doesn't understand the stakes."

"I wasn't trying to insult her. Don't get your feathers ruffled." Brax flashed one of his winning smiles, the same smile that he'd used to get out of trouble more times than Luke could count. "Just remind me once things calm down for good to make fun of you until I run out of breath for finally falling for a woman."

"I'll do that right after I remind you to grow up. How's that sound?"

His burner phone rang. Brax grew serious as he perched on the edge of Luke's desk to listen in. "Yes?" Luke answered, glancing at his brother.

"All's well," Weston assured him. "Your lady is working her fingers to the bone over here. I don't think I've ever heard keys clicking so fast."

Like that was what he wanted to hear about. "Has she found anything?"

"Oh, definitely. She hacked the security footage around the office building—not in Ballard's offices, mind you, but the ones nearby. That way he won't know somebody's been looking around. She managed to pick up clear shots of a pair of big guys who tag along with him wherever he goes. You can plainly see them from a camera across the street getting in and out of his car.

She ran a facial recognition scan, and their names are Nick Masters and David Brooks—both ex-CIA, both with filthy records."

"A perfect resource for a man with no scruples."

"Exactly."

"What about those detectives? Anything there?"

"Claire is working on them as we speak. I'd guess they'll be easier to get to than these two psycho meatheads. The odds of catching one of them without Ballard nearby is greater. They're regular guys...detectives, probably with wives and kids."

"So their pressure points will be closer to the surface. Easier to find and use against them."

"Correct again. You'll get the hang of this yet."

"Everybody's a comedian all of a sudden."

There was noise in the background, making Luke's heart clench. The sound of her voice did that to him, the longing he couldn't shake. Wanting to have her there, with him, where he could see and touch her and know she was okay.

"She found something," Weston murmured. "Let's see."

"What is it?" Luke exchanged another glance with Brax, whose eyebrows were lifted high enough to practically blend in with his hairline.

"Oh. Oh, this is good. This works in our favor." Weston's dark chuckle was punctuation at the end of that statement. "I'll let the lady tell you what we're looking at."

Moments later, Claire's voice washed over Luke like a gentle rain. Just the sound of it helped him breathe easier.

She launched straight into her report. "Looks like our friendly neighborhood detective has a bad habit. There are two mortgages on Arellano's house, and he's in credit card debt up to his eyeballs."

"What is it? Drugs, drinking, women?"

"Judging by the locations of these ATM transactions, I'd say gambling."

Brax shook his head and let out a low whistle while Luke pressed on. "Any sign of interference?"

"A big flashing red sign. Man, the guy even took an early withdrawal from his IRA. His checking account was nearly in the negative. But suddenly...poof! A whole bunch of money showed up across a number of different accounts like a benevolent fairy waved a wand."

"How much?"

"There's a lot of zeroes. Let's put it that way."

"They weren't even sneaky about it."

"Eh, they were pretty sneaky," she chuckled, "but I'm sneakier."

He grinned. "Of course. I can't forget that."

"I'd say he's your way in. From what I'm seeing, Fisher is just plain dirty. He's been written up for excessive force a half dozen times in four years and has a string of citations for other offenses. How does he even have a job?"

"Somebody's convinced somebody else to look the other way," Luke decided. "How about Arellano's record?"

"Clean as a whistle."

"He's our way in, then." Luke offered Brax a smirk. "Let's see how Detective Arellano feels when the tables are turned and he's the one being tailed."

It was early evening by the time they found him, his car parked outside a Chinese take-out restaurant a few miles from the rancher he and his wife called home. There were no kids in the picture, but that didn't make him any less vulnerable—not with a gambling habit like his.

With Brax keeping lookout, Luke waited in a narrow alley between the restaurant and the dry cleaner next door. It wasn't more than a few minutes before a man in a rumpled suit emerged holding a plastic bag in one hand.

Detective Brandon Arellano wasn't at the top of his game, not even close. Luke was able to grab him and steer him toward the alley without even a hint of force. He wondered if the guy was fully aware of what was happening to him. It wasn't until they were standing face-to-face that the detective blinked hard, shaking his head a little. "Oh. It's just you."

Luke blinked, a little thrown by this reaction. "Who did you expect, Detective?"

"Not you. What are you doing?" Arellano looked back and forth, up and down the cramped passage. "Are you insane, trying to pressure me like this?"

"Who said anything about pressuring? I thought we might have a little chat, is all. You've been so interested in my life as of late, it seemed rude not to be interested in yours."

It was then that Luke noticed something.

The man looked like death warmed over, as Sheila Patterson was prone to saying. Even in the few days since Luke had last known the displeasure of the man's presence, Arellano had lost weight. The buttoned collar of his shirt was loose around his neck, his Adam's apple sticking out more prominently than before. He hadn't shaved in at least two days, and his eyes were ringed in dark circles. "What happened to you, man?" Luke asked, dropping any pretense of threat.

"It's none of your business. And if I were you—"

"You aren't me. For one, I don't look like somebody

reanimated my corpse. What's going on? Don't pretend everything's fine because I know things about you. And something tells me I'm not the only one."

"What's that supposed to mean?"

"Read the racing form lately?"

Arellano's already pale skin turned ashen. "That's none of your business."

"Listen to me." Luke lowered his brow along with his voice, locking eyes with the detective. The man was terrified, sweat rolling down his face and neck. It was time to take a calculated risk. "I know Ballard's blackmailing you."

The risk paid off. Arellano's eyes flew open wide in time with the dropping of his jaw. "Wh-what?"

"You heard me. It doesn't have to be this way. The man is a disease, isn't he? He finds your weak spot and works his way in. So, what is it? He found out about your gambling and threatened to spill to the department? I mean, they can't have a degenerate gambler on the force, now, can they?"

"Watch it," Arellano snarled. "You have no idea what you're talking about."

"Don't I? I have the feeling I'm right. Call it instinct or the way your body language is taking to me. You're scared out of your wits, man. Like I said, it doesn't have to be this way."

It was clear the man didn't want to buckle. He wanted to stay strong and pretend he didn't have the first clue what Luke referred to, but there were limits to a man's resolve.

He leaned against the wall with a heavy sigh. "You're right. He found out about the gambling and threatened to go the captain unless I agreed to play along. I mean, what was I supposed to do? It seemed like the answer to a prayer. Only..." He averted his eyes.

"Only you didn't want to play along once you figured out what that would involve?"

A single nod. "Fisher...he's a complicated man. He doesn't, uh, care much about going by the book. I didn't know that Ballard already knew him, though. Not until this whole thing started. And I didn't know how far he was willing to go. I couldn't do the things Ballard wanted us to do." He shuddered, shaking his head.

Luke fought to put things together. He looked down at the bag Arellano still carried and noticed how light it looked. The condition of his clothes, the sweat stain around his collar, the stain on his tie.

An even uglier picture started to come together.

"You told him you wouldn't play his game," he murmured, "so he forced your hand."

"He took my wife. He *took* her." There were tears in the man's eyes when they met Luke's again, and the pain in his voice was almost enough to stir sympathy. "He's going to kill her if I don't see this through. I believe him."

Luke muttered a curse, hands linked on top of his head. This was worse than any of them had imagined. "We can get you out of this."

Arellano let out a miserable laugh. "You can't believe that. Not knowing what you know, Patterson. You don't seem like a stupid person."

"You're right, I'm not. Which is why I know we can get all of us out of this, but we've got to be smart. Which means you've got to play on our team from now on."

"Don't you get it?" Arellano snarled like a trapped animal—which, in essence, was what he was. "It's quid pro quo. Claire's life for Amanda's. He wants Claire Wallace dead. He requires it, or else Amanda dies."

Luke looked away as the man started to cry, both sorry for him and more than a little uncomfortable. "He's not a disease… He's the devil incarnate."

"He is. I wish I'd known. I swear, I didn't know. I wouldn't have accepted his deal if I thought Amanda would get roped into it. She's innocent. She didn't even know about the blackmail money. I don't know where he has her—" His voice lifted in pitch, taking on a note of panic.

Luke took Arellano by the shoulders and shoved him against the cold brick wall to shake him out of his spiraling. "Okay, all right. You've gotta stay calm and rational for Amanda's sake. And you have to accept help when it comes your way. This isn't like before. I'm not Ballard. I'm not trying to trick you. There's a way we can all get what we need, but we have to work together. You need us, and we need you."

Arellano took a few deep, shuddery breaths before pulling himself together, standing straighter than before. "You said you have a plan?"

"I do."

"And this is a Ballard-proof plan?"

"Only if I have your full cooperation."

He nodded, firm now. "Okay, Patterson… Let's hear it."

Chapter Twenty

If there was anything Claire knew for sure about herself, it was that she was no hero.

She sure hadn't been one the day of Julia's murder, had she? She sat there and let it happen, watching in mute horror with her knuckles in her mouth to hold back a scream. Running like a scared rabbit afterward, barely keeping herself from breaking into a run. Not exactly heroic.

She hadn't been heroic in the days since then, either. If anything, Luke was the hero. He kept her safe, took care of her, made sure she didn't starve or set up camp under the freeway with a cat who thought he was a dog as her only friend and protector.

He had even come up with this absolutely insane plan.

She was no hero—not then, not now. And for better or worse, she was still in possession of her wits, which meant she was scared to death. Any sane person would be. So many things could go wrong.

Yet it was the only way. That was the cherry on top of a melted sundae. This plan of Luke's—crazy though it might've been—was the only way out of the madness.

Her heart pounded hard enough to make her sick; her hands were slick with sweat. She clutched the steering wheel tighter, pressing down on the gas pedal. Her poor car was just about at its limit now, its engine whining as dust kicked up behind the wheels. She sped along through the outskirts of San Antonio, just like she was supposed to.

And she had never felt lonelier in her life.

Focus. Breathe.

This had to go off cleanly. There couldn't be any doubt.

Ballard had to believe she was no longer a threat, which meant making him believe what was about to go down. She had to sell it.

"You okay?"

Brax's voice was in her ear and it brought her a measure of peace. A sliver, anyway. But it was better than nothing. "Define okay," she replied with a shaky laugh.

"You're doing great. You've got this. Just follow the plan and we're home free."

"Right." She forced herself to breathe again when she noticed she'd been holding her breath. Her entire body was tensed tight enough to hurt. This was only the beginning of things, so she had to calm down if she was going to get through it.

"We went through all this last night, right?" Brax was warm. Calm. Encouraging. He had that way about him, she noticed. His personality complemented those of his brothers. He was a sweetheart, a charmer. "You can go through the steps backward and forward."

"Right."

"Just live it out the way we planned. You know what you're doing."

"I hope that's the case when the time comes for the next step…"

"You wanna know something I've learned?"

"Please." Anything to distract her from the doubts circling her head like water circling a drain.

"You can't think too far ahead when you're in the middle of acting out a plan. You can only focus on the step you're on and pull it off the best you can. Think too much about what'll happen next and you'll mess up what you're trying to do right now."

"Got it. That makes sense." For instance, it wouldn't do her any good to run the car off the road, would it? She focused on her driving while doing her best to make it look like she was trying to get away.

If anybody had ever told her she'd end up being pursued by the cops one day, she would've laughed herself sick. Meek little Claire Wallace, who'd never said boo to a ghost? Who carried spiders outside rather than kill them outright? Why would the police have any reason to chase her?

Life had a funny way of making the impossible real. Tangible. Nauseating.

"The bridge is coming up," Brax reminded her. As if she needed the reminder. It took effort to bite back a snarky comment, which of course, would've been the result of fear. "You know what to do."

"I do." She pushed the car harder, forcing it to speeds it had probably never reached before. If anything, driving fast and being dangerous was a treat. She had spent her whole life playing it safe, keeping her head down, avoiding notice.

To think, it took the threat of being murdered to make her life a little more interesting. "All things being equal, I liked life the way it was."

"What?" Brax's soft chuckle rang through her earpiece.

"Never mind."

The San Antonio River sparkled up ahead, a ribbon cutting through the otherwise dusty, empty land outside the city. It would keep flowing south from the springs where it originated, eventually hooking up with the Guadalupe River miles downstream.

She approached the drawbridge with her heart hammering, her breath coming sharp and fast. A glance at the clock on the dash told her they were right on schedule. Everything was going according to plan, right down to the exact time she'd reach the bridge.

And down to the car speeding her way from the other side of the river.

"Here they come." She knew Brax could see them but felt the need to say it anyway. "I think my heart's going to explode."

"I promise you, it won't. Just stay the course. You can do this. You can do anything. You've made it this far, and you can keep going." Did he know how tense he sounded? How close his voice was to sliding into a bark? She probably didn't sound much better.

The tires hit the metal bridge and made an almost ear-splitting noise at this speed, but she kept going. This was it. There was no going back. Might as well put on a show.

She made it roughly three-quarters of the way over the bridge before the approaching car cut her off, skidding to a stop sideways across the other end, blocking her way through.

Claire slammed her foot on the pedal and the brakes shrieked. Her body pressed against the belt hard enough to take her breath away, but that was only a thought in the background of her mind.

"Okay. On my count. Five…four…three…two…one."

Claire took a deep breath before she threw the car into Reverse and backed away from the car blocking hers, which she knew held Detectives Fisher and Arellano.

Only there was no time to get away. The drawbridge

started to raise behind her, cutting her off in that direction, too. She was out of options. Her heart would surely give out on her by the time this was over, wouldn't it? It had to. She couldn't stand the strain.

Even if all of this was going exactly according to plan, exactly according to schedule. "It's going perfectly," Brax reminded her. "You're doing great. Time to move to the next step."

Right. So easy. How would he feel if he were the one about to do what she had to do? Would he sound so calm and reassuring if he was in her place?

"Claire. You have to move." He didn't sound so calm now. He was downright demanding. "Go. Now."

Her hands fumbled with the buckle while the detectives got out of their car. She had to remind herself that Arellano knew what was happening. He was in on it.

Could they trust him? That was what made her hands so sweaty, sliding off the handle when she first tried to open the door. "Don't forget your earpiece!" Brax shouted, and she was glad he did. She plucked it from her ear and dropped it into her pocket before she opened the door and stepped out of the car.

This was it. This was for all the marbles.

Luke, please help me.

"Hands in the air!" Fisher bellowed, leveling his gun at her. Moonlight glinted off the metal. Her hands shook as she raised them, her gaze darting over to his partner. This was not the time for a trigger-happy cop to get ahead of himself.

"Stand down," Arellano ordered. "I've got this." Claire could only hope he was right, that Fisher wasn't as desperate to shut her up. She let out a shuddery breath when he holstered his weapon.

But that didn't mean she was out of the woods.

She crept closer to the edge of the bridge where a low railing was all that stood between her and the water. Was it cold? Was it rushing fast? She could only hope not.

Make sure you go to the side of the bridge facing upstream. Right. This would all fall apart if she made a stupid, tiny mistake.

"I know you're working for him!" she called out. At least her voice sounded strong, like she wasn't quite as terrified as she felt. "Ballard. I know he has you both in his pocket. That's why you're doing this."

"Keep your hands in the air!" Arellano was either serious about wanting to stop her or he was a very good actor. Wouldn't that be the ultimate kick in the head—a double-cross on a double-cross?

What if he'd been lying the whole time? What if there was nothing wrong with his wife? What if Ballard had him tell that story to make himself seem sympathetic? To lure them into a trap?

No. There was no room for doubt. She had to believe. She had to trust the plan.

Arellano shook his head with a stern expression. "You don't know what you're talking about!"

One step closer to the railing. Another step. Her knees threatened to buckle. She couldn't let that happen. That would ruin everything. "I do!" she shouted, and she let her heartache and disappointment and fear come out. And her disgust—deep, pulsing, bile-flavored disgust. "You're in this with him! You accepted his dirty money, his promises, and look where it got you! This is wrong! You know it is! I didn't do anything wrong! I never killed anybody—he's the killer, not me!"

"Just stop talking," Fisher warned. "This doesn't have to end badly for you. But it does have to end. You can't run from the police forever. Your best bet is to come with us, Claire. You said you didn't do anything. You have no reason to run."

The railing was within her reach. Did she have to guts to do this? Well, she'd had the guts to do everything else so far. This was just one more thing she would never have imagined before now, not in her wildest dreams.

"You're lying!" Was she laughing? It seemed unthinkable. There was nothing funny about this. But there were all sorts of reasons for a person to laugh. Like when a situation was beyond the absurd, which applied to this situation.

The water was just below her, rushing audibly. Or was that the blood rushing in her ears? If only Luke was here with her. If only she could hear Brax's voice again, but keeping the earpiece in was dangerous. Not only because one of the men at the end of the bridge might see it. The last thing she needed was for the thing to short out while in her ear.

"Come with us and you'll see." Fisher's voice was deceptively quiet, bringing to mind a snake. That was what he was, too. A snake in the grass, lying in wait. Lying in general, in fact. She almost laughed again.

"I don't think so. I don't think I'll make it to the police station. Isn't that right, Detective?" She looked at Arellano, willing him to go along with what was supposed to happen next. Everything hinged on what was about to happen next. He had to sell this just as much as she did—more than she did. In another few moments, her part would be over.

"Just come with us, Claire," he shouted. "This can all be finished. But you have to stop running. We're not the only people looking for you."

"You think I don't know that?" Her hip bumped the railing. This was it. Everything would come down to this. She stiffened her spine against the fear threatening to break her. "But Ballard wants me dead. Stop pretending he doesn't. Stop lying for him!"

"Claire…"

"Have a little courage!" she screamed. "A little integrity! How do you sleep at night, doing what you do for him? You cowards! You filthy, lying, murdering—"

"Enough!"

Arellano's deep, bellowing voice mixed with the sharp, sudden crack of a gunshot.

Oh, Luke. Help me.

Claire closed her eyes and went over the railing, into the dark water below.

Chapter Twenty-One

It was like watching a horror movie unfold in slow motion. Only this was too real.

Claire's limp body seemed to float through the air, falling, falling. How could it take so long for someone to fall off a bridge? It wasn't such a long drop—they'd chosen that particular bridge not only because it sat in an empty area, but because the drop wasn't so far. Hence, it being a drawbridge, too low for anything to pass underneath without it opening.

He braced himself for impact almost like it was his body about to hit the water. It might as well have been. Claire was his life, nothing less than everything that mattered.

She hit the river with a splash, roughly where they'd worked out her impact. Close to where he was waiting under the bridge. He waited a second before letting go of the dummy dressed in clothes identical to Claire's, floating it facedown.

He then ducked under the surface, taking hold of Claire before the river's current pulled her out of reach. She was panicked, struggling against him even though everything was going according to plan. He guided the mouthpiece to her lips, his scuba gear allowing him to breathe underwater. She had to breathe, too.

And she could once she settled down and let him insert the device into her mouth. She clung to him the way he clung to her with all his might. She was safe. She would be okay.

She was, after all, dead.

Well, not exactly. Thanks to the blank Arellano had fired and the dummy Luke had set loose, to Fisher it would look like Claire was out of commission and no longer a threat. With the report coming from both detectives, Ballard would have no choice but to believe she was dead.

Now all they had to do was wait, holding on to each other beneath the water's surface. He could just make out beams of light shining down from the bridge. Flashlights. Arellano probably wanted to make sure his partner saw the lifeless dummy before it rounded the bend and floated out of sight.

It was a long fifteen minutes, with Luke keeping watch on the riverbank and waiting for the signal. When a bright light flashed from inside the trees, he knew they were in the clear. Brax had been keeping watch and was satisfied that both cars were gone. They'd made sure to leave no trace of Claire in her car. Just the keys, so one of the men could drive it off the bridge and somehow make it disappear.

They'd wipe out all memory of Claire's existence. At least, that was what Ballard would believe.

Or so they hoped.

Luke pulled Claire to the surface with him where she tore the respirator from her mouth and gulped fresh air. "I can't believe it worked," she whispered, her teeth chattering.

"You don't trust me now, Kitten?" He tried to keep his voice light and teasing. Like it was completely normal for them to take a swim in the river in the middle of the night. For her to pretend she'd been shot and pitch herself off the side of the bridge.

God, how he loved her. Her strength and courage. He wasn't even sure whether he'd have the guts to throw himself off a bridge, no matter whether the fall had been planned or not.

He held on to her as he swam for shore, where Brax waited with a car and towels. "You were perfect," Brax whispered, wrapping one of the towels around Claire while Luke pulled off his goggles and slid the oxygen tank off his back. "I told you so."

"You told me." Her voice was shaky, though it was clear she was trying to sound cheerful and relieved. And she had every right to be relieved—she'd cheated death.

"Let's get you back to the house." Luke guided her into the back seat of Brax's car, noting the way she shivered until her teeth chattered. He had a feeling there was more to it than feeling chilly, still soaked from the river. He made a point of holding her close while Brax drove, trying to warm her, trying to comfort her.

Sure, she was out of the worst of it. Safe, now that Ballard thought she was dead. That didn't mean the enormity of what she'd just done wouldn't hit her from all sides. The thought of what might've gone wrong. What if Fisher had fired on her instead? He didn't have the first clue what was happening, that his partner had gone into business with the enemy to save his wife's life.

Would she be safe now? Luke hoped so. He didn't hold anything against the guy for getting himself trapped in the spider's web. Ballard knew how to choose his prey, how to wrap them up so they couldn't escape.

"You're sure they won't find the dummy?" Claire lifted her head from his shoulder, looking up at him with eyes that seemed a lot bigger than usual.

"They won't. It'll end up in the Guadalupe before long, and from there, it'll sail into the Gulf. It'll be enough for them to hide or destroy the car, so there won't be any trace of you lying around. By the time that's finished, the dummy will be gone for good. Nothing to worry about."

"I hope you're right…" She wanted to believe him, he knew she did. Though the fact that there was any doubt didn't exactly thrill him.

He guessed he'd be afraid to bask in victory if Ballard had burned him so many times. Not only Ballard—life had burned Claire again and again for years. No wonder she was hesitant to rest easy.

If he had his way, that would never happen again.

"So, what now?" Claire's head found his shoulder and she let out a soft sigh while she snuggled in. He stroked her wet hair, still heavy with the smell of the river.

"First, we shower."

She snickered. "I thought that went without saying."

"Then, we settle you in so you can get some sleep. You can't burn the candle at both ends forever. We spent all last night going over the plan. Clearly, the effort was worth it. Now you need to sleep."

"You know I appreciate how much you care about me, right?"

"Right." He sensed there was something more to it than that.

"But I don't need you to tell me to rest. I know I need to sleep. I wasn't talking about this very night. What's our next move?"

Brax met his gaze in the mirror, eyes crinkling at the corners. He could afford to smile, couldn't he? Claire wasn't the love of his life. If they were still kids, that little grin would've earned Brax a punch in the arm.

A punch in the arm sounded good right about then, all things considered.

"Can't it be enough for now to rest and regroup?" he asked Claire in a softer voice than before. "You faked your death not forty-five minutes ago. If anything you've ever done has earned you the right to unplug for a minute and recharge, it's what you just pulled off."

She went silent, which he wasn't sure was a good sign. His mom would go silent like that whenever she was good and frustrated with his dad.

Which was why he didn't push Claire to answer.

The ride to the safe house felt like it took years, thanks to the roundabout route Brax followed to get them there. "Just in case," he muttered more than once, taking them down unlit roads, sometimes doubling back. Once he felt comfortable there was no one on their tail, he took them the rest of the way to the safe house.

It was dark and empty. Weston and Chance had made it their business to be seen around town earlier in the evening prior to settling in at home—well before Claire had played out her one-act drama with Detective Arellano—just in case Ballard had been watching for signs of life from them.

Brax entered first, checking for any signs of trouble before waving them in. Luke hurried Claire up to the front door, an arm around her waist, his head on a swivel. They couldn't be too careful, even now.

Once they were inside and he could see for himself that all was well, he allowed himself to breathe. No one could ever call him lazy or out of shape, yet the events of the evening had left him with a bone-deep exhaustion now that the rush of adrenaline had tapered off.

"You okay?" Brax asked while Claire went to shower

off the river's stench. The frown lines creasing his brow revealed his concern.

"Fine. Glad that's over, for sure." Luke opened a bottled water and downed half in one desperate go, signaling dehydration. "Is it possible to sweat bullets while you're underwater?"

"You were worried about her."

"No kidding. Of course, I was. It was the longest few minutes of my life between her rolling onto the bridge and falling off."

"She's gutsy, I'll give her that. She held up under pressure." Brax elbowed him, and a little of his usual good humor flashed in his smile. "You chose well."

Brax couldn't understand, so Luke didn't bother to explain the finer details. There had been no choice involved. Life had put them together, and something about Claire had spoken to something inside him. Maybe his protective nature sensed someone in serious need of someone like him.

Rather than try to explain, he stripped off his wetsuit and ducked into the shower once Claire was finished. Her skin was pink, like she'd scrubbed it within an inch of its life. He couldn't blame her. Even though he'd been covered while underwater, he soaped up twice and rinsed in water as hot as he could stand before stepping out.

He found her sitting on the bed, combing her hair, and his heart swelled with love and relief. Was this how it would always be? Every time he saw her, even if she were engaged in something so commonplace, would he have this same reaction? He hoped not, on reflection, since he planned on their lives being very dull and ordinary once Ballard was out of commission. He wouldn't carry the constant fear of losing her.

"In case I didn't make it clear to you before now, you

were amazing." He dried off and dressed quickly before he sat next to her. "You couldn't have done any better out there. I hope it doesn't come off as condescension when I tell you how proud you make me."

Her hand closed over his. "You don't sound condescending at all. I'm just glad it's over and I don't have to dread faking my death anymore."

Rather than give him time to draw her into his arms, she all but jumped up from the bed. "I know how to finish this."

Luke barely held back his surprise at this sudden announcement—and the absolute dead-eyed certainty with which she delivered it. "You do?"

She gave a single, firm nod. "I do. I've been tossing the idea around in my head like a computer program running in the background while we worked out the plan for tonight." She managed a faint smile.

"Okay. What's the idea?" There was an intensity in the way she moved, the hard glint in her eyes. As much as he wished he could take away any reason for her to look and act that way, there was no denying how proud she made him. Her ingenuity, her capability, her courage.

"Ballard loves nothing more than feeling secure, right?" She didn't pause for an answer, rolling on through. "He finds people to do his dirty work for him. He has eyes everywhere, reporting back to him. He wraps himself in layers of firewalls and cameras and monitoring, like he's protected against the entire world."

"Only a man who poses a threat to the entire world needs to go to those lengths," Luke mused.

Claire nodded. "Exactly. And it's all an illusion. It takes nothing more than a person with awareness of how he does things and the skill to get around his defenses to take him down."

"You're the person with the awareness and the skill."

"I am." She raised her chin like she dared him to argue, but he wouldn't have argued for anything in the world.

"What does that mean?"

"I'm going to use his security system against him. Against all of them."

Chapter Twenty-Two

Whatever special something Brax Patterson had, he could've made a mint from bottling and selling it.

"I told you he'd come through." Luke grinned once his brother had confirmed success on the first step of this latest part of their plan. What would be the end of everything, if it all played out the way they needed it to.

No. The way *she'd* make it play out. It was all in her hands now, and Claire could almost taste victory. So long as Ballard kept acting predictably, she'd be fine. And if there was one thing she'd finally started to understand about Ballard, it was his lack of imagination.

Anyone could've predicted what he'd done so far, if they were willing to sink to his level and think like a power-hungry, greedy sociopath.

Her one advantage over him so far was that total lack of imagination. He hadn't imagined her to be strong, smart or capable. He'd looked at her—or through her the way so many people had all her life—and seen nothing. Nobody.

Talk about a blow to his ego. How much of his desperation to find her stemmed from his fear of what she could do to him and how much came from his crushed pride?

Luke switched on the burner phone's speaker. "You

got it?" Claire asked. Khan took this as an invitation to leap into her lap, wanting all her attention as always.

She kissed the top of his head anyway. He was her spoiled brat.

"I got it." It was clear Brax was smiling, proud of himself. "It was easier than I thought. The ladies at that company need to get laid. She was too glad to stop and chat with me for a little while on her way to her car."

Claire rolled her eyes. "Or maybe you're the most charming devil who ever lived and whoever she was, she couldn't help but fall under your spell."

"Stop. You're making me blush."

Luke snickered. "Okay, okay. Back to business. You have the key card, which means we have access to the building tonight. Weston secured the new laptop and is on his way with it. Claire knows what to do when she gets her hands on it."

She nodded her agreement while wondering how true that was. There she went again, doubting herself when she'd been so sure, so completely certain. She saw it all clearly, each step, everything she had to do.

All that was left was actually doing it.

Weston had followed her instructions to the letter, finding a machine with the capabilities she was looking for. The power she needed, the speed. Speed would be their weapon. When the ball started rolling, it would have to roll fast.

And she'd be the one pushing it along.

The hardest part might very well have been waiting to get started. At least there was one task to keep her occupied—hacking into the security feed.

"You're sure you won't be noticed?" Luke leaned in behind her, squinting at the screen.

"This is the least of our worries, believe me. Nobody

considers a hack to their security cameras—and even if they do, they expect the hack to shut down the system. I'm not shutting it down. I'm looping the same twenty minutes on repeat, so it looks like nothing out of the ordinary is going down while we go to work."

"While you go to work, you mean."

She took a second to kiss his cheek before turning back to the security feed. "You're too sweet. We both know darn well you'll be working, too." No way would she walk into the building alone. Even if she had the nerve to go in on her own, Luke wouldn't allow it.

"If you do your job fast, there won't be anything to do on my end. I'll be downright bored."

She withheld her comment. It was nice to imagine things going smoothly, but a beaten dog still flinched when a hand came its way, even if it hadn't been beaten in a long time.

It hadn't been too long since Ballard had killed people who used to mean a lot to Claire.

She couldn't shake the pit of fear in her stomach when she imagined Ballard taking the person who meant the most.

For his sake, she kept a positive attitude—on the outside, at least.

It was after midnight by the time they rolled out, taking two cars. She rode with Luke and Weston, while Brax and Chance took the second vehicle. If anything went south, it was better to have two cars involved, so whoever was in a position to flee might be able to.

However, she strongly doubted any one of the four Patterson brothers would leave any of the others behind. They might not have shared blood, but they were brothers in every other respect.

This would be the last time she'd ever visit Passage Digital. Rolling into the adjoining parking garage was like stepping back in time, reminding her of better days. She might never have exactly been thrilled to work here—it was always a means to an end, a stepping-stone, a paycheck—but life had been much less complicated then.

And lonelier. There was no Luke back then. He'd been nothing more than a memory.

In the end, it seemed like a fair trade-off.

"You ready?" He put the car in Park and turned to look at her. The hard set of his jaw and narrowed eyes spoke to his strain and his worry for her.

The least she could do was stiffen her spine. "Yes. I'm ready." She carefully slung the pack onto her back, knowing Khan didn't like being jostled around too hard. He'd already been through enough, the poor thing. They both had.

"You sure it was a good idea to bring him?" Weston asked in his "concerned dad" voice. He was such a cop.

Luke knew better. "There's no separating those two. She'd sooner leave me at home than she would that cat-dog hybrid of hers." She smiled, but didn't bother correcting him. He wasn't entirely wrong.

They used the key card that Brax had swiped from the girl he'd flirted with earlier to access the building without setting off any alarms. Though even with the easy entrance, there was no time to dawdle.

They dashed to the elevator and picked the floors in question, planning to split up. "You have your terminal numbers and access codes?" she asked, though she knew they would. They were professionals, not about to lose something so important. Still, double-checking put her mind at ease.

Brax took one floor. Chance, the next. Weston exited

after him, leaving Luke and Claire to get off the elevator on the floor she used to work on. Again, the sense of past and present overlapping threatened to overwhelm her. She took a deep breath and pushed it aside.

Luke kept watch, using his earpiece to confirm his brothers were in place and had successfully logged into their machines. "They're in," he muttered. Claire took a seat, leaving Khan and the pack under the desk. She then opened the laptop and plugged in the precious drive she'd been guarding with her life—the one holding the files Julia had lost her life over.

Something inside her took over. Something bigger than her, some deeper intelligence in her subconscious. So long as she could relax and trust her instincts, she'd be fine.

It was the rest of them she worried about.

"Okay. Phase one." She clicked the button and let the program run. Each of the computer terminals Luke's brothers had accessed would appear to be the ones attempting to access the network, to dig deep into the files in which Claire had hidden the video of Julia's murder.

Meanwhile, Luke used a tablet to monitor the building's real-time security feed rather than the loop Claire fed to the security guards' monitors. "They're unaware," he reported. "Business as usual." She only half heard him, now facing the almost impenetrable layers of security put in place to stop her.

Almost impenetrable…but not entirely.

"Phones are cut," she whispered. "There's no communication out of the building. Radio frequencies jammed, too." Luke reported this to his brothers, confirming the next phase's completion. Even if the security guards caught wind of their presence, they wouldn't be able to call the police or request backup from Ballard's cronies. There wouldn't be any communication among them, either.

However, there was the risk of one of them trying to check in with another for some other reason, and she knew it. They would probably confirm all was well at the quarter hour and more likely at the half, and they'd know there was a problem when their radios didn't work.

It was twenty-four minutes past.

Was that sweat trickling down the back of her neck?

"How's it going?" Luke whispered behind her.

She never took her eyes from the screen. "It's going." Even if the guards caught wind of something being amiss, the Patterson brothers had log-in credentials for four terminals each and directions for where to find them. They'd already planned out their next target, and the next. The point was to keep security thinned out, running from floor to floor, chasing ghosts. Luke was watching for any approaching guards so he could give his brothers the heads-up to start moving.

He muttered a curse. "Here we go." She knew that meant security was onto them. "Chance, you need to move. Now."

Her hands flew faster than ever. They were already running out of time.

"Brax. On to your next terminal. Move."

Cold sweat ran down the back of her neck and pooled between her breasts. The progress bar inched, signaling the decryption in progress. It wasn't moving fast enough, yet she knew it would only take a minute for the process to wrap up.

Which was the longest minute of her life.

"Weston, you've got two on you, approaching from above and below." There was extra strain in Luke's voice, which was more of a sharp bark at this point. She could almost taste the fear for his brother.

Come on, come on, faster. Weston will be trapped soon.

Luke's hand cupped her shoulder. "Claire, you've gotta pause it."

"I can't. We're too close."

"I have to help Weston. I have to get them off him. They'll kill him, you know they will. I'm closest, so it has to be me."

He left the tablet on the desk next to the laptop. "Stay here. Don't move. I'll be right back, I swear." He took her by the back of the neck and silenced anything she might've said by pressing a hard, desperate kiss against her mouth.

She watched the live feed with her heart in her throat, tracking the guards closing in on Weston's floor as victory slipped through her fingers like sand.

Chapter Twenty-Three

"Come on. Come on, Luke." Claire chewed her lip hard enough to pierce the skin, watching as Luke moved between floors via the camera feed on his tablet.

This wasn't something she'd prepared for or thought out in advance.

This gut-twisting, nauseating dread.

The feeling that she was watching her life crumble in real time.

What if he got shot?

What if they killed him?

There would be nothing for her to do about it, nothing she could say. A decryption program wouldn't bring him back. Wouldn't erase the guilt. The pain. The loss.

Khan was restless in the pack at her feet. He sensed her anxiety; he always did. She couldn't find the breath to comfort him. Who was going to comfort her if she lost Luke?

And it was all her fault.

There was movement from another section of the screen, another camera's feed. Chance was on his way to his next terminal—only he'd end up on a floor where two guards currently patrolled, weapons drawn.

"No," she breathed, her heart sinking. Her stomach

clenched and threatened to expel everything in it. Only the thought of Khan's reaction at being thrown up on stopped her.

She had no way of warning him. Why hadn't she thought to get an earpiece for herself? She could only watch and let things unfold. She was utterly powerless.

The same powerlessness she'd felt all her life. Every day for so long. No power. No say in how things unfolded.

And she was tired of it.

She realized there was something she could do.

Because at this point, what did it matter? If they were going to die, it had better be for a good reason.

She turned to the keyboard and clicked the key to continue the decryption program. Luke had asked her to put it on pause—for once, she shouldn't have listened to him. They were losing valuable time. Every second she wasted was one more second in which the Patterson brothers risked their lives.

If anything, starting the process again would mean drawing security away from them and toward her.

Could she stand that? Could she take that onto herself?

"Yes," she decided. "Because they're doing this for me." Khan meowed, signaling his agreement.

Every second lasted an hour. Claire's gaze darted back and forth between the tablet and her screen. Luke had vanished from sight.

She couldn't breathe. Her lungs wouldn't take in air.

No, there he was. Darting up a flight of stairs, hugging the wall. Weston was behind him. The pressure in her chest lessened.

But they weren't out of the woods yet, not even close.

Those guards must have cloned themselves, she decided. They were spreading everywhere.

Just another minute. Maybe two. That was all they needed.

Her head snapped up at the sound of a door closing. She held her breath. Her muscles froze, like the first few seconds after waking up from a nightmare.

Only this was no nightmare...this was very, very real. And somebody was on the floor with her.

Her head might not have moved, but her eyes did. She looked down at the tablet and could still see Luke, Weston. Chance. Brax.

It wasn't one of them.

One of the guards? There was no telling how many of them existed, so it could've been one of them. The progress bar crept so slowly. Could she stall?

Footfalls. Closer now. Tears filled her eyes, but she found the ability to move in time to knuckle them away. There was no time for tears.

What would Luke do? What would he want her to do?

She turned away from the computer with her hands raised, blocking the screen as best she could with her body.

Her heart stopped when she saw who she was facing.

No wonder he'd moved so slowly. He'd been playing with her. Again.

"Hello, Claire." Vance Ballard flashed the sort of smile he usually saved for the media with his Mr. Good Guy persona. "You have no idea how hard I've been looking for you. How you've inconvenienced me. And I don't enjoy being inconvenienced."

"You don't look surprised to see me," she whispered.

Every ounce of her wanted to look at her screen, at the tablet, but she didn't dare take her eyes off him.

Only an idiot would take their eyes off a snake when it slithered its way closer.

"That's because I'm not surprised." He came to a stop, his feet planted and arms folded. With his chin raised, he looked at her over the tip of his nose. "I didn't buy that whole fake death for even a second."

She gulped. What did that mean for Arellano's wife? And why was she worried about either of them right now? "Y-you didn't?"

Tipping his head to the side, he looked like a disappointed parent. "Oh, come on, Claire. We both know you. You aren't brave enough to face down two armed law enforcement officers without there being another plan in place. The moment those two nitwits came to me with the news, I suspected you had something up your sleeve."

"You could've come after me right away. Could've put my name back on the news, offered a larger reward—"

"No. That wouldn't do." He shook his head. "You had to believe that I believed it—which meant releasing that detective's wife, as much as I hated doing so."

At least that part had worked. "Why let her go?" she asked. "If you knew it was all a trick?"

"Detective Arellano had outlived his usefulness—and I couldn't run the risk of him alerting you. I let him leave town with his wife, let him leave and never come back. I don't care very much." He snickered. "It's not like anyone would believe his story anyway…"

Where were the guys? Where were the guards?

Where was she on the decryption?

She licked her parched lips. "We could back him up, you know."

"You won't be alive long enough to back him up,

Claire." He laughed softly, but there was a hardness in his eyes. That hardness was always there. It always had been. She had only tried to ignore it back in the day when he was nothing but her boss.

He had always been empty.

"You think you're going to kill me now?" She snickered the way he had. *Let him see how good it felt to be laughed at.* "You've tried all this time... You think you'll succeed now?"

"You were stupid enough to walk in here and make it easy for me." He threw his hands into the air with a dramatic sigh. "Come on, Claire, I know you. I know everything about you. Which was why I knew you couldn't have been brave enough to face those men if you weren't absolutely certain they wouldn't kill you."

"I wasn't certain... The other one could've shot me. And the fall from the bridge could've—"

His sharp bark of laughter cut her off. "Please. A cowardly thing like you? Sure, you might take a risk to avoid capture, but we both know you would've collapsed and trembled like a leaf if you hadn't gone into that situation with at least a fair degree of certainty of your success."

Before she had the chance to tell him off, he continued, "I know everything there is to know about you. Don't you understand that by now? How did you think I was able to track down your former foster families?"

A lump lodged in her throat. She pressed her lips together to keep from letting out a sob.

The corners of his mouth twitched, and she realized he enjoyed watching her suffer in silence.

"I know your pain points. I know your weaknesses. Information is my stock-in-trade, Claire. You ought to know that by now. Isn't that what this is all about?"

"Information?"

"And the power it holds. Mind you, only the right sort of person can wield that power. Only they can take that information and turn it into something useful. Even the sharpest blade is nothing in the hands of a rube."

"I'll keep that in mind."

"You will keep nothing in mind." His playful, toying expression shifted, hardened.

He reached into the inner pocket of his suit jacket and pulled out a semiautomatic. "Though I'm glad we had this time together, Claire...really, I am. I wanted to explain myself to you before bringing an end to your useless little life."

"Useless?" She forced herself to not flinch away from the sight of the gun and maintain eye contact. "I created the program you're going to use to steal that all-powerful information you have such a craving for. How does that make me useless?"

"Because you would've left it lying there! All that knowledge. All that power. Right within your grasp, and you would've let a golden opportunity pass you by! Too concerned with honesty and integrity and all the pretty words people use to mask their weakness. Their aversion to doing what needs to be done to get them what they want."

"I didn't want that. Neither did Julia."

"Which is why you are both expendable. The world is no place for the weak, Claire. I'm only culling the herd."

She went cold when he raised the gun and leveled it at her. His hand trembled, but only slightly. He would make the shot.

Which was when the sweetest sound in the world met her ears.

The soft chime of a program reaching its conclusion.

There was no holding back her smile. "Thank you, Mr. Ballard."

His brow furrowed, his gun still pointed at her chest. "For what?"

"For giving my decryption program the time it needed to complete its job."

It was all worth it.

The terror. The running. The pain. Knowing her life could end at any time.

It was worth it just to watch the brief flash of fear wash over his face.

"You're lying." He lowered the gun but charged at her anyway, shoving her aside and bending over the laptop. "What have you done?"

"What I came here to do." She eyed the tablet, willing somebody to come. Quickly.

"Which was?"

"You knew I recorded Julia's murder." She spat the last word. "You knew somebody was watching from another terminal. I bet you tried to find the file, too. But even you couldn't manage that. But little old me...? I hid it where you'd never think to look—and even if you did, you'd never recognize it after encryption or know how to decrypt it yourself. Always using other people to make up for your inadequacies."

This was almost fun, and it might've been if the question of whether the Pattersons had survived didn't hang over her.

Whether Luke had survived.

"No. No! What have you done to it?" He pocketed the gun. His hands flew in a blur over the keys while curses poured from his mouth.

"What have I done to you, you mean?" Yes, she had strength now, the strength she'd always possessed. Only it was a lot easier to let it show while the monster in front of her fell apart.

She watched as he floundered. Nobody could ever have explained how satisfying it would be to watch him panic this way.

"I should thank you for coming up here to see me, since that was what gave me the time I needed to finish running the program. I knew once I started asking questions, you wouldn't be able to help yourself. You would have to grandstand."

"Quiet," he growled, still working and breathing hard.

"What are you trying to do? Delete the file? Destroy it? What about the external drive hooked up to the machine? It has all the files Julia sent me. All the proof of what you planned to do with our app. You should try to destroy that, too, before the information falls into the wrong hands."

He swore again. "You'll pay for this, Claire Wallace."

"You first."

He stood upright, taking a step back from the machine when the display changed.

There were now only four words on an otherwise black screen.

<Files Sent. End Program.>

"What does that mean?" His eyes were wide and oh so panicked when his head snapped around. "What did you do?"

"You did it." She jerked her chin toward the laptop. "You tripped the program I created. All you had to do was keep your hands off and there wouldn't be anything but files on that machine. Just there, nowhere else."

"And now?" he bellowed, his face red and sweat rolling down his neck.

"Now you've sent the files to the entire San Antonio Police Department."

Panic turned to horror. "No...you're bluffing."

"Julia's murder. The files she sent me with your intentions to steal data from your clients. It's all there, and now they have it."

"Lies!"

"Wait and see. I expect they'll be opening their email anytime now. It won't take long for the police to come knocking." When he only stared at her in slack-jawed surprise, she shrugged. "I know you, too, Mr. Ballard. I knew you wouldn't be able to leave well enough alone. You're the one who delivered your own death blow, you monster. I hope it was all worth it."

He shook his head as his body began to tremble. "Lying," he murmured. "Buying time."

"I'm not."

"You are."

"Just wait and see."

They stood that way for what felt like forever but might have lasted no longer than moments. Eye-to-eye. She would never forget the thrill of knowing she'd taken him down. Of watching realization begin to dawn when she didn't flinch, didn't falter.

He knew she was telling the truth.

Which was why he reached into his pocket for the gun and leveled it at her chest. "You're dead."

Chapter Twenty-Four

It had been too long.

He'd left Claire alone for far too long.

"Luke, slow down." Weston took the stairs behind him, urging him in a soft voice.

Easy for him to say. Could Weston slow it down if it meant leaving the woman he loved unguarded for even a minute?

He didn't take the time to answer; instead, he opened the door to Claire's floor and swept over the area in front of him with narrowed eyes. It looked empty, just as it had been before.

But something was different.

The air...there was a charge in it. Someone else was there, out of sight.

Claire was talking. He could just make out the sound of her voice. And while Luke wouldn't put it past her to hold a full conversation with the cat—

He took off, moving as swiftly as he was able while staying silent.

He should've known. How had he not seen this happen?

His gun was drawn; the sound of his brothers whispering in his ear as they kept track of one another's locations was mere background noise as he zeroed in on his target.

And the man who'd just aimed a gun at her chest.

"You're dead," Ballard spat.

Luke took it all in at once, all in the time it took his heart to beat.

Ballard looked like death, which was fitting considering who he was and what he'd done. Soaked in sweat, shaking, chalky.

And Claire. In spite of the semiautomatic that was now pointed at her chest, she looked...

Triumphant.

Luke mimicked Ballard's position, aiming at the man's head. He didn't want to have to go that far, especially since he didn't want to take the risk of Claire being shot, but if it meant distracting Ballard long enough to spare her life, then he'd stop at nothing.

Which, he feared, was Ballard's mode of thinking as well. He would stop at nothing to end Claire's life.

"Ballard. It's over."

Ballard turned his head just enough to take in the sight of Luke aiming at him. "You're right. It is. But not for me."

"Yes. For you." Ballard returned his gaze to Claire. "Hey, I'm talking to you," Luke barked. "Look at me, Vance."

Ballard snorted. "Don't turn that tactical knowledge on me. Using first names, trying to talk sense. Letting me believe you're on my side, that this can all end well. We both know it won't."

"I need you to look at me, Ballard." If he felt more comfortable with last names, then so be it. "You're right. We both know this won't end well. But you'll only make it worse if you shoot her."

"Worse?" Ballard laughed—it had an edge to it, threatening to cross over into something like madness. "Worse than what? If what she told me is true and the entire police department has the files now, I'm finished. But I can at least know I made her pay. I can take that memory with me, at least."

"You wanna make her pay?" Luke glanced at Claire just long enough to take in the sight of her, trembling and wide-eyed. He didn't dare take his eyes off Ballard longer than that.

"Wouldn't you?"

"Yeah. I guess I would, if I were you. I'd want to make the person responsible for my downfall suffer for what they did to me."

"We can agree on that, then."

"But killing her isn't the answer. I'm serious," he insisted when Ballard laughed again. "You end her life, it's over. It's finished. She's gone. That's not suffering, is it?"

Ballard was silent, though the gun remained unmoving.

"Now, shooting me? Killing me? That's suffering."

"No," Claire whispered.

Luke shot her a look. This wasn't the time for her to try to be heroic.

"Are you listening, Ballard? Do you hear what I'm saying? You shoot me and she'll suffer."

"Why would she?" There was that sneer Luke had expected. "Don't tell me the two of you are in love."

"I've loved her since we were kids. You were right," Luke admitted with a sigh. "There was a connection. Thanks to a convenient name change when I was adopted, there was no way for you or your men to figure out how we knew each other. Your instincts were right on the money, though. I've loved her since we met in a foster program years ago. She remembered me and came to me for help."

"I thought so."

"Yeah, you're a smart guy." Luke looked at the gun in Ballard's hand. "I love her, and I think she might love me, too. But even if she doesn't, you know her well enough to know that she'll blame herself for the rest of her life for getting me killed. Do you see what I'm saying? Kill her now, and it's over."

Luke pointed his pistol at the ceiling, his other hand raised at shoulder-height. "Vance. Look at me."

"Don't do this!" Claire begged.

"Quiet." He maintained his focus on Ballard. It didn't matter at this point whether he aimed at the man or not. Getting a shot off at Ballard would still put Claire in danger—he might squeeze the trigger as his body reacted to being shot.

Luke could just about see the wheels turning in the man's head.

He wanted to hurt Claire; he wanted to see her suffer.

Wanted to watch her die in front of him for taking away everything he'd ever held dear. All his power. His prestige.

"Shoot me and she'll crumple like a dry leaf," Luke promised. "And let's face it, Vance. I'm just as responsible for this as she is. More so, even. If it wasn't for me, she never would've made it this far. You would've caught her long before now and put an end to this. I'm the one who hid her. I'm the one who worked the fake-out with the detectives."

"And you know what?" he concluded with a grim smile. "I loved every second of it, because it meant giving you what you deserve—making you pay for what you've done."

Ballard looked from Claire to Luke and back again. The gun didn't move. Didn't even tremble.

It wasn't working. None of what Luke tried was working.

"Stop trying to play the hero, Patterson." Ballard snickered. "I'm not impressed with your mind games. And if you're responsible for this, then you deserve to suffer just as much as she does. I think making you watch her die before you do should be apt punishment."

"No!" Luke shouted and lunged, knowing he wouldn't be fast enough.

He wasn't fast enough.

But someone else was.

Khan.

"What the—" Ballard let out a cry of pain and surprise when claws dug into his arm. The cat had leaped from the backpack to protect his owner, latching onto Ballard's gun arm, and holding on for all he was worth.

And that was all the time Luke needed.

He threw himself at Ballard, driving him to the floor where they landed in a tangle of arms and legs.

The man barely noticed since a cat who thought he was a dog still held on tight, claws sinking through Ballard's sleeve. "Get it off! Get it off!" he screamed.

Luke pried the cat free and set him loose while he pinned Ballard to the floor. "You're finished," he spat, disgust and rage finally coming to the surface now that Claire was out of this monster's crosshairs.

"No!" Ballard struggled, still holding the gun now pinned between them. He kicked, screamed, bucked in the effort to throw Luke off him. "No, this isn't how it ends!"

Luke took hold of his wrist, pressing hard with two fingers just below the heel of his hand. No matter how a person fought to hold their grip on an object, there was no fighting that pressure point.

Ballard's hand fell open long enough for Luke to

snatch the weapon away. He slid it across the floor before delivering a sharp blow to Ballard's jaw, knocking him unconscious.

It was over.

What a weak, pathetic monster he'd turned out to be.

"What do you think you're doing?" A familiar pair of thugs ran from the corner office with their guns drawn—it had to be Ballard's, Luke realized, and probably had a separate entrance. That was how he'd managed to get up here without them knowing about it.

Weston had been waiting by the stairwell all along and jumped into action, followed by Chance and Brax.

When one of the thugs aimed at Chance, Weston drove his head into the man's stomach, knocking the wind from his lungs before they both hit the floor. He took the man by the wrist and slammed his hand against the floor once, then twice, before the gun fell free.

Chance and Brax made quick work of the second attacker, who quickly realized he was no match for two skilled gunmen at once. He raised his hands, dropping his pistol. He might have even looked relieved that it was all over. Chance zip-tied him while Weston did the same with his thug.

Claire. Where was she?

Luke stood, allowing his brothers to make short work of the unconscious Ballard. He looked around, his chest heaving. "Claire?" he panted. "Where'd you go?" There hadn't been any shots fired. What could've happened?

She emerged from under one of the nearby desks with Khan in her arms. "Is it over?"

Emotion swelled in his chest. He nodded, opening his arms. "It's over. Thanks to that attack cat you're holding."

Weston laughed. "There I was, wondering if it was a good idea for you to bring him with us."

"Good boy. Good boy." Claire's tears soaked into the cat's fur while Khan licked his paws like he hadn't done anything out of the ordinary, like he hadn't saved his owner's life.

Then again, Luke thought as he took them both in his arms, *it could've been pride in a job well done*. He thought it might've been, knowing the cat in question.

"I thought I was about to lose you." Now that it was over and he was holding her trembling body next to his, he could admit that much.

"You thought that? You thought it?" Her eyes were sharp when they met his, sharp enough to surprise him. "What did you think you were doing back there? Offering yourself up to him. You know he could've killed you, right?"

"I wouldn't have let that happen." He smoothed sweaty hair back from her forehead and cheeks. "So long as I knew he didn't have you in his crosshairs, I could've taken care of myself."

"You're sure about that?"

"You doubt me now, Kitten?" He pressed his lips to her forehead, eyes closed, thanking anything and anyone listening that the woman in his arms was exactly who she was.

Even now, having come so close to dying, she would think to scold him for putting himself in harm's way.

"Cops are a minute away," Brax announced with a satisfied smile.

That smile lasted only a second before the stairwell door burst open and a team of security guards poured onto the floor.

"So much for security." Chance smirked, his hands raised. He approached the men and explained what had taken place, that the police were on their way and all would be settled when they arrived.

Luke was only dimly aware of this as he held on to Claire. He had all he needed right there.

"Did you mean what you said?" Her voice was muffled, her mouth near his shoulder, but he heard the hope there.

"I said a lot of things. Which thing in particular?"

"You know what I'm talking about. Loving me." She lifted her head, her baby blues searching his. "Is that true?"

"You don't know by now?" He had to laugh in disbelief. "Do you think I go to these lengths for just anybody? Because I'll tell you right now, I don't. Only for people I love more than anything else in the world."

Tears filled her eyes, but they weren't the tears left behind after a close call.

They held joy. Wonder. He knew how she felt.

"You know I love you, too, right?" She giggled softly, a little giddy. "I can't believe I never said that before now. I just figured you knew."

He kissed her softly, tenderly, a kiss filled with every hope and dream he had for their life together.

And it would be spent together, because he couldn't remember how he'd lived without her.

And he certainly couldn't have imagined a future without her.

He didn't want to try.

But that would have to wait, since now the sound of sirens filled the air. They had some serious explaining to do to the police.

Chapter Twenty-Five

It was all so beautiful.

Claire had appreciated the beauty of the land surrounding the Pattersons' cabin during her first visit with Luke over six weeks ago. Even then, she'd been able to recognize how special a place it was. Peaceful and perfect, like the modern world hadn't quite made its way there yet.

Now? Without the threat of imminent death hanging over her head?

It might as well have been heaven.

Especially considering who was there with her.

"Fishing is actually a lot more fun than I ever imagined it would be." Claire cast off, waiting for the hook and fly to hit the water and send ripples out over the otherwise still lake. She reeled her line in just a little, knowing now that the motion would attract any nearby fish.

Luke had taught her a lot.

He smiled with a wry grin, careful to keep his voice soft to avoid scaring away the fish. "That's easy for you to say. You're a natural."

"I have a good teacher." And yes, she was slightly better at it than he was, which helped her enjoyment. But she wasn't about to say that out loud.

She loved him and knew he loved her and would for-

give a lot of things, but there were times when a girl knew
not to tread on a man's ego.

It had been a magical few days together for sure, and
exactly what they both needed now that the hectic mess
of clearing her name was over. Now it was nothing more
than a memory.

Though it was still a fresh memory, she knew it would
fade with time.

And Luke would help. Just the way he always did.

The information that she'd sent out to the police department had been more than enough to put Vance Ballard away for the rest of his life, along with the man who'd
murdered Julia in such cold-blooded fashion.

There was plenty of additional evidence against Ballard's murderous bodyguard and the other one along with
him. Julia's murder was only the tip of an iceberg that
ran wide and deep. It was a comfort to know those men
would get what they deserved. Even if it wouldn't bring
back any of the lives they'd taken.

She drew a deep breath and let it out slowly, the way
she always did whenever the still-fresh reality threatened to close in on her. How close she'd come to losing
her life. Or, worse, to losing everything that had ever
truly mattered.

Luke hadn't been lying that day, describing how she
would suffer if he'd died because of her.

But he hadn't.

She took another deep breath and reminded herself
it was safe to be happy. Safe to feel secure. Safe to feel
loved.

The early-morning sun framed Luke's profile. He took
her breath away, even after weeks of seeing him constantly. Would it always be like that?

"What are you thinking about?" He glanced her way

with another little smile before reeling his line in just a bit to attract attention.

"Hmm? How did you know I was thinking about anything?"

"I know you, Kitten. That mind of yours never stops working." He smiled wider. "And I could feel you staring at me."

"Was I staring?"

"It sure felt that way."

She laughed at herself. "I guess you're nice to stare at."

"Thank you. You're not so bad yourself."

"Anyway," she continued, turning back to the water, "I was thinking about how grateful I am to have the cabin to ourselves for a little while. I know I've said it before, but your parents are the best."

"They know quality when they see it." He winked.

"Obviously, since they took to you the way they did."

"You're in a sweet-talking mood today. Not that I mind, of course."

"I guess I'm feeling generous since I've already caught three fish, and you've caught... How many again?"

"Shush, woman. I should've known you would lord it over me."

She eventually stopped giggling. "Really. I meant what I said. You, your brothers... You're a special group. I never could've imagined them welcoming me the way they have." She didn't bother saying anything about what they'd done to ensure her safety. By then, they'd rehashed the details of that day at the Passage Digital office and the days leading up to it more than enough.

"They know quality when they see it, too."

"It's easy for you to brush it off—not that you're not taking me seriously or anything. I know you are. But you've known what it means to be part of a family a lot longer than I have. It's still new to me."

He kept his gaze trained on the water, speaking slowly. "You have all the time in the world to get used to it…if that's what you want."

If that was what she wanted? She wanted nothing more in the entire world than to be with Luke for the rest of her life. Longer than that, if possible. Forever.

But she wouldn't push for anything more than this. For now, this heavenly trip was more than enough. Focusing on just the two of them and being happy.

This time, she felt Luke's gaze on her instead of the other way around. "Where did you go?"

"You mean, other than right here? On the lake with you?"

He wasn't buying it. "Yes. Other than right here. You went someplace else."

Darn him for being so observant. "It'll take me some time to get used to living like a regular person, I think. I've spent so much of my life closed off from others. I didn't want to trust. I didn't want to run the risk of getting hurt. I figured it was easier on my own." She shrugged. "You know all this."

"I do. And I understand. It's not like I adjusted right away to knowing I had a family around me, either. It took time to get used to that new mindset." He offered a soft chuckle. "More than six weeks. In case you happen to find that relevant."

"Gee. Why would that matter?" They laughed together as softly as they could for the sake of the fish.

"So long as you're happy, Kitten. That's all I want."

And she knew it, and she loved him more than ever for it. Somebody in the world wanted her happiness above all else—her safety and well-being, her fulfillment.

The fact that this person happened to be Luke was the icing on the cake.

"I'm happy right now. I'm happy with you." She leaned over to kiss him, but the kiss was cut short by a tug on her line.

"Again?" Luke laughed, grabbing the net in case she needed help. She was much better at reeling her catch than she was at first, so there was no need for him to splash around in the water for her sake.

"What can I say?" She held up a sizable, shining, wriggling trout with a proud smile. There was no helping it.

"Are you putting something special on the hook? Are you bribing these fish?"

She laughed as he took the hook from the trout's mouth. That was something she still couldn't bring herself to do, even averting her eyes when he did it. Catching and cleaning and eating them was one thing.

There were limits, though.

"Yeah, I'm bribing them in some weird way so they'll bite. You figured out my trick."

"Are you sure you aren't, though?"

"What?" She looked his way when curiosity won out over squeamishness. "What are you talking about?"

"There's…something…else on the hook." Luke plopped the fish into the basket between them, then bent to rinse something off in the water.

"What is it? I didn't put anything special on there… You're right here with me, you see what I'm doing." Curious, she leaned over his shoulder.

He stood and turned to her.

And held out a ring.

She dropped her pole in favor of crossing her hands over her chest, where her heart had suddenly started pounding. "What…? How…? What…?"

Luke offered the sweetest smile. "Should I bother answering those questions?"

She couldn't answer. Somebody had stolen her words. All Claire could do was shake her head while her eyes remained glued to the ring. White gold. Diamond solitaire. Sparkling in the sunlight.

He lowered himself to one knee. "I didn't intend to do this here and now, but with the direction the conversation took, it seemed like a natural time to ask you to marry me."

She gulped. "Oh. My gosh."

"I'll take your reaction as surprise and not horror."

"Oh, no! Not horror. Definitely surprise." Her head felt like it was about to fall right off, she was so surprised.

"You didn't know I was planning to propose?"

"I hoped…" she admitted, trembling, "but I didn't know. I didn't want to assume anything."

"Which is one reason of many for me to ask you to marry me, Claire Wallace." There was so much love shining on his face, looking up at her the way he was, holding out the ring. "You've been the one for me all our lives. The one person I could never forget. You've always been part of my soul."

Her breath caught and her eyes filled with tears.

"You always will be," he murmured. "And I fully intend to spend the rest of my life reminding you of how lovable you are. Because you are. You're worthy of adoration and support and protection and everything I could ever offer. More than that, but I'm nothing special. I'm not a superhero, I swear. Though I'll do everything in my power to be that for you. I'll be anything and everything you need."

She shook her head as tears spilled over. "You're already everything I need and more than I ever dreamed

I'd have. I don't think I could be happier than I am right now at this moment."

"Is that a yes?"

She giggled and nodded. "It's an absolute yes."

There was no time to say anything else before he was on his feet again and she was in his arms. He kissed her, filling her heart with so much love. And joy. And hope.

Finally, she had hope for her future.

And thanks to Luke, she had the courage to dream.

"I love you." He touched his forehead to hers while his arms locked tight around her, holding her close enough that she could feel his heart pound in time with hers. "Thank you for saying yes."

"I love you, too. Thank you for asking." She opened her eyes. "Wait. Where did the ring come from?"

"My pocket. Where do you think?" He laughed at himself. "I pulled it out when you were looking away. Come on, you have to give me points for originality."

"Oh, you definitely won some points."

"Speaking of which…" He took her left hand in his and slipped the cool band over her finger. It was a perfect fit.

Just like the two of them.

"There goes the rest of my day." Claire held out her hand, moving her finger, admiring the diamond's sparkle. "I don't think I'll be able to take my eyes off this ring."

"Wow. I killed two birds with one stone, then. No pun intended."

"What do you mean?"

He offered a wink, nodding to the poles lying on the ground. "If you're distracted, I might actually be able to catch more fish than you."

"Something tells me it'll take more than a sparkling diamond for you to manage that, Luke Patterson."

Still, she was willing to give him this one since he'd given her so much more. A lifetime's worth of more.

And they had only just begun.

* * * * *

DANGER ON MAUI

R. BARRI FLOWERS

In memory of my beloved mother, Marjah Aljean, a devoted lifelong fan of Mills & Boon romances, who inspired me to do my very best in finding happiness and success in my personal and professional endeavours. To H. Loraine, the love of my life, whose support has been unwavering through the many wonderful years together; and the loyal fans of my romance, mystery, suspense and thriller fiction published over the years.

Lastly, thanks to my fantastic editors, Allison Lyons and Denise Zaza, for the opportunity to lend my literary voice and creative spirit to Mills & Boon Heroes.

Prologue

He's hot, Jena Sutcliffe had to admit, as she admired from afar the tall, fit and handsome dark-haired man at Linc's Tavern on Wharf Street in Lahaina, a happening town in West Maui in the County of Maui, Hawaii. She doubted he even noticed her, even if most considered her to be attractive and a good catch, with long and luscious raven hair and pretty blue eyes. But Maui was full of good-looking and sexy young women, many of whom seemed to be at the club that night and were all over him like an expensive suit. Or was that just her imagination? Jena turned her focus to another dark-haired hottie, who was sitting at the bar all by his lonesome and, like her, appeared to be taking it all in, as if to size up both the competition and the hot women. Again, he never seemed to lay his eyes on her, as she apparently wasn't what he was looking for.

His loss, Jena told herself dismissively as she sipped her Lava Flow drink and pushed back at the thought of wanting to get the attention of Mr. Hot Stuff. After all, what was it they said about the definition of insanity? Hadn't she already been burned in the past by tall, dark-haired, handsome and virile men who looked like him? Why put herself through that agony again?

Jena turned away from the man, content to finish off her drink and head home alone. She did need to get up early for work at a hotel, where she was an event planner. *Who knows, maybe I'll meet my sexy knight in shining armor at the next big event*, she told herself while not holding her breath. She made her way through the crowded bar, imagining one of the knights in shining armor would follow, sweep her off her feet, and it would be the start of something great.

By the time she left the place and climbed into her orange Subaru WRX, reality had set in and she drove home. Jena was unaware that someone had gotten into another vehicle and began to follow her.

IF HE HAD a dollar for every woman who never looked his way, underestimating him or just what he was capable of, he would be a very rich man right now. And then his true worth might be better appreciated. Until such time, he would allow his actions to speak for him and his victims would be forced to carry the brunt of it. Right to their early graves. And he would continue to have his revenge and take joy in the thrill of the kill. As well as the solace of knowing there was little that could be done to stop him. Not till he'd had enough of dishing out the type of pain that he had been given.

He followed the Subaru to a condominium complex on Lower Honoapiilani Road, allowing her to park first while pretending to be just another tenant coming home. Perhaps from a night out on the town, like her. Only his presence was much more sinister than that. Quickly parking, he left his vehicle and surreptitiously made his way inside the building. He happened to catch her scaling the stairwell and followed, noting she went to the third floor.

By the time he got there, he saw the door to her unit close. After making sure there were no prying eyes around, he walked up to the condo. Using his instincts that told him she was all by her lonesome, he rang the bell, calculating that she would at the very least be curious as to who he was. Hadn't that proven to be true time and time again? Gullibility was always their downfall. Why should it be any different on this occasion?

She did not fail, opening the door like clockwork and smiling at him as though greeting an old friend. "Can I help you?" she asked politely.

He grinned innocently and replied in a deceptive tone of voice, "Yes, I believe you can."

Using a stun gun, he placed it to her skin and she reacted accordingly with the electrical shocks doing a number to her body and brain, giving him complete control of his latest victim as he entered the condominium to finish what he'd so cleverly and joyously started.

Chapter One

At 10:00 a.m., Daphne Dockery sat on an uncomfortable wooden chair in the Aloha Land Bookstore on Front Street in Lahaina, pasting a perfect smile on her heart-shaped face as she signed copies of her latest bestselling book, *The Accident Killer.* As an award-winning true crime writer, Maui, Hawaii, was the last stop on a late summer book tour to push the unsettling real-life story of serial killer Oscar Preston, who made the deaths of his fifteen victims appear to be accidents till the frightening truth emerged and he was made to pay for his heinous crimes. Daphne planned to take full advantage of the idyllic setting in paradise for some much-needed rest and relaxation away from her hometown of Tuscaloosa, Alabama, after a difficult year that included a bad breakup with her ex-boyfriend, Nelson Holloway, and a scary encounter with an obsessed fan, Marissa Sheffield. Thankfully, Marissa was now in jail and Nelson probably should have been, given his unfaithfulness and questionable practices as a hedge-fund manager.

But Daphne hoped to put them behind her and focus on where she went from here as a newly single—but not necessarily looking for love and companionship—woman, thirty-two years of age, who had landed on

Maui on a new mission. Apart from some fun in the sun and on the sand, along with taking a dip in the warm waters of the Pacific Ocean, she'd come to research her next book, tentatively titled *A Maui Mass Murder*. It was about a workplace love triangle on the island that resulted in a murder-suicide, taking the lives of five people last year, including a pregnant woman. The subject matter hit home for Daphne painfully. As an only child, her own father had snapped when her mother threatened to leave him and his abusive ways, resulting in him shooting her mother to death before turning the gun on himself.

Her own tragedy, when Daphne was only seven years old, set her on a course in which, as an adult, she wanted to delve into the backstory of violent criminals, criminality and victims to help others better understand the dynamics involved and learn to cope with it. After earning her Master of Arts degree in journalism and media studies from the University of Alabama and landing a job with a local news station as an investigative journalist, she needed greater autonomy to investigate hard-hitting stories and share them with the public on a larger scale. Hence, she turned to writing true crime books and found success there with seven bestsellers to date and had contracted for three more books with her publisher. This included the next crime topic Daphne had chosen to write about and had been approved by her supportive editor, Gordon Yung, at Lefevre and Weigel Publishing.

But first, there's still the matter of wrapping up one more book signing for my current title, she thought, as Daphne glanced down at the fresh flower lei that hung over a scarlet-and-black-printed faux-wrap dress on her five-seven slender frame, worn with comfort-able-to-walk-in moccasin flats. She again put on her best face and twinkled big blue-green eyes at the tall thirtysomething man with a medium build and dark hair in a mushroom cut. He was wearing a red shirt adorned with sunsets and palm trees and loose-fitting black jeans. Slightly crooked but intense brown eyes with flecks of gold were locked on hers as he held the hardcover book in big hands to his chest.

"Aloha." She spoke in a friendly voice, wanting to break the intensity of their staring game, as if to see who would blink first.

"Aloha." He kept his own voice level. "Welcome to Maui."

"Happy to be here." She wondered if he could say the same, judging by his anxious demeanor. *Better get this over with,* she thought, *and move on to someone less intimidating.* "Would you like me to sign your book?" Daphne assumed that to be the case, as he had waited in line rather than simply taking the book to the ca-shier to purchase.

"Yeah," he responded tersely, and handed it to her. "Make it out to Tommy."

"Okay." She used the pen the store provided and scribbled his name on the blank first page, followed by her usual words: *Thanks for taking the time to show up. Hope you find the read to your liking and pass it on to others interested in true crime. Daphne Dockery.*

She handed the book back to him and, in keeping up with Hawaiian lingo said lyrically, "Mahalo."

"Back at you," he said stiffly, and walked away.

Wouldn't want to get on his bad side, Daphne half joked to herself as the next person in line, a frail elderly woman with ash-colored hair worn in stacked layers approached. "Aloha."

"Aloha." Her face creased with a smile. "I'm a big fan of your books. In fact, I've read every single one of them."

Daphne blushed. "That's so nice to hear," she told her genuinely, never taking such comments for granted with so many books for readers to choose from out there.

"It's obvious that you put your heart and soul into each book."

"I try to," Daphne agreed, knowing this was what separated true crime narrative nonfiction books from criminology books, in essence. Being herself and freely prefacing each book with her own experience as a victim was what made her books popular and kept Daphne going as well in a cathartic sort of way. She took the book from her.

"You can make that out to Olivia Righetti."

"Will do." Daphne happily signed her book, feeling more confident that she wanted it for all the right reasons, as opposed to the last person perhaps.

"Hope you enjoy your stay on the island," Olivia said. "There's a lot more to do than being cooped up in a bookstore signing books, you know."

Daphne chuckled. "I promise to take some time to explore the sights, sounds and spirit of Maui."

The woman crinkled her eyes and took Daphne at her word, and Olivia gave a little wave as she walked off. Daphne took a sip of her bottled water on the table, which included stacks of books spread out strategically, as her throat felt dry from talking. Never mind that her hand was sore from signing books. But she would never complain about something that was part of the process for success as a top-selling author and remaining high on the bestseller lists for nonfiction.

"Nice to know you're up for taking in what the island has to offer," said a resonant voice that drew Daphne's attention. She looked up into the very deep brown-gray eyes of a chiseled face that belonged to a most handsome Hawaiian man. His curly black hair was in a textured fringe cut that went agreeably with the rest of him, which included at least a six-foot, three-inch sturdy frame and long legs. He was dressed in casual attire apropos of Hawaiian living, consisting of a tropical print shirt, dark straight-fit chino pants and brown Venetian loafers.

When she could get her mouth to move, Daphne chuckled and responded wryly, "I wouldn't have it any other way."

He grinned easily. "Good to hear."

As she tended to do when nervousness got the better of her, Daphne flipped her long and layered raven hair that was styled in a U-shaped cut. She managed to look past his good-looking face to the copy of her book he was holding. "Who do I make that out to?" she asked, if only to get back to the business at hand and not the man himself.

He slid the book across the table up to her. "Ken should be fine and whatever else you'd like to say that I can brag to my buddies about."

Daphne laughed, trying to imagine him bragging about having a signed copy of *The Accident Killer* to anyone. Somehow, he didn't seem the type to take such a thing too seriously. "You have yourself a deal," she quipped. "Ken and a bit more to say mahalo for coming in today."

"Wouldn't have missed the chance to pick up a signed copy of your latest true crime book as a serious fan of narrative nonfiction of this kind," he insisted.

"I see." *Guess my reach truly is far and wide, with a readership that apparently knows no bounds*, she told herself as she signed the book and handed it back to him, realizing there were others waiting in line before she could call it quits and move on to the rest of her important agenda while on Maui. "Hope it lives up to your expectations."

Ken grinned from one side of his wide mouth that appealed to her all on its own as perfectly kissable were the circumstances different and amenable. "I'm sure it will. Have a safe trip back to the mainland whenever you return."

"Thanks." Daphne smiled back and watched briefly as he headed to the cashier while wondering about his life story as, she assumed, an island resident. Was he single and available? Judging by his laidback clothing, trying to figure out what he did for a living was almost impossible, as in this tropical environment it could be anything from a business owner to a lecturer. Or maybe he was a resort worker or involved with technology. She supposed some things were best left to the imagination as Daphne welcomed the next book buyer before her, happy to see the line was starting to thin. Which meant she would soon be able to get the most out of her stay on the island, including her investigation into the mass shooting at the workplace.

HOMICIDE DETECTIVE KENNETH KEALOHA, a member of the Maui Police Department's Criminal Investigation Division branch of the Investigative Services Bureau, couldn't seem to get his mind off Daphne Dockery, the stunning true crime writer he met earlier in the day at her book signing. In fact, if the truth be told, she looked even better in person than the photograph on the back of her book, *The Accident Killer*, which he fully intended to read with interest. But he couldn't actually relay that to her in front of other book buyers, lest she get the impression he was trying to hit on her. Another place, another time, that might not have been too far from Kenneth's mind, as she was definitely his type with the luscious and long dark hair, enticing aquamarine eyes and streamlined physique. But in this instance, he thought it was probably best that he kept this view of the gorgeous author to himself.

As for her true crime book, given the subject matter involving a serial killer named Oscar Preston, who murdered fifteen people ten years ago in Mobile, Alabama, and was suspected of killing ten others, Kenneth was admittedly curious about her take on the ruthless killer who was given the moniker the "Accident Killer" and his ultimate capture and conviction. It was that same year that another serial killer, Trevor Henshall, operating out of Honolulu, Hawaii, and dubbed the "Paradise Foot Killer" strangled to death ten women in some twisted foot fetish and fixation on their beach walks. One of those women, Cynthia Suehisa, was a close friend of Kenneth's. Like him, Cynthia was a native Hawaiian who'd had her whole life ahead of her before it was snuffed out like a candle's bright flame. At the time, he was a detective for the Honolulu Police Department's Criminal Investigation Division, investigating crimes of violence. In spite of killing Henshall when he refused to surrender, Kenneth had been unable to prevent his friend from becoming a murder victim, dying in his arms.

Two years later, Kenneth transferred to the Maui PD, as much for a fresh start as to put the darkness of Cynthia's untimely death behind him to the extent possible. He had learned the hard way that crime would follow him wherever he went as a police detective tasked with going after bad people. At thirty-three, with no love life to distract him, his sole focus these days was pretty much solving serious crimes to the best of his ability. With homicides topping the list.

That included his current investigation. A serial killer was terrorizing attractive women with long dark hair on the island of Maui. Nicknamed by the local press the "Maui Suffocation Killer," the unsub suffocated his victims to death by putting a plastic bag over their heads and faces. Thus far, nine unlucky women had been murdered due to asphyxia over the past eight months. The last one, Jena Sutcliffe, met her fate a week ago. Another woman, Ruth Paquin, was nearly killed around the time of the third fatality but managed to survive the attack. Unfortunately, due to the brain injury she suffered, all she could tell them was that the killer was a dark-haired male, maybe of medium build, with only a vague description beyond that. Using what they had in trying to piece it together, a task force had zeroed in on a suspect.

Zack Lawrence was a thirty-eight-year-old fitness instructor and self-described ladies' man. He also happened to have been present at all the bars the victims had been seen at the night they were killed. Though there was no solid evidence to make an arrest, there was reason to believe Lawrence could be the man they were after. Starting with a prior conviction for attempting to smother to death an ex-girlfriend. Then there was the fact that he had been trying to date at least one of the victims, but was apparently rebuffed by her.

At the moment, they hoped to catch him in the act. Or at least an attempted act of abduction and murder. Which was why they were currently conducting an evening stakeout of the suspect at Popi's Tavern on Lower Main Street in the town of Wailuku, the county seat and commercial hub of Maui County. Kenneth was undercover at a table across from Detective Tad Newsome. At thirty, between his perpetual tan, lean frame, blue eyes, and short blondish-brown hair in an undercut style, he could easily have passed for a surfer instead of a cop, Kenneth believed. They pretended to be sipping Mai Tais, which was actually only orange juice.

At another table were FBI agents Kirk Guilfoyle and Noelle Kaniho, giving the guise of being a loving couple. In reality, at forty-five with a shaven bald head and landing strip goatee, Guilfoyle, African American with coal black eyes, was ten years older and happily married to his high school sweetheart; while Noelle had a longtime boyfriend and looked younger than her age with short and cropped blond hair and brown eyes behind fake vintage glasses. Kenneth nodded to them, making sure everyone was on the same page, before directing his attention to the bar, where working undercover as the decoy was Detective Vanessa Ringwald. The twenty-five-year-old green-eyed, single mother fit the prototype of the Maui Suffocation Killer's victims. She was slender and attractive with long and layered dark curly hair and baby bangs, that would normally have been worn in a high ponytail while on duty. She had on a sexy multicolored flare dress and strap sandals in doing her part to get the suspect to make his move.

Kenneth peered at Zack Lawrence, who was sitting beside Vanessa. The suspect was about his own height of just under six-three and every bit as in shape, with blue eyes, an oval face, and dark brown hair worn in a skin fade comb-over style. *I suppose I could see why women might be attracted to the man*, Kenneth mused, taking a sip of the orange juice. The only question was whether, like the Pied Piper, he led them down a road from which there was no coming back.

When Vanessa gave the signal that Lawrence appeared to swallow the bait and that they were leaving together, Kenneth acknowledged this. Stressed, he made sure that the other undercover law enforcement personnel knew what was about to go down. That included texting the detectives who were hanging around outside in case they were needed as backup.

"Get ready to head out," Kenneth informed Newsome.

"Ready when you are," he responded eagerly.

As Vanessa and Lawrence walked past them, with the suspect having a territorial hand on the small of her back, Kenneth waited till the last possible moment to follow and set things in motion. Outside, they allowed the suspect to lead Vanessa across the fairly well-lit parking lot to his car, a silver Porsche 718 Boxster Convertible, where they hoped to find the tools of his trade for smothering his victims before swinging into action, and Lawrence appeared to try to kiss the detective on the passenger side. She turned her face at the last moment, with the kiss hitting Vanessa's chin.

Law enforcement converged on the two before Lawrence could get Vanessa into the car. Kenneth had his department issued Glock 17 semi-automatic pistol out and aimed at the suspect's shocked face. Just as he was about to come to Vanessa's rescue, she had turned Lawrence around, twisted his arm and handcuffed him roughly while announcing in a confident and harsh tone, "Detective Ringwald, Maui PD. You're under arrest."

Lawrence, who looked flustered, was defiant. "For what? Wanting to get together with what I believed to be a like-minded pretty woman who came on to me only to try to entrap me?"

"You did that all on your own," she insisted with a snap. "Did you really think you could charm me with your empty words?"

"Not a chance," Kenneth quipped, approaching her. "She's not nearly that easy."

"You've got that right." Vanessa made a comical face at him. "What took you so long, Kealoha? For a moment there, I thought I was going to have to take a ride with this creep."

Kenneth chuckled, knowing it would never have come to that. He placed his firearm back in its leather holster. "Since you seemed to have things well under control, we took our own sweet time." He turned the suspect around to face him and stuck a search warrant in the pocket of his blazer. "This gives us the right to take a look inside your car."

Lawrence scowled. "Go ahead. Look all you want. As I've said all along, I've got nothing to hide."

"We'll see about that," Kenneth countered, hopeful they had found their perp before he could do any more damage. "Don't move," he warned him, though it was clear that Vanessa and the others had the upper hand in keeping the suspect from even thinking about fleeing.

Putting on a pair of nitrile gloves, Kenneth took a look inside the Porsche, searching for anything incriminating that might link Lawrence to the serial killings. Regrettably, he found nothing, but would leave it to the crime scene technicians to dig deeper. When emerging from the vehicle, Kenneth noted a frown on the face of Detective Tad Newsome, who said, "We may have a problem."

"What is it?" he asked anxiously.

"Just got the call. A young woman's body was discovered by her neighbor in Kahului. It looks like she was a victim of foul play in a manner reminiscent of the Maui Suffocation Killer's victims. The neighbor reported seeing a man, fitting the general description of the serial killer, fleeing from the residence." Newsome ran a hand across his jaw, glancing at the suspect. "Lawrence may not be our guy, after all."

"What a shock." Lawrence rolled his eyes sarcastically, then narrowed them at Kenneth. "Sorry to disappoint."

Though frustrated, Kenneth had to admit he was thinking the same thing regarding the guilt of the suspect. Or lack thereof. Given that they had been surveilling the fitness instructor ever since he left the gym on Kolu Street in Wailuku, Zack Lawrence just might have bought his ticket to freedom. Unless he had crossed the line with Vanessa and she chose to press charges on something akin to assault on a law enforcement officer. Still, he hated giving the smug suspect the pleasure of knowing they had screwed up. But the reality was that Lawrence could well be innocent as a serial murderer. "We'll hold on to Mr. Lawrence for the time being," Kenneth ordered while Vanessa pondered the notion, to be on the safe side. Even then, Kenneth had a sinking feeling that the real unsub had struck again while their attention was occupied elsewhere.

Twenty-five minutes later, this had been more or less confirmed as Kenneth stood in the crime scene—a spacious bedroom in a single-story mission-style house on Mokapu Street in Kahului, a town in central Maui that was home to the Kahului Harbor and main airport in Maui County. The Hawaiian victim was identified as Irene Ishibashi, a thirty-one-year-old fashion designer. Between traditional furnishings, she was lying atop a cotton quilt on a platform bed, fully clothed in a blue square-neck dress and mules. Long black hair in a mermaid style surrounded a narrow face, marred by the clear plastic bag covering it, her features distorted grotesquely as she undoubtedly fought desperately for air that fell far short of what was needed for survival. One of the two plush pillows was beside the body with facial impressions that suggested it may have been used by her attacker in the aftermath of the suffocation to further ensure its success. As there was no sign of forced entry, Kenneth believed that the victim had likely opened the door voluntarily to her attacker, either recognizing the person or doing what way too many people did naturally when someone rang the bell. Opened the door first and asked questions later. Only in this instance, there would be no later for Irene Ishibashi.

"What's your take on this?" Kenneth almost dreaded to ask as the Maui County medical examiner and coroner did a preliminary examination of the victim.

Dr. Rudy Samudio was brown-eyed, thin, and in his

sixties, but barely had any gray in his short raven hair in a pompadour cut. Wearing latex gloves, he removed the plastic bag from the dead woman's head, then turned her face from side to side as if a rag doll before responding bleakly, "My initial assessment is that the decedent died from asphyxia, almost certainly as a result of that plastic bag cutting off the flow of oxygen to the brain."

Kenneth sighed. "I was afraid you'd say that, but not really surprised, considering."

Samudio pointed to what appeared to be small burns on the deceased's neck. "It looks like the killer used a stun gun on the victim."

"Suspected as much," Kenneth said, recognizing the signs.

Samudio wrinkled his thick nose. "I'd say the so-called Maui Suffocation Killer has struck again with a nasty vengeance," he said flatly.

That too pretty much went without saying as Kenneth wrestled with the stark reality that the unsub had been anything but brought to his knees. Quite the contrary, he had once more managed to kill and evade capture. For now. Allowing the Crime Scene Response Team to take over in searching for evidence, Kenneth left the home that, by all appearances, seemed orderly in spite of the homicide that had taken place there. This suggested to him that the methodical serial killer was, as before, quick and decisive in his actions, taking care not to create disorder where not needed to carry out his crime.

"We need to cut Zack Lawrence loose," Kenneth informed Vanessa outside near some fishtail palm trees and landscape lighting, where she had been interviewing the neighbor who reported the crime, an elderly widow named Mary Cabanilla, before an officer escorted her away. "He's not our serial killer."

"I gathered that." Vanessa had put her hair back into her customary ponytail. "Especially after taking Mrs. Cabanilla's statement. According to her, when she saw a man dart out of the victim's front door and hightail it down the street, Mrs. Cabanilla sensed something was up and went to check on her neighbor, only to find Irene Ishibashi dead. The witness provided a description of the man she saw running away. Not precise, but slightly different from the surviving victim's portrayal of her attacker, which we can blame on her brain injury."

"That gives us something to work with," Kenneth said matter-of-factly, planning to have a sketch artist drop by to see Mary Cabanilla.

Vanessa drew a breath. "As for Zack Lawrence, he's definitely arrogant and annoying, but apparently not a killer. He's just a heartbreaker for gullible women. But not me," she emphasized.

"Didn't think so." Kenneth managed a grin. He'd heard that she was starting to see someone outside the force, but did not pry. Any more than she had about his pretty much nonexistent love life these days, though not from lack of wanting to find that special someone who got him and vice versa. But he wouldn't force the issue. If it happened, it happened. If not, then he guessed it just wasn't in the cards for him. "Other women might do well to run as far away from the man as possible."

"I'm with you there," she agreed, and argued emphatically, "I'd say the same for any women unfortunate enough to come into the crosshairs of the Maui Suffocation Killer. Assuming they lived to talk about it."

Kenneth's lips became a thin line. "Yeah, there is

that," he conceded, knowing that only one, thus far, had escaped death at the serial killer's hands. "With any luck, we'll catch the unsub before he can add to his list of victims."

"Right." Her face expressed doubt. "Until then, we'll stay on it."

"Yeah." Kenneth gave a determined nod and watched as Vanessa went to confer with Detective Tad Newsome and FBI agents Guilfoyle and Kaniho. Kenneth took out his cell phone, knowing it was up to him to try and explain to the Assistant Chief of Investigative Services Bureau, Martin Morrissey, how the stakeout of Zack Lawrence had gone awry while the real killer was targeting another victim.

Chapter Two

Daphne was up early in the Kiki Shores luxury ocean-front villa on Kai Malina Parkway in Kaanapali. The beautiful and popular resort was on the west shore of Maui. As much as she would have liked to have slept in for another hour or so in the comfortable king-sized bed in the large primary bedroom, with a second bed-room serving as her temporary office, that would have to wait for another day. There were things to do and people to see, one in particular. Having done her re-search, Daphne had found out that the lead investigator in the murder-suicide case she was working on was a homicide detective named Kenneth Kealoha. From ex-perience, she had learned that interviewing detectives working the investigations provided just the right con-text needed to ensure the true crime book balanced in its factual basis and verisimilitude while keeping the readers engaged throughout. *Hopefully, Detective Ke-aloha will be cooperative and not just blow me off,* she thought while tying her hair up.

After putting on a blue T-shirt and gray shorts, Daphne stepped into a new pair of white running shoes, ready to break them in. She spotted a small gecko on the cream-colored wall as she passed beneath the swirling fern-leaf ceiling fan and across the villa's ceramic tile flooring. Moving past the vintage furnishings with a modern feel, she headed out for a quick morning run on Kaanapali Beach. It included three miles of pristine golden white sand and an endless view of the clear waters of the deep blue ocean. Then there was Black Rock, the hot spot on the nearshore for cliff diving. She wondered if she could muster up the courage to give it a try during her stay. Beyond that, she could see the Hawaiian islands of Lanai and Molokai. There were a few other runners out, but well spaced from one another. One tall and tanned male runner acknowledged her before picking up speed, as if to show off his powerful legs. She chuckled within. *At least I can be myself here and not be bothered by anyone*, Daphne mused, knowing full well that being somewhat of a celebrity— at least in Tuscaloosa—was not all it was cracked up to be. Attracting the wrong attention could become a nightmare as thoughts of her stalker, Marissa Sheffield, filled Daphne's head.

She shut this down, determined not to give in to an ordeal that was now over. Once back in the villa, she took a shower, dressed and grabbed a bite to eat at the Kiki Shores restaurant. Then Daphne got in her rented Chevy Malibu, equipped with a GPS navigation system, and used the voice directions to make her way to the Maui Police Department on Mahalani Street in Wailuku.

At the front desk, Daphne was told by the thirty-something burly male desk officer where to find Detective Kenneth Kealoha. When she reached his cubicle, there was a tall and dark-haired man standing by a wooden desk with his back to her. Clearing her throat to get his attention, Daphne uttered, "I'm looking for Detective Kealoha..."

The man turned around and locked solid brown-gray eyes with her, looking just as shocked as she was. "You found him," he said equably.

"Ken." The word blurted out of Daphne's mouth even before she began to put the pieces together in sizing up the man she'd met yesterday at her book signing.

"Daphne Dockery, the true crime writer," he said in return, an amused grin playing on his full mouth. "Ken is short for Detective Kenneth Kealoha, which I'm sure you've probably already figured out."

She blushed. "I gathered that much."

"Feel free to stick with Ken, if you like." Kenneth stared at her and stuck out his hand. "Have to say, I didn't think we'd see each other again. At least not so soon." He laughed wryly as they shook hands.

"Neither did I," she had to admit, having no idea of who he was the first time around, while feeling the sensations of their skin contact.

"You're not stalking me, are you?" he asked playfully.

"Not funny." Daphne made a face. She considered stalking serious business, having been a victim of it.

Kenneth seemed to pick up on her uneasiness with the subject matter. "Poor choice of words," he said contritely. "Sorry about that." He paused. "So, what can I do for you?"

Daphne smoothed a thin eyebrow. "I need your help," she said tentatively, commanding his contemplation. "Or to get some information from you."

"Go on," he prodded gently.

She took a breath. "I'm writing a book about the

murder-suicide involving the Takahashi family that took place on the island last summer. Since you were the lead detective on the case, I was hoping to talk to you about it to help fill in some of the blanks."

"I see." Kenneth shifted his weight to one leg. "As much as I'd love to help you, Ms. Dockery, right now I'm in the middle of a major investigation."

"Please call me Daphne," she told him, sensing that it had suddenly seemed to become more formal between them. But she didn't come there simply to be turned away. Not without giving it her all. "I understand that you're busy, Ken," she allowed in a friendly voice, "but I just need a little bit of your time. I can pay you…"

He frowned. "I don't want your money."

Did I just insult him unintentionally, or what? Daphne asked herself. "Perhaps this was a bad idea," she said. "I'll just have to work my way around this part. Maybe you could direct me to one of the other detectives who was involved in the investigation?"

Kenneth met her eyes and she could tell he was having second thoughts. "I'm probably your best bet to get what you need," he spoke evenly. "And while we're at it, I have a few questions of my own for you."

"Oh…?" She cocked a brow curiously, wondering if his questions were professional. Or more of a personal nature?

He didn't follow up on that, instead asking, "Can we get together this afternoon, maybe for lunch?"

"That works for me," Daphne agreed, perhaps too eagerly. "Lunch is a good time to talk." Especially if they could do so at a relatively quiet place.

Kenneth concurred. "Where are you staying?" She told him, knowing it was asked for the right reasons, coming from the handsome detective, who then said, "I can meet you at the Seas Grill in Whalers Village at one."

"I'll see you there," she said, knowing of the swanky outdoor shopping center on Kaanapali Beach, having already acquainted herself with it during a walkthrough.

He grinned crookedly. "Look forward to it."

"Me, too." Daphne smiled back, wishing she wasn't so attracted to him, if only to keep her focus on the mission at hand. But then again, she saw no harm in admiring the detective, who seemed to be just as taken with her, even while remaining somewhat aloof.

Kenneth walked her out halfway, introducing her to some of his colleagues along the way. Daphne could tell that they had each other's backs in the tough world of law enforcement, which was important in being able to solve cases and stay on the same page along the way. While she didn't necessarily have that type of almost-familial bond as a writer, Daphne did have a close relationship with her editor, Gordon, and some others at her publisher. She hoped to someday be able to find it again on an intimate level, but was not about to get ahead of herself in the process.

BEFORE THEY WENT their separate ways, Kenneth gave Daphne the once-over and admitted that she was just as stunning as when he first laid eyes on her the day before. Maybe even better when she wasn't half hidden behind a table, so he could take in her tall and slender physique in a white eyelet top with puffed sleeves, slim-leg stone-colored pants and dark double-zip booties to go with the good looks and stylishly long dark hair. What was he thinking in nearly passing up the opportunity to get to see her again? Yes, he was busy with the serial killer case they were all under pressure to solve. But not so much that he couldn't give some of his time to help the bestselling author with her latest book. Having had a front-row seat in the investigation of Norman Takahashi—who murdered his pregnant wife, mother-in-law, teenage daughter, and her boyfriend before killing himself—Kenneth could certainly provide some details that would undoubtedly strengthen the book's credibility.

Besides that, he realized that Daphne could be of benefit to him as well with her previous title. Writing about another serial killer might have given her some insight that he could tap into in his current investigation. Having an opportunity to get to know the striking writer a bit better was something Kenneth could hardly afford to pass up as a bonus. When he got back to his desk, he got on his laptop for a cursory background check on Daphne Dockery ahead of their sitdown. Googling her, he saw that she was thirty-two, from Tuscaloosa, Alabama, lost her parents at an early age as an only child, gotten a master's degree in journalism and media studies from the University of Alabama and worked as an investigative journalist for a local news station before authoring seven international bestsellers. In celebrity status news, he noted that Daphne had split from her wealthy and older boyfriend, Nelson Holloway, seven months ago. Apparently, no one had taken his place in her life since.

He must have been a jerk or flat-out crazy to have let her slip away, Kenneth thought, feeling that Daphne was someone he could imagine fighting tooth and nail to hang on to, had they been together. But then he couldn't get into the head of her ex or Daphne, for that matter, to know what drove them apart. Given his own shortcomings in the relationship department, he wasn't exactly in a position to make judgment calls on others. Right now, he would settle for spending a little time with Daphne before she headed back to Alabama.

Shortly before 1:00 p.m., Kenneth pulled his department-issued dark sedan into the Whalers Village parking lot on Kaanapali Parkway. He walked to the Seas Grill restaurant and saw Daphne standing near the door when he arrived. "Aloha."

"Aloha," she said back, adding before he could ask, "No, I haven't been waiting long."

"Good." He gave her a sheepish smile while opening the door and they went inside. After being seated by the window, Kenneth looked at the menu and said, "I'm starving. See anything that looks interesting to an Alabamian?"

"Everything, actually." Daphne chuckled and studied her menu before settling on an organic Caesar salad and fish taco.

"Good choices," he said, and went with the chopped garden salad, fries and a cheeseburger. Both ordered fresh lemonade. "So, what would you like to know about the Takahashi family mass murder?" Kenneth decided to get right to it, troubling as it was to have to relive the tragedy that rocked Maui last year.

Daphne pulled a voice recorder out of her hobo handbag. "Do you mind?"

"Please do," Kenneth said, wanting as much as her to ensure accuracy if he was to be quoted for the book.

She cut the recorder on and asked without prelude,

"What drove Norman Takahashi to commit this horrific act of violence?"

Kenneth took a breath thoughtfully. "Simply put, jealous homicidal rage. Takahashi, forty-six, an associate professor in the University of Hawaii Maui College's Mathematics Department, learned that his thirty-eight-year-old wife, Jenny, was carrying another man's child and wanted out of the marriage. This apparently caused Takahashi to go off the deep end at the couple's home. He used a 20-gauge pump-action shotgun to mow down his wife, the couple's eighteen-year-old daughter, Sarah, her twenty-year-old boyfriend, Lucas Piimauna, and Jenny's sixty-two-year-old mother, Donna Duldulao. Then Takahashi used a .22 Magnum revolver to shoot himself fatally in the head."

Daphne cringed. "What a shame," she muttered sadly.

"Tell me about it," he concurred.

"Did the weapons belong to Takahashi?"

Kenneth lifted his chin and nodded. "Yes, he had a permit for both firearms and they were registered with the Maui PD."

"Oh, that makes it all the more tragic," she said with a catch to her voice.

"Yeah. We can always debate about more gun control legislation, but at the end of the day if someone is hell-bent on doing something like this, the firearms are accessible, legal or not."

"So true." She paused. "Did alcohol or drugs play a role in Takahashi's actions?"

"Most likely. According to the toxicology report, there were excessive amounts of alcohol and fentanyl in his system at the time of the murder-suicide."

"Figures." Daphne gave him a knowing look. "Still, losing it like that through gun violence, whatever the triggers, and ending the lives and futures of the victims, including himself, boggles the mind."

Kenneth had to agree. "It never gets any easier having to investigate these types of crimes. Not to say that murder-suicide is all that common on the island. But it does occur, even in paradise." He stopped and looked at her. "Of course, you already know this, since that's what brought you to Maui. Along with your book signing."

She acknowledged as much with her expression. "I only wish it had been under better circumstances, apart from the signing. But this is what comes with the territory in writing true crime books. It's something I believe I was meant to do."

Kenneth knew he didn't have the full story of her background, having skimmed over her prefaces. After the food arrived, and she stopped recording, he inquired further, "What got you into writing nonfiction books on crime?"

Daphne's voice shook as she answered, "My dad killed my mom, before putting the gun up to his own head and committing suicide. I was seven at the time and had to be taken in by an aunt. Lovable as Aunt Mae was, life wasn't quite the same from that point on"

"I'm sorry to hear that." This had to have affected her in ways Kenneth could not imagine. Losing both parents at such a young age was something he wouldn't wish on his worst enemy, given the normal stresses young people dealt with growing up.

"I suppose I knew then that I wanted to do something with my life to address violent crime in all its ugliness and help people to better deal with it to one degree or another."

"Seems like you've succeeded," he pointed out, lifting his cheeseburger. "I've seen some of the reviews of your books and it appears as if readers are all in for whatever story you choose to dig into."

"Thanks." She blushed while forking lettuce from the Caesar salad. "We all have our calling. It's up to us to try to do the best we can with that."

"True enough."

Daphne tasted the lemonade and asked, "So, what drew you into becoming a detective?"

Kenneth wiped his mouth. "I've been asked that a time or two." He sat back musingly, sipping his own lemonade. "Guess I've had an interest in law enforcement for as long as I can remember," he said. "After getting a bachelor's degree in criminology and criminal justice at Chaminade University of Honolulu, I ended up working for the Honolulu PD. I've been with the Maui PD for the last eight years."

"Living on Maui obviously agrees with you." She laughed. "Of course, who wouldn't like being in this oasis day in and day out?"

"Maybe you should give it a try yourself," he tossed out jokingly, assuming she was happy living in Alabama. "Yes, it can be a paradise, excluding the times when it's not."

"Well, there is that," she conceded with a chuckle. "Still, I could probably get used to the constant sunshine and nice weather, gorgeous beaches, swaying palm trees and the like."

And I could get used to having you around to get to know on a deeper level, Kenneth told himself honestly, but didn't go there, believing it to be unlikely that she would stay once her research was completed. No reason to set himself up for disappointment. On the other hand, there was nothing preventing them from friendship or whatever on a short-term basis. "Do you have more questions for me?" he asked coolly.

"I do," Daphne confessed, and turned her recorder back on. "What can you tell me about the man Jenny Takahashi was involved with?"

Kenneth sat back. "His name is Francis Hiraga. They were physician colleagues at the Maui Medical Center. Hiraga, an ER doctor, had apparently hoped to marry Takahashi and raise their child together. At the time of her murder, Hiraga was at a medical conference on Kauai, and was cleared of any involvement in the crime."

"And yet he was involved, in spite of the separation," she pointed out remorsefully, "having to live with the what-ifs for the rest of his life."

"Yeah, that's true," Kenneth said, sensing Daphne was reliving the death of her parents. He, too, found himself relating to this sense of loss in his own life with the death of someone he was close to.

When it was his turn again to ask the questions, Kenneth paid for the lunch and they went outside and sat on a bench beside a cluster of bamboo palm trees. It was there that he recounted the murder of his friend, Cynthia Suehisa, by a serial killer in Honolulu, the same year that Oscar Preston, the subject of Daphne's book *The Accident Killer*, was committing serial murders in Mobile, Alabama.

"I'm so sorry to hear about your friend," Daphne expressed.

"Though it was a long time ago," Kenneth admitted

mournfully, "it still hurts." He sighed. "In any event, your book about Preston interested me, as much for its parallels to the Honolulu serial killer case as a current set of murders on Maui I'm investigating, thought to be the work of a serial killer."

"Really?" Her eyes grew wide. "I've been so consumed with my book signing and research that I didn't even pick up on this. Tell me more…"

Knowing he wasn't compromising the investigation with basic information, Kenneth said, "He's been dubbed by the press as the Maui Suffocation Killer, as the unsub kills his victims, who are all attractive dark-haired women who were at a nightclub prior to their death, by suffocating them. So far, there have been ten victims that we know of." Even in so saying, Kenneth couldn't help but think that Daphne herself fit the profile of the dead women. Did she contemplate this as well?

Blinking, while otherwise remaining poised, she said evenly, "Sounds like something that would make a great true crime book, once the killer has been brought to justice."

"I suppose so," he acknowledged, considering this was her forte. "Which brings me to your last book."

"What would you like to know?"

In that moment, they brushed shoulders and Kenneth felt an electric shock surge through him. He assumed she felt it, too. Pushing that aside, he confessed, "I haven't started reading it yet, but since you've written about a serial killer, what's your view on what makes them tick that might provide some insight into the mind of the Maui killer on the loose?"

Daphne paused while meeting his eyes. "Well, in

the case of Oscar Preston, he got a pathological thrill out of fooling the authorities and public into believing the murders he committed were accidents—be it by drowning, falling from a high-story building, tinkering with brakes and other means. It was only when the dots were connected and it told a different story, that it led to Preston's downfall. But, based on Preston and other serial killers I've written about, the common denominator appears to be a lust for killing, often fueled by hatred and rage, along with favorable circumstances that lowers the risk for identification and capture."

Kenneth nodded. "That seems to fall in line with my way of thinking," he told her. "While we haven't been able to nail down the specifics of the Maui Suffocation Killer's motivation, it's a good bet that the victims are being targeted based on physical characteristics and opportunity."

"I agree," she said. "And knowing I fit the bill, doesn't make me particularly comfortable at the moment."

"Nor should you be," he told her bluntly, believing that this knowledge could well save her life, should it come to that. "Being on your guard for anyone acting suspicious while on the island is probably a good idea, just to be on the safe side."

"Now that you mention it, there was a man at the book signing yesterday who kind of gave me the creeps."

"Oh…?" Kenneth gazed at her. "How so?"

"Nothing I can really put a finger on," Daphne said. "It's just the way he was checking me out, as if sizing me up for the kill." She laughed. "Likely nothing more than the overactive imagination of a true crime writer. He was probably harmless."

"Probably." Kenneth wondered what the odds were that the serial killer would come to a book signing for a book about a serial killer. Sounded crazy. But stranger things had happened. Hadn't they? "Do you remember what he looked like?"

"Not so much," she admitted. "There were a lot of books signed, yours included, making the faces and body shapes almost a blur after a while. He was just a regular guy. Though I would probably recognize him if I saw him again."

"Hopefully, you never will," Kenneth told her. "If only because he rubbed you the wrong way, which may be worth missing a book sale."

Daphne chuckled. "You're right about that."

He took out his cell phone and Kenneth realized the time had gotten away from him. In spite of enjoying this, he said reluctantly, "I have to get going."

"Me, too." She stood first. "Once you finish reading *The Accident Killer*, if you have any other questions, I'll be happy to answer them."

"Good to know." Kenneth liked the sound of that and was sure he would take her up on the offer. Except for the fact that he was a notoriously slow reader and doubted she would be around much longer. "Why don't I get your number and give you mine, in case either of us have any further questions."

"Deal." Daphne grabbed his phone and punched in her number and then put his number in her phone. "There," she said, flashing a nice smile.

He couldn't resist smiling back. "Good luck with the

research for your book. And enjoy the rest of your stay, no matter how long it may be."

"Mahalo." She chuckled cutely. "I have to get used to saying that."

"You will," he assured her.

"Hope so." Daphne laughed naturally. "When in Hawaii and all that."

He grinned, imagining her being in his native state for a long time. "Right."

"Well, I'll let you get back to work," she said. "I'm just over there in those villas, so I walked here."

Kenneth glanced in that direction, glad that she was close by and in one of the safest areas on the island in the Kaanapali resort. "Good," he told her. "Catch you later." He wondered if that opportunity would present itself. Maybe he should just ask her out and be done with it. She smiled at him and walked away while he admired the confidence in her stride.

Chapter Three

Honestly, Daphne felt as though she could have talked with the handsome police detective all day. Or at least she was comfortable enough with him that time seemed to almost stand still in his formidable presence. She had totally gotten Nelson out of her system and was amenable to becoming involved with someone new. Kenneth certainly seemed to hit the right marks as a person she could imagine having a romance with. Too bad he lived on Maui and she had made a comfortable life for herself in Tuscaloosa. Still, change could be good for you. Right?

Wrong, if it means not being entirely on the same wavelength, Daphne told herself as she sat in a swivel club chair on the lanai, enjoying the sights and sounds of Hawaii while sipping from a goblet of red wine. Been there, done that with nearly disastrous results. She was better off by herself if the alternative meant being in an unhealthy relationship. A long distance one didn't seem like a good idea, either. But what about a fling? Not really her thing. Still, she imagined that Kenneth was a great kisser and probably an even better lover.

Let's not get ahead of ourselves, she thought, in spite of feeling warm at the notion while noticing wide-eyed as a gecko make its way across the floor. For all she knew, Kenneth was seeing someone right now. If so, she wasn't about to try and come between him and another woman. Hadn't cheating been the motivating factor for a jealous Norman Takahashi losing it and killing his pregnant wife and three others? That type of potentially deadly tripartite Daphne felt she would just as soon avoid, thank you.

But what if Kenneth were as free and available as she was? While pondering that, against the backdrop of her main mission on the island, Daphne also considered that he was in the middle of a new serial killer investigation that admittedly had her spooked a bit. It wasn't lost on her that she resembled the nice-looking females with long dark hair that the killer was apparently targeting. She had to watch her step, even while still determined to complete the research for her next book. Being paranoid was not a good mix for a true crime writer who was thorough in gathering the information she needed for her writing projects. Daphne cringed nevertheless when thinking about the woman who'd stalked her, Marissa Sheffield, in what turned out to be a dangerous obsession. Daphne had initially made the mistake of being genuinely flattered by what she had believed was simply an adoring fan. So maybe it wasn't such a bad thing after all to be a little paranoid while keeping a proper perspective.

When her cell phone rang, Daphne's heart did a little leap, thinking it was Kenneth missing her already. Instead, she saw that the caller was her editor, Gordon Yung. Mindful of the time difference between Hawaii and New York, she realized that it was 8:30 p.m., Eastern Daylight Time. Or past the point in the day when he would still be in his office. She accepted the video-chat request and Gordon's face appeared on the small screen. Asian American and in his mid-forties, he had short black hair in a French crop cut and sable eyes behind aviator eyeglass frames.

"Hey," he said in a friendly tone.

"Aloha," she told him, smiling.

"Hope I'm not catching you at a bad time while living it up in paradise?"

"You're not. I'm just sitting on the lanai of my villa, enjoying a glass of wine before heading out again."

"Good for you." He grinned. "Heard from the publicist that the signing was a big success."

"It was," Daphne concurred. "Everything I could have hoped for."

"Then it was worth it setting you up with the Maui bookstore."

"Definitely." She flashed her teeth and recalled her initial meeting with Ken, who turned out to be Detective Kenneth Kealoha.

"How's the research coming along for your next book?"

"It's coming," she told him. "I spoke with the lead detective in the investigation and got his input on the murder-suicide. He's made himself available if I need more info."

Gordon pushed up his glasses. "That's terrific. Looks like you're well on your way."

"Yes, I believe so." Daphne tasted the wine. "Have to interview a few more people and get some other basic data, then I'll head home." Somehow saying it made her wish this weren't so. Especially when she could see herself spending more time on Maui. Maybe with Kenneth beyond being a helpful detective.

"If you need to stay in Hawaii a bit longer for some R&R, then do so," he suggested. "Tuscaloosa will still be there when you get back."

"I'll keep that in mind." She smiled thoughtfully. "Beyond the research, rest and relaxation, I think I may already have the subject matter for my next book."

"Really?" Gordon peered at her with curiosity. "Do tell?"

Daphne told him about the serial killer on the loose known as the Maui Suffocation Killer and how this was in direct contrast to the idyllic beauty of the island.

"Sounds interesting, in an unfortunate way," he said.

"I think so, too. But it's too soon to know if this is what I should be looking at," she stressed.

"With your track record, if another serial killer story captures your fancy, I say go for it."

"Mahalo, Gordon." She welcomed his support, which seemed to always be there as she navigated her way from newbie to bestselling author in demand by the media and social media for what she brought to the table.

"Anytime."

After disconnecting the chat, Daphne finished the wine and did a little work on her laptop. Half an hour later, she hopped into her car and took the short drive to a gated community in Kahana, where she was allowed entrance, and pulled up to a Bali Craftsman-style two-story home on a cul-de-sac on Hua Nui Way. It was the house where Norman Takahashi perpetrated a mass murder-suicide. She got out and, using her cell phone, took a couple of pictures of the exterior, including the mature trees bordering the property.

She went onto the lanai porch and rang the bell. When the door opened, an elderly frail Hawaiian man with white hair in a comb-over style greeted her. "Aloha." His brown eyes crinkled at the corners.

"Aloha," she said.

"You must be the writer, Daphne Dockery."

"Yes." She gave him a thin smile. "And you're Ralph Takahashi?" she assumed, Norman Takahashi's father, who moved into the property a few months after the crime occurred.

"Yes. Come in."

Stepping inside, Daphne took a sweeping glance of the living room with its warm contemporary furnishings before turning back to its current owner. "Thank you for seeing me."

"No problem," Ralph said. "Can I get you a mock-tail?"

She smiled. "That would be nice."

"Make yourself comfortable." He proffered a thin arm toward a leather chair.

As she sat down, Daphne pondered the events that would forever change the dynamics of the household. Ralph handed her the nonalcoholic drink with a mixture of fruit juices and said somberly, "This is where it happened…"

She saw the pain in his face and felt badly for forcing him to relive the memory, but believed it was important for readers to visualize the horrific incident. "I'm sorry for your loss," Daphne uttered sincerely, and couldn't help but think back to her parents' deaths.

"So am I." Ralph sat in an upholstered rocking chair.

"But it happened and there's nothing that can change that." He paused. "But maybe your writing about it can help other families avoid what I've had to go through."

"I hope so." More than he realized. She asked him a few general questions about the day of the murder-suicide and if there had been any indications that his son would resort to such drastic measures.

"I knew Norman was having a difficult time dealing with Jenny's betrayal, but I never thought he would take it that far. Ending her life was bad enough. But killing Sarah and Lucas in the prime of their lives and Donna, who was a good person, was unforgivable." Ralph sighed heavily. "I only wish Norman would have talked to me about what he was thinking of doing. Maybe I could've talked him out of it."

"People who commit these types of acts often tend to keep to themselves till the very last moment for fear of being talked out of it," Daphne hated to say, but believed. "Your son's sense of betrayal, right or wrong, clouded his judgment to everything else in his life at that moment. I doubt that you would have been able to stop him," she said, hoping to soften the blow of survivor's guilt.

"Perhaps you're right." He gazed out the window musingly. "Feel free to have a look around or take pictures, if you want, for the book."

"Mahalo." Daphne took him up on his offer and did so as quickly as possible before leaving. It wasn't till she was back on the road and returned to Kaanapali Beach for a casual stroll along the popular beach walkway that ran the length of the ocean side of the resort that Daphne had the distinct feeling she was being watched.

HE WATCHED HER like a hawk, but smartly kept his distance. It wouldn't do him any good if she spotted and recognized him, now would it? He slowed down as she slowed down. Picked up the pace when she did. She definitely intrigued him as much for her beauty and guts as her ability to write about people like him. Yes, she got him, even if she had no idea just how much. But soon she would find out what it felt like to be on the receiving end of a serial killer, instead of simply trashing them for a gluttonous audience, hungry for good reading material to detract from their own miserable lives.

Cozying up to the police detective in charge of the Maui Suffocation Killer investigation was a smart move on her part to gather information and maybe more. He supposed she intended to write a future book on the subject. Whatever her intentions—or the detective's, for that matter—it would not save her in the end. Like the others, she needed to be taught a lesson. A fatal one. But not yet. He still had time to work with before she tried to leave the island. From what he'd gathered in overhearing the two at the Seas Grill earlier, the true crime author was doing research on an incident last year where a guy killed his wife and others before taking his own pathetic life. This indicated she was staying put for the time being.

That was further supported by her going to talk with the old man, apparently in relation to the murder-suicide that took place at that house. He'd followed her there and back to Kaanapali, careful not to tip his hand, thereby taking away the element of surprise. When they met face-to-face, it would be on his terms, not hers. And certainly not when the detective was tagging along, who hadn't yet been able to figure out who he was or what he was up to. Not till it was too late for the author. As had been the case for the other victims who never saw him coming before he overwhelmed them and took their lives.

He pretended not to notice as Daphne Dockery moved away from the Kaanapali Beach walkway and headed toward the Kiki Shores villas. Having followed her there before, he knew what unit she was staying in. As such, no need to take any chances in pursuing her at the moment. Instead, he gave her no reason to be suspicious of him in particular as, while wearing sunglasses to hide his eyes, he continued to walk down the pathway, seemingly uninterested as she glanced back, as though expecting someone to come after her.

Not yet. All in good time. *See you soon, Daphne*, he thought, suppressing a laugh of amusement and confidence that she would soon be his for the taking.

THE SUFFOCATION SERIAL KILLER TASK FORCE meeting was held that afternoon in the Maui PD conference room. Kenneth was seated in a faux leather chair around the mahogany boat-shaped table as his boss, the Assistant Chief of Investigative Services Bureau, Martin Morrissey, spoke at the podium. Fifty years old and on his second marriage, he had only recently been promoted to the position. Under pressure from the Chief of Police, Wendy Kutsunai, to bring this case to a close, Morrissey pulled no punches in making it crystal clear that he expected real results, sooner than later. "Allowing the unsub to run rings around this department is not an option," he stressed, standing tall at six-five, with a sturdy build, steel blue eyes and shaved bald head. "One death under my watch is one too many. But ten women suffocated to death by some maniac is totally unacceptable. We all need to work harder to get this guy, before he kills again."

When Morrissey turned it over to Kenneth, he knew that there was no beating around the bush. They had screwed up in focusing on Zack Lawrence. Owning up to this was less of a problem than having to admit that they were no closer to nailing the real serial killer than after his first kill. At least it felt that way to Kenneth. In fact, they did have bits and pieces of information that gave them something to work with. But they needed to tie it all together in a meaningful way to identify the unsub and put an end to his reign of terror brought down on women in Maui.

Kenneth stood beside the large touch-screen monitor and, using a stylus, displayed the unsettling grotesque images of all ten victims, the clear plastic bags over their tortured faces. "These women all died needlessly at the hands of the so-called Maui Suffocation Killer as a result of asphyxia," Kenneth said painfully, "while being initially brought under the unsub's control by a stun gun." He proceeded to mention their names one by one out of respect and as a reminder that all were once attractive, vibrant human beings before their lives were extinguished by the fiendish killer. "Venus Delgado, a twenty-nine-year-old yoga instructor, Deena Moanalani, a thirty-year-old hula dancer, Yolanda Monaco, a twenty-three-year-old waitress, Tracy Lowndes, a thirty-four-year-old wife and mother, Harriet Zulueta, a twenty-eight-year-old actress, Nichole Ciminello, a twenty-two-year-old registered nurse, Gwynyth Johnston, a twenty-nine-year-old psychologist, Luana Quesada, a twenty-seven-year-old real estate agent, Jena

Sutcliffe, a thirty-three-year-old event planner, and Irene Ishibashi, a thirty-one-year-old fashion designer. All had visited bars or nightclubs the same night they were killed."

Kenneth switched to a single image, also with a plastic bag on her face. "Ruth Paquin, age thirty-one and an elementary school principal, is the only known survivor of the unsub. She was also attacked after being at a nightclub." He showed another picture of her after recovery as an attractive, brown-eyed woman with long black hair worn in a wavy razored shag. "Due to her ordeal, Ms. Paquin had a brain injury and has only been able to give us limited information on her attacker." Kenneth paused before putting on the monitor a photograph of their onetime chief suspect. "Zack Lawrence was once thought to be our unsub. Unfortunately, he fell off the radar when, aside from lack of hard evidence, Irene Ishibashi's corpse was discovered at a time when Lawrence had been under surveillance."

Lastly, Kenneth put up a digital sketch of a thirty-something blue-eyed male with longish black hair in a textured crew cut. "This person may be Ishibashi's killer," he said in a hopeful tone. "According to the victim's elderly neighbor, Mary Cabanilla, a man resembling this digital image, courtesy of our forensic sketch artist Patricia Boudreau, was seen running from Ishibashi's residence. We can only assume that this person of interest may not only be responsible for Irene Ishibashi's death, but the murders of the other victims of a serial killer on the island—till proven otherwise. In other words, we need to identify the unsub in a hurry, and bring him in for questioning."

"We're working on that, even as we speak," Detective Vanessa Ringwald said matter-of-factly. "The forensic composite sketch has been released to the public in hopes we can identify the unsub."

"Good," Kenneth said, eyeing her still seated at the table. He understood that a sketch derived from the recollections of a woman pushing eighty, who admitted she was stressed out at the time, was still a long shot at best.

"Forensics is trying to see if any prints or DNA can give us something to go on in identifying a suspect in Ishibashi's murder," Detective Tad Newsome pointed out as he stood against a wall.

Kenneth nodded. "We'll see if they can come up with anything." Thus far, their serial killer had managed to avoid leaving behind any scientific evidence. Could that change?

FBI agents Noelle Kaniho and Kirk Guilfoyle added their thoughts to the discussion, with Noelle believing that, between their law enforcement agencies, it would not be long before a suspect was behind bars. Or as she put it, "He's running out of places to hide and we're never going to give him a moment's rest from looking over his shoulder."

Guilfoyle, a veteran of the Bureau, was more pragmatic, if not as determined to catch the serial killer. "We've been down this road before. Even with our best efforts, these types of crimes are not always solved overnight. Serial killers, by definition, are able to take two or more lives and get away with it on the short-term. And sometimes that turns into long-term. Can you say Trevor Henshall, Ted Bundy, Lonnie Franklin Jr., Gary Ridgway? Need I go on? Let's keep working together and get this bastard."

"Couldn't have said it any better myself," Kenneth

stated with an edge to his voice. "Now comes the hard part, tracking him down before he can do more harm."

Morrissey gave Kenneth a stern look and said, "That's what I'm expecting of you and the task force. Bring the perp in and let the justice system do its job."

Kenneth gave him a respectful salute, but understood where he was coming from. It was all part of what was expected in his line of work. Either deliver or get out of the way and someone else would. He had no intention of walking away anytime soon. Not unless there was a good reason for his doing so. Somehow, he ended up thinking of Daphne.

AFTER LEAVING THE police department, Kenneth got onto Highway 30 and headed home. He continued to think about the alluring true crime writer and fantasized about spending the night with her. Or even the day in bed, for that matter. But that was getting way ahead of himself, wasn't it? Maybe getting involved with some-one who could be leaving the island any day now was a very bad idea. Maybe she was still caught up with her ex, Nelson Holloway. Kenneth didn't do well with re-bound relationships. Not that he'd been involved in any romance in a serious way, as it turned out. If Daphne were to be willing to meet him halfway—wherever that was—then it could be a game changer of sorts.

The possibilities of romancing the writer waned in his head as Kenneth neared his house on South Lauhoe Place in Lahaina. It sat nestled on nearly three acres of land with great views of the ocean and Hawaiian islands of Molokai and Lanai. He'd purchased the single-story three-bedroom, two-bath plantation-style home two years ago, with investment savings and a small loan from his parents. Though he welcomed his little slice of island paradise and the privacy it afforded him from the rat race, Kenneth would gladly share what he had should the right person come along. Or was that asking too much?

He drove through the palm tree–lined driveway and reached the house. Inside, he walked across the engineered hardwood flooring, admiring the open floorplan that included floor-to-ceiling windows, a great room, gourmet kitchen and tropical ceiling fans in every room. He had outfitted it with an eclectic mix of vintage and contemporary furnishings. Front and back lanais offered him a spot to chill and enjoy the sights and sounds of his property that had a security system in place for further peace of mind.

After grabbing a beer from the stainless steel refrigerator, Kenneth flopped onto the armless sectional sofa. Barely noticing the gecko that scurried across the floor fearlessly, he picked up the copy of *The Accident Killer* from the bamboo coffee table, intending to read a couple of chapters at best. But the more he read, the more Kenneth found himself riveted. He wound up reading the entire thing and it gave him more insight into the dark mind of Oscar Preston and, by virtue, a greater sense of what they were up against in dealing with the Maui Suffocation Killer unsub.

Chapter Four

Daphne was already up bright and early when her cell phone rang. Seeing that the caller was Kenneth, she was eager to answer. "Hey," she uttered, tempering her enthusiasm.

"I read your entire book last night," he said flatly.

"Really?" This surprised her. Given his full-time duties in law enforcement, she had expected him to take his sweet time finishing the book.

"Yeah, I wasn't expecting that, either. But the truth is, I couldn't put it down. You did a terrific job, Daphne."

She reveled in his compliment. "Thanks."

"I have a couple more questions for you about it," he said. "I was hoping you could come over to my place for dinner tonight. I'd like to cook you a traditional Hawaiian meal before you leave the island, if you're game."

Daphne chuckled. "You cook?"

"Of course." Kenneth laughed. "Does that surprise you?"

"Not really," she lied. "Guess I'm just not used to men cooking for me."

"Maybe it's time to change that. So, are we on?"

"Yes, I'd love to experience a genuine Hawaiian meal while I have the chance," she agreed, unable to hide her excitement in dining with him and otherwise spend quality time. The fact that he could actually cook, which was not exactly her own strong suit when it came to anything extravagant, was another feather in his cap. "What time?"

"How about six?"

"Works for me."

"I live in Lahaina, so it won't be a problem to swing by and pick you up," Kenneth offered. "While letting the food work its magic."

Though it sounded appealing in an old-fashioned way, Daphne saw no reason to put him out. If he was doing the cooking, the least she could do was come to him. "I'll drive to your place. With a GPS navigator, it should be no problem getting there."

"All right," Kenneth said. "See you around six."

"Shall I bring wine?" Daphne wondered, feeling the need to contribute in some fashion.

"Not necessary. I have several varieties to choose from."

"Okay." She got his address and hung up, curious about how his investigation was going. As with her last book, she could only hope that the killer would be brought to his knees before he could hurt anyone else. *I'll ask Kenneth for an update tonight*, Daphne thought, as the notion of one day writing about the disturbing subject continued to intrigue her.

Gazing out the window at the inviting waters of the ocean, she decided to go for a swim before everyone else at the resort beat her to it. Minutes later, she had put on an orchid-colored one-piece swimsuit, grabbed a long towel and headed out. It didn't take long before she had walked across the sand, dropped the towel and dove into the water. Having excelled on the swim team in high school, Daphne immediately felt in her element as she started off with freestyle swimming and switched effortlessly into the breaststroke and backstroke, before ending up where she began. She took measured breaths and felt the strain on her muscles while swimming through some ripples in the water. Even though there were no other swimmers in the vicinity and very few beachgoers, she felt a bit uneasy as though someone were spying on her.

Don't allow your imagination to run away with itself, Daphne chided herself. *No one's out to get you.* The one person who might have been was safely locked up in Tuscaloosa. And there was no reason to believe a serial killer had truly set his sights on her of all people. Was there?

By the time she had swam back to the shore, Daphne had chalked up her jumpiness to nothing more than misplaced paranoia just for the sake of it. After drying herself a bit with the towel, she padded across the sand and went back to the villa.

DAPHNE DROVE TO the Lahaina Banyan Court Park on the corner of Canal and Front Streets, where she had arranged to meet the sister of Jenny Takahashi, Katie Lacuesta. The park, which featured the largest banyan tree in the country, was near the Lahaina Harbor. After parking, Daphne approached a woman of medium build in her late forties with short gray hair in a choppy cut and hazel eyes.

"Katie?" Daphne asked to be sure.

"That's me," she responded with a tender smile.

"Daphne Dockery." They shook hands and Daphne

thanked her for taking time away from her day to meet with her.

"I'm happy to help you get a more vivid picture of my sister," Katie expressed maudlinly.

They sat on a bench and, after getting permission to record the conversation, Daphne jumped right in. "Tell me a bit about Jenny?"

Katie's eyes lit. "She was a vivacious person, a great doctor and loving mother. Jenny never expected to fall out of love with Norman and in love with Francis, but it happened."

Daphne waited a beat before asking gingerly, "Did you know Jenny was pregnant before she was killed?"

"Yes," Katie responded equably. "We talked about everything that was happening in her life. Though the pregnancy was unexpected, she still looked forward to being a mother again and starting over with Francis."

"And he felt the same way as the *other man* in her life?" Daphne needed to ask.

"Very much so. He wanted to marry Jenny. They were in love. Francis embraced the idea of becoming a dad for the first time." Katie's voice broke. "To have this taken away by Norman out of spite was unconscionable. Just as it was to murder my niece, Sarah, and my mother, along with Sarah's boyfriend, Lucas. I hope Norman rots in hell."

Daphne gave her a moment while collecting her own thoughts. "Had Jenny expressed concern over telling Takahashi that she was leaving him?"

"Of course. But she never thought Norman would go that far in exacting revenge," Katie insisted. "Jenny would not have put her own needs ahead of the lives of those she loved. She would have stayed with Norman if it had come down to that, had she known he would commit a cowardly act of murder and suicide."

After a few more questions for clarity, Daphne ended the interview, knowing that Jenny Takahashi's spirit would live on in her sister and the coworkers she left behind. Including her erstwhile lover and father of her unborn child, Francis Hiraga.

Back at the villa, Daphne spent a few hours on her laptop doing research for her book, wanting to tell as complete a story as possible in presenting the truth to her readers.

When it was time to get ready for her dinner date, Daphne freshened up, brushed her hair and left it down, and changed into a floral-print midi dress and low-heeled slingback pumps. In spite of being a little nervous in what amounted to her first romantic-type outing with a man since breaking up with Nelson, she was more enthusiastic to see if it might lead to anything down the line. Or should she not look too far ahead when the time they could be together was getting shorter by the day?

The short drive down Highway 30 East, took her onto the Punakea Loop, and to South Lauhoe Place, where Daphne ended up at Kenneth's door. He was standing there, sporting a big grin and looking dapper in a yellow Oxford shirt, brown khaki pants and cognac-colored derby shoes. "Right on time," he said. "E komo mai. That means welcome."

She smiled while thinking that was a good step to feeling at home with him.

"You look nice," Kenneth said sincerely as he perused her.

"Thanks." Daphne flashed her teeth. "I could say the same about you."

"Mahalo." It was his turn to blush while knowing he wanted full well to make some kind of impression on her by cleaning himself up. "The food is just about ready."

"Smells delicious."

"It'll taste even better." He grinned at her confidently. "Feel free to look around while you wait."

"All right, I will," she said, taking him up on the offer with a warm smile.

On that note, Kenneth proceeded to head back into the kitchen, where he had prepared authentic cuisine he'd learned from his parents. That included Hawaiian green salad, mango-glazed baby back ribs, steamed white rice and sautéed mushrooms, and pono pie for dessert. He hoped he hadn't overdone it. That would be up to Daphne to decide.

"Your place is lovely," she gushed as he handed her a goblet of pineapple wine while they stood by the back lanai.

"Thanks. I like it," he had to admit while tasting his wine. But he also felt it lacked a woman's touch to truly make it a home. This made him curious about her place of residence. Would she ever be willing to leave it? "I'm sure you have a place that fits your needs."

Daphne sipped the wine, marveling at its taste, then said, "Yes, I'm happy with it." She paused. "Doesn't mean I couldn't be just as happy somewhere else, if it was meant to be."

Kenneth nodded musingly. "Yeah, I'm with you there." He wondered if he would truly be willing to leave the island. Yes, he loved it on Maui for all the right reasons. Still, if the right powers of persuasion were there, then why wouldn't he entertain relocating?

"Have you ever been to Alabama?" Daphne seemed to read his mind.

"Can't say that I have," he hated to admit.

"You should visit sometime. You don't know what you're missing."

Kenneth met her pretty eyes challengingly. "I think I have some idea."

"Oh, really?" Her eyes batted coquettishly. "What idea might that be?"

He pretended to think about it, enjoying this easy flowing banter between them. *I'll bite the bait*, he thought. "Let me put it this way, if you're representative of Tuscaloosa, then yes, I'm definitely missing something worth seeing."

Daphne flashed her teeth. "Good answer."

Kenneth laughed, but was dead serious. They would go down that road later. "Let's eat."

As they sat in wicker dining chairs around the rustic trestle gathering table and dug into the food, Daphne proclaimed, "It's delicious!"

"Mahalo." He couldn't help but grin, happy to cook for someone other than himself for a change. Even better would be to share the cooking duties. He imagined she could teach him a dish or two from her part of the country. And then some.

He watched as she scooped up white rice and said, "So, now that you've finished my book, what else would you like to know?"

Kenneth collected his thoughts while taking a bite of his salad. "First of all, let me just say again that I thoroughly enjoyed the book. Reads like a novel, but with all the twists and turns of a real-life crime story as it unfolds."

"That's the only way readers will connect without losing their attention," she contended.

"Makes sense." He stuck his fork into a mushroom. "How did you get Oscar Preston to grant you an interview? I assumed that most serial killers preferred to keep us guessing as to the nature of their criminal behavior."

"Actually, it's just the opposite," Daphne said. "The majority, if not all, serial killers are narcissists and only too happy to boast to the world about their killing ways and the ins and outs of it. Preston couldn't wait to tell his side of the story, no matter how disturbing and self-serving it was."

Kenneth frowned at the thought of the perp getting his kicks from bragging about committing multiple murders, but understood the value in the public knowing. "What took the authorities so long to figure out that the so-called accidental deaths were no accidents at all?" he asked curiously.

"Preston was smart enough to cover his tracks well for a period of time in that the deaths by accident and set far enough apart were plausible." She lifted a rib and took a bite. "But every ego-driven killer eventually becomes overconfident and slips up, as he did."

Kenneth thought about the Maui Suffocation Killer and wondered if he had slipped up as Daphne asked interestedly, "Any new developments with your local serial killer?"

"As a matter of fact, there has been a development," he answered, knowing that it had already been made public. "A digital sketch of a person of interest has been released. We're hopeful it's the break we've been looking for."

"Do those sketches really work in terms of giving a strong resemblance to the suspect?" she questioned, forking salad. "Or are they more likely to result in a flood of people claiming they know the person, even though they don't, throwing you off in the process?"

"The sketches aren't meant to replace a witness identification or photograph of a suspect," Kenneth pointed out. "Even if only reasonably accurate, it can be enough to get someone to recognize the person and lead to an arrest, no matter how many misses come with it. Of course, the sketches are only one tool in our arsenal in trying to nab criminals."

"I know that," she said ruefully. "Didn't mean to suggest otherwise. You guys have a difficult job to do and I can't imagine how the rest of us could ever rest comfortably if you weren't there to separate us from them."

"We all play our roles," he told her modestly, finishing off his rice and mushrooms. "I'm glad to be able to give it my all in getting the bad guys off the streets. Writing true crime books is every bit as important in the scheme of things to inform the public about what happens when we miss the signs all around us, emboldening criminals to continue to carry on as they see fit."

"I suppose." Daphne dabbed a napkin at the corners of her sexy mouth. "You're definitely good for my ego."

Kenneth laughed. "Just telling it as I see it." And he imagined there was much more to unravel in her appeal as a woman. "Hope you saved room for pono pie."

She smiled. "I think I can manage a bite or two."

"Good. So can I." He stood and began clearing the table.

"I can help," she insisted, getting up and grabbing used dishes.

Kenneth liked working in unison with her. He hoped they could put that to practice in other ways. Even if it wouldn't last. Half an hour later, they were out on the front lanai with their wineglasses and Kenneth felt compelled to say, "I have a confession to make."

"Uh-oh… Not sure I like the sound of that." Daphne looked at him warily. "You're married and you forgot to mention it before now? Or something even more unsettling?"

"No, not married. And no other dark secrets." He tasted the wine thoughtfully while meeting her eyes. "I did a little snooping about you. Or, more specifically, your relationship status. Saw that you broke up with Nelson Holloway." Kenneth wondered if he should have kept his mouth shut. "What can I say, I was curious about where things stood in your love life."

She sighed. "You could have just asked me. If so, I would have told you that Nelson and I ended things months ago."

"Sorry," Kenneth voiced shamefully. "Didn't mean to pry. Or maybe I did," he admitted, "but I should have just asked, as you say." He paused. "So, what happened between you two?"

Daphne sipped the wine. "Nelson was a jerk," she snapped. "And I was a fool for ever believing a word he said. End of story."

"That's good enough for me." Kenneth didn't want to push it any further for what was obviously a sore point for her. Still, again he wondered why Holloway would blow his chance with Daphne, something Kenneth could never imagine doing were they together.

"And what about you?" she asked curiously. "Why aren't you with someone?"

He considered the question before responding, "The short answer is I haven't met anyone I've clicked with to be in a steady relationship."

"What about the long answer?" she pressed.

Kenneth knew she expected nothing less than the truth. And he wanted to give it to her if there was to be any chance that something could develop between them. "I was once involved with someone. We started out as friends and seemed to be heading in the right direction toward something more serious. But then tragedy struck." He sucked in a deep breath. "Cynthia, that friend, was killed and everything we hoped to have together died with her."

Daphne gazed at him. "She's the person you mentioned who was a victim of a serial killer in Honolulu?"

Kenneth nodded solemnly. "Yeah. Cynthia ended up being the last of ten victims Trevor Henshall murdered," he said resentfully. "Though I tried, there was nothing I could do to save her."

"I'm sorry you had to go through that." Daphne put a hand on his arm. "Nothing quite prepares you for that type of loss."

"You're right. It sucks, but it's just something you have to deal with."

"I know."

He held her gaze and understood that, in losing her parents to violence, she too had been put through the ringer and was also doing her best to live in the present while never forgetting what was unforgettable. "Anyway, that's my story. Doesn't mean I'm giving up on finding love that can last a lifetime, marriage, children, the whole bit."

"Neither am I," she told him, a softness in her inflection. "I want those things too someday."

Without judging whether or not this was something either could see in the other as a future partner, they found themselves sharing a tender kiss. Kenneth did not try to stop it, welcoming the taste of her soft lips on his, even while having no expectations. Nor did he pursue it further when Daphne pulled away and, just like that, it was over.

Chapter Five

"We've positively ID'd the suspect in the murder of Irene Ishibashi," Vanessa Ringwald said excitedly at the PD. "Name's Ben Hoffman, age thirty-six. Hoffman was one of Ishibashi's ex-boyfriends. He's currently unemployed."

Kenneth was not quite ready to pop open the champagne bottle just yet this morning. But he was certainly open to any news that indicated they could be closing in on a killer. "So the digital sketch did the trick in lining up with his real mug?"

"Yep, that and his fingerprints," she answered. "Dead giveaway."

Kenneth cocked a brow. "Explain?"

"I can do that," Tad Newsome pitched in. "Forensics was able to pull a print off the plastic bag over the victim's head, as well as another matching one from a sliding glass door at Ishibashi's house. They ran them through the system and came up with a hit for Hoffman. Obviously, he slipped up in his hurry to get in or out. Turns out, he's been arrested and served time for domestic violence and a DUI."

"Looks like we've caught a needed break," Kenneth said, not wanting to let this slide through their fingers.

"The sketch of the suspect was spot on." Vanessa pointed at her laptop screen. "Check this out. Here's Hoffman's mug shot and the digital sketch. Pretty much a dead ringer."

Kenneth was inclined to agree, crediting Mary Cabanilla for having a sharp eye in describing the man she saw leaving the scene of the crime. As well as Patricia Boudreau, their forensic sketch artist, for masterfully interpreting the description. "Let's get an arrest warrant and bring Hoffman in—the sooner the better," he stated, knowing that time was of the essence in capturing what could be the Maui Suffocation Killer.

"We're on it," Vanessa said, getting on her cell phone to get the ball rolling.

An hour later, Hoffman's black Volkswagen Tiguan was spotted on Halia Nakoa Street in Keopuolani Regional Park, with the driver matching the suspect's description. When police tried to pull the car over, Hoffman bolted. He led them on a high-speed chase to a residence on Kaikoo Place, where the suspect lived and was now barricading himself inside.

Wearing a ballistic vest and armed with a .40 caliber Glock 23 pistol, Kenneth sped to the scene, feeling they had a serial killer cornered and there was no way out for him, other than to surrender. Or be killed. His choice. The man had obviously decided against allowing the initial police he encountered to bring him in. Kenneth could only hope they could flush him out peacefully and interrogate him for some answers.

His mind drifted to the kiss between him and Daphne, which Kenneth could still feel on his lips. He had no idea what it meant, only that she had managed to stir something in him that he hadn't felt in a long time and he wanted to pursue it further. Assuming she was of the same mind. When he reached the location on Kaikoo Place, it was already flooded with cop cars and the Special Response Tactical Team was in place, awaiting further instructions.

Presenting his ID, Kenneth stepped inside the perimeter that had been set up around the two-story modern-style house, where neighbors had been evacuated as a safety precaution. Rendezvousing with other detectives and FBI agents behind a police van, Kenneth asked about the suspect, "Has Hoffman said anything?"

"Only that he won't come out," Newsome stated. "If you ask me, I think he's just posturing, hoping against hope that we'll back off."

"Yeah, right." Vanessa rolled her eyes. "Like that's going to happen."

Kenneth frowned. "Is anyone in the house?"

"It doesn't appear so," she answered. "According to one of Hoffman's neighbors, he lives alone."

"Let's hope that's true," Kenneth said. "Last thing we need is a hostage situation." Nevertheless, he didn't want to take any chances, ordering that a hostage and crisis negotiator be brought in to try and defuse the situation.

"I agree," Agent Noelle Kaniho said. "If Hoffman has anyone in there, he's desperate enough to try and use them as a shield to save his own neck."

"That's classic fugitive MO," Agent Kirk Guilfoyle argued. "But if he is alone in there, flushing out the suspect with all the means we have at our disposal shouldn't be much of a problem. That's assuming Hoffman wants to come out of this alive."

"One can only wonder," Kenneth said, when sud-

denly a shot rang out from the house, sending everyone
ducking for cover with weapons drawn. Peeking behind
the van, Kenneth could see movement from an upstairs
window. The suspect apparently had no desire to end
things peacefully. Another shot came from the house
in Kenneth's direction, shattering a window in the van
while forcing him to stay low to keep from being hit.
"Everyone okay?" he asked nervously.

"Yeah, we're all still in one piece," Noelle said.

"Seems so," Vanessa concurred. "But barely. He's
clearly out to get us before we can get him."

That appeared to be the case as more shots rang out,
forcing the Special Response Tactical Team to return
fire. There was no indication that the suspect had been
hit, as he used the house for cover while peeking out the
window but not standing directly in front of it.

"I'll try to talk him down," Kenneth said, not both-
ering to wait for the crisis negotiator. Or standing pat
till the suspect had been shot dead. "I need a bullhorn."
He was handed one and, while still crouching behind
the van, spoke directly to the suspect. "Ben Hoffman,
I'm Detective Kealoha, Maui PD. We need you to come
out with your hands up. No one needs to get hurt. Least
of all yourself. So far, none of us have been hit by your
gunfire. Let's not change that. Otherwise, all bets are
off."

"I'm not going back to jail!" Hoffman shouted. "Irene
got what was coming to her. She refused to let me back
into her life."

"What about the other women you killed?" Kenneth
asked. "Did they deserve to die, too?"

Without giving an answer, a single shot was fired.
Only this time it was within the house. Panicked, Ken-

neth tried talking to the suspect again. No response. There was a sinking feeling amongst them that Hoffman may have turned the gun on himself. But now was not the time to take any risks on their lives. "Let's give it a few more minutes and then we'll go in," Kenneth said, wanting to give them every opportunity to take the suspect into custody. Or lower the chance that he could still pose a threat, should they enter the house.

The hostage and crisis negotiator, a thirtysomething woman with short reddish-blond hair in an asymmetrical cut, arrived and attempted to pick up where Kenneth left off. "Mr. Hoffman, I'm Aiysha Nixon, a crisis negotiator. If you can hear me, please say something and we can try to negotiate your surrender."

When there was still no response, Kenneth could see the writing on the wall. "He's either seriously injured by a self-inflicted gunshot. Or dead. We need to find out either way."

Aiysha tried to speak to the suspect one last time, and when Hoffman did not or could not reply, she acquiesced to Kenneth and gave the go ahead to enter the premises. With the Special Response Tactical Team and armed detectives leading the way, a battering ram was used to force open the suspect's front door.

The house was in disarray as Kenneth went inside, equipped with a search warrant along with the arrest warrant. Scaling the carpeted stairs, he reached the second story and kept his firearm in readiness before entering the primary bedroom, where the suspect was unresponsive on the floor, apparently from a self-inflicted gunshot wound to the head. Next to him was what looked to be a 9-millimeter Luger semiautomatic handgun. There was no indication that the suspect had been wounded by law enforcement. But Ben Hoffman was still clinging to life.

Kenneth hoped he would pull through for all the obvious reasons as the suspect was rushed to the Maui Medical Center to try and save his life.

DAPHNE WAS STILL feeling giddy from kissing Kenneth last night. Though it was something she wanted to happen and was happy that it had, the timing seemed off to go much further at that point in time. Still a bit unsettled with the knowledge that a woman he'd been so close to had been the victim of a serial killer, the last thing Daphne wanted was to allow misplaced feelings to cause either of them to do something they might later regret. But if what she was starting to feel for him was real and vice versa, she hoped the opportunity would still be there for them to delve into the possibilities. Whether it was nothing more than a fling in paradise or something that had much more to offer for the long run.

She reached the Maui Medical Center on Mahalani Street and parked her car in the lot before heading inside. Doctor Francis Hiraga, the lover of Jenny Takahashi, had agreed to speak with her. Daphne was greeted by him in the busy lobby.

"Aloha," he said. "I'm Dr. Hiraga. Or you can call me Francis."

Daphne debated this as she studied him. In his early forties, he was around six feet and of slender build, with black eyes and short raven hair worn in a bowl cut. He had a three-day stubble beard and wore a white lab coat over scrubs. "Nice to meet you, Francis," she decided, given the nature of their meeting.

He shook her hand and said, "I only have a few

minutes to talk. Let's go to a room where we can have some privacy."

She followed him down a hall and into what looked to be a small lounge with a picture window. He sat in a gray tub chair and invited her to sit in the one beside it, after which Francis furrowed his brow and remarked sadly, "You know, I miss Jenny every single day."

"I'm sure you do," Daphne said sympathetically. "Losing someone like that is every person's worst nightmare."

Francis eyed her. "Sounds like you're speaking from experience?"

"Good observation." She told him about her parents' tragic deaths while getting his permission to tape the conversation.

"I'm sorry that happened to them," he said sincerely. "I have to say, though, that I never imagined in a million years that Norman Takahashi would do something so horrible as to take the lives of Jenny and our unborn child, their own daughter, Sarah, Jenny's mother and Sarah's boyfriend, Lucas. Then kill himself. It's just crazy. Why couldn't he have let Jenny go and moved on with his life?"

"That's something we'd all like to know." Daphne only wished she could get into Takahashi's head to try and understand why he and others like him felt such rage that a preference for death overcame the normal sanctity of life. "Did Jenny express any concern to you about leaving her husband?"

Francis scratched his pate. "Of course, it was of concern to her. But only because she didn't want to hurt him. The truth is she was worried more about how this would affect Sarah. Jenny didn't want her to be too confused and unsettled about being torn between two parents. But things hadn't been good between Jenny and Norman for a long time. She tried to ignore it, till she couldn't any longer."

Daphne reacted, remembering how things between her and Nelson had deteriorated over time and no amount of apologizing on his part could repair the damage. She was thankful that things had not escalated into violence between them. "How have you been holding up since the tragedy?" she asked the doctor poignantly.

"Truthfully, there's been good days and bad days," he said pensively. "I keep asking myself if there was something I could have done differently, short of never having fallen in love with Jenny and been given her love in return. I'd never want to take away the brief time we had together. She wouldn't have wanted me to."

"I believe you. I don't think she would have." Daphne looked at him and said understandingly, "As for what you could have done differently, we all tend to second-guess ourselves when things like this happen. In most instances, none of us can control what happens when people choose to do unpredictable or deviant things. We just move on with our lives as best as possible."

"I suppose you're right." Francis got to his feet. "Well, I have to get back to work. Never a dull moment around here."

"I can only imagine," she said, shutting off the recorder and standing. They stepped back into the hall. "Thanks for speaking with me. I know how difficult it was to do so."

"If you writing about it can bring some sort of closure to the ordeal of the past year, it was well worth it. Good luck with the book."

"Mahalo." Daphne smiled and was about to leave when she heard a commotion. She looked over her shoulder and saw a man being wheeled toward them on a gurney. There was blood coming from a hole at the side of his head, *undoubtedly from a bullet*, she thought, having seen this before as an investigative journalist.

"Code blue, Dr. Hiraga," she heard someone shout. "The patient has a self-inflicted gunshot wound to the head."

"You'll have to excuse me, Ms. Dockery," he said, his thick brows twitching with concern.

Daphne stepped aside, watching as he sprang into action, taking charge as the patient was moved hurriedly down the hall in an attempt to save his life. As she headed in the opposite direction, a bit shaken by the incident, Daphne found herself staring up into the face of Kenneth.

"WHAT ARE YOU doing here?" she asked him, trying to read into his eyes.

"I could ask you the same thing," Kenneth responded evenly, sensing that she wasn't seeking medical attention. A good thing.

"I came to talk to Francis Hiraga regarding his relationship with Jenny Takahashi."

"Oh, right." He should have guessed that, knowing that Hiraga was on staff and an important part of the story that ended in murder, mayhem and suicide. "How did it go?"

"As well as could be expected," Daphne said. "Losing the love of your life can be hard to overcome."

Even as she uttered the words, Kenneth could tell that she regretted saying them in recalling his own love loss. He wasn't quite ready to call Cynthia the love of his life, though, in spite of her early death. They were never given the opportunity to cross that threshold. Meaning such a love for him had yet to play out. "It's fine," he assured her.

Daphne nodded, then regarded him suspiciously. "You never told me what you were doing here." She glanced in the direction from which she had come and back. "The man who was just brought in…"

"His name's Ben Hoffman," Kenneth said tonelessly. "We were attempting to arrest him on suspicion for the murder of Irene Ishibashi when he holed himself up inside his house. Before the arrest warrant could be served, he shot himself. But not before trying to take out a few of us along the way. Fortunately, no one else was hurt."

"Thank goodness." Daphne breathed a sigh of relief to that effect and then a lightbulb seemed to go off in her head when she asked, "Are you saying that you think Hoffman is—"

Kenneth finished for her. "Yes, we have good reason to believe he may be our Maui Suffocation Killer…"

Before he could mention the DNA evidence and physical evidence indirectly linking Hoffman to the murders, Dr. Hiraga approached them, looking frazzled with fresh blood staining his lab coat. If he was surprised to see Kenneth and Daphne together, he didn't show it. "Detective Kealoha," he said with familiarity, no doubt from the investigation into the death of his married lover, Jenny Takahashi.

"Doctor," Kenneth acknowledged him.

"I understand you wanted an update on the condition of the patient brought in with head trauma from a gunshot?"

"That's right." Kenneth eyed him. "How is he?" Hopefully, they could keep the suspect alive at least long enough to question him, if not to be held accountable for his alleged crimes.

Francis shook his head. "I'm sorry to say that Ben Hoffman succumbed to his injuries. We did everything we could to save him. Unfortunately, it was not to be."

Kenneth had little choice but to accept that as he nodded at the doctor and turned to Daphne, who also seemed to be digesting the news and its implications as it related to the terrorizing of women on Maui by the serial killer.

Chapter Six

"So, is the nightmare really over on the island?" Daphne asked later that evening.

They were at the Lahaina Second Friday Town Party in Campbell Park, right off Front Street. It was part of the Maui Friday Town Parties, where each Friday of the month one of five locations, starting with Wailuku and ending with Lanai, came alive with arts and crafts, live music and entertainment, and plenty of food choices. Basically, a big party with everyone invited. Kenneth thought it might be nice to show her another good side of island life to balance the not so good.

"One can only hope that's the case," he answered tactfully. The DNA found on the murder weapon—a plastic bag—that was responsible for the asphyxiation of Irene Ishibashi belonged to the dead suspect, Ben Hoffman. Similar plastic bags were confiscated from his home. A stun gun was also found among Hoffman's possessions that may have been used to subdue the victims. Open-and-shut case for him being the Maui Suffocation Killer? For some reason, Kenneth was not quite ready yet to make that call. It still troubled him that when given the opportunity after admitting to the murder of Irene Ishibashi, Hoffman chose to take himself out of the equation with a fatal shot to the head rather than confess to being the Maui Suffocation Killer. Was this a deliberate attempt to keep them forever guessing? Or was another killer still at large, waiting to strike again? "I'm guardedly optimistic we've got our man."

Daphne made a face. "That doesn't exactly sound convincing."

Kenneth was impressed at her ability to read him like a book. Maybe those instincts came with being a writer. Or this author, in particular. He flashed her an awkward grin. "I'm not totally convinced," he admitted truthfully, without elaborating. "Everything's pointing toward Hoffman as our killer. But it's in my nature to not jump the gun prematurely. Until we've fully cross-checked his history and the timing with the serial murders apart from Ishibashi's death, and wrapped up the forensic investigation in that regard, I'll stick with a guardedly optimistic approach that the nightmare on Maui has run its course."

She smiled. "Makes perfect sense. Guess that's what makes you a first-rate homicide detective."

He reacted modestly. "Not sure about the first-rate part, but I try not to leave any stones unturned for every investigation I'm involved in."

"That's a good way to look at it," she said. "Kind of how I feel in writing true crime. There's no half stepping where it concerns making sure I've covered all the bases in telling the story."

"Based on the one book of yours that I've read," he told her with a grin, "there's definitely no half stepping in your style or substance." Kenneth realized that this applied to her as a woman as well. Something that kept him wanting to get in deeper with her as a man.

Daphne laughed. "Thanks. Now two-stepping is a different thing altogether. Though I can hold my own on the dance floor, I basically have two left feet."

"I doubt that," he said, picturing her as being a good fit in his arms in partner dancing. "I'd love to try the two-step with you sometime." No matter that he'd never done it before. He otherwise felt comfortable moving his feet on the dance floor.

"Hmm. If you're that courageous, then I'm in."

"Cool." He took that as a future date and fully intended to hold her to it while also looking beyond the dancing and to another activity they might be able to move their bodies in. "So, I guess hula dancing is out?" he joked, as they passed a stage that featured barefoot hula dancers strutting their stuff, alongside fire dancers, to the sounds of chanting and Hawaiian music.

"Uh, you probably guessed right." Daphne chuckled. "Looks like fun, though."

"I'll take that as a maybe," Kenneth said, believing she was as up to stepping outside her comfort zone in dancing as he was.

She wrinkled her nose. "Okay, I'll go along with the maybe."

As they continued to walk around, sampling food from vendors, Kenneth noted that Daphne suddenly seemed unsettled. "What is it?"

She grimaced while looking this way and that. "This may sound crazy, but I've had the strangest feeling that someone has been watching me."

His eyes narrowed. "When you say watching, do you mean as in stalking?"

"Yeah. I haven't actually seen anyone I could point out," she admitted. "It's just a feeling, maybe brought on after practically watching a serial killer breathe his final breaths before my very eyes. Probably shouldn't even have mentioned it."

"I'm glad you did," Kenneth told her sincerely. "I trust your feelings. Where there's smoke…" Maybe there was fire. Or something akin to it. He recalled that he'd joked about her stalking him when they met for the second time and she all but hit the panic button. Why? "Have you been stalked before?"

Daphne sighed. "Yes," she admitted. "Two months ago, an obsessed fan named Marissa Sheffield showed up at various signings and events in Tuscaloosa and elsewhere in and out of state. I didn't realize just how fanatical and dangerous until she demanded that I hire her as my assistant while insisting that we were bound to be best buds. When I tried to get her to back off, told her I didn't want an assistant or best friend, she became agitated and actually threatened me with bodily harm. It was really scary."

"I'm sure it was," Kenneth said, knowing this went well beyond your everyday adoring fans. "Where is she now?"

"In jail, charged with first-degree stalking, a Class C felony," Daphne replied with satisfaction. "At least she was when I left for my book tour."

"Hmm…" Kenneth wondered if her stalker was out on bail now. "Does she know you're in Hawaii?"

"I don't think so. Though my book tour schedule is public and easy to learn though my publisher's website, she would have no way of knowing I was planning to stay on Maui for a while, researching my next book."

"Maybe not." He scanned the park for any signs that they were being watched. No one stood out as being focused on Daphne. That didn't make him feel any more comfortable. Kenneth knew that any smart stalker would make it a point not to draw attention to him or herself. "I'll check on the status of Sheffield," he said. "In the meantime, if you still feel someone is following you, trust your instincts. If you see anyone who rubs you the wrong way, get a description of them and don't try to approach."

"I will and I won't," she promised to his last words of advice. Daphne touched him and said, "Thank you."

Kenneth again felt the heat of her fingers against his skin. It made him want to touch in return and experience even more of the sensations while hoping they were having the same effect on her. But he held back, as this was neither the time nor place to test the waters. Or maybe it was and he felt it was best not to go there just yet while they contemplated what they wanted or expected from one another. "Happy to do what I can to keep you safe while on Maui," he told her candidly. And in the process, Kenneth realized Daphne's safety and well-being was becoming important to him, wherever she happened to be. But especially in the face of danger. Perceived or real.

THE NEXT MORNING, Daphne went jogging on the walking trail, which meandered alongside the Kaanapali golf course. It reminded her of her favorite jogging path in Tuscaloosa and offered a beautiful view of the landscape up high and a perfect rainbow. She wondered if Kenneth was a jogger. Though they had not talked about his fitness routine, obviously he worked those muscles some way. She imagined them working out together, both in and out of bed. But would it ever happen? She could see them potentially in a serious relationship. Never mind the fact that they lived in two different places and hadn't progressed any further than a hot kiss and few sizzling touches. Those alone, however, had lit something in her that Daphne was sure he felt, too, and would need to be addressed one way or another before she had to leave.

With her hair tied in a low ponytail, she reached the top of the hill and sucked in a deep breath while taking it all in. It was gorgeous, which she expected in visiting Maui. What she hadn't anticipated was having an actual serial killer at work in real time on the island during her visit, apart from the murder-suicide of the previous year that she was writing about. Thank goodness Kenneth and his colleagues had apparently put the brakes on the now infamous Maui Suffocation Killer. When the dust settled, she would certainly delve into it more deeply as she contemplated pursuing it as a true crime book.

For now, she had her plate full with the possibilities on both the personal and professional front up in the air. As she headed back downhill, Daphne instinctively looked over her shoulder, as if expecting a stalker to be hot on her trail. There was no one. *Guess I've been overdoing it in looking for something or someone that wasn't there*, she told herself. *Get a grip.* She decided to heed her own advice as Daphne continued to jog peacefully, giving an occasional wave to an early golfer or other runner.

When she arrived back at the villa, she went through a bottle of water and took a phone call from Gordon, her editor, who was checking up on her while fishing for her thoughts on the idea she put forth for her next book. "Heard that the Maui police had found their serial killer, who took his own life rather than be held accountable for his actions."

"So it seems," she told him. "The PD is still working on filling in the gaps before closing the case for good."

"I see," Gordon said. "And where do you stand on writing about it, once you've completed your current book? I don't mean to rush you or anything," he stressed. "There's plenty of time to decide where you go from here."

"It's fine." Daphne understood that he was just doing his job in wanting to keep the fires burning while the coals were hot. Who knew how long she would be writing narrative nonfiction crime stories before deciding to call it quits and focus on other things? Such as becoming a wife and mother. Not to say that she couldn't wear multiple hats at once, if need be. On the contrary, she was more than capable of continuing to be a writer and having a family. "I'm still contemplating the subject matter," she said honestly. "By the time I've wrapped up *A Maui Mass Murder*, I should have a much better idea of what my next project will be."

"Fair enough," he said acceptingly. "Hope you've taken some time to explore the island."

She smiled. "I have done some exploring and would like to do more before I head home." Of course, she could extend her stay, if need be, for one reason or another, including further exploration of Maui and all its wonders.

"Good for you. I hope to make it there one of these days myself. Think I'll try Oahu first, though, as I've heard so many good things about it."

"All are true," she assured him as Honolulu had been her first stop in Hawaii for the book tour. When another call came in from an unknown caller, Daphne cut the conversation short to take it out of curiosity. "Hello?"

"Hi," the female caller said nervously. "My name's Roxanne Sinclair. I was told that you're writing a book about the Takahashi murders and suicide on the island last year."

"Yes, I am." Daphne wondered how she got her number.

"I was having an affair with Norman Takahashi at the time," she claimed. "I thought he was in love with me. Then he finds out about Jenny being pregnant and in love with another man and goes berserk. If you're interested in what I have to say, we can meet for coffee."

Daphne was wary. Was this woman stalking her? Of course, she was interested in this unexpected twist to the story of Takahashi's life, if true. It would certainly add another element to the book. But what if it was fabricated in order to lure her into a trap?

"I'm not in this for money," Roxanne insisted, "or anything else. I just felt I was keeping this inside long enough and it needed to come out. But if you're not up for it, I understand."

"It's not that," Daphne told her, still with her guard up for some reason. "Do you have proof, like a photograph, that you and Takahashi were involved?"

"Yeah, sure." She made an indecipherable sound. "I just sent two pics to your phone."

Daphne pulled them up. They showed a man and woman in what could be described as being pretty cozy with one another. Daphne recognized the man as Norman Takahashi. He was slender, brown-eyed and had short gray-brown hair worn in an undercut style. Based on his appearance, it had to have been taken in his last year or two of life. She looked at the much younger African American female. In her early twenties, she was attractive with a light complexion and had long dark hair and big brown eyes. To Daphne, it was at the very least proof that Takahashi knew her.

"I have text messages between us," Roxanne said. "I can show you."

Knowing that she wanted the book to be as complete as possible, Daphne agreed to meet with her for coffee. What harm could there be in that?

An hour later, Daphne stepped inside the Coffees and Creams Café on Kaanapali Parkway in Whalers Village. She spotted a young woman who resembled the one in the pictures sitting at a corner table. "Roxanne?"

"Yes."

"I'm Daphne Dockery."

"Hi." She stood at around Daphne's height and build. Her long straight raven hair was loose with arched bangs. She was wearing a Hawaiian print T-shirt, frayed-hem denim shorts, and flip-flop sandals. "Thanks for meeting with me."

"You made it hard not to," Daphne had to admit. "I have to ask, though, where did you get my number?"

Roxanne did not flinch when she responded, "From school. I'm a student in the Mathematics Department at the University of Hawaii Maui College. You left your number there for Norman's successor, Professor Lynda Miyahira, whom I work for as a teaching assistant. Just as I did for Norman."

"I see." Daphne had, in fact, spoken briefly to Professor Miyahira by phone and planned to visit the college to get more background information on Takahashi. She smiled at his former student-lover. "Let's sit," she told her and both ordered cafe mochas and freshly baked pastries.

Roxanne nodded. "Okay."

There was small talk till their orders arrived and, with her voice recorder turned on, Daphne jumped right in. "So, how long were you seeing Professor Takahashi?" she asked inquiringly as she tasted her drink.

"For six months before his death," Roxanne answered matter-of-factly.

"He's quite a bit older than you."

"I know, but it didn't feel like it," she argued. "We just made a connection and were able to get past the age difference."

Daphne tried to imagine getting involved with one of her professors in college. She couldn't fathom it for all the right reasons. But what if he had been able to play on her vulnerabilities? Might she have found herself in a similar situation of awe, seduction and perhaps raging hormones? "Did Takahashi's wife, Jenny, know about your affair?"

Roxanne paused, her lower lip trembling. "Yeah. I told her, thinking it would help Norman to get past his reluctance to leave her." She sighed. "Guess I only made things worse. Two days later, he killed Jenny and himself, along with their daughter and the others…"

Daphne tried to come to grips with Takahashi refusing to accept his wife's betrayal and wish to leave the marriage, even while finding it perfectly acceptable to be engaged in an affair of his own. How selfish and outdated was that way of thinking? She suspected that Takahashi had cheated on his wife with other naive college girls. Perhaps Jenny had gotten wind of it before Roxanne, giving her license to pursue an affair of her own, falling in love with Francis Hiraga. Even if that were not true, she still had the right to want out of the marriage and Takahashi should have allowed her that much, whether he remained in a romantic relationship with Roxanne or not.

"Can I have a look at those text messages?" she asked her.

"Sure." Roxanne pulled them up on her cell phone and handed it to Daphne. She scanned them and read the explicit love and lust notes that made it clear that Takahashi had been stringing her along into believing they had a future together.

Daphne handed her back the phone and asked bluntly, "Why would you want this exposed now, months after Norman Takahashi was dead and the relationship over? And how did the police not know about this in the course of their investigation?"

"Norman used burner phones when we communicated outside the office or bedroom, to try and hide the affair," she said. "Apparently, the police never figured it out. But now I need people to know there was another side to Norman than the one who went berserk." Roxanne wiped crumbs from her mouth. "He never laid a hand on me and was a good man deep down inside. He was just caught up between the past and a possible future with me and didn't know where to go with it."

Keep telling yourself that, Daphne mused sarcastically. Whatever decency Takahashi may have shown his young girlfriend, he threw it out the window where it concerned his own daughter, who wasn't much younger than Roxanne. Not to mention his pregnant wife, mother-in-law and another innocent victim. The carnage he'd left behind could not be easily swept under the rug. Even by someone who obviously cared deeply for him.

"I'll make sure that Norman Takahashi is given a fair shake insofar as the different sides of his character in writing the book," Daphne promised while remaining focused on its nature as a crimes-of-murder project. She took a final sip of her coffee.

"Mahalo." Roxanne seemed pleased with this. She stood and Daphne followed, the two shaking hands like old friends. "Good luck with your book."

"Thanks." She smiled at her as they walked out of the café and went their separate ways. Daphne contemplated the amazing twists and turns that always seemed to come with her profession. That included the serendipitous meeting of a certain homicide detective and any potential romance between them.

Chapter Seven

Martin Morrissey summoned Kenneth into his office for an update on the Maui Suffocation Killer investigation. Or more specifically, whether the death of Ben Hoffman meant the case had been effectively closed. Kenneth only wished he could say that were true. It would make things a whole lot easier for him and the other members of the investigative unit and task force. But he wasn't going to lead his boss astray by giving him a false read of the situation. Or jumping the gun in wrapping this up with a nice ribbon on top if he wasn't quite ready to go there yet.

Morrissey's brows twitched as he towered over his U-shaped gray desk, peering down at Kenneth seated in a stacking chair. "So, where are we in the investigation now that Hoffman is dead?"

"Better off than we were when he was alive," Kenneth said humorlessly. He knew that wouldn't cut it. "We believe that Hoffman is all but certainly responsible for the asphyxiation murder of Irene Ishibashi, based upon the DNA evidence and his own final words as a vindictive ex-boyfriend of the victim. Not to mention taking his own life rather than giving himself up. Ballistics was able to match the bullet removed from Hoffman's head to the shell casing and 9-millimeter Luger semi-automatic handgun found by his body, both with his fingerprints on them. All things considered, it stands to reason that given the MO, the presumption is that he also murdered nine other women. But I'm still not quite there yet to pin those on him."

"What's holding you back?" Morrissey demanded, pressing large hands on the desk.

Kenneth wanted to say a gut feeling, over and beyond the lack of evidence. *That won't fly*, he thought, instead saying frankly, "The timeline, for one. So far, we haven't been able to conclusively show through forensics or surveillance videos that Hoffman was present or in the vicinity at the time the murders occurred. This doesn't mean he wasn't. Only that it leaves open the door that he was a copycat killer. That's what we need to figure out before putting this case to rest. Officially."

"Well, get it done," he ordered, softening his hard stance. "The families of the victims deserve some real closure. That can't happen as long as this case continues to hang over us."

"I understand." Kenneth took this as his cue that the meeting was over. He stood, bringing them closer in height, making him feel less intimidated by the Investigative Services Bureau assistant chief. "We'll finish this," he promised while refusing to put a date and time on it.

After leaving the office and Morrissey, who had gotten on his cell phone to probably update the police chief, Kenneth was approached by Vanessa Ringwald. Her green eyes were wide with curiosity when she asked, "So, how did it go in there?"

"Just as you might expect." Kenneth took a breath.

"Morrissey wants results that he can pass on to his boss and the families of the so-called Maui Suffocation Killer. I told him we'd deliver, but only when everything fits right to do so."

"Everyone wants this over," Vanessa contended. "With Hoffman out of the picture, we're clearly on the right track."

"We just have to be sure there's not more than one train to derail," he said wryly.

She nodded. "Yeah."

Kenneth thought about Daphne and her sense of being stalked. "I need you to check on the status of a woman named Marissa Sheffield. She was arrested for stalking Daphne Dockery in Tuscaloosa, Alabama."

Vanessa raised a brow. "Long ways from Maui."

"My thinking also," he said evenly. "Ms. Dockery seems to think someone may be following her around as she researches her next book on the island. If there's even a possibility…"

"Got it!" Vanessa smiled without further comment on his clear interest in the author beyond an official capacity other than to say, "I'll see what I can find out."

"Good." Kenneth rubbed his hands together. "In the meantime, I think I'll pay a visit to the only known survivor of the Maui Suffocation Killer, who may or may not have something to say about Ben Hoffman."

KENNETH DROVE DOWN South Puunene Avenue toward Wailea, a popular resort community in South Maui, where Ruth Paquin lived with her mother. Since her near-death experience with a serial killer, the grade school principal had been unable to return to work, still suffering from the brain injury caused by the attack.

After turning onto Piilani Highway, he soon took a left on Wailea Alanui Drive and entered the Wailea Heights condominium complex, parking in the lot.

Passing by swaying palm trees and plumeria plants, Kenneth walked down a winding pathway to the ground floor unit and rang the bell. The door opened and a petite sixtysomething woman with ash-colored hair in stacked layers, whom he recognized from his previous visit as Ester Paquin, Ruth's mother, greeted him. "Detective Kealoha."

"Mrs. Paquin." He gave the widow a nod. "I was wondering if I could have a word with Ruth regarding the investigation into her attack?"

Ester reacted. "Yes, please come in." Kenneth stepped onto bamboo flooring in a small living room with rattan furniture. "I'll go get her," she told him. "Won't you sit down?"

"Mahalo." He sat on a wicker sofa while wondering if Ruth would be of any help to him in possibly identifying her assailant.

When Ruth entered the room alongside her mother, Kenneth thought she looked even frailer than the last time he saw the school principal. She had small brown eyes and her once long dark brown hair had been cut into a short messy style. "Aloha, Detective Kealoha," she spoke tentatively, then sat beside him.

"Hi, Ruth." He gave her a moment before asking gently, "How have you been?"

"I'm getting better," she said. "It's been an adjustment not being able to work, but my doctor tells me I'm responding well to treatment so I should be able to return to the school soon…"

"I'm happy to hear that," he said sincerely. "You

probably have heard that a suspect in your case has been identified. His name is Ben Hoffman. He died from a self-inflicted gunshot injury."

"Yes, I saw the story on the news." Her chin dropped. "I was shocked."

Kenneth took a breath for what came next. "Here's the thing. We need to be certain that Hoffman was in fact the person who tried to kill you."

Ruth eyed her mother and back. "I don't understand?"

He took out his cell phone and pulled up Hoffman's mug shot. "I need you to take a good look at this photo, Ruth," he told her. "To the best of your ability, does this look like the man who assaulted you?"

She studied the image for a long moment before saying, "My memory's still a little hazy, but seeing his face, it doesn't seem to be the same person who attacked me."

"Are you sure about that?" he pressed.

"I think so." Ruth's voice shook. "The attacker's face was rounder, eyes more closely set. Maybe it's all in my head, still playing tricks on me…"

Or not, Kenneth told himself. He wasn't sure just how much more reliable the witness was this time than before. Yet the mug shot didn't square with her initial description of the assailant, which she apparently maintained. In Kenneth's mind, this lent itself to the real possibility that they could be looking at two killers. One mimicking the killing method of the other.

Kenneth promised Ruth and her mother that he would keep them informed on any new developments in the case, even as he tried to keep an open mind himself on whether or not Ben Hoffman was actually their serial killer.

"Hey, just got news on your stalker, Marissa Sheffield," Kenneth spoke on a cell phone video chat.

"Oh…" Daphne tensed as she awaited what came next while sitting on a Louis XV armchair in her villa.

"Yeah, I'm afraid she was able to make bail," he said with a catch to his voice.

"Figured as much," Daphne muttered realistically, even if against her wishes. Should she be concerned?

Kenneth seemed to read her mind. "As far as we've been able to determine, she hasn't left the state of Alabama. Presumably, she'll stay put and won't bother you anymore."

"That's good to know," she said with a chuckle.

"Apart from that, do you know how to ride a horse?"

Daphne hadn't seen that abrupt detour coming. "Of course." She almost felt as though it went without saying. "When I was young, I rode horses every summer on my grandparents' ranch. Why do you ask?"

"An ex-cop friend of mine, Jared McDougall, who happens to be an expert in criminal background analysis, has a ranch Upcountry in Makawao," Kenneth told her. "I'm headed there to get some feedback from him on my current investigation and thought you might want to tag along. Since he worked on the Takahashi case, he can give you some insight on that as well, if interested. Jared usually likes to talk shop while riding one of his horses."

"Yes, I'd love to go with you," she said excitedly. "Haven't ridden in a while, but I'm sure that won't be a problem. I enjoy riding horses. I've also wanted to experience Upcountry Maui before I leave the island. It would certainly be a bonus to get Jared's take on Norman Takahashi."

"Great, then it's a date!" Kenneth's voice lifted an octave. "I can pick you up in half an hour."

"That sounds fine." Daphne looked forward to the adventure and liked the idea of it being a date, even if a working one. She gave him her unit number, but said she would meet him in front of the villas to save time.

"Be sure to dress accordingly," he teased her.

She laughed. "I will."

It was only after she got off the phone that Daphne began to wonder if she had anything to wear that was appropriate for horseback riding. Or would she need to go shopping with little time to spare? In going through her things, she settled on a pink short-sleeved sun shirt, boot-cut jeans and some comfort faux-leather boots she'd brought along. She put her hair in a high pony-tail and applied suntan lotion and was ready to go.

With a little extra time on her hands, Daphne went to her laptop for a quick peek at info on Upcountry Maui. She saw that it was located on the western slopes of the Haleakala volcano and included the Haleakala National Park. Looking up Makawao, it was known as a paniolo town for Hawaiian cowboys and had a yearly Makawao Rodeo every Fourth of July. Seemed like a place she would love and imagined Kenneth as a cowboy, caus-ing her to warm at the thought.

When Kenneth showed up on schedule, Daphne hopped inside the car. "Hey," he said, grinning at her.

"Hey." She smiled back, taking in his solid green polo shirt, jeans and paddock boots, while thinking that his attire more than measured up to her imagina-tion. Including the Western felt black cowboy hat he wore. She chuckled. "You really are a cowboy at heart."

"Yeah, a little bit." He laughed and said, "Have

something for you." Kenneth reached into the back seat and brought up a straw cowgirl hat, handing it to her. "Didn't want you to feel left out."

"How sweet." Daphne blushed and stuck it on her head, fitting perfectly. "Now I truly do feel the part. Mahalo!"

He grinned. "All set?"

"Yep," she said out of the corner of her mouth. "Let's go Upcountry."

During the drive on Highway 380, Daphne mentioned her unexpected sit down earlier with Norman Takahashi's girlfriend. "She had photos and text messages that backed up her story that they were having an affair."

"Wow," Kenneth said with surprise. "How did we miss that in the investigation?"

"Apparently, she kept this to herself until now," Daphne told him. "She wanted me to know so I could show a different side to Takahashi in the book, as someone she was in love with and claims loved her back."

Kenneth smirked. "Funny way for Takahashi to express this great love," he uttered sarcastically. "By leaving her wanting for someone who's no longer there. Never mind the hypocrisy of the jealous rage he exhibited in mass murder and suicide."

"I know." Daphne was in full agreement. "Takahashi was some piece of work."

"You're telling me." Kenneth made a grumbling sound. "My morning wasn't much better. Seems like the one survivor of the Maui Suffocation Killer, Ruth Paquin, doesn't believe that Ben Hoffman is the man who tried to kill her."

"Seriously?" Daphne's lower lip hung. "What does this mean?" she wondered.

"It means that either Paquin's judgment can be justifiably called into question," he replied, "or we could be dealing with a copycat killer. Meaning her would-be killer is still at large."

"That's a scary thought," Daphne had to say. Like everyone else, she had hoped that Hoffman's death would have spelled the end of the serial killer terrorizing dark-haired women on the island. What if this was a false assumption?

"Yeah, scary." Kenneth turned onto Piiholo Road. "I'm hoping Jared will have some thoughts about this to chew on."

"We'll see." She felt unsettled about where this investigation might be headed while at the same time wanting to see it through to its conclusion as a true crime story to possibly write about. Moreover, Daphne was happy to take this excursion with the detective as a way to spend as much time together as possible, with neither of them knowing where it was going.

JARED MCDOUGALL WAS ten years Kenneth's senior and someone he looked up to. After more than two decades in law enforcement, moving from the San Antonio Police Department to the Maui PD, he'd had enough. He chose an early retirement to buy a ranch, where he could raise horses, give riding lessons and offer scenic tours by horseback and trail rides. Though Kenneth didn't see himself calling it quits for the foreseeable future, he could see the day when he would hang it up and maybe get some prime property and more acreage of his own Upcountry to have a greater laidback life with

a significant other he could start a family with. Someone like Daphne.

Jared was waiting outside when they drove up to his
large Dutch colonial house on Waiahiwi Road. Single,
he was the same height as Kenneth, but a thicker build
and tanned from spending much of his time in the sun.
When he was introduced to Daphne, in true cowboy
style, Jared tilted the brim of his wool Western hat hiding curly gray-blond hair with a receding hairline, and
aiming weathered gray eyes at her, said, "Read your
last two books. Both kept me engrossed throughout."

"Thanks." She blushed. "I do my best to try and keep
them real, yet readable."

"I can tell," he said. "So, you two ready to saddle up
and we can talk?"

"Let's do it," Kenneth told him, and imagined how
sexy Daphne would look on a horse.

"It'll be fun to ride and get a better appreciation of
your land," she spoke eagerly.

Jared grinned. "Happy to show you around."

They went to the stables and Kenneth and Daphne
came out with quarter horses and Jared a Clydesdale
he'd named Grace after his mother. Kenneth would have
happily helped Daphne climb atop the horse, only she
did it on her own effortlessly and started riding as if
she owned it, adding another layer to his fascination
with her. She seemed just as taken with his own riding ability, which he'd also learned as a boy from his
grandfather, who had a cattle ranch on Oahu. If Jared
picked up the vibes between him and Daphne, he didn't
let on, choosing to focus on their purpose for paying
him a visit.

"Let's start with Norman Takahashi," Jared said as

they rode down the trail surrounded by green grass, sloped land and koa trees. He faced Daphne, riding between the men. "I'm sure Kenneth told you I helped in the investigation."

"Yes, he mentioned that," she said. "I was hoping that with your expertise on criminal background analysis, you'd like to weigh in on what propelled Takahashi to take such drastic measures in murdering four people and killing himself." She threw in the new revelation that he'd been having an affair at the time.

"I'd be happy to shed some light on this," Jared said. "As far as the infidelity, I'd heard some whispers to that effect, but nothing that stuck. Kudos to you for getting Takahashi's mistress to come out of the woodwork with her story."

"I believe it was eating away at her and she felt this was the best way to find closure," Daphne indicated.

"She was probably right. Keeping things bottled up, no matter how difficult, is rarely a good thing." Jared took a breath and continued, "With respect to Norman Takahashi's willingness to end so many lives as a respected professor and father, in my view, he had a narcissistic personality that made him believe it was his way or no way. Moreover, I think he had a male-superiority complex that, in his mind, had Takahashi believing he had a right to do what he damn well pleased. But his wife, well...that was a different story. Especially with another man's child in the mix."

"Interesting," Daphne said, guiding her horse down the trail. "But why couldn't he simply have gone after his wife, if Takahashi couldn't bear to have her with another man? Why murder his daughter, her boyfriend and his mother-in-law for his wrath?"

"Good question," Jared said. "Of course, only Taka-hashi can answer that definitively, if he weren't in the grave. But based on my analysis of mass murder-sui-cide in general, the killer is usually trying to make a statement, albeit homicidal. Takahashi likely decided his actions were justified in taking out his rage on any-one who happened to be present when triggered to the point of no return."

"What about the mental-illness angle?" Kenneth asked curiously, knowing that such actions were typi-cally thought of as the work of someone who was crazy.

Jared jutted his chin. "Only a small percentage of killers, whatever the type, suffer from mental illness," he pointed out. "The rest may try to justify their behav-ior because of the standard dynamics, such as anger, depression, jealousy, resentment or any combination thereof."

Daphne gave a little chuckle. "You really do know your stuff."

Jared laughed. "After reading your books, I could say the same for you."

She blushed. "Thanks."

"I agree with you both," Kenneth said admiringly as they picked up the pace. It was his turn to shift the con-versation to the current serial killer case. He'd hoped they would have been able to close the investigation, but it still lingered in the air like the high humidity that characterized the island. He brought Jared up to date on what he hadn't already known. That included the lack of connecting DNA evidence between the killings and inconsistency with the presumption of Ben Hoffman as the Maui Suffocation Killer and the only surviving victim's belief that he didn't fit the description of the attacker still in her head.

Jared took a moment or two to collect his thoughts and said, "As you know, Kenneth, most serial killers are successful because they tend to leave few rock-solid clues, such as DNA and fingerprints at crime scenes for us to collect. So it's no surprise that it's not laid out in a neat package to point toward the perp definitively. That being said, serial killers make mistakes like everyone else. The fact that Hoffman's prints tied him to one murder could've just been sloppiness. Or indicative that his was only a single kill and a copycat killer, assuming Hoffman was even trying to confuse authorities. It may have been just happenstance that he used the same MO as the serial killer to murder his victim. I mean, there's only so many ways one can kill."

Kenneth lifted the brim of his hat. "Are you saying you think the serial killer is still out there?"

"Or could the surviving witness be off base with her reluctance to identify him as her attacker due to the brain trauma she suffered from the attack?" Daphne asked.

"You don't know what you don't know," Jared answered cryptically. "Obviously, if the serial killer never strikes again, one can make a strong case for Ben Hoffman as the culprit, given that the addictive nature of serial murder suggests that one will keep killing till caught or dead. Short of that," he said thoughtfully, "without having studied the extent of Ruth Paquin's brain injury, she may not have gotten a good enough look at her attacker to be able to identify him. But if I were to go with my gut instincts, I'd say that it's more likely than not that this thing may not be over with the death of Hoffman."

As Kenneth exchanged uneasy glances with Daphne while keeping the horse steady, his cell phone rang. He managed to take the phone out of his pocket, answering, "Kealoha." After listening to Detective Tad Newsome reveal some news, Kenneth told him levelly, "I'm on my way."

Daphne regarded his face as Kenneth stiffened. "What is it?"

"There's been another woman killed," he responded solemnly. "From the looks of it, with a plastic bag over the head and all, it appears that she was suffocated to death in the manner perfected by the Maui Suffocation Killer."

Chapter Eight

Kenneth would have preferred to drive Daphne back to her Kaanapali villa. But given that it was nearly twice the distance to get to from Makawao as the crime scene in Kihei, a bustling city in South Maui, going directly there was a no-brainer. Then there was also the fact that, sensing a story that fit into her wheelhouse as a potential true crime book with dramatic twists and turns, for better or worse, she had insisted on accompanying him as an interested observer. Or as she'd put it, "If this so-called Maui Suffocation Killer is truly still at it, alive and well, I'd like to be there to check it out for myself as a writer interested in island criminality in real time."

"How can I argue with that?" he'd said, knowing he was fighting a losing battle.

"You can't," Daphne told him determinedly. "I promise to stay out of your hair."

And I'd really love to run my fingers through your luscious long hair once it's down, Kenneth couldn't help but think in glancing at her ponytail while tempering his attraction to her. "Okay, you can come," he agreed. His only concern had been trying to protect her from the horrors of crime scenes. Or this one, in particular, that appeared to be the mark of a serial killer. Not that she needed his protection as someone who obviously was no stranger to immersing herself into crimes of violence as a top-notch researcher and writer. "Just keep away from the crime scene as a noncop, so as not to hurt the investigation," he warned and she agreed, accordingly,

Driving on Haliimaile Road, Kenneth soon came to Uwapo Road in North Kihei, where he swung right before entering the Kihei Creekside Apartments. After parking, they got out and he showed his ID to get them through the crime scene barrier.

"Remember not to touch anything," Kenneth said habitually, as they approached the building.

Daphne formed a tiny smile. "I'll keep my hands to myself."

He nodded, knowing that she would not be a problem. Entering the first-floor unit, where police activity was underway in securing, collecting and photographing evidence, they were met by Detectives Newsome and Ringwald in the open-concept living space, congested with traditional furnishings and people moving about on the travertine flooring.

Newsome glanced at Daphne, wrinkling his nose. "What's she doing here?"

Kenneth understood that Newsome's curiosity was probably getting the better of him, but her presence wasn't his call. Before he could respond, Vanessa said supportively, "What do you think? Ms. Dockery is probably here to research her next true crime book. Am I right?"

Daphne smiled thinly. "You could say that. At least I'm thinking about it. At the moment, I'm just an observer."

"Which I have no problem with," Kenneth made

clear, peering at Newsome. "I've already advised her to not interfere as we do our jobs."

He backed down. "It's cool."

"Then let's get back to business," Vanessa said, "sad as it is and indicative of just what we didn't want to believe."

Kenneth shifted his gaze from her to Daphne and back again. "What do we have?" he asked characteristically, bracing himself for the gory details.

Vanessa frowned. "The victim, an African American female, age twenty-three, was found in the bathtub fully clothed. A plastic bag was left over her head, resembling that of the other victims of our serial killer."

"Including the murder of Irene Ishibashi," Newsome noted. "Only it's highly doubtful that the latest homicide was committed by Ben Hoffman, seeing that he's dead."

Unless it occurred before Hoffman took his own life, Kenneth thought, which admittedly was a long shot at best. He asked routinely, "And the name of the victim?"

"Roxanne Sinclair," Vanessa said, "according to her driver's license and student ID from the University of Hawaii Maui College."

Kenneth watched the color seem to drain from Daphne's face, prompting him to ask, "What is it?"

"I know her," she stammered. "Or at least we've met."

"When?" he asked.

"This morning." Daphne's voice quavered. "Roxanne was the student romantically involved with Norman Takahashi," she explained. "I can't believe she's dead."

Neither could Kenneth, considering. His brows drew together in assessing this. The timeline took Hoffman completely off the table as a suspect, while opening up new possibilities. Could Takahashi's murder-suicide be connected to a serial killer? Or were the two events totally separate and coincidental? Had Sinclair's killer been stalking Daphne and murdered the college student as a consolation prize?

"I want to see her," Daphne demanded.

"Probably not a good idea," Kenneth indicated, knowing how much it stuck with you seeing dead bodies, no matter how much one got used to it.

"Maybe it's a different woman," she suggested. "If not, since I was probably one of the last people to see Roxanne alive, we need to be sure it's her and go from there."

All things considered, her argument made sense, Kenneth knew. Even if he had little reason to believe the driver's license and student identification ID'd the wrong person. He agreed to allow Daphne without touching anything to see the victim while needing to do the same himself.

They made their way inside the small bathroom that had a separate tub from the step-in shower. A quick glance by Kenneth at the granite countertop showed the typical items such as an electric toothbrush, hair and facial products, and one used facecloth. His eyes locked in on the mirror above the sink, where a red magic marker was used to write the alarming words, *I'm Still Here. The Other Idiot was a Copycat.*

Kenneth winced. If this was the work of the Maui Suffocation Killer, had he targeted the victim at a night-spot and bided time before going after her? Or had the unsub changed his m.o.? Kenneth caught Daphne reading the disturbing message, before he homed in on the bathtub. The decedent was seated in front of the faucet, wearing a print T-shirt, denim shorts and was barefoot. Her twisted face, surrounded by long and straight dark hair, was covered with a clear plastic bag, obfuscating her appearance somewhat, but still identifiable. Kenneth asked Daphne, "Is this the same woman you met with this morning?"

Looking at her with horrified eyes, she turned away and uttered, "Yes, it's her—Roxanne Sinclair..."

Putting his arm around her, Kenneth said, "Let's get you out of here." He led Daphne from the bathroom, feeling her shaking at what she'd witnessed. "Sorry you had to see that." He tried to comfort her as they reached the living room area.

"I needed to," she insisted, pulling herself together. "Whoever murdered Roxanne may have been trying to send me a message."

"What kind of message?" Kenneth regarded her keenly. "Other than the one the unsub left on the bathroom mirror for us to find."

Daphne's face reddened. "The kind that says I'm watching you and may come after you next."

The thought of anything happening to her chilled him to the bone as Kenneth contemplated the notion of the two cases merging somewhat, even if on different levels. What if Daphne's sixth sense about being stalked was real? Only instead of a crazed fan, the stalker was a serial killer?

Vanessa weighed in. "Until we can get to the bottom of this, I suggest you watch your back, Daphne, if you plan to remain on the island for a while."

"I will," she promised, and eyed Kenneth. "The last thing I want is to be the target of a killer. But I won't be driven off like a scared rabbit, either. I have a job to do and intend to complete it."

"I understand," he said calmly while knowing he would need to do his part to keep her safe as long as she was on Maui. Even then, Kenneth was regretting the day when she would have to leave. But as long as she did so on her own two feet instead of in a casket, he would have to live with it. He motioned to Newsome and asked, "Who reported the crime?"

"No one we can identify," he said vaguely. "It was an anonymous call."

Which suggested to Kenneth that it came from the killer, who clearly wanted them to discover the body, along with this troubling message. "Let's see if we can trace the call," he said, knowing it was a long shot as the caller had likely used a burner phone.

Newsome nodded. "You got it."

Kenneth told him and Vanessa to double down on seeing if any of the victim's fellow tenants saw or heard anything as well as checking for surveillance videos. Someone had to know something, he reasoned while wondering if the unsub could actually be a resident at the apartment complex.

When Rudy Samudio, the medical examiner and coroner, arrived, he immediately went to do a preliminary examination of the decedent. Emerging, he had a dour look on his face as the decedent's body was bagged and carted away by his staff. "I thought this was behind us," Samudio groaned. "Apparently, I was mistaken."

"What's your initial take on the cause of death?" Kenneth asked him point-blank, sharing in his frustration.

"The decedent's death was all but certainly the result

of suffocation," he answered without prelude, "caused by the plastic bag over her face, blocking the needed oxygen to the brain to survive." Samudio added, "Burn marks on her neck and arm are consistent with those made by a stun gun."

"Why am I not shocked?" Kenneth remarked sarcastically.

"Did you see the cryptic message the killer left on the bathroom mirror?" Newsome asked the coroner.

"How could I have missed it?" Samudio rolled his eyes. "Looks to me like you have two different killers—one dead and one very much alive."

"That seems to be the clear takeaway." Kenneth rubbed his jaw. "How long would you say this latest victim has been dead?" He needed to know, to be sure they were actually dealing with a second killer. Or the actual serial killer.

Samudio contemplated for a moment. "Pending a thorough examination, based on body temperature and other factors, I'd say that the deceased has been dead anywhere from two to four hours."

Kenneth could see a reaction from Daphne while validating in his own mind that Roxanne Sinclair couldn't possibly have been murdered by Ben Hoffman. It meant that the Maui Suffocation Killer was alive and well. Something they would have to deal with before the Suffocation Serial Killer Task Force could be officially disbanded.

"I'll take you back to the villa now," Kenneth told Daphne, believing that she had seen enough. As had he. But this was his job. She hadn't signed up for morbid crime scenes like this, even as a bestselling and coolheaded true crime writer.

HE STOOD AMONGST the bystanders outside the yellow crime scene tape, hidden in plain view as the police went about their work investigating the murder of Roxanne Sinclair. In spite of leaving them a message taking credit for killing her, while separating himself from the copycat killer Ben Hoffman, he wasn't about to turn himself in. Or confess right then and there to being the Maui Suffocation Killer. On the contrary, his work as a killer was far from over. Not when there were plenty of other women ripe for the picking, like perfect red apples. They needed to suffer as he had over his lifetime, getting little to no sympathy from anyone. Now was his time to shine and he gladly took on the challenge, daring anyone to try and stop him.

He watched as Daphne Dockery and Detective Kenneth Kealoha emerged from the building. Both looked weary. Or was it wary? He laughed within at the thought. The true crime writer had inspired him, making him want to go further than he'd ever thought possible in being a serial killer. Her books, especially the most recent one, had captured his fancy. She had, given him a whole new reason to try and outdo his predecessors as a hardhearted but clever serial killer. Roxanne Sinclair had been one example of that as an impromptu but necessary person to target for death. Before she realized the serious error of her ways in inviting him in, it was much too late to do anything but accept her fate as the next hapless victim of a bona fide killer.

Just as Daphne Dockery would soon be forced to do. She believed she was safe under the watchful eye of the detective, whose interest in the pretty true crime writer seemed to go beyond the call of duty. But he knew better. She would never be able to escape the trap he was setting for her, as long as she remained on the island. Even on the mainland, she could not rest easily, for he was just as capable of laying a hurt on her there from which she would never recover. Or be miraculously rescued by Detective Kealoha, as if she belonged to him. And only him.

No, the writer was his and it wouldn't be long before it was time to give her what she deserved. The type of oxygen-depriving death that the other women had suffered till their breathing stopped altogether. Then maybe someone else could write a book about famous true crime writers having the tables turned on them. He laughed again in his head while maintaining a calm and concerned facade for anyone who might look his way.

He watched as Daphne and the detective got into his vehicle, taking them away from the crime scene and its terror the murder had caused to spread around the apartment complex like a wildfire. But paradise came with a price. He would exact his revenge for being wronged while creating his own brand of pleasure for doing what he saw as right and ready to be carried out at the time and place of his choosing.

He effortlessly separated himself from the gathering, knowing he had gotten away with murder once again. It was time to chill and wait for the next person to die a cruel death. Until then, he would bask in his triumphs, knowing there was little that could be done to interfere with his actions. Which was unfortunate, as he had no plans to let up. Not when women like Daphne Dockery were out there, waiting to experience death, which he intended to deliver time and time again.

"I DON'T REALLY feel like going back to the villa yet," Daphne surprised herself by saying once they got inside the car. Or maybe the circumstances gave her the courage to put it out there and see what happened.

"You want to go for a drink?" Kenneth asked as they pulled onto the street. "I've got a little time to work with as the investigation unfolds."

"How about we go back to your place?" There, she said it. Would he take the bait and run with it? Or would duty call and need to be put on hold?

"We can do that." His tone was unreadable, but Daphne read his body language behind the wheel that told her they were very much on the same track. Or was that more wishful thinking on her part?

"Good," she said, leaving it at that while knowing she wanted him and had to believe he wanted her just as badly. In spite of the fact that they were both caught up in murder investigations that had mysteriously merged. And that her planned time on the island was coming to an end. It was certainly not long enough to think in terms of what sex might mean beyond being all hot and bothered for one night. But why give it a lot of thought, if he hadn't brought up? Just enjoy each other's company on a day they could both use a distraction.

Neither of them had much to say during the rest of the drive, even if Daphne's thoughts were filled, thinking about wanting him like she couldn't remember wanting someone. This was intermingled with concerns about whether or not she was being stalked by a serial killer and if she should be worried that her life could be in danger. Or was the murder of Roxanne Sinclair unrelated to the book she was writing and Daphne's presence on Maui?

When they arrived at the house, Kenneth asked, "Can I get you something to drink?"

"Beer would be nice," she said. Though not much of a beer drinker, Daphne had a taste for it at the moment.

"Beer, it is." He walked into the kitchen and grabbed two bottles from the refrigerator, opened them and handed her one in the great room while commenting, "It's been quite a day."

"That's for sure." She sipped the beer, gazing into his wondrous brown-gray eyes. "Do you think Roxanne was killed by the same man responsible for most of the other suffocation deaths? Or could he be the actual copycat killer?"

"Good question." Kenneth drank beer thoughtfully. "We'll have to see about that. If I had to make a call on this, I'd have to say that whoever murdered Roxanne is the real deal, insofar as wearing the moniker, the Maui Suffocation Killer. He obviously went through great lengths to illustrate this, including the message on the mirror. Why Ben Hoffman decided to kill his ex-girlfriend, Irene Ishibashi, in the same manner, who knows? I can only assume that he was hoping to throw the authorities off. Might have worked, too, if not for the prints he left behind."

"Not to mention the apparent real killer seems determined not to let someone else take credit for his crimes," Daphne said, unnerved at the mental image of Roxanne in the bathtub with her face anguished from dying the way she had.

"Yeah, there is that," he conceded, locking eyes with her.

"Then there's this…" She tilted her face upward and kissed him, tasting the beer. The kiss lingered for a time before she pulled back and met his gaze. "In case you're wondering, I want you."

"I think that goes both ways." Kenneth's voice deepened. "Forget the *I think* part. I want you, too." He lifted her chin and they kissed again, this time with an even greater sense of urgency, as he slipped his tongue inside her mouth and she reciprocated. She could feel his erection straining to be released, deepening her yearning for him.

"Shall we go into your bedroom and continue this?" Daphne asked.

"Absolutely," he told her without hesitation.

"Do you have protection?" she thought to ask, taking another sip of the beer. Though the desire to be with him was overwhelming, Daphne knew it was wise to act responsibly for both of them at this stage of whatever was going on between them. Even so, she was sure he was good father material, should the day come that they were ever to go down that road in a relationship.

"Yes. Always." On that note, Kenneth took her hand and led the way into the bedroom.

Daphne glanced at the vintage oak furniture before narrowing her focus on the rustic panel bed, imagining them soon on it. Kenneth took their beer bottles and set them on the dresser before cupping her cheeks and resuming their kissing. Its intensity actually made Daphne feel lightheaded. All the more reason why she relished the thought of what was to come next.

Chapter Nine

Kenneth was beyond aroused as he watched Daphne strip naked, showing off her perfect body with full and firm breasts, small waist and shapely legs. She waited till last to undo her hair, shaking it into place as it cascaded down across her narrow shoulders. Seemingly just as enamored with his undressing, she laid atop the rustic tweed comforter and waited for him to join her. Grabbing the condom packet from the nightstand drawer, he tossed it on the bed, before commencing to what had been in his fantasy from practically the first time he laid eyes on the gorgeous author.

A sweet dream come true, Kenneth thought as he climbed onto the bed with the ceiling fan spinning overhead and kissed Daphne. She was tasty and tantalizing. *I could kiss her forever*, he mused, intoxicated by her scent. He forced himself to break away from the passionate kiss, wanting to pleasure her in other ways while resisting his need to be inside her. He kissed her chin and neck, moving down to her breasts, teasing her taut nipples with his lips and teeth, all the while running skillful fingers up and down her body, till settling between Daphne's legs, pleasuring her while she moaned softly.

Abruptly, she grabbed his hand to stop and uttered hoarsely, "I'd rather take that first journey together. Please…"

"I'd like that, too," he said, giving in to her wishes, more than happy to oblige as his own hunger for her threatened to explode. He put the condom on. Fitting himself perfectly between her moist thighs, Kenneth drove inside her, going deeper with each thrust as they kissed passionately and the sense of primordial needs enveloped them like a shroud, separating them from everything else in the sometimes dark and dangerous world at large.

He wasn't sure if she climaxed first or him, or if they reached that apex in unison, as Kenneth had been so caught up in the frenetic movement and harmonious moments between him and Daphne that he simply enjoyed the ride and was more than content to allow nature to take its course. It did, and then some. Only when they came out of it to catch their breaths, did their bodies stop trembling with satisfaction and their heartbeats slowly return to normal.

"Wow," was all he could think to say as Kenneth lay beside her, feeling the breeze from the ceiling fan cool them off.

Daphne giggled. "How about mind-blowing!"

"That works." He laughed. "It was definitely more than worth the wait."

"So, you were waiting for this?" she teased him.

"Yeah, assuming we ever reached that point, which I was in no way taking for granted," he assured her. "If so, I was sure it would be amazing."

"Glad to know you have good instincts." Daphne

chuckled and ran her foot along his leg. "Guess we both do, leading to this moment."

"But hopefully not the last." Kenneth touched her leg draped over his, the creamy skin still damp from their sexcapade. He certainly didn't intend to put any pressure on her, knowing full well that she wasn't going to remain on the island forever. And with a serial killer still on the loose and possibly eyeing her as a victim, could he really blame Daphne for wanting to leave as soon as she could? Kenneth sought to moderate his words. "I think what I'm trying to say is that I like being with you, in bed and out. I don't have any expectations, but as long as you're around…"

"I get it," she said, "and I feel the same. I'm enjoying your company, too, for as long it lasts. No pressure either way."

"Agreed." Kenneth welcomed her words of encouragement, but was still pained by the thought of time running out for them to explore this further to see if it might lead to something much more significant than sex, meals, horseback riding and joining forces on the true crime front. Not to mention their paths spilling over into his current investigation. But none of that should detract from what had just happened and how good it made him feel. Should it?

I WONDER WHAT he's dreaming about? Daphne asked herself as they lay in bed in the middle of the night, with Kenneth cuddling her in his powerful arms. Hopefully her. And where this could go between them if they grew serious about each other and weren't frightened off by barriers such as long distance. And careers that might not always be in sync, even if they seemed to be a natural fit in many ways. *I'm not about to pressure him into something that he's not ready for*, she thought. Maybe she wasn't ready, either. Or maybe she was more than ready to be in a steady relationship again. Even get married and have two or three children. But only with someone who shared her vision of exactly what it meant to be committed to another person in body and spirit. Rather than like her ex who thought only about himself at her expense. Kenneth was different, Daphne knew. But that didn't mean they were meant to be together. Not yet, anyway. Right now, she just wanted to enjoy the intimacy that had thoroughly captivated her a few hours ago, giving them much-needed relief from the cases of murder swirling all around them like sharks in the water. Whatever either of them needed to do to stay ahead of the curve in their respective occupations, she was sure they would find a way. No matter the obstacles that came when dealing with people who liked to kill other people for one disconcerting reason or another.

When Kenneth began to stir, Daphne found herself aroused again and wanting more of him. Was he ready to go another round? Only this time without the sense of desperation that dictated their actions the first time together?

"You awake?" she whispered to him as if someone might overhear them.

"Yeah, I am now," he said sluggishly. "Can't sleep?"

"I can, but I'd rather not right now." Daphne was amazed at just how assertive she had become around him. Where had this come from?

"Hmm…" Kenneth kissed her shoulder. "Did you have something else in mind?"

She turned her head and kissed him on the mouth.

"Yes, I do." She slipped a hand between his legs. "But only if you're up for it."

He chuckled. "I'm sure I can manage." After kissing her again, he lifted up and said, "Give me a moment."

Daphne waited for him to get another condom and come back to bed, whereby she took control, kissing and touching him all over while thrilling in the way his body reacted to this stimulation. He did the same to her, titillating her slowly and very surely, before she had worked herself into a frenzy. After putting on the protection, Daphne climbed atop Kenneth and guided herself onto him. He ran one hand through her hair and used the other to hold her hip firmly as she rode him like the quarter horse she'd ridden on his friend's ranch. Only Kenneth was decidedly all human male to corral. When she couldn't hold back any longer, she allowed herself to climb the mountain of sexual delight to the very top, and held his trembling body tightly as he joined her in sheer bliss. Afterward, all Daphne could think of was that she was falling in love with the handsome and sexy police detective, both scaring and beguiling her, before she fell asleep in his arms.

KENNETH ALMOST HATED to have to reconvene the Suffocation Serial Killer Task Force so soon after they had hoped it might be on its last legs, giving way to future task forces fighting crime on the island. He'd much rather be in bed, making love to Daphne as they had off and on last night. He hadn't been able to get enough of her. And she had made it clear that this worked in reverse as well, giving them both something to chew on. Instead, here he was, forced to come to grips with the reality that their serial killer investigation was apparently far from over and may have moved in a different direction with links to a mass killing on the island.

He swallowed, while standing at the podium in the conference room, and said, "I know we thought this task force had just about wrapped things up with the confirmed suicide of Ben Hoffman, thought to be the Maui Suffocation Killer. But new evidence has surfaced to indicate otherwise." Kenneth used the stylus to control visuals shown on the large touch-screen monitor. He brought up a split image of Hoffman and Irene Ishibashi. "While there's strong reason to believe that Ben Hoffman was responsible for the suffocation death of Irene Ishibashi in what appears to be a copycat killing, it's very likely that the actual serial killer is still out there…"

Kenneth put up a graphic image of the latest woman to die. "Yesterday, Roxanne Sinclair, age twenty-three, was found fully clothed in her bathtub at an apartment in Kihei with a plastic bag over her face. According to the autopsy report, the victim's death was caused by asphyxia, the same as ten other women on Maui over the last eight months or so. Only one of those can be accounted for with a suspect." He paused while switching to a picture of the note left on the mirror. "This message came from the purported killer of Sinclair, taking full credit for it while discrediting Ben Hoffman as being the real Maui Suffocation Killer. It's something we have to take seriously," Kenneth pointed out, "given that another young woman is dead and, with the estimated day and time of death, unless Hoffman has reemerged as a vampire, he's not our guy.

"Another possible twist to this sordid tale has emerged." Kenneth displayed side-by-side images of

Norman Takahashi and Roxanne Sinclair. Pausing for a moment to collect his thoughts, he said with ambiguity, "According to Sinclair, she was the secret lover of Norman Takahashi who, last year, killed his pregnant wife, teenage daughter, her boyfriend and Takahashi's mother-in-law before shooting himself to death. Sinclair has provided photographs and text messages to true crime writer Daphne Dockery to support this claim. Now Sinclair is also dead, apparently at the hands of a serial killer, who appears to be changing his m.o., with no evidence that he and the victim ever crossed paths at a nightclub. Whether there is a direct connection between the cases or it's purely coincidental, it bears looking into as part of our overall investigation in solving the current case." What Kenneth left out of the equation for now was his fear that the still-active Maui Suffocation Killer may have set his sights on Daphne. As yet, she was the one person who was indirectly connected, through meeting with Roxanne Sinclair, to the Takahashi mass murder-suicide and the serial killings of now ten women on the island. Had the killer gone after Roxanne Sinclair in the course of stalking Daphne to muddy the waters somewhat in the investigation?

These were questions that Kenneth was determined to get to the bottom of while doing what he could to protect Daphne to the extent possible. As it was, there was only so much he could do at the moment. He didn't have the authority to assign a full-time detail to follow her around day and night. Nor was he able to stop Daphne from insisting on going back to the villa and continuing her own work in doing research for her next book. That was her right as a professional writer and bestselling author. Right now, his best bet for safeguarding Daphne was to try and solve the Maui Suffocation Killer case by IDing the unsub and getting the serial killer off the streets and behind bars, once and for all.

On that front, the task force was in full agreement. Kenneth listened as Agents Kirk Guilfoyle and Noelle Kaniho took turns in reiterating the Bureau's full support and resources in assisting them in the investigation. Detectives Tad Newsome and Vanessa Ringwald were, as always, on board in doing whatever it took to bring this case to a close. And though he would have preferred that Ben Hoffman was their man and no one else had to die, even Assistant Chief of Investigative Services Bureau, Martin Morrissey, recognized that, with Roxanne Sinclair's suffocation murder, a killer remained on the loose. Their job was to leave no stones unturned in pursuit of justice for her and the other victims of the Maui Suffocation Killer.

DAPHNE DROVE DOWN Maui Lani Parkway en route to the University of Hawaii Maui College, located in Kahului, where she was meeting up with Kenneth to speak with Lynda Miyahira. Roxanne Sinclair was a teaching assistant for the mathematics professor, who'd succeeded Norman Takahashi in the position. Aside from wanting to get some further insight on Takahashi, Daphne wondered if Professor Miyahira had any knowledge of Roxanne's life outside the school that might help lead to her killer. At least this was something Kenneth was interested in learning, with Roxanne being the latest victim of the Maui Suffocation Killer, who was no longer believed to be buried with Ben Hoffman.

I never thought I'd be drawn into this serial killer investigation, Daphne told herself. Certainly not before officially taking it on as her next true crime book. But the fact that Roxanne had been murdered just hours after interviewing her made the confluence all but impossible for Daphne to dismiss. Was she at all responsible for the young woman's death? Perhaps as a warning to not dig any deeper for the book? Or was something even more sinister at play here, with a serial killer deciding to bring her into his orbit, starting with going after Roxanne?

Quite naturally, Daphne was unsettled at the notion. As was Kenneth, who had questioned whether it was wise to continue doing research for her book as long as his case was ongoing. But facing danger was not new to Daphne. Hadn't she stood her ground when up against a stalker? And even found herself face-to-face with notorious serial killer Oscar Preston. Although he was shackled at the time, with a burly correctional officer in the room, it was still a dangerous environment for her in interviewing the killer. Though she surely did not court trouble, she understood that there was invariably a certain risk versus reward in writing true crime. Backing away from it now would only make her question her career choices later. She couldn't let a serial killer dictate the life she led. Any more than Kenneth could when he went into law enforcement and went about investigating crimes.

Daphne knew deep down inside that he understood this, in spite of natural reservations about her staying the course, the circumstances being as they were. How could he not? The fact that he respected what she did was one reason she was attracted to Kenneth. Another was their off-the-charts sexual chemistry, which brought them together in bed last night and gave her another reason for falling in love, aside from the physical attraction. He only wanted her to remain safe. Having him around was half the battle. The other half was seeing if there was more to look forward to between them.

She turned onto West Kaahumanu Avenue and made her way to the college's Mathematics Department, where Daphne found that Kenneth had beaten her there, waiting outside the professor's office. "Hey," he said, grinning slightly.

"Hey." She colored, thinking about the hours they had spent in bed last night, much of it awake with plenty of sexual action. "You could have gotten started without me."

"We're in this together," Kenneth reminded her. "Let's see what Professor Miyahira can tell us about Roxanne Sinclair and more."

"All right," Daphne agreed, and went inside the small office.

When seeing them enter, Lynda Miyahira stood up from her ergonomic desk. In her mid-thirties, she was small with short and layered brown hair with blond highlights and coal eyes behind square glasses. "Hello," she said nervously.

"Hi, I'm Daphne Dockery. Thanks for seeing us." She understood how difficult it must be.

"Detective Kealoha," Kenneth said somberly.

Lynda shook their hands and said, "I just can't believe Roxanne is gone. She was a great teaching assistant and a good student with her whole life ahead of her."

"I know," Daphne offered sympathetically, knowing no words could suffice.

"Please have a seat," she told them.

They sat in vinyl guest chairs and Lynda remained standing, leaning against her desk. Kenneth motioned for Daphne to take the lead, prompting her to say, "I met with Roxanne yesterday. She wanted to talk about her relationship with Norman Takahashi for the book I'm writing."

Lynda nodded to that effect. "Yes, I told her about your book and wanting to get some background information on Professor Takahashi," she voiced maudlinly.

"Roxanne said she'd been having an affair with the professor before he died," Daphne stated, wondering if she knew about it, having been in the department at the time.

Shock registered across Lynda's face. "What?"

She didn't know, Daphne mused instinctively. "Roxanne provided proof that it was going on. She was in love with him and believed, whether true or not, that he loved her as well."

"I don't know what to say." Lynda touched her glasses. "I had no idea that Professor Takahashi would get involved with his one of his students and teaching assistant. Roxanne certainly never divulged this to me, though I knew she took Norman's death pretty hard. I just thought it was due to what happened." She drew a sharp breath. "Now Roxanne's been murdered—"

Kenneth leaned forward. "This is where I come in," he said evenly. "We suspect she was the victim of a serial killer."

Lynda put a hand to her mouth. "Oh, no."

"Do you happen to know if Roxanne was seeing anyone recently?" he asked.

"We didn't talk much about her personal life. She pretty much kept to herself," Lynda insisted. "However,

Roxanne seemed to be on friendly terms with another teaching assistant in the department. Joshua Winningham. I can't tell you anything more than that."

"It's a start," Kenneth said. "I need to get in touch with Winningham."

"I can give you his cell-phone number."

As she did just that, Daphne thought to ask, "Did Roxanne ever indicate that someone was stalking or harassing her?" *That would be one way for a serial killer to target a victim before victimizing,* she thought.

"She never told me anything like that," Lynda said. "Maybe you could talk to some of the students in her classes. I can provide you her class schedule."

"That would be helpful," Kenneth told her.

Daphne eyed Lynda and asked curiously, "What can you tell me about Norman Takahashi when he was with the department? What type of professor was he?"

Lynda considered this. "Most people in the department liked Norman," she asserted. "He was approachable and truly seemed to care about his students and wanted them to excel in mathematics."

"Did he ever have any complaints about sexual harassment or other inappropriate behavior with students?" Daphne asked straightforwardly. "Or other staff, for that matter?"

She shook her head. "Not that I'm aware of. You can check with the director of the department, Doctor Mitzi Yamane. But from what you've told me, evidently Professor Takahashi had no boundaries for what he was willing to do and with whom. I'm only sorry that Roxanne had to be swept up in his troubled life."

"So am I." Daphne couldn't help but wonder if that extended after Takahashi's death, with Roxanne winding up in the crosshairs of a serial killer.

Chapter Ten

As fortune would have it, they were able to track down Joshua Winningham in an accounting class. Pulling him out in front of classmates might not have been the best thing to do, but with another woman murdered, Kenneth didn't have the luxury of cutting him some slack. Once they had Joshua in the hall, he studied him. The suspect was in his mid-twenties, tall and lanky, with a low fade brown-man bun and blue eyes. Flashing his identification, Kenneth said toughly, "Detective Kealoha, Maui PD, Criminal Investigation Division."

He was about to introduce Daphne, when Joshua gazed at her and stated, "You're Daphne Dockery, the true crime writer."

"Yes, I am," she acknowledged.

"I went to your book signing," he said. "Along with Roxanne."

"Really?" Daphne flashed Kenneth a thoughtful look.

"Yeah. We thought it would be fun." Joshua furrowed his brow. "I assume that's why you're here. You're investigating what happened to her, right?"

Kenneth wasn't sure if he was merely playing innocent along with being perceptive. Or what. "That's correct," he told him.

Joshua winced. "Murdered. I'm still trying to process this."

"I understand that you two were friends?"

Joshua leaned on one leg. "Yeah, we were." He shifted his weight to the other leg. "We hooked up a couple of times, but that was before she got involved with some older dude."

Kenneth knew that person to be Norman Takahashi. "What older dude?" he asked.

"She never said," Joshua claimed. "Had my suspicions, but it wasn't any of my business." His eyes widened. "You don't think I had anything to do with her death, do you?"

"That depends." Kenneth pursed his lips. "We have reason to believe that Roxanne was involved with Professor Norman Takahashi." He watched Joshua react as though he knew or suspected as much.

"Yeah, I thought so, too," he conceded. "Saw them hanging together from time to time, but she claimed it was just as his TA. Who was I to question it?"

"After Takahashi murdered his pregnant wife and others, then killed himself, do you know if Roxanne got involved with anyone else?" Daphne asked pointedly.

Joshua pinched his long nose. "If so, she never mentioned it to me," he said. "But then again, it wasn't in her nature to talk about her relationships. If you know what I mean."

Daphne eyed him. "Would she have confided in you if she thought someone was stalking her?"

"Probably." His expression changed as if a thought had popped into his head. "Come to think of it, I did get this weird text from her yesterday. Didn't think any-thing of it till now."

"Do you have your phone?" Kenneth asked, assum-ing that was the case.

"Yeah." He took the cell phone out of his jeans pocket and brought up the text message. Kenneth read with Daphne. It said, I'm Still Here.

They exchanged looks as Kenneth remembered the disturbing message left on Roxanne's bathroom mir-ror that this mimicked in part. It apparently was sent by her killer, no doubt meant to double down on being the actual Maui Suffocation Killer instead of an imposter.

After Joshua produced an alibi for the time of Rox-anne Sinclair's murder, he was allowed to return to his class with Kenneth reasonably convinced that he had nothing to do with her death.

Daphne followed Kenneth to a place called Loraine's Grill on Hookele Street for lunch. After they were seated and ordered teriyaki glazed chicken to go with potato salad and fresh brewed coffee, Daphne had to ask, "If that text did come from Roxanne's murderer, what's he trying to prove? That he can play games with people's lives and get away with it?"

Kenneth sipped some water. "That seems to be the gist of it," he muttered. "Appears as though the unsub was counting on the text being discovered through Joshua Winningham's cell phone and the authorities being able to put two and two together in knowing that it was the calling card of the Maui Suffocation Killer. Or, in other words, it seems like the perp is intent on taking credit for the murders he committed, which now stands at ten, not counting the murder of Irene Ishibashi by Ben Hoffman."

"So, how will you be able to catch him?" she asked, as if the police hadn't encountered this type of thing enough to know how to use every method at their disposal to eventually trip up the perpetrator.

"By trying to outthink the killer," Kenneth said bluntly. "That is to say, working hard to figure out his next moves before he makes them. He obviously is enjoying taunting us and probably feels invincible. They all do, till they discover that's not the case and we either slap the cuffs on and haul them off to jail or they wind up dead themselves, one way or another."

Daphne grimaced. "In the meantime, young women like Roxanne Sinclair are left to take the brunt of the killer's rage."

"Unfortunately, it happens." Kenneth sighed. "More often than I care to admit. We can't read killers' minds to stop them ahead of time. But we damn sure can do everything in our power to try and prevent as many deaths as possible."

"I know that," she told him, never doubting the seriousness in which he took this. Especially having lost a close friend to a serial killer. Writing true crime gave her an added perspective on how law enforcement was able to come together through adversity and track down some of the worst criminals, even if the process could be agonizing at times. She was sure that would be the eventual outcome in this instance, too. But until such time, women on Maui were still left to the whims of this psychopath.

Kenneth gave her an earnest look. "I don't want anything to happen to you."

Daphne took that to heart. "Trust me, I feel the same way. But there are no guarantees, are there?" she stated honestly. "No woman wants to see her life come to an end by a serial killer. We can only try to outlast them while living our lives." She realized it wasn't as simple as that no matter how many times she said it. The female victims in her book were proof of that.

"You're right," he spoke calmly. "You can't hide under a rock. Just do me a favor, don't let your guard down, even as you live that life. If something were to ever upend it..."

His voice broke and Daphne instinctively reached across the table to touch his hand. "Don't worry. I'm not a quitter," she promised him. "I have so much to live for." *You're one of those things*, she thought in spite of not knowing where they were headed.

Kenneth relaxed as he squeezed her fingers gently. "Okay."

HE FELT BETTER in listening to her speak with confidence, given the dangers poisoning the atmosphere. Still, as long as a killer remained at large, Kenneth knew he could not rest easily where it concerned Daphne. Though they hadn't known each other for very long, it was long enough for him to know that what he was beginning to feel for her was real and could be lasting, if things were to work out between them. If last night's torrid action in bed was any indication, that was a distinct possibility that he longed to explore further.

After the food arrived, he waited till they began to eat. Then, gazing at Daphne's face, Kenneth said, "About last night..."

She looked up from her plate. "Are we talking about anything in particular from last night?" she teased him.

"How about everything." He gave a half grin, aroused at the carnal thoughts, but resisted going further. "Let's just say, I enjoyed our time together."

"That's a relief." Daphne blushed. "For a moment there, I was starting to wonder."

"Don't," Kenneth made clear as he sliced into the teriyaki glazed chicken. "Just so you know, though, I'm not a fling type of guy." He needed to put that out there for a reaction.

Her lashes fluttered. "And I'm not a fling kind of girl," she argued, sticking her fork into the potato salad.

"So, where is this going?" He angled his face while hoping this wasn't a mistake.

"You tell me." She drew a breath. "We live and work in different states, an ocean apart, Kenneth. I thought we both understood that going in?"

"I do understand," he confessed. How could he not? "That doesn't mean I have to like it."

"I don't like it, either," Daphne insisted. "But it is what it is. Why ruin a good thing by making a big deal out of something neither of us is willing to do anything about at the moment to change the status quo?"

Kenneth chewed some food and grudgingly admitted, "You're absolutely right. My bad. Shouldn't have mentioned it. I overstepped."

"I want you to feel free to say whatever's on your mind," she told him, sounding sincere.

"You, too," he said, still having regrets about causing friction between them. That was the last thing he wanted. Especially when there was enough pressure on them in their professional lives. And his own intent to keep her from falling into the clutches of a demented killer but still respecting Daphne's right to coexist on her own terms while visiting the island. *I can't blow it just because I'm falling hard for her and can't stand the thought of this coming to an end anytime soon, if ever*, Kenneth told himself. But what choice did he have, other than giving in to the reality that she had her life elsewhere and he had his. End of story. He tried to pivot in a different direction and smiled, causing his eyes to crinkle at the corners. "Okay, how about we pretend I didn't just put you on the spot and keep an open mind on things between us?"

Daphne flashed her teeth. "Yes, an open mind sounds great."

"Cool." Kenneth smiled again while already wondering if he could ever be satisfied with a short-term involvement, even if more than a fling. Especially when he knew deep down inside that he wanted to be able to share a bed with her every night and do all the things daily that couples did together. But was this a bridge too far to cross?

THAT AFTERNOON, Daphne went jogging along the Kaanapali Beach walkway, bypassing casual walkers, while taking in the swaying palm trees and endless ocean with waves crashing against the shore. She was still assessing her luncheon with Kenneth and whether or not they were on the same page as far as where things were headed between them. Yes, they agreed that neither were into one-night stands as a substitute for a real relationship. Yet, neither seemed willing to commit to anything more. For her part, she had no strong ties to keep her in Tuscaloosa. But relocating to Hawaii to be with someone who had yet to clarify exactly what he felt for her, assuming it was more than sexual gratification, wasn't an option. She needed more from Kenneth if he expected more from her.

Am I asking too much of him? Daphne mused. Or should she settle for less than what she wanted in a man? She had so much to offer, beginning with all the love he could ever ask for. But she needed the same in return. Would she ever get that from him? She jogged through Whalers Village and ended up on Kaanapali Parkway lined with monkeypod trees. She ran down the sidewalk that bordered the resort hotels and condos, sidestepping a few geckos along the way.

Daphne thought about the murder of Roxanne Sinclair. What were the odds that someone connected to mass murderer Norman Takahashi would find herself a victim of a current serial killer? It seemed more than pure coincidence to Daphne. Yet, she found it a stretch to link the two directly, other than that Roxanne had a bad run of luck on both fronts. *The other connection between the two is me*, Daphne told herself as she crossed over to the golf course side of the street. Had her research on Takahashi played a role in his former lover's death? Daphne couldn't get herself to accept this. Especially given that she had never sought Roxanne out. Never even knew she existed until she was contacted by her.

No, whatever reason the serial killer had for targeting Roxanne, who fit the profile of the other victims of the Maui Suffocation Killer, he was solely responsible for her death. Daphne could only pray that the perpetrator was ultimately held accountable for his crimes.

Just like Oscar Preston and the other killers she had written about.

As she ran up the hill on the sidewalk, Daphne took note of the man mowing the golf course fairway. She guessed him to be in his early thirties, on the lean side, with messy dark hair in a sideswept style. Though he was busy at work on the grass, his eyes seemed transfixed on her. *What's his problem?* she asked herself. Or was she only imagining him leering at her? She averted her gaze and continued past him, wanting to believe she had been spooked because of the latest events with a killer at large.

But when she turned around at the top of the hill and began her descent to return to her villa, Daphne saw that the man was now standing next to the mower, maybe ten feet from the sidewalk, as though waiting for her. He was wearing a uniform and his long arms were crossed as he gave her a menacing look. *Definitely not imagining his dislike for me*, she told herself as a chill coursed through her perspiring body.

Daphne wondered if he had been stalking her. How had she not noticed him before? Moreover, she couldn't help but wonder if he was also a serial killer, using the golf course as a convenient cover. She locked eyes with him and he broke into a laugh as if entirely amused. Or sending her a warning that he was onto her and coming after her. Impulsively, she whipped out her cell phone and took a quick picture.

"What do you think you're doing?" he demanded, clearly unnerved at the prospect of being photographed.

"I could ask you the same thing," she shot back. "Or is harassment part of your mowing duties?"

"Who's harassing who, lady?" His thick brows knitted. "Get the hell away from me, if you know what's good for you."

"I have a pretty good idea what isn't." Daphne didn't need to be told twice. She hightailed it away from the creepy guy, who continued to glare as she put some distance between them, but for some reason she still felt threatened.

KENNETH WAS AT his desk when he got the call from Daphne informing him that she was suspicious of a Kaanapali golf course groundskeeper. All things considered, he took her concerns seriously as she sent him the picture she took of the man. *He does look somewhat ominous,* Kenneth had to admit to himself. Could he have been stalking her? Or worse, be sizing her up for the kill?

"I'll check him out," Kenneth promised in the video chat.

"Thanks," Daphne said. "Maybe I'm freaking out for no reason. Or maybe there's every reason to."

He wanted to suggest she stay at his place for now, but Kenneth had already been rebuffed before and didn't want to put any further pressure on her. "It was the right thing to have me look into the groundskeeper," he said. "Can't be too careful right now."

"You're right. No woman on the island can afford to be." Daphne made a face. "Certainly not the women fitting the profile of those attacked by a serial killer. That includes me."

"You'll be fine," Kenneth promised, forcing himself to offer a smile to that effect. "If you see him checking you out again, or anyone else who gives you cause for concern, let me know."

"I will." She smiled self-consciously. "Well, I have to get some work done. Catch you later."

"All right." He disconnected and wondered if that was an invitation to visit her tonight. Or vice versa? Either way, Kenneth knew that he didn't want what they had to end anytime soon. Wherever that happened to take them. He got on his laptop and looked up the Kaanapali golf course that Daphne described. Kenneth called and spoke to the course manager, Ricarte Ribucan.

After sending him the photo, Ribucan quickly identified the man as Matthew Hamilton, age thirty-four, who had worked for the golf course for two years and apparently given them no problems. When Kenneth did a criminal background check on him, he discovered that Hamilton had been arrested for making threats against a neighbor and being accused of stalking a coworker. Neither charge resulted in a conviction. In Kenneth's mind, that was still more than enough to haul him in for questioning.

Newsome volunteered to do the honors, picking up the person of interest without incident. "He tossed out a profanity or two, but wisely didn't do anything stupid," the detective told Kenneth as they looked at Hamilton through a one-way window.

"Whether he did anything stupid remains to be seen," Kenneth said. He headed into the interrogation room where the suspect was seated.

"What's this all about?" he demanded while running a hand through his hair.

Kenneth sat on a wooden chair in front of him, a metal table separating them. "You make a habit of intimidating women?"

Hamilton narrowed his eyes. "I don't know what you're talking about."

"We received a complaint from a Kaanapali jogger that you were harassing her," Kenneth accused him.

Hamilton muttered an expletive. "I say it was the other way around," he claimed.

Kenneth flashed him a warning look. "You'll have to do better than that. Unless you want to spend some time in police custody."

"Okay, I was checking her out. No harm in that."

Maybe not, Kenneth conceded. For the moment, he was more interested in what else the suspect may have been up to. "So you say," he told him tonelessly. "Problem is, stalking someone is a crime."

"I never stalked her—or anyone else," Hamilton spat. "If she told you that, she's lying."

Kenneth peered at him. "A woman was murdered yesterday in Kihei between five and nine p.m. Can you account for your whereabouts then?"

Hamilton shifted uncomfortably. "Yeah, I was hanging out with my buddies playing pool at Krista's Lounge on Lower Main Street in Wailuku. Ask any of them."

"We will," Kenneth assured him. Then he decided to see if Hamilton had an alibi for the times the other deaths occurred that were attributable to the Maui Suffocation Killer.

By the time he delivered the news to Daphne that evening at her villa, Kenneth had become convinced that Matthew Hamilton was no longer a suspect as a stalker or serial killer, but was still a jerk.

Daphne concurred on the last point. "Glad to know he checked out anyway as having an alibi in not being a serial killer."

"Yeah, that's true." Kenneth sipped the red wine he had brought along. "Better safe than sorry, though," he told her, not taking anything for granted where it concerned her health and well-being.

"Always," she agreed, tasting her wine. "Guess I sometimes read people wrong as far as their intentions."

"We can't be sure what Hamilton's intentions may have been if given the opportunity. He's been warned that if he even looks in your direction again…"

Daphne smiled at him, running a hand along Kenneth's jawline. "Thanks for having my back, seemingly time and time again."

"It's pretty easy to do," he admitted, kissing the inside of her hand. "Especially when your back is so soft and wonderful to touch. Not to mention the rest of you."

"Hmm…" She showed her teeth. "So you like touching me, do you?"

He grinned desirously. "More than I can say."

Daphne lifted her chin and kissed him. He tasted the wine from her lips. "You can always show me, to prove your point."

"It would be my pleasure." Kenneth kissed her this time, returning the favor, making sure it was a potent kiss that was a good start in the romantic business of touching and more. They went into the bedroom and resumed what he had started. After stripping off their clothing and putting on protection in the hope that they might end up in her sleigh bed, Kenneth made love to Daphne. He wanted to make sure she achieved every bit of pleasure he was capable of giving before his turn came to enjoy the total fulfillment he got from being with her.

When it was over and they were cuddling, Kenneth

thought about telling Daphne that he might be falling in love with her. But he held back out of fear that coming after red-hot sex, the timing might not be right. Last thing he wanted was for her to believe it was his libido speaking rather than his heart. Instead, he was content for her to fall asleep in his arms, while Kenneth contemplated how she might take the news and where she stood with the future on the line.

Chapter Eleven

The following morning, Kenneth left Daphne sleeping as duty called. The Maui PD had received a request from the Portland, Oregon, Police Bureau to assist in the arrest of Rodney Okamoto, who had been charged with murder in a hit-and-run collision that left one teenage pedestrian dead and another critically injured. A tip led Portland authorities to believe that Okamoto, thirty-seven, had fled to the island, where he had relatives living in the resort area of Kapalua in West Maui.

It was close enough to Kaanapali that Kenneth agreed to join in on capturing the fugitive. Especially when he had been spotted entering a nearby store on Napilihau Street. Meeting up with Vanessa Ringwald and Tad Newsome in the parking lot, and members of the Maui PD's Crime Reduction Unit, Kenneth had already removed his duty handgun as he asked, "Is the suspect still inside?"

"Yeah," Newsome said. "Been in there about ten minutes. Not sure what he's buying, but he's taking his sweet time doing so."

"Either that, or Okamoto knows we're onto him and is holed up inside with hostages," Vanessa said. "Aiysha's been called to the scene," she added of their hostage-and-crisis negotiator, Aiysha Nixon.

Kenneth nodded. "Good." The last thing they needed was a bloodbath, assuming the suspect was armed. Just as he was about to confer with the Crime Reduction Unit on contingency plans, the suspect emerged from the store holding a bag of items in his hand. He was short with a medium build and dark hair in a buzz cut. Without preface, Kenneth yelled out, "Rodney Okamoto, you're under arrest for a felony hit-and-run. Drop the bag."

Okamoto took a long moment to weigh his options, before doing the smart thing and obeying the order. "Okay, you got me." After setting the bag on the ground, he raised his hands, fell to his knees, and they converged. Kenneth was the first to reach the suspect, slapping on handcuffs and reading him his rights before handing him over to the Crime Reduction Unit for eventual extradition back to Oregon.

"Glad that ended well," Vanessa said, putting her sidearm back into its holster.

"Me, too," Kenneth told her, wishing that were true with all crimes they were tasked with investigating and apprehension of suspects. No such luck. It continued to weigh on him that the Maui Suffocation Killer remained at large and clearly had a thirst for killing that would likely not stop till they forced him to do so.

"I'm checking out some surveillance video near the Kihei Creekside Apartments," Newsome told him as if reading Kenneth's thoughts. "Hopefully, we'll see someone coming or going during the timeline of Roxanne Sinclair's death that will eventually lead to identifying the unsub."

"Let me know what you find," Kenneth spoke routinely while fearing that the culprit had more than likely been able to successfully execute his escape through tried and true methods that had worked thus far.

"Speaking of our unsub," Vanessa said, "I heard that the lone survivor, Ruth Paquin, has returned to work."

"Really?" Kenneth voiced with surprise, believing she would need more time to recover.

"Yeah. Guess her doctors felt she was ready. At least something good has come out of this."

"I agree," he said. "Getting on with her life is the best way to triumph over the type of adversity the unsub put her through."

As Kenneth headed back to his car, he got out his cell phone and called sketch artist, Patricia Boudreau. "Hey, can you meet me at the Manikiki Elementary School in Kihei and bring along your digital drawing tablet?"

"Sure," she answered. "Who will I be sketching?"

"The person who attacked and tried to kill Ruth Paquin. I'm hoping, now that she's back at work, her memory is sharper and she can give us a better description of the unsub."

"Okay," Patricia said. "See you soon."

Disconnecting, Kenneth kept his fingers crossed that Ruth would be up to the challenge. He got in his car and called Daphne, wondering if she was up yet. "Hey," she said after two rings.

"Hey." He liked the sound of her sleepy and sexy voice. "Did I wake you?"

"No," she insisted. "Just enjoying my morning coffee and wishing you had hung around long enough to have breakfast together."

"I'll take a rain check on that." Kenneth welcomed

the notion of having meals with her, day and night. "Had to respond to a fugitive-at-large call. It ended with no one getting hurt, excluding the teenagers the suspect mowed down in Portland."

"That's awful," Daphne moaned. "At least you're okay."

"Yeah." He was much more concerned about her safety, if the truth were told. But he appreciated the thought nonetheless. "Anyway, I'm on my way to see the lone survivor of the serial killer about putting out a new sketch of the unsub. She's apparently recovered enough from the victimization that I'm hoping she can do more to help us find the attacker."

"Good luck with that." Daphne made a sound from tasting her coffee. "I have exciting news of my own. My publisher has booked me to appear this afternoon on the *Aloha, Maui* television show to talk about my book."

"That's great," Kenneth said. "Congratulations."

"Thanks. Every little bit of promo counts, right?"

"Absolutely. I'll try to make it to the studio to check you out."

"Hope to see you," she said. "If not, you can catch it on TV."

"Okay." He hung up and started the car. Dating a gorgeous bestselling author in demand was something he was wrapping his mind around. Were they dating now? Or just enjoying each other's company till it was time to say goodbye?

When Kenneth arrived at the school on Lipoa Parkway, he was met in the parking lot by Patricia Boudreau. In her early thirties, she was tall and slender, with red locks in a pixie cut with an undercut at the nape of her neck and green eyes. "Hey," she said, smiling while clutching her drawing tablet.

"Let's see what we can get from Ms. Paquin," he said evenly. They headed to the front door and showed identifications before being let in and led to the principal's office. Ruth was seated at her L-shaped desk. Next to it was an areca palm plant. Kenneth smiled thinly and, after introducing her to Patricia, said, "Sorry to barge in on you like this, but when I heard you were back at work, I was hoping you could give us a better description of your attacker."

"I can certainly try, Detective Kealoha." Ruth took off her cat eyeglasses. "Please have a seat." They sat in side chairs across the desk. "Heard about that poor young woman who was just murdered. How awful." She gave a weary sigh. "Will this ever end?"

"Yes, it will," Kenneth tried to assure her. "With your help, we'll catch him." He realized this was a tall order. But given that she had correctly rejected Ben Hoffman as the man who tried to kill her, giving them a better visual of the unsub could go a long way.

"I'll do my best," Ruth promised, pressing her hands together as if in prayer.

Patricia opened her tablet before saying gently, "Try to think back to when you first saw your assailant and what he looked like. Even the smallest details would be helpful. Take your time."

Ruth sat back in her faux leather swivel seat, closed her eyes for a long moment and said, "He seemed to be in his mid-thirties, was tall and had a medium build, I think."

"That's good," Patricia encouraged her. "What color was his hair?"

"Dark, maybe black or dark brown," Ruth responded.

"Long? Short?"

"Short."

"Curly? Straight?"

"I'm not sure," Ruth told her. "I think maybe it was short on the sides and fuller at the top."

"Okay." Patricia worked on the tablet. "What about his face?"

"Hmm... It was kind of an oblong face."

Patricia repeated the words as she drew. "What color were his eyes?"

"Dark brown, I believe," Ruth said, wringing her hands.

"Were they more close set? Or wide set?"

"I think wide set."

Patricia held the tablet up. "Like this?"

"Yes," she answered.

Kenneth wondered just how sharp her recollections were, given the brain trauma she suffered. Were buried memories able to be brought back to the surface over time?

"How about his nose?" the digital sketch artist asked. "Do you remember if it was long, short, crooked, fleshy, roundish?"

"I think it was fleshy and had a slight hump as if it had been broken," Ruth indicated. Patricia asked about the unsub's mouth and chin, and with the latter, if there was any facial hair. "Not that I can remember," she was told.

A few minutes later, Patricia said, "Tell me if this looks like the man who attacked you?" She slid the tablet across the desk.

Ruth put her glasses on and then picked up the tablet, studying the digital drawing. She put a hand to her mouth. "Yes, that's him…" She dropped the tablet as if it were a hot coal.

Lifting it, Patricia gazed at Kenneth and showed him the drawing, which he assessed. "Are you sure this is the man who attacked you?" he had to ask, knowing this was not an exact science, even for expert witnesses. And even harder for those victimized to give an accurate description.

"I think so." Ruth swallowed. "It all happened so fast, but that looks like the man in my head."

"Do you recall seeing him at the club you were at that night?" Kenneth asked.

Ruth stared at the thought. "I may have seen him there," she suggested. "If so, we never spoke. Not till he attacked me."

"What did he say to you then, if you can recall?" Kenneth pressed.

She sucked in a deep breath and her voice shook when answering, "You're going to die, like the others."

When they left the building, Kenneth regretted forcing the principal to relive the dark memories, but knew it was necessary to make the nightmares go away for her and the community in general. "Let's get this sketch out there as soon as possible," he told Patricia. "If this is indeed the unsub, we need the public's help in identifying him."

"I'm on it," she said. "Like Ruth Paquin, none of us females on the island can sleep very well at night while this bogeyman remains at large."

"I know." Kenneth gave her an understanding look and thought about Daphne as a temporary island resident. Unless he could change that, once this case was solved.

DAPHNE SAT ON the cream-colored couch on the set of
Aloha, Maui, located on Hoohana Street in Kahului,
with her hair tucked into a low chignon and wearing
a yellow maxi shirtdress and dress sandals. Though
she had been interviewed on live television more than
once, she still managed to get butterflies, as if the entire
world hung on her every word. Of course, she knew this
wasn't true, but still wanted to make a good impression
nevertheless in promoting the book. Beside her was the
attractive host, Betsy Leimomi, slender and in her thirties with hazel eyes and long layered blond hair with
cappuccino highlights.

When it came time for them to chat, Daphne readied
herself mentally as Betsy said on cue, "Our first guest
today is international bestselling true crime writer,
Daphne Dockery. Welcome to *Aloha, Maui,* Daphne."

"Thanks for having me," she responded appropri-
ately.

"So nice of you to come to our little island for your
book tour," Betsy said sweetly. She held up a copy of
The Accident Killer. "I've read this and, folks, it's a real
page-turner. Why don't we jump right in, Daphne, and
you can tell us a bit about the book?"

"I'd love to." Daphne showed her teeth. She gave a
short summary of serial killer Oscar Preston and the
horrific crimes he committed. Or just enough to whet
the appetite. "The book chronicles his life of criminality, the victims' backstories, the system of justice at
work, the trial, the verdict and so much more."

Betsy giggled. "Sounds fascinating. What other tid-
bits can you give us?"

Daphne picked out a few more points of interest before saying, "I'm afraid you'll have to read the book to find out the rest."

"Quite understandable," the host said. She lifted the book again. "Read this. For fans of true crime and gripping narrative nonfiction, I promise you won't regret it." The subject matter switched to Daphne's next book, for which Betsy said coolly, "I understand you're currently doing research on another frightening true crime, one that took place on Maui last year involving mathematics professor Norman Takahashi, who went ballistic and killed a bunch of people, himself included. What can you tell us about this for a sneak peek?"

Daphne outlined the basic premise of the mass murder and suicide that rocked the island, promising a chronicling of events that included adultery, betrayal, pregnancy, mass murder and the killing of oneself. She finished with, "There's a very good reason why the truth is described as more frightening and disbelieving than fiction. Stay tuned."

After the break, Daphne noticed Kenneth. How long had he been there? He sported a big grin, causing her heart to flutter. She hoped it wasn't evident to the host or audience. Otherwise, she might have to explain just how much her feelings had grown for the police detective. Before they had a chance to talk about it and how strong his feelings might be for her.

When the director signaled to Betsy it was time to talk again, she gazed at her guest and said, curiosity in her tone, "As you probably know by now, Daphne, we are currently being terrorized on Maui by a serial killer in our midst, referred to by some as the Maui Suffocation Killer. If you don't know, sorry to have to spring this on you as a visiting author hoping to catch some rays, sand and surf in between researching your next book."

Daphne gave a little laugh. "Yes, I am somewhat familiar with the serial homicides and the investigation," she admitted, glancing in Kenneth's direction, while mindful of sharing any sensitive information.

"Well, that's a relief." Betsy chuckled, feigning wiping her brow. "Now that we have that out of the way, as the author of a string of true crime bestsellers and clearly an expert on serial killers, in general, can you share some thoughts on the Maui Suffocation Killer? And whether or not you think that the authorities are doing enough to catch this guy and make it safe for us women to resume enjoying paradise, without the need to constantly look over our shoulders?"

Talk about being put on the spot, Daphne mused, regarding the second question. But she understood that it was the talk show host's job to push the envelope to keep viewers interested. That didn't mean she was about to step on any toes in the ongoing criminal investigation. Certainly not Kenneth's, as someone she knew was giving his all in trying to nab the perpetrator. Keeping her breathing measured, Daphne made eye contact with him and then faced Betsy, saying to her smoothly, "Regarding the serial killer on the loose on the island, all I can say is that, though it's rare in our society, some men and women do decide to kill people for various nonsensical reasons. I can only hope that this one is brought to justice as soon as possible, for all our sakes." She waited a beat for that to settle before taking on the other question squarely. "As for those investigating these crimes, I'm confident that they're doing everything possible to bring this case to a close. The

Maui PD takes their job seriously, just as I take mine, and with any luck, they'll catch the killer before anyone else has to die."

"Couldn't have said it any better myself," Betsy claimed before giving the book one last plug and saying, "Mahalo, Daphne, for taking time out of your busy schedule to talk with us. We wish you all the best with your latest and future books."

"Mahalo," Daphne said dynamically, shaking her hand and walking off the set. Kenneth was waiting when she got to the back of the studio. "You came."

"Yeah." He gave her a broad smile. "You were amazing."

She cast him a doubtful look. "You sure you're not just saying that for my benefit?"

Kenneth laughed. "Positive. No need to embellish what everyone here believed as well. You killed it."

Daphne sensed that he had second thoughts about using those last three words as she pondered the serial killings that included Roxanne Sinclair as the latest victim.

Chapter Twelve

"I've seen that person before," Daphne said, studying the digital sketch of the suspect in the attack on Ruth Paquin.

"Really?" Kenneth looked at her as they stood on his lanai. "Where?"

"Hmm…" She seemed to strain her mind. "The book signing. Yes, he was there."

"Was he?" Kenneth voiced skeptically, given that the sketch was based on a description that Ruth could have been mistaken with after her attack.

"Yes," Daphne repeated, a firmness to her tone. "I'm almost positive that this is the same man I told you about who creeped me out at the signing with the weird way he was looking at me, like he had a disdain for me or something."

"As I recall, you said you couldn't describe him," Kenneth pointed out.

"I also said I would probably recognize the man if I saw him again," she countered. "Okay, this isn't an actual photograph of him or in a lineup, but it seems to be a pretty good representation, all things considered."

"Uh-huh," he said, going along with it.

She wrinkled her nose. "If Ruth Paquin and I share

a mental image of the same man, don't you think it's worth looking into?"

Kenneth was warming up to the notion. "Maybe."

"I assume the bookstore keeps surveillance video. If so, they could still have video of the signing and a real image of the man in question, who just might be a serial killer when he's not reading true crime books."

"You're right." Kenneth couldn't argue with her logic. At the very least, if they were talking about the same man who attacked Ruth Paquin and presumably ten other women, seeing him on video could go a long way toward identifying him. "What do you say we head over to the bookstore?"

Daphne's face lit teasingly. "I thought you'd never ask."

They drove to the Aloha Land Bookstore and met with the manager, a fortysomething woman named Mireille Lacuesta with brown hair in an A-line cut. "Nice to see you again, Daphne," she expressed, her brown eyes brightening.

"You, too." Daphne smiled, then introduced Kenneth. "This is Detective Kealoha of the Maui PD's Criminal Investigation Division."

Mireille eyed him curiously, shaking his hand. "How can I help you?"

"We'd like to take a look at your surveillance video from Daphne's book signing, if you still have it."

"As a matter of fact, we do," she said. "We usually keep it for thirty-one days before taping over it. May I ask what you're looking for?"

"Not what but whom," Kenneth answered vaguely, adding, "We'll know when we see it, as part of an ongoing investigation."

"All right. Follow me."

They were led to a small windowless room that held the security system equipment. Mireille sat in a mesh chair at a corner desk and started searching through the video. "Let's see what we've got," she muttered.

"Stop there!" Daphne voiced after a short while and Kenneth realized he was looking at himself at the signing, causing him to blush. He wasn't sure the bookstore manager picked up on it. The thought of how far he and Daphne had come on a personal level since then moved him. He only wondered how far they could still go before whatever they had ran its course. "The man we're looking for would be before the elderly woman who should be just ahead."

"Okay. Tell me when," Mireille said, and backed up the video some more.

"There!" Daphne practically shouted as she froze the image. "That's him," she told Kenneth.

"You're sure?"

"Positive. I remember his clothes…and him," she insisted.

He asked Mireille to zoom in, which she did, allowing Kenneth to study the somewhat grainy image better. He could certainly see a resemblance between the medium-sized, dark-haired man who looked to be in his mid-thirties and the digital sketch. Moreover, if Kenneth weren't mistaken, he could swear that the unsub seemed to be making an attempt to avoid staring directly at the security camera, as though he knew precisely where it was located. *Why would he want to do that, if he didn't have anything to hide?* Kenneth asked himself. Perhaps there were more than a few skeletons in his closet.

"Can you go back a little more?" Daphne asked. Mireille rewound and was asked to stop. "Tommy."

Kenneth saw when the man in question handed Daphne his book. "Tommy?"

"That's the name he gave when asking me to write something in the book," she asserted. "It's come back to me."

"All right." Kenneth contemplated this, wondering if this was the unsub's real name and could be used to track him down.

"What's he done?" Mireille inquired. "Or shouldn't I ask?"

"You have a right to," Kenneth reasoned. "For now, he's simply a person of interest." There was no reason to tell her prematurely that they could be looking at the Maui Suffocation Killer paying her bookstore a visit. She didn't pry any further. "Can you make me a copy of this section of the video?"

"Of course," Mireille said.

"Beyond that, I'd like to take a look at your outside surveillance video from around the same time," he told her, hoping they might catch a break and get an even better image of the unsub on Front Street.

"Sure thing," she told him.

The outside video missed the suspect's face altogether, catching only the back of his head and clothing. Kenneth made a mental note to have detectives check the security footage of nearby shops.

"Can you check to see if this man used a credit card to pay for my book?" Daphne asked the manager. "Using the name Tommy, Tom or whatever?"

"I can try."

Kenneth considered this unlikely if this Tommy was

their serial killer, since using a credit card could give away his identity. Something that the unsub had worked hard to conceal. But missteps did occur, even for killers and psychopaths.

As it turned out, Mireille was unable to narrow down the purchase of Daphne's title using some facsimile of Tommy to correspond with the timeline as a credit transaction, leading Kenneth to believe the man in question had likely paid for the copy of *The Accident Killer* in cash. But it still told him that the unsub had decided for whatever reason to buy a book about a serial killer and, at the same time, may have been using it as a means to surveil Daphne as a prelude to killing her.

"So, what happens now?" she asked outside the bookstore.

"First, I take you back to the villa," Kenneth responded equably. "Then we'll see if the video of the unsub can be enhanced even more so it can be circulated with motion and still shots, to go along with the digital sketch of the suspect. Hopefully, this will help lead us to a positive ID and we can bring him in for questioning."

Daphne nodded and frowned. "I hate to think that a serial killer was close enough to touch at the signing, but far enough away to stay hidden in plain sight."

"Maybe he overplayed his hand this time." Kenneth felt optimistic they had made a breakthrough that could pay off. "We'll see how it goes."

After walking her to the door, Kenneth gave Daphne a quick kiss, having wanted to do that all day but resisting the temptation, knowing that the more passionate they became, the harder it would be to ever let her go. Was it too selfish on his part to want her to remain on

the island once her research was over and the danger
that a killer had brought to Maui abated?

DAPHNE WORKED ON her laptop, trying to stay focused
on finishing the preliminary investigation into anything
and everything that played a role in the life and times
of mass killer Norman Takahashi. It was such a tragedy, killing his pregnant wife and his own daughter,
along with two others and himself. This brought back
fresh memories of losing her parents in a similar fashion. Never knowing what it was like to experience a
normal life growing up had shaken Daphne to the core
and made her wonder if such would ever be possible
in a relationship and with a family of her own. Her ex,
Nelson Holloway, had only reinforced her fears that she
was doomed to remain on her own, with no kids to look
forward to doting over.

Then Kenneth had entered her life and given Daphne
reason to believe that what they had was real. It certainly felt that way. At least for her. But though he had
intimated strong feelings for her, until he was more direct on where things stood between them, she couldn't
put her life on hold. Or risk having her heart broken on
sexual chemistry and promising possibilities alone. *I
can't put myself through such disappointment again*,
Daphne mused as she refocused on prepping for her
next book. And weighing on her mind nearly as much
was the ongoing serial killer investigation on the island
that she had unwittingly become a part of. First, with
the murder of Takahashi's lover, Roxanne Sinclair, believed to be by the killer. And now, with the real likelihood that the unsub had brazenly come to her book
signing, potentially posing a real danger to her should

he remain on the loose. But running away from Maui before things were resolved one way or the other between her and Kenneth wasn't something Daphne was prepared to do. Was this a wise decision?

When a knock on the door was followed by the loud words, "Housekeeping," startling Daphne, she put the laptop to sleep and padded from the room in her bare feet, knowing that she did need some fresh towels. The moment she opened the door, having never bothered to look through the peephole, Daphne regretted it. Standing there was someone she thought she would never see again.

Marissa Sheffield looked like her. At least at a glance. She was attractive at twenty-seven, five years younger than Daphne, but the same height and slender build. She had the same heart-shaped face and bold blue eyes that could have passed for blue-green. Her once long and layered black hair had been cut, perhaps to make it harder to track her, and was now in an unruly inverted bob style. She was dressed in a sleeveless beige tank top with tapered boyfriend jeans and white sneakers.

Her wide mouth cracked an amused one-sided grin. "I can see you're surprised to see me, Daphne."

That was an understatement, to say the least. Forcing words to her mouth, Daphne's voice trembled when she said, "How did you find me?"

Before Daphne could react to prevent it, her stalker had barreled her way into the villa, almost daring Daphne to get in her way. Though her first instinct was to run as far as she could while screaming for help, curiosity got the better of Daphne as she went inside, though keeping her distance.

Marissa looked around and marveled, "Hey, this is really nice."

Daphne narrowed her eyes. "Are you going to answer me, or what?"

"Sure." Marissa flopped onto a leather suede armchair. "To tell you the truth, it wasn't all that difficult. On your website, you were only too happy to talk about your book tour in Hawaii that ended on Maui. Then I picked up bits and pieces on your new book deal and plans to write about a murder-suicide that took place on the island. I put two and two together to figure out that you were still here, waiting for me to find you." She giggled like a teenage girl. "Voilà, here I am."

Daphne frowned. "How long have you been on the island?" she asked, remembering the feeling of being followed.

"Long enough," Marissa responded vaguely. "All that matters is this is where I'm supposed to be, with you."

You're sick, Daphne told herself, but didn't dare say it out loud at risk of ticking her off. Who knew what her stalker was capable of? "You have to leave, okay?" Her voice was measured but with resolve. "I'm here for work, not play."

Marissa regarded her unaffectedly. "I can help you. As your personal assistant, remember? Just tell me what you need."

Daphne ventured a step closer. *Maybe if I'm straight with her, this can end peacefully*, she thought. "What I need is for you to leave me alone, Marissa. I thought I'd made myself perfectly clear in Tuscaloosa. I don't need an assistant or friend. I'm hoping you'll respect that and go away. If you do, I won't call the police and report you for stalking me again."

Marissa shot to her feet, scowling, causing Daphne to take an involuntary step backward. "I'm not going back to jail. It was awful in there. If you try to put me there again, you'll be sorry."

I'm already sorry for letting down my guard, Daphne told herself. But she had to stand her ground. Otherwise, she might never be rid of her. Especially since the authorities weren't able to hold onto her. "You don't have to go to jail, Marissa," she spoke softly. "But I think you do need help. Following someone around against her wishes is not cool. I get that you like my writing and all, but this has got to stop."

"No, it doesn't!" Her voice raised a couple of eerie notches as Marissa got up into her face. "Why can't you see what I can? We were meant to be friends. I love your books and can offer my suggestions to make them even better in the future. Don't mess this up for us, Daphne." Her thin brows lowered over her narrowed eyes. "I won't let that cop come between us."

"What?" Daphne played innocent to her direct threat against Kenneth.

"You heard me," she snapped. "I've seen him with you. And I'm guessing he wants you to move here." Her lower lip hung down angrily. "Where does that leave me as your number one fan? We both belong in Alabama. Not Hawaii."

I'm not sure where I belong anymore, Daphne told herself truthfully. If it was to be with Kenneth, she would know soon enough. What was clear, however, was that her stalker was unwilling to take no for an answer. Making her all the more dangerous. "I need time to think," she told her, hoping this would get her to leave long enough to have her arrested. "Can you give me that much?"

Marissa ran a sunburned hand through her hair thoughtfully. "Yeah, I can." Another pause, then a stark warning, "But don't take too long."

"I won't." Daphne pretended to play nice. "So, where are you staying?" That would make it easier to pass on to the police.

"Never mind," she snorted smartly. "I'm going…for now." She regarded her with a menacing stare. "See you later."

On that note, Marissa rushed out of the villa as if she had somewhere better to be. Daphne quickly locked the door and took a moment to get herself together. She had managed to avoid a confrontation that could have ended in disaster. But how long before Marissa came back, crazier than the last time? Or could she be taken into custody first?

Daphne went back into her interim office and grabbed her cell phone off the computer table. She punched the redial for Kenneth and when he answered, she said unsteadily, "You won't believe who just paid me a visit."

"Who?"

"Marissa Sheffield, my stalker from Alabama," Daphne made clear.

"Marissa Sheffield was there?" Kenneth asked in disbelief.

"Yes." Daphne raised her voice. "She tracked me to Maui," Daphne hated to say it. "What's more, she threatened us both." She sucked in a deep breath before stating flatly, "And I'm afraid she means business."

Chapter Thirteen

Kenneth's mouth was agape as he stood inside Daphne's villa before reiterating what he'd asked earlier on the phone, "Marissa Sheffield actually showed up here?"

"In the flesh," Daphne informed him. "She was standing right where you're standing now. Only it was much more unnerving."

"Sorry you had to go through that." More than he could say as Kenneth hated that the unstable stalker had given Daphne a whole new cause for concern on Maui.

"I thought you said Marissa never left Alabama?" Daphne's arms were folded petulantly.

"She hadn't," Kenneth defended his previous words. "At least not at that point. Somehow, she was able to evade tracking and make her way here."

"She's been following me...us," Daphne uttered. "Who knows for how long? Point is, she's clearly dangerous, Kenneth. Unless you arrest her for stalking and, I don't know, violating the conditions of her bail, there's no telling what she may be capable of."

"I agree," he spoke in earnest, troubled that the stalker had threatened him as well. "Which is all the more reason why I'd like you to stay at my place, with a security system, till we can find her. We've issued a

BOLO for Marissa Sheffield, using both her mug shot and your description of her current look, and should be able to take her into custody in short order. Still, it's best to be on the safe side." Beyond that, Kenneth liked the idea of having Daphne close by as long as an elusive serial killer was also on the loose and even more of a threat to her health and well-being. If being accosted by a mentally unstable stalker could do the trick, so be it.

"Okay," Daphne relented. "Maybe it is a smart idea to not ask for trouble if I can possibly avoid it."

Kenneth wondered if there was a dual message in there somewhere. "I do have a spare bedroom that you're welcome to use, if you like." Far be it for him to presume she'd want to share his bed every night, and even during daylight hours, simply because it was something that worked for him for as long as she remained on the island. "I have no problem setting up boundaries, if that's what it takes to keep you out of harm's way."

"Boundaries aren't necessary," Daphne stressed. "But it's only fair that I have my own space, when needed. At least till we know where this is going between us."

"I understand," Kenneth told her. How could he not? After all, he was just as uncertain about what would become of them once she had completed her research and needed to return to the life she'd made for herself in Tuscaloosa. Would she welcome him there with open arms? Would relocating to Maui be out of the question for her when it came right down to it? Now was not the time to tackle those questions but rather get her to safer ground.

"Mahalo," Daphne uttered, stepping up to him and

wrapping her arms around his waist. "We'll have a nice long talk once we're past all this unwanted drama."

"Yeah." He held her close, wishing it could last a lifetime. Maybe it could. If that drama, which included a demented stalker and diabolical killer, didn't swallow them whole. And with it, any hopes for the future.

"Any news on Marissa Sheffield?" Daphne asked Detective Vanessa Ringwald the following morning when she showed up at Kenneth's house.

Vanessa shook her head. "Not yet. We're checking all the local accommodations to see if she's staying at any of them. So far, nothing. But don't worry. She can't hide forever. We'll get her."

"Hope so." Daphne gave her a little smile, thankful that the detective had been nonjudgmental in finding her staying with Kenneth temporarily. Though the idea of it becoming a more permanent situation appealed to her on a serious level, Daphne didn't dare cross over into the realm of thinking prematurely. For one, Kenneth hadn't invited her to stay. For another, the nature of what they meant to one another still had not been defined in terms beyond the surface. So she would wait, focusing instead on the moment at hand. Her stalker was out there somewhere, looking for another opportunity to come after her.

Kenneth, who was holding a mug of coffee as they stood in the kitchen, said, "Vanessa's right, Daphne. Now that we're onto Sheffield, it's only a matter of time before we track her down. In the meantime, I'm assigning an officer to remain outside in case she shows up here, my excellent security system notwithstanding. And should you want to go out, which I suspect is a given, to continue your work or whatever, he'll follow and keep an eye on you."

Daphne frowned. "Is that really necessary?" It almost felt like she was a prisoner rather than someone who made a good living writing about criminals who ended up in prison.

"I'm afraid so," Kenneth insisted. "Best not to take any chances that Sheffield could give us the slip and go for broke to get to you."

"He's right," Vanessa pitched in. "I've seen or heard about cases like this when obsessed stalker fans crossed over into homicidal maniacs."

Unfortunately, Daphne was also familiar with such incidences of stalking that ended in tragedy. The murder of musician John Lennon by Mark David Chapman and actress Rebecca Schaeffer by Robert John Bardo came to mind. She had no wish to become a fatality and yesterday's news by being defiant toward those who wanted to help keep her safe. "Fine," she told them. "Whatever you think is necessary."

Kenneth grinned at her. "Good."

Daphne got a warm feeling inside as she thought of them cuddling last night without the sex, illustrating that what they had went beyond carnal impulses. She smiled back at him and left it at that, while lifting up her mug of coffee from the slate countertop.

When her cell phone rang, Vanessa answered it with, "Ringwald," listened and told the caller, "We're on our way." Disconnecting, she turned toward Kenneth, a bleak look crossing her face. "There's been a report of a woman's body being found at the Lei Motel on Wharf Street in Lahaina. Appears as though she was suffocated with a plastic bag over her head."

For whatever reason, Daphne got a bad feeling that the victim was none other than her stalker, Marissa Sheffield. If true, the thought that she had fallen prey to a serial killer bothered Daphne, making her feel guilty for unwittingly bringing the obsessed fan to the island, resulting in the loss of Marissa's life.

IT WASN'T DAPHNE'S stalker after all, Kenneth knew, as he studied the victim. She was slender and around five-six, sitting in a tufted armchair in the small motel room. Her narrow face was covered by a plastic bag, twisted in agony from being suffocated. Long thin dark hair in a curly down style was swept to one side. She was fully clothed in a floral print V-neck ruched dress and block heel black sandals while wearing an orchid flower lei.

"According to her driver's license," Agent Noelle Kaniho said, "the victim's name is Ashley Gibson. The twenty-five-year-old lived in Westport, Connecticut. Her body was discovered by a housekeeper."

"Based on Ms. Gibson's clothes," Kenneth said, "I'd say she's been like that all night."

"Must have been a hell of a night," Agent Kirk Guilfoyle suggested sardonically. "Gibson had apparently been vacationing on the island, according to a front-desk worker, and was particularly keen on its nightlife."

Kenneth wondered if the killer had followed her from one of the hot spots. Or even left with her, unsuspecting of what was in store. He homed in on what looked to be a burn mark at the base of her throat. "He used the stun gun on her to gain complete control."

"Seems that way," Vanessa said sadly.

"There's no quitting with this guy," Guilfoyle bemoaned. "Not that I would expect the unsub to throw in the towel, as long as he can find victims to asphyxiate the life out of."

Kenneth furrowed his brow. "The Maui Suffocation Killer moniker has definitely gone to the perp's head," he speculated. "He's getting more and more brazen with each kill, putting us on notice that he's very much still in business and having fun in a maniacal fashion." Kenneth was thoughtful. "But since it's likely that we're looking for a man named Tommy, who we now have on video, along with a digital sketch, I think we're closing in on him, whether he likes it or not."

"You could be right about that," Noelle agreed. Putting on a nitrile glove, she lifted the victim's pale hand, studying the long, pink-colored fingernails. "Looks like there's dry blood beneath them. My guess is that it belongs to her attacker. Can you say DNA?"

"Yeah, definitely some DNA there," Kenneth agreed, "most likely from the unsub." Of course, he understood that even if that were the case, they still needed a match to identify the person.

They were joined by the medical examiner and coroner, who griped, "This is starting to get annoying."

"I think it's way past the starting point," Kenneth said, being real about it.

"You're right, unfortunately," Rudy Samudio admitted, putting on his latex gloves. He immediately began his preliminary examination of the decedent, noting the DNA beneath her nails. Afterward, he said, "I hate to sound like a broken record, but the victim almost certainly was killed due to asphyxia sometime between one and five a.m. But she did manage to scratch her assailant."

"Or in other words, Doc, we're talking about another victim of the serial killer?" Guilfoyle put forth.

Samudio nodded. "No reason to believe otherwise at this point, given the similarities between the victims and manner of death. It'll be up to you guys to make the final call."

"It's been made for us," Kenneth spoke bluntly. "Now we just need to stop him before the next victim crosses his path."

As the crime scene technicians took over and interviews commenced with other motel guests and staff, Kenneth thought of Daphne, knowing she had feared the victim was the person stalking her. The fact that this possibility bothered Daphne so, in spite of the danger Marissa Sheffield posed, told Kenneth everything he needed to know about what a special woman Daphne was. Not that he hadn't already realized that before now. It only added to the growing number of reasons why he was crazy about her in a perfectly sane way. He stepped away and phoned her. "Just wanted you to know that your stalker wasn't the latest victim."

"I'm happy to hear that," Daphne uttered, "weird as that may sound."

"Doesn't sound weird at all," Kenneth told her. "You're not the type who would wish a horrible death on anyone. Not even Marissa Sheffield."

"You're right about that. She's become a real problem, but no one should have her life taken away at the hands of a serial killer."

"Sheffield has managed to avoid that fate, for now," Kenneth warned. "Hopefully, we'll find her before the perp manages to target her. Or your stalker takes another crack at threatening you."

"I'm with you on both fronts," Daphne said. "But I think you know that."

"I do." He was beginning to know her all too well and wouldn't have it any other way. "I have to go," he told her and reminded her to be careful while feeling comforted in knowing the muscular and veteran officer he had assigned to Daphne would be there to safeguard her should trouble come her way.

"ALOHA," FRANCIS HIRAGA said to Daphne over the phone, surprised to hear from him.

"Aloha," she responded.

"I don't know if you're interested in this or not, but I'm about to head over to the cemetery to pay a visit to Jenny's gravesite on the one-year anniversary of her death. I thought you might like to come for some added perspective when writing about the tragedy."

Daphne had not expected such an invitation. Her first thought was to pass, but then she remembered why she was on Maui in the first place. She couldn't allow the uneasiness of a stalker and a serial killer on the loose to cloud her judgment as a true crime writer unafraid to take chances. Surely, Kenneth understood that? Moreover, she did have Officer Jose Menendez ready to step in between her and danger. What little she knew of the six foot four brawny and baldheaded fortysomething widower with a horseshoe mustache was that he was a no-nonsense kind of guy and took his job seriously. That was good enough for Daphne as she felt the same about her occupation. She told Francis, "Yes, I would like to see where Jenny is buried." She assumed her mother, daughter, daughter's boyfriend and even Norman Takahashi himself were in the cemetery as well.

"Mahalo," Francis said and gave her directions. "See you soon."

Daphne texted Kenneth about her plans, then hitched a ride with Officer Menendez to the Heavenly Palms Cemetery on Waiale Road in Wailuku, following a slight detour to a local florist, where she purchased a bouquet of fresh lilies. "I'll be right here if you need me," Menendez told her, standing outside his vehicle. Daphne nodded and headed across the grass to the nearby gravesite, where Francis was placing red roses against the white marble headstone.

He lifted and turned when he heard her. "I appreciate you coming."

"Thanks for inviting me," she told him, and set the bouquet beside his flowers.

Francis bowed his head. "Nice of you to do that."

Daphne's eyes twinkled. She glanced at the gravesites of Sarah Takahashi, Donna Duldulao and Lucas Piimauna while noting that Norman Takahashi's grave was nowhere to be found. Gazing back at Francis, Daphne said thoughtfully, "I know how difficult this must be for you." Even now, whenever visiting her parents' graves, she grieved in wondering why their lives had to end in such a tragic way.

"It was a boy," Francis reflected on his unborn child. "We were going to name him Makoa, which means fearless and courageous in Hawaiian."

"It's a good name," Daphne said sincerely.

"Yes, I think so." Francis paused, staring down at his Oxford shoes. He looked up at her. "So, how's the research coming for your book?"

"I'm just about done with it," she answered. "At least the part I needed to do on the island."

"Good." He grinned. "If you want to take a picture of Jenny's grave for the book so people can always remember her, feel free to do so."

Daphne nodded to that effect, but declined, feeling it was unseemly, even if a common element of many true crime books. Some things, she believed, should be left alone.

"I saw you on television," he commented. "I thought you did a nice job talking about your books and the serial killer we're currently dealing with on Maui."

At the reference to the serial killer case, Daphne looked instinctively at Officer Menendez, who was watching them and wouldn't take long to close the gap if needed. Turning back to Francis, Daphne tried to picture him as the Maui Suffocation Killer, but somehow that didn't seem to be a good fit. Or could she be unwisely thrown off by him being an ER doctor who was supposed to save lives, not take them?

"Everyone's a little spooked by such a killer being loose on the island," she told him candidly. "True crime writers who happen to be female are no different."

"Is that why the officer is over there—to protect you?"

Daphne didn't deny it. "You could say that." She saw no reason to mention that the protection was more about a stalker than a serial killer, though knowing Kenneth, this was his way of trying to keep her safe from both offenders.

"Figured as much," Francis said. "Well, you're safe with me."

She gave him a confident smile. "Good to know."

"I will say that I was blown away when the man whose life I tried to save on the day we met, Ben Hoff-

man, was believed at that time to be the Maui Suffocation Killer."

Daphne smoothed a brow. "The evidence seemed
to point toward that conclusion till the killings started
again."

"And Hoffman wound up being a copycat killer,"
Francis contended.

"So it seems," she said musingly, not ruling out that
Hoffman did what he did without any inspiration beyond his own homicidal impulses.

"This may sound odd, and I'm not even sure why I'm
mentioning it, but on the day Roxanne Sinclair died, I
had a voice-mail message from her asking if we could
meet because we had something in common." Francis
furrowed his brow. "She said she'd been having an affair with Norman Takahashi. Before I could call her to
get together, she was dead and they said it was the work
of the real Maui Suffocation Killer."

Daphne processed what he'd just said, again glancing at the officer and back suspiciously. "Did you tell
this to the police?"

"No, I didn't think it was relevant to their investigation," he argued. "It was probably a bad move on
my part."

"You think?" Her voice was thick with sarcasm.

Francis reacted. "Since I still have the voice-mail
message, I'll send it to Detective Kealoha, who I hear
is working the case."

"That's a good idea," she pressed, knowing Kenneth
would want it as potential evidence. Daphne wondered
if the doctor could have killed Roxanne as a way to get
revenge for Takahashi killing Jenny. Or as the Maui
Suffocation Killer getting back on track after Ben Hoff-

man's possible copycat killing took away from the serial killer's infamy.

Seeming to sense her misgivings, Francis took a step back and said, "Just in case you're wondering if I murdered Roxanne Sinclair, I can assure you I did not. I was stuck in the ER that entire day and well into the night. Pretty easy to verify. Same is true for last night, when I understand another young woman was killed."

"Okay." Daphne took him at his word, knowing that Kenneth would follow up on his alibi for both murders. She breathed a sigh of relief nevertheless as it appeared that Francis Hiraga was still grieving the loss of his lover, but was not a killer. Which indicated that someone else was out there continuing to mark women for death.

Chapter Fourteen

Probably the last person Kenneth, or Vanessa for that matter, expected to hear from was Zack Lawrence, the fitness instructor who had once been their number one suspect as the Maui Suffocation Killer. But given that he claimed to have information on the investigation, they had little choice other than to hear him out. Kenneth drove into the parking lot of the Wailuku Gym on Kolu Street owned by Lawrence as Vanessa muttered, "Think Mr. Casanova is just looking for some attention to stroke his ego?"

"We're about to find out," Kenneth said, trying to keep an open mind. "My guess is that Lawrence has no desire to stay on our radar by getting us over here just to mess with us."

"Hope you're right. We've got better things to do with our time than play games."

"You've got that right." Kenneth was certainly in no mood for games. Not when too many lives were at stake as long as a killer remained on the prowl and dangerous as ever.

They left the car and headed toward the gym, bordered by Golden cane palm trees. Inside, the large gym had all the latest equipment and was in full swing with users exercising. Kenneth spotted Zack Lawrence at an elliptical machine, flirting with a fit and tanned brunette-haired young woman, before he left her and approached them, wearing designer workout clothes and black cross-training shoes.

"Hey, thanks for dropping by," Lawrence said casually as if they were old friends.

"Gee, you're welcome," Kenneth responded wryly.

Lawrence grinned crookedly at Vanessa and said, "Nice to see you again, Detective Ringwald."

"Wish I could say the same," she stated, sneering at him.

"Why don't you tell us why we're here, Lawrence," Kenneth spoke impatiently, "and we'll be on our way."

"Yeah, sure." Lawrence looked around the gym. "Let's go to my office."

Kenneth eyed Vanessa and back. "Lead the way."

They went inside a spacious office with modern furnishings and a ceiling fan spinning. "Do you want to sit down?" Lawrence proffered his long arm at a rust-colored velvet sofa.

Both declined and Vanessa said hotly, "You said you have some information pertaining to our serial killer investigation."

"Yeah, I think so." He walked over to his ergonomic T-shaped standing desk and grabbed a sheet of paper, bringing it back over to them. "I happened to see this sketch of the suspect you're looking for on my laptop and realized that I know this guy."

"Really?" Kenneth glanced at the sketch and back.

"Well, not really. I mean, we weren't friends or anything," Lawrence said, shifting from one foot to the other. "I saw him at a couple of clubs where I hang out. At least it looks like the guy."

Vanessa pursed her lips. "You need to do better than that, Lawrence," she snapped. "Do you have anything worthwhile for us or not, beyond some less than convincing belief that he looks familiar?"

"All right, all right." Lawrence lifted his hands as if in mock surrender. "If it's the person I think he is, he came up to me one time and asked what my secret was for getting women. I told him there is no secret. It's as plain as day and tried and true over the centuries. Look good, smell good and give them what they want. Simple, really."

"I don't think so," she snorted. "Not all women fall for that, sorry."

"Don't be." He shrugged. "Win some, lose some."

While he was apparently charming more women than not, with Vanessa being the exception to the rule, Kenneth was much more interested in the other man. "How did he respond to this?"

"It angered him," Lawrence indicated. "He accused me of making it difficult for men like him. I said it was just the opposite. All you needed was to follow the formula and have confidence in yourself. He didn't respond well to that, either." He rolled his eyes dismissively. "Some dudes just don't get it."

"Did he ever tell you his name?" Kenneth asked interestedly.

"Yeah, I believe he said it was Tommy."

Kenneth looked at Vanessa. The presumed name of the suspect had not been made public as yet. This appeared to give more fuel to the likelihood that this was the same man who had come to Daphne's book signing while fitting the description she and Ruth Paquin gave of the unsub.

"Did he give you his last name?" Vanessa asked.

"Just Tommy."

Kenneth peered at him. "Have you seen this Tommy at your gym?"

"No." Lawrence shook his head. "Not exactly the type who was into staying in shape, if you know what I mean. Still, I'm a believer that anyone can better themselves if they're willing to take that first step. So, I gave him my card."

"How generous of you," Vanessa said sarcastically.

Kenneth eyed him. "If you happen to run into Tommy again at a club or he decides to show up here, let us know."

"Count on it." Lawrence ran a hand along his jawline. "Is this guy really the serial killer every woman I know is freaking out over?"

"That's yet to be determined," Kenneth said truthfully. "We count on people like you to help us find him and possibly prevent someone else from dying."

Lawrence nodded. "I'll keep my eyes open," he promised. "And ask around, in case someone else I know has information to pass along about him."

To Kenneth, this would have to do. They left the gym with him feeling as though they had turned a corner in the pursuit of the suspect who went by the name Tommy and seemed to pose a clear and present danger to attractive women with long dark hair on the island.

Outside, Kenneth remarked to Vanessa, "You were a bit hard on Lawrence, don't you think?"

"Yeah, probably," she admitted. "It's not like he didn't have it coming. I've met too many men like him, including my ex, who thought they were all that and seemed to have no problem playing head games with women."

Kenneth understood that she still had a chip on her shoulder from being forced to raise a child alone after her ex-boyfriend absconded his obligations, but all men weren't like him, or Zack Lawrence for that matter. Kenneth suspected she knew that, even if feeling the need to vent. "At least Lawrence gave us more to work with in getting some perspective on this Tommy. If he's who we think he is, the man seems to be taking his own inadequacies out on his victims."

Vanessa frowned. "That's a scary thought."

"Which is why we need to locate him," Kenneth said, a sense of desperation in his voice.

"We'll find him," she said with determination.

As they headed across the parking lot, Kenneth got a call from Daphne. He answered casually, "Hey, how did it go at the cemetery?"

"It was interesting," she told him, piquing his curiosity.

"How so?" He glanced at Vanessa, who was checking her own phone.

"Francis Hiraga said he received a voice mail from Roxanne Sinclair on the day she died, hoping they could meet, given their common ground with Norman and Jenny Takahashi. Francis says they never met and apparently has an alibi for Roxanne's time of death," Daphne pointed out. "Anyway, he's supposed to contact you about this. I thought it might be relevant to the current investigation, one way or the other."

"It is," Kenneth assured her. "Thanks for the heads-up. We'll certainly look into this."

"Okay." Daphne paused. "So, how's the search for Marissa progressing?"

He noted the concern in her tone. "She was apparently spotted loitering outside a supermarket in Kahului. Seems as if we just missed her."

Daphne groaned. "She's hard to catch."

Sounds like someone else we're searching for, Kenneth told himself sourly. "That won't last," he promised, then thought to ask, "How's Officer Menendez's presence working out?"

"Good," she assured him. "He's doing his job, watching over me."

"Happy to hear that." Short of being with her around the clock himself, Kenneth believed that Menendez was a good man to have on the job till they were able to make some arrests.

"My editor's calling," Daphne said. "I should probably get this."

"You should." Kenneth wanted her life to go on as normally as possible under the circumstances thrust upon her. It would be better all the way around when they could operate without the cloud of homicides and stalking hanging over them. Then see where things went. "Bye," he said, and hung up.

"Everything okay with Daphne?" Vanessa asked.

Kenneth brought her up to date regarding the unexpected connection between Francis Hiraga and Roxanne Sinclair.

"Hmm…" Vanessa batted her lashes. "Talk about six degrees of separation."

"Yeah, I know. It's strange. Yet not so much," Kenneth said when thinking about it.

"Could Dr. Hiraga actually be involved some way in Sinclair's murder?"

"He claims to have an alibi for her time of death. We'll have a chat with him and see if there's cause for further investigation," Kenneth told her. "But as it stands, Hiraga doesn't fit the description of the unsub we're looking at, even if the Tommy name is a moniker."

"Good point," Vanessa said as they reached the car. "Still, the way this case is going, one never knows…"

"True enough." Kenneth acknowledged that it was troubling to see some symmetry between a closed case and one still very much open. Was there anything to it? Or was this merely playing into the hands of a ruthless serial killer seeking to add to his number of homicides?

In the car, Vanessa turned to Kenneth and said unevenly, "This is probably none of my business, but what's going on between you and the true crime writer?"

You're right, it is none of your business, he thought. Yet, Kenneth felt the question wasn't unreasonable, considering the time he had been spending with Daphne. He also had a good working relationship with Vanessa, ever astute, and also considered her a friend. "Daphne and I have hit it off," he replied candidly.

Vanessa chuckled teasingly. "Tell me something I don't already know."

Kenneth glanced at her and back to the road. "Guess it wasn't that hard to figure out. She's a wonderful person, beyond the bestselling author."

"Just as are you, Kealoha, beyond the hard-nosed police detective," she told him. "I think you make a great couple."

He grinned musingly. "Mahalo."

"I just hope you don't blow it," she warned.

"You and me both," he concurred behind the wheel. "Long-distance relationships can be tricky, though. Not that we've delved into that much as yet."

"Trust me, all relationships can be tricky," Vanessa said matter-of-factly. "That doesn't mean we don't do what's necessary to keep them going, if the connection's strong enough. I'm just saying."

Kenneth laughed. "I'll keep that in mind. Maybe you missed your calling, Ringwald. Psychologist might have been more apropos."

She chuckled. "Actually, I was thinking that crime writer might suit me. I certainly have my fair share of murder investigations to draw upon. But not till I log in a few more years of detective work to add to that. Anyway, we're talking about you, not me. Go with your heart and the rest will take care of itself. And that's my two cents."

"But worth its weight in gold," Kenneth told her sincerely, giving him more to ponder, with Daphne never leaving his thoughts for long and with good reason.

DAPHNE SPENT THE early afternoon on her laptop, doing an online question-and-answer session as a guest blogger for a popular true crime blog. She tried to keep her answers short and sweet but deep enough to hold the attention of viewers. It was a welcome detour from dodging stalkers and serial killers, though she felt confident that with the Maui PD searching for them, neither would be able to stay on the loose for very long. She knew that Kenneth, in particular, was doing everything in his power to take both into custody. Of course, with the unsub yet to be officially identified beyond a man named Tommy, the hope was that this could be accompanied by scientific and other hard evidence to lead to an arrest and conviction of the serial killer of at least eleven women.

In spite of wanting to see Marissa Sheffield off the streets and out of her life for good, Daphne did find solace in the fact that she hadn't been the most recent victim of the Maui Suffocation Killer as Daphne had feared. *I wouldn't wish that type of death on my worst enemy,* she told herself. Troubled stalker or not. But that hardly meant she wanted to give Marissa a pass for following her to Maui and threatening both her and Kenneth. Even though she was sure he could take care of himself, Daphne didn't doubt that crazy people were capable of doing crazy things, no matter the obstacles. As such, she wouldn't feel at ease until her obsessed stalker had been located and the threat was over.

Until such time, Daphne preferred to focus on self-promotion and wrapping up the research needed for her next book, *A Maui Mass Murder.* Beyond that, there was still a strong possibility that once the Maui Suffocation Killer investigation had come to a conclusion, she would write about it as well, including the unexpected crossover of elements between the two murder stories. She wondered how this might fit in with things between her and Kenneth. Would they be able to move forward at the end of the day? Or would love not be enough to conquer any roadblocks they would surely face if they were to make this work?

Feeling restless, Daphne put her hair up and threw on some jogging clothes, having checked out of the Kiki Shores Villas to stay at Kenneth's house, gladly accepting his invitation to do so as both a matter of practicality and an opportunity to be closer to one another. She peeked through the venetian blinds and saw that Officer Menendez was in his car on duty. Meaning that he would spot Marissa if she somehow showed up at the house.

Stepping outside, Daphne took in Kenneth's beatific property before going for a jog, while marveling at the amazing views of Molokai and Lanai, along with the ocean itself. *If there truly is such a thing as paradise*, she thought, *this is pretty close to it*. She only wondered if that would be enough to keep her on Maui much longer.

Chapter Fifteen

After interviewing Francis Hiraga and checking out his alibi, Kenneth believed the doctor had nothing to do with the death of Roxanne Sinclair. Or, for that matter, the other serial killings, with Hiraga also able to account for his whereabouts. Still, Kenneth found it somewhat eerie that Hiraga and Sinclair were forever bound by Norman and Jenny Takahashi's infidelity and murder-suicide; with Sinclair now a victim of a serial killer, indirectly linking the homicide cases.

Oddly, Kenneth considered that, apart from writing a book on the Takahashi tragedy, Daphne had unwittingly become a part of his current investigation with the prime suspect, a man named Tommy, attending her book signing and potentially eyeing her as a victim. The fact that the unsub had killed Roxanne Sinclair shortly after she met with Daphne was equally troubling to Kenneth, giving him all the more reason to want to keep her safe, over and beyond protecting her from Marissa Sheffield.

I can't let anything happen to Daphne on my watch, he thought with determination, as Kenneth headed to the Police Department's Crime Lab on Wili Pa Loop in Wailuku. Not the way he felt about her. She needed to know just how strong those feelings had become before she left Maui. Then they could go from there as to how she responded, with his hope that it would be positive in moving ahead.

In the crime lab, Kenneth joined Tad Newsome in meeting with forensic analyst Farrah Ueto at her workstation. In her early thirties and of medium build, with jet black short hair in a blunt cut and small black eyes, she had recently worked in the Scientific Investigation Section of the Honolulu Police Department before transferring to the Maui PD. Wearing a white lab coat, she smiled at the detectives and said, "Aloha."

Kenneth, feeling antsy, cut right to the chase. "Were you able to come up with anything from the blood beneath Ashley Gibson's fingernails?"

"Yes," Farrah answered concisely. "We've collected the DNA that Ms. Gibson was able to get by apparently scratching the skin of her assailant deep enough to draw blood. It was not a match for the victim's own DNA, to be clear," she stated.

Newsome angled his face in anticipation. "So, who does it belong to?"

"Unfortunately, we don't have a name yet," Farrah told him. "The DNA profile was submitted to CODIS, hoping something would click in either the Arrestee or Convicted Offender Indices or Forensic Index." She sighed. "So far, the Federal DNA Database Unit's search for a match has not made a hit."

Kenneth frowned, hoping that this Tommy's full name would surface, giving them a direct line to the suspect. "Guess we couldn't get that lucky," he spoke sardonically.

"Don't give up," Farrah told him. "As you know,

these things can take a while. If the unsub is in the system, we'll find him, and then you can make an arrest."

"Can't happen soon enough," Newsome griped. "This killer doesn't know the meaning of taking a break. He needs to be stopped."

"We're doing the best we can," she said. "Just as you are. The moment I hear anything, I'll let you know."

"Okay," Kenneth said, realizing that she wasn't a magician at producing results that weren't there. But he sensed that the unsub's DNA would eventually lead to a breakthrough.

Farrah shared this thought when saying, "His DNA is bound to show up elsewhere. A serial killer can only hide his genetic code for so long. Given the number of people he's killed, it's amazing that his DNA hasn't already produced a match."

Newsome wrinkled his nose. "Yeah, I keep telling myself the same thing. Little good that's done."

Kenneth shared his frustrations while knowing they both understood how this worked. Even serial killers could delay the inevitable for a time. Only in this instance, there was precious little of it to waste before the unsub went after someone else.

"WE'VE GOT A situation here," Jared McDougall said mysteriously over the phone.

Kenneth, who was at his desk, sat up. "What is it?"

"A hiker passing through the north end of my property has discovered what appears to be human remains, half buried."

Kenneth reacted. "Can you tell if it's a male or female?"

"A shoe sticking out of the dirt suggests a female."

Jared sighed heavily. "Needless to say, I'm pretty shaken up about it."

"I understand," Kenneth told him, pondering the sobering news. He hated that his friend should have to deal with something like this in retirement. Never mind the fact that someone was dead, likely the victim of a homicide. "We're on our way."

An hour later, a team of investigators had descended upon McDougall's ranch, homing in on the area in question that consisted mostly of weeds and dirt softened from recent rainfall. While waiting for the remains, still yet to be officially identified as human, to be unearthed, Kenneth took note of the gold ballet flat, darkened by dirt, that seemed to be about a size eight or eight and a half, and certainly appeared to be a woman's shoe.

When the remains were brought up, still intact, a veteran forensic identification officer named Stefanie Chadwick declared them to be those of a human female. As he processed this, what first caught Kenneth's attention was that the head of the badly decomposed victim was covered by a clear plastic bag. Wearing a red cold-shoulder top and high-rise flare jeans, she was slender and, he estimated, about five feet six inches tall with long dark hair. The other ballet flat was still attached to her foot. The similarities between the female and the victims of the Maui Suffocation Killer sent chills down Kenneth's spine.

With this section of the property now an official crime scene, police investigators, FBI agents and crime scene technicians combed the area for clues on what, to Kenneth, was a homicide with far-reaching implications. He estimated that the victim had been deceased for months or more, possibly predating the first known victim of the serial killer around eight months ago. Were there more bodies buried? More victims elsewhere on the island?

Kenneth walked over to the twentysomething female hiker, Gail Broderick, who made the grisly discovery and was clearly shaken up by it. "I've run this route, or close to it, with Mr. McDougall's permission, maybe three times a week," she said, her thick red hair in a mini braided ponytail.

"Have you seen other hikers in the vicinity?" Kenneth asked.

Gail shook her head. "Not that I can recall. I've pretty much had the area all to myself, as I live just up over the hill, and no one comes this way." She frowned. "At least I didn't think so. Who would do such a thing?"

Kenneth could think of one suspect, but saw no need to freak her out even more in saying that a serial killer may be responsible. And could even be one of her neighbors. "That's what I intend to find out," he promised her.

Minutes later, Kenneth caught up with Jared McDougall, who had just been interviewed by FBI Agents Noelle Kaniho and Kirk Guilfoyle. They were standing on grass near Jared's house.

"If you have any more questions," Jared told them toughly, "you know where to find me."

Guilfoyle nodded. "Fair enough."

As they walked away, Jared lowered the brim of his Western hat and said gruffly, "They're treating me like I'm the criminal."

"Just doing their job," Kenneth told him feelingly. He didn't believe for one moment that his friend had anything to do with the dead body found on his ranch as someone who had spent a good part of his life putting real criminals behind bars.

"Yeah, I know," he muttered acquiescently.

"Sorry about this, Jared."

"I can't believe someone used my land as a dumping or burial ground for this poor woman," he said, kicking his boot at the grass.

"Neither can I." Kenneth gazed across the land thoughtfully. "Depending on how long she's been dead, it could have preceded your ownership of the property."

"Yeah, there is that possibility. Still, the fact that it happened at all, and I'm left to deal with it, is a hard pill to swallow."

"I know." Kenneth's brow creased. "Even harder is that, considering the manner of death, she may have been murdered by the same unsub we think killed at least eleven other women."

"That thought crossed my mind, too," Jared said, running a calloused hand across his mouth. "If so, there has to be a way to stop him."

"We're working on it," Kenneth stated firmly, while knowing that only action at this point would suffice. Particularly if the culprit had just raised the stakes even more.

DAPHNE WAS SHOCKED to hear about the dead woman discovered on Jared McDougall's property. More disturbing was the apparent manner in which she died, being suffocated like the female victims of a serial killer. Was there a connection? Or were they two entirely different acts of criminality? "Do you know how long she's been dead?" she asked Kenneth as they stood on his back lanai.

"That will be up to the medical examiner to determine," he responded, holding a beer. "Judging by her condition, I'm guessing she's been dead for some time."

Daphne grabbed the beer bottle and took a drink before handing it back to him. "Any idea who she is? I mean, has anyone been reported missing in the past few months or beyond that?"

Kenneth considered this. "We've had our fair share of women reported missing," he told her. "In most instances, it was simply a matter of miscommunication. Or the person showed up elsewhere, with a reasonable explanation. There was one local woman who went missing about a year ago. The search for her turned up empty."

"Could this be her?" Daphne wondered.

"Possibly," Kenneth said musingly, drinking beer. "She was in pretty bad shape, so it may take a while to make a positive identification."

"Do you think she could have been killed by the same unsub blamed for the suffocation deaths of those other women?"

"Too soon to tell," he said, a catch to his voice. "The similarities are certainly troubling, to say the least. If so, this would open a whole new can of worms. Hopefully, forensics can obtain DNA from the remains to give us some answers."

Daphne found her mind churning as a true crime writer, always willing to consider every angle. "If this was the work of the same serial killer, could the perpetrator be a ranch hand or other employee of Jared's?" After meeting the former detective, she saw him as an honorable man and couldn't imagine him being a killer. Much less a serial killer.

"We're looking into that," Kenneth admitted. "At the moment, we're just trying to wrap our minds around this."

"I understand." She took the beer bottle from him again and sipped. "Did you speak with Francis Hiraga?" she asked curiously.

"Yeah. His alibi checked out." Kenneth took the bottle, drinking from it. "Also ruled out his involvement in the other serial homicides. Seems that Roxanne Sinclair contacting Hiraga that day was coincidental to her murder."

"Glad to hear that," Daphne spoke sincerely. She hated to think that the doctor could have been doubling as a homicidal maniac. Nor was she keen on having to mix and match her current book with a possible new one. "Anything new on Marissa?"

"Nope." Kenneth frowned. "Wherever she's holed up, Sheffield's keeping a low profile. But she won't be able to touch you. As soon as she resurfaces, we'll make an arrest."

"Okay." Daphne had to accept this, even if a part of her was still concerned that Marissa would make her move when least expected. What Daphne didn't know was just how far her crazy fan would be willing to take this. Or, for that matter, how Marissa would react if cornered by the police. *Hopefully, it can all end with no one getting hurt*, Daphne thought.

Kenneth turned her his way and took Daphne's mind off the dark side of human nature with a kiss. She welcomed this, feeling the need to be with him, returning the stirring kiss full-fledged. They took it to the bedroom, and made love with the same passions that had brought them together the other times. Daphne's emotions ran high and when things settled down, she was left to wonder how she could ever return to a life on the mainland that didn't include the entirely addictive, intelligent and sexy man she had fallen in love with.

AT THE MAUI PD's Forensic Facility in Wailuku on Wili Pa Loop, Kenneth watched as the medical examiner and coroner, Dr. Rudy Samudio, was performing the autopsy on the unidentified victim. "While sparing you the grisly verbal details of carnivores going to town on the decedent's remains and rigors of decomposition over a period of time, her actual death was caused by asphyxia that came from having the plastic bag over her head. Given that she was lying in a shallow grave, she was all but certainly a victim of homicide."

Kenneth winced at the sight of the corpse. "How old was she at the time of death?"

"I'd say between twenty-five and thirty years of age."

The age range fit as far as the victims targeted by the Maui Suffocation Killer. "Can you tell if she was sexually assaulted?"

"I need more time to assess that," he responded, "but as of now, I'm not seeing any indication that she was raped or sexually victimized."

"Were you able to collect any DNA?"

"Yes." He lifted the bones of her hand. "It appears as though there is blood beneath a couple of the nails, like she scratched her assailant. Samples of the DNA have been sent to the crime lab for analysis."

"Good." Kenneth could only hope the DNA had not been corrupted over time. "How long ago was she killed?" he asked acutely, his interest more than just in passing.

"Based on the condition of the remains, I estimate that she has likely been dead for anywhere from ten months to a year," Samudio said, examining the corpse while wearing latex gloves.

"Hmm…" Kenneth muttered. *That would make it two to four months before the first known victim of the serial killer,* he thought. Could there be another killer at large?

Samudio seemed to read his mind as the coroner said, "You're probably wondering if your Maui Suffocation Killer got started sooner than suspected. Well, that will take further investigation on both our parts, Detective. But if I'm basing it on the manner of death and the consistency with the murders attributed to a serial killer, I'd have to say it's a good possibility that we're talking about the same perpetrator. Now as to why he would bury this one and not the others, that will be up to you to figure out."

"We will." Kenneth nodded musingly. "When do you think you'll be able to make a positive ID of the victim?"

"We hope to be able to identify the decedent through dental records," Samudio responded, "along with the victim's clothing and a ring she was wearing. These things take time, though. I'll keep you posted."

"Mahalo," Kenneth said, gazing again at the victim and wondering if she could speak to them in terms of clues left behind in identifying her killer. If so, Kenneth wanted to try and hear her loud and clear in helping to bring the unsub to justice. In the meantime, he had to entertain all possibilities as to who the victim was, who decided to take her life and if there was in fact a connection between this murder and the similar homicides currently being investigated.

I don't like where this is going, Kenneth told himself after departing the forensic facility and heading to his vehicle. Why the hell had a young woman ended up buried on Jared McDougall's ranch? Instincts told Kenneth that Jared's hands were clean. But could the same be said for those he employed? Could any of them have decided that the unidentified female's life was worthless? If so, did this feeling extend to nearly a dozen other women? Or had this been a one-off, much like the murder of Irene Ishibashi by Ben Hoffman, a copycat killer, while an actual serial killer remained at large and as dangerous as ever?

Kenneth drove off with these questions weighing heavily on his mind, while knowing that within them lay the answers that would tell him everything he needed to know in solving the case of the latest homicide victim as well as the pending homicides by suffocation that deserved resolutions.

Chapter Sixteen

In the conference room, Kenneth stood by the large touch-screen monitor for his latest update at the meeting of the Suffocation Serial Killer Task Force. He had packed a lot into this and as such wasted no time getting to the nitty-gritty of where things stood. "I don't think I need to convince any of you just how trying these past months have been in working this case. Though we're still not quite at the finish line just yet, the progress made leads me to believe that realization is imminent."

He used the stylus to put the face of an attractive dark-haired, blue-eyed woman on the screen. "Her name is Willow Hudson, age twenty-five," he said. "Last week, Ms. Hudson's remains were discovered on the property of our former colleague Jared McDougall's ranch in Makawao. She was positively identified through dental records, along with the clothing and a gemstone ring she wore when she went missing ten months ago." Kenneth put the image of this evidence on the screen for a moment or two before switching back to her picture. "At the time of her death, Ms. Hudson was employed by the Transportation Security Administration as a screen officer at the Kahului Airport. I'll get back to that later."

He took a breath before clearing the screen and saying, "The good news here is that, after a thorough search of Jared McDougall's property, no other human remains were found, leading us to believe that Hudson's death was a one and done insofar as the location to bury her remains." Kenneth furrowed his brow. "The bad news is we think that Willow Hudson was the first victim of a serial killer named Tommy, and given the moniker the Maui Suffocation Killer by the media, whom we believe murdered twelve women in total by suffocating them with a plastic bag."

He put all the victims' images on the screen together, allowing that tragic reality to settle in before removing all but the faces of two victims. "Through CODIS and the Federal DNA Database Unit, DNA taken from beneath the fingernails of Ashley Gibson and Willow Hudson, the presumed most recent and first victim of the serial killer, were a match. Meaning that the DNA belonged to the same person, whom we believe to be the killer of both women."

Kenneth frowned. "Unfortunately, as good as this news is, it still does not identify the unsub by name. Apparently, up to this point, he's been able to avoid arrest or conviction, where his DNA would have provided an identification." Using the stylus, Kenneth brought up the image of a white male with dark hair in a mushroom cut, brown eyes and a medium build. "His name is Emerson Thomas Gladstone, age thirty-seven. Approximately two months before Willow Hudson went missing, Gladstone was employed at the Kahului Airport as a ramp agent. After Hudson accused him of sexual harassment, Gladstone was fired and said to be bitter because of it. Prior to his stint at the airport, Gladstone was employed as a ranch hand at the very property Jared McDougall owns, but before he purchased the ranch. We think Gladstone had it in for Willow Hudson and this killing mentality escalated in targeting other women of similar physical characteristics."

Kenneth sighed. "We believe that Emerson Thomas Gladstone was selectively using a version of his middle name, Tommy, such as when he attended a book signing by true crime writer Daphne Dockery." He showed the surveillance video of the suspect at the signing, then put up the digital sketch of the unsub with a split screen of Emerson's photo ID while an employee at the Kahului Airport. They were nearly identical. "Gladstone, or Tommy, was aptly described by Ruth Paquin, the only known victim of the killer to survive, as well as by Ms. Dockery and even Zack Lawrence, our original prime suspect as the serial killer.

"To shorten this long story, we believe we have more than enough probable cause to get a search warrant to collect Gladstone's DNA and look for other evidence," Kenneth pointed out. "And to make an arrest, pending the results of our findings."

Martin Morrissey, second in command of the Investigative Services Bureau, stood and said in a booming voice, "You've made your case, Kealoha, and a compelling one at that. You'll get the warrants. Bring Gladstone in before he can do any more harm on the island."

"You got it!" Kenneth took that as a good sign. Now they needed to finish this once and for all. Certain that Emerson Thomas Gladstone was the Maui Suffocation Killer who had terrorized women on Maui for months on end, it was past time to hold him accountable for his crimes of violence. Then Kenneth could turn his attention to the woman he hoped to spend the rest of his life with as his wife and mother of his children, sharing an all-around happy existence together wherever they lived. But first things first. They needed to apprehend a serial monster.

DAPHNE HADN'T PLANNED THIS, but she decided to actually begin writing her next true crime book, *A Maui Mass Murder*, while still on the island. With the research completed and an outline written, it seemed a good idea to do the first few chapters in the comfort of Kenneth's house. She had converted one of his spare bedrooms into a temporary office, which he had encouraged her to do. Though she was a little homesick, they both wanted to spend more time getting to know one another if they were to have any chance at turning what they had forged into a lasting relationship.

Tuscaloosa isn't going anywhere, Daphne told herself as she stopped typing on the laptop to gaze out the large window, where palm trees were swaying and the otherwise tropical setting was inspiring to her as a writer. But she knew that she couldn't remain in Hawaii forever. At least not as long as Kenneth appeared to drag his feet in exactly where he saw things heading for them. Or was she expecting more from her dream man than his reality?

I won't overthink this, she thought. What they had was real. Even if some things still needed to be ironed out like dress fabrics and shirts. She needed to be patient and let things move at their own pace. Fortunately for her, Daphne didn't need to wait to be in touch with her feelings for Kenneth. She was certain that the rest would soon take care of itself.

When she heard a sound outside the room, Daphne assumed it was either the house settling or the wind echoing within, as was often the case. She got up anyhow to check it out, padding across the hardwood floor in her bare feet. At a glance, she didn't see or hear anything else out of the ordinary. *Guess it was nothing*, she mused. Still, though she felt safe there with Officer Menendez outside, along with Kenneth's often masculine presence, something nagged at Daphne that just didn't quite set well with her. Call it women's intuition. Writer's awareness. Or whatever.

She peeked out the window and saw Menendez sitting in his car. No indication that anything was wrong. Yet, why did she feel otherwise? Perhaps it was because her stalker, Marissa Sheffield, had somehow remained at large for days since their encounter, as though biding her time before coming out of the woodwork and going on the attack. Even more troubling to Daphne was that the serial killer named Tommy, who Kenneth had identified as Emerson Thomas Gladstone, a former airport ramp agent, was apparently still on the loose as well. Though his arrest for the murder of Willow Hudson and eleven other women was impending, neither Daphne nor any women on the island could afford to take this for granted. Or lower one's guard.

As Daphne contemplated this and whether or not she should go check on Officer Menendez, or call Kenneth, the power suddenly went off. Fortunately, it was in the afternoon and sunny, so there was no difference in the lighting inside. She wondered if there had been a power outage in the area. Or was it just this house?

I better speak with Officer Menendez and see what's going on, Daphne thought nervously. She stepped into some slip-on flats while haphazardly putting her hair into a low and loose ponytail. The moment Daphne opened the door and gazed directly at the person on the other side, she realized it had been a very big mistake.

WITH ARREST AND search warrants in hand, members of the task force and Special Response Tactical Team arrived at Emerson Thomas Gladstone's apartment complex, Beaubien Gardens, on Lower Honoapiilani Road in Lahaina. There was no sign of the suspect's red GMC Terrain Denali SUV. Believing that he could still be inside, no one was about to take any chances of running into an ambush. While wearing a bulletproof vest, Kenneth took out his Glock 17 pistol from its holster and led the way toward the ground floor unit. He banged on the door and shouted that they were there to execute a search warrant, hoping it would be the ticket inside to apprehend the suspect.

When this was repeated and there was still no response, Kenneth gave the order to use a battering ram to force open the door. As they stormed inside the one-bedroom apartment and across ceramic tile, he noted the sparse contemporary furnishings and untidiness of the place. On a lift-top wooden storage coffee table, Kenneth spotted a copy of Daphne's true crime book, *The Accident Killer*, bringing him back to the unsettling thought of the serial killer suspect being at her book signing. The idea that she had been sized up by him for victimization grated on Kenneth.

"It's clear," Vanessa told him. "Whether Gladstone had a sixth sense or just got lucky, he's not here."

Kenneth frowned, though having suspected as much. "He won't get very far."

"Look what we've got here." Agent Noelle Kaniho came into the room holding with nitrile gloves three firearms. "Found these ghost guns in the bedroom."

"Not surprised that the perp would have illegal weapons," Kenneth remarked of the unregistered firearms that had no serial numbers.

"There's more where those came from," Agent Kirk Guilfoyle said. "In a storage closet, Gladstone has stashed three short-barreled ghost gun rifles, a couple of high-capacity magazines and several double-bladed knives, among other things. Looks as though the man is getting ready for war."

"All the more troubling." Kenneth sighed, realizing the suspect was a greater threat than any of them realized. Not to say that being a certified serial killer wasn't bad enough. It was to Kenneth, and stopping Gladstone cold was front and center for him. "We need to put out a BOLO for Gladstone and his vehicle."

"It's done," Tad Newsome stated. "By the way, we found crystal meth and marijuana in the bathroom. Gladstone's some piece of work."

"Yeah, right." Kenneth rolled his eyes with disdain. "An extremely treacherous piece of work."

"And one whose DNA we now have," forensic analyst Farrah Ueto declared. She was holding two evidence bags with latex gloves. "Took the suspect's toothbrush and used razor. Between the two items, we should be able to extract DNA that can be compared with the matching DNA profiles from an unidentified perpetrator taken from underneath Ashley Gibson and Willow Hudson's fingernails to see if there's a hit."

"Good work," Kenneth told her. "Go get it done and get the results."

"Will do," she promised.

"In the meantime," Kenneth said, his tone deepening to illustrate the level of heightened concern, "all things considered, we have to assume that Emerson Thomas Gladstone is in fact the Maui Suffocation Killer, and is armed and extremely dangerous. Every second he remains on the loose puts someone's life in danger."

In Kenneth's mind, that included Daphne, which was all the extra incentive he needed to go after Gladstone as though his own life depended on it. That mentality was put to the test minutes later when, while on the road, he got a call from Vanessa, who said in an urgent voice, "Gladstone's SUV has been spotted on Highway 30, not far from your place. It may not mean anything, but just thought you should know while we attempt to bring him in."

"Thanks, Vanessa," Kenneth said into the speaker-phone as he tried to keep his heart rate steady. "Officer Menendez is stationed outside the house. In any event, I'm just minutes away, so I'll stop and make sure everything's fine. When you catch up to Gladstone, let me know."

"I will," she assured him before disconnecting.

In spite of wanting to believe otherwise, Kenneth had a gut feeling that the suspect's presence near his house may not have been coincidence. He tried to call Menendez for some reassurance but only got the officer's voice mail. "Come on, pick up!" Kenneth pleaded out loud. When there was no answer, he knew something was wrong. Gladstone, or Tommy, was going after Daphne and Menendez stood in his way.

While calling for backup and emergency medical services to come to his house, Kenneth pressed down on the accelerator, knowing full well that it might be left up to him to save Daphne's life. And in the process, give him and his one true love a chance at a lifetime of happiness.

BEFORE DAPHNE COULD REACT, she felt the stun gun placed on her neck, sending electrical shocks and intense pain throughout her body. Her brain suddenly turned to mush and her arms and legs went limp as she collapsed into the robust arms of her grinning attacker, Emerson Thomas Gladstone. "Nice to see you again, Daphne Dockery," he said amusingly. "In case you've forgotten from your book signing, my name's Tommy."

He chuckled and Daphne felt herself being dragged roughly across the floor and pulled up onto the sectional sofa, where she was put into a sitting position, which she could neither prevent nor control. "Oh, and in case you're wondering about Officer Menendez, he's incapacitated at the moment." Gladstone laughed sarcastically as he knelt down to eye level with her. "Couldn't allow him to interfere with my plans for you, Daphne. You see, ever since I read your book, I knew that I wanted you to join the other good-looking women with long dark hair in death. It's a perfect fit to have a true crime author essentially write her own story for another author to tell one day."

Gladstone chuckled at his own morbid sense of humor and Daphne realized she was unable to speak and couldn't clearly comprehend what he was saying to her. She still retained enough in her head to know that he was a serial killer intent on killing her. If only she could make herself think clearly and move her limbs freely, which were trembling involuntarily. *I don't want to die*, Daphne managed to think. But with Menendez unable to come to her rescue and no ability to contact Kenneth for help, her chances of survival were getting lower with each passing second.

"Before you breathe your last breath very soon now, Daphne," Gladstone said, as he removed a clear plastic bag from the pocket of his gold twill jeans, "which, trust me, will be even more painful than what you're experiencing now, I may as well tell you that it all started with that bitch Willow Hudson. She cost me my job, when all I wanted to do was get to know her. I made her pay dearly for that. Never thought they would ever find her body, but I guess I didn't bury her deep enough to keep the critters at bay."

He laughed. "The other women, including yourself and Roxanne Sinclair, who I couldn't resist killing after she met with you, and to throw you and the cops off balance in trying to figure out just who was responsible, reminded me of Willow, as good-looking snobs or otherwise thought they were hot stuff. And how ordinary guys like me are always ignored by and we're sick of it. I know I am. You're about to join the others, and Detective Kealoha will find your corpse waiting for his return. I'd love to see the look on his face, but I'll be long gone by then. Say hello to Willow and Roxanne for me, Daphne."

He pulled the plastic bag over her head and face and Daphne immediately gasped for air, her lungs on fire. She felt dizzy and even more disoriented, her body aching, when someone came up behind Gladstone and pepper-sprayed him in the face and eyes. As he bolted to his feet, bellowing while rubbing his eyes, someone apparently used his own stun gun on him, pressing it into his throat as Gladstone went down.

His attacker quickly yanked the plastic bag off Daphne's head and she fought to catch her breath and regain her equilibrium as the normal feeling began to return to her brain and body.

Gladstone's attacker went back and used the stun gun again on the serial killer, as though to pay him back in some small measure for his heinous crimes. Only as she gained clarity and heard the person say, "I wasn't about to allow that creep to hurt you, Daphne. Unlike his other victims. Sorry I couldn't get here sooner," did Daphne realize that the improbable person to come to her rescue was none other than her obsessed stalker fan, Marissa Sheffield.

"Marissa..." Daphne managed to get out of her mouth in utter disbelief.

"Yeah." She smiled. "It's me. I tried, but just couldn't stay away."

Even as she tried to process this and get her feet to move, Daphne realized before Marissa did that Emerson Thomas Gladstone had recovered enough from the pepper spray and stun gun and become a threat again. Only, this time, he likely would want to kill them both.

KENNETH ARRIVED AT his house and saw Officer Menendez slumped over the steering wheel. He opened the driver's side door and checked his pulse. He was still breathing, having apparently been shot in the neck, something his bulletproof vest was unable to prevent. "Hang in there, buddy," Kenneth told him sorrowfully. "Help is on the way."

Leaving him, Kenneth recalled seeing Gladstone's

SUV parked just down the road. No doubt for a quick escape. *Please don't let me be too late to stop him from killing Daphne, the woman I love,* Kenneth told himself, sickened at the thought of losing her to that madman. When he got to the back of the house, he could see that the power line had been cut, knocking the security system out. By the time the security monitoring company would have sent someone over to have a look, the damage would already be done. Daphne would be dead.

Slipping quietly through the back door with his sidearm out, loaded and ready to use, Kenneth could hear Daphne utter, "You won't get away with this, Tommy," though her words were a little incoherent. This told him that Gladstone had likely used the stun gun on her.

As Kenneth anguished over this and what else the creep might have done to her, he heard another female's unfamiliar voice say, "Leave Daphne alone. Kill me instead."

Kenneth recognized from her mug shot that the woman was none other than Marissa Sheffield, Daphne's obsessed fan. What was she doing in his house? He didn't get the sense that she had come there with Gladstone. Or was necessarily a threat to Daphne at this moment.

Once he had Gladstone clearly in sight, Kenneth could see him brandishing what looked to be a .40-caliber semiautomatic gun. Daphne placed herself between Marissa and Gladstone and told him firmly, "Let her go, Tommy. It's me that you want."

There was mocking laughter from Gladstone, who said smugly, "Thanks for offering to be her sacrificial lamb, but I think I'll take two for the price of one."

Kenneth begged to differ. "I wouldn't count on that,"

he snapped, approaching him with his gun aimed at his head. "You're under arrest, Emerson Thomas Gladstone, for too many crimes to mention at the moment. Drop the gun and put your hands up. Now!"

"I don't think so," Gladstone retorted defiantly.

In a swift move, catching Kenneth off guard, he turned the gun on him and fired. In a split second, Kenneth dove to the floor, but kept his own pistol aimed at the suspect. Under normal circumstances, he would have taken the offender out with one clean shot between the eyes. But this wasn't a normal situation. The last thing he wanted was to have to kill someone under his own roof. Especially when he intended to ask Daphne to live there. And so, in that instant of reflection and quick decision-making, Kenneth fired two bullets in rapid succession. One hit Gladstone squarely in the shoulder of his shooting arm, the bullet tearing through it, causing the gun to fly out of his hand. The second shot hit him smack dab in the kneecap, shattering his right leg in the process.

As Gladstone howled like a wounded animal and went down in a heap of anguish, Kenneth scrambled to his feet and rushed toward him like a man possessed as Gladstone tried to stand. Tackling him and bringing him down hard, Kenneth spat again, "You're under arrest, Tommy," and clocked him with a solid blow to the jaw, knocking him out stone-cold.

Not trusting that to last for long, Kenneth handcuffed him and stood, only to find Daphne running into his arms. "Is he going to live?" she asked shakily.

"Yeah, he'll live," Kenneth assured her confidently. "Gladstone's not about to get off that easily by dying before spending decades behind bars."

"Good." Daphne winced. "Thought I'd lost you for a moment there," she uttered.

"Not a chance." Kenneth ignored some aches and pains he felt from dropping to the floor as well as taking Gladstone down and landing awkwardly on top of him. "I was thinking the same thing about you," he admitted while checking her out. He could see a small burn mark on her neck from the stun gun.

"I'm fine," she insisted, touching the spot self-consciously.

"We'll get you checked out, anyway," he told her, sensing she had been put through more than met the eye. Daphne didn't argue the point.

Both looked toward Marissa, who suddenly looked like a lost deer in the woods. "What about her?" Kenneth asked warily, wondering how she had managed to evade capture, only to choose now to reappear as someone who seemed intent on stalking Daphne. "Or do I want to know?"

As Daphne struggled to find words, the front door burst open and Vanessa and Newsome ran in with their guns drawn. Agents Guilfoyle and Kaniho followed, along with members of the Special Response Tactical Team.

"One suspect is down," Vanessa stated while glancing suspiciously at Marissa.

"But apparently not for the count," Guilfoyle said in assessing Gladstone's condition.

She smiled satisfyingly. "That's good to hear."

"The sooner he's out of my house, the better," Kenneth told them in a huff.

"EMS should be here any moment now," Vanessa stated.

Kenneth nodded, though frankly he was more interested in making sure Jose Menendez pulled through and that Daphne was given a clean bill of health after her ordeal.

Newsome went to Marissa and, without being privy to the full story, placed her under arrest as a wanted fugitive stalker. Seemingly accepting her fate, Marissa put up no struggle. She looked at Daphne and said contritely, "I'm sorry."

Daphne met her gaze and voiced quietly, "Thank you." After she was led away and they were given a moment alone, Daphne uttered, "I want to help Marissa."

Kenneth raised a brow. "Really?" *What am I missing?* he thought.

"She saved my life," Daphne told him. "Tommy or Emerson Thomas Gladstone tried to suffocate me to death, just like the other women he went after. He confessed to it all like this was just a disgustingly sick game to him, as some type of payback against women who bore some resemblance to Willow Hudson after she rejected his advances. I honestly thought I was going to die." Daphne sighed. "Whatever her faults as a fanatical admirer, if Marissa hadn't shown up out of nowhere when she did…"

"Then I might not have been given the chance to tell you that I'm deeply in love with you, Daphne, and want you to stay on Maui as my wife," Kenneth said, deciding there was no better time than now to lay his heart on the line. He was also grateful that, against all odds, Marissa Sheffield had swooped in like an angel and saved the day. *Will wonders never cease?* he mused.

Daphne met his eyes affectionately. "You do?"

He held her gaze in earnest. "Yes. At least for the next few years till I can put in for an early retirement," he explained. "Then we can move to Alabama, Alaska, hell, even Australia, if you want. Just so we're together and can have a good environment to raise a family, with as many children as you want." He knew she would be a great mother, whether they had one, two, three kids or more.

She took an agonizingly long moment before Daphne flashed a brilliant smile and said vivaciously, "Yes, I'd be delighted to live on the island as your wife and be the mother of our children, Kenneth. Since I'm also very much in love with you, I wondered just how long it would take for you to ask me to stay."

"Is that so?" He threw his head back with an amused laugh. "Apologies for keeping you waiting." But hearing her say she loved him made it well worth the wait as far as he was concerned.

"Apology accepted." She wrapped her arms around his neck. "With respect to someday living in Alabama, Alaska, Australia or elsewhere, I think not. Who wouldn't want to live in Hawaii, on Maui, for a lifetime of joy with my handsome husband, even after you retire from the Maui Police Department, which doesn't need to be anytime soon? Island living may not always be perfect, with the likes of such frightening criminals as Norman Takahashi and Emerson Gladstone marring the Maui landscape from time to time, but true paradise is what you make of it. Right? From where I'm standing, we can make the most of it for many, many years to come."

"Well said," Kenneth told her endearingly. "Yeah." He kissed her on the mouth passionately and then looked her in the eye. "I fully intend to hold you to that for the rest of your life, Daphne Dockery."

She beamed and declared lovingly, "I wouldn't have it any other way, Mr. Kealoha," while punctuating this with another solid kiss.

Epilogue

Three months after Emerson Thomas Gladstone's reign of terror on Maui had come to an end, the Suffocation Serial Killer Task Force had finally been able to close the case and disband. On a Friday night, Kenneth and Daphne went out for celebratory drinks with Vanessa Ringwald, Noelle Kaniho, Tad Newsome, Kirk Guilfoyle and Martin Morrissey at a popular hangout for law enforcement called Ngozi's Bar on Lower Main Street in Wailuku.

"Never doubted we'd nail the bastard," Morrissey argued over his mug of beer.

"Not even a little doubt?" Kenneth teased him, appreciating the pressure they had all been under. But it was never so overwhelming that any of them were prepared to ever throw in the towel and allow evil to prevail.

"None," the Assistant Chief of Investigative Services Bureau maintained. "Not with the experienced and tenacious team we put together."

"I agree wholeheartedly," Kenneth had to admit, tasting his beer.

"Same here," Guilfoyle voiced loudly. "Gladstone

was never going to get away with it. Or keep the killings going."

"Not a chance," Newsome went on the record while drinking beer. "Perps like him are always too confident for their own good."

Kenneth nodded. "Till biting off more than they can chew as it relates to violent criminal behavior."

"He'll need a full stomach for where he's headed," Morrissey laughed.

Vanessa grinned. "Getting a helping hand from a terrific true crime writer who definitely knows her stuff didn't hurt matters any," she said, raising her beer mug to Daphne.

"Hear, hear!" Noelle sang, lifting her beer mug as well, with everyone else following suit.

Daphne blushed. "Not sure just how much of a hand I gave, but hanging out with this guy," she said, pointing to Kenneth beside her at the table, "made it hard not to want to be involved on some level with getting to the root of the crime story." She drank beer. "That's not to say being targeted by a serial killer was anything I would have ever volunteered for."

While this elicited chuckles from the group, Kenneth could only manage a sideways grin. Knowing just how close she came to becoming another victim of Emerson Thomas Gladstone made Kenneth practically nauseous. But the fact that she had survived gave him joy beyond words. "Believe me, Daphne, I never wanted you to have to come face-to-face with Gladstone and in my own house, no less," he said sincerely.

"You had no way of predicting his moves or malicious mind at work," she reasoned.

Kenneth allowed this much. "Beating him at his own game, though, is something we can both take pride in."

"I couldn't agree more," Daphne stated, smiling warmly, and then gave him a kiss to back it up.

"Music to my ears." Kenneth savored this and took a moment to reflect on the investigation. As it turned out, the DNA found on Gladstone's toothbrush and razor had proven to be a perfect match for DNA taken from the suspect. In turn, CODIS had successfully linked the previous unknown DNA left under the fingernails of murder victims Willow Hudson and Ashley Gibson, the first and last victims of the Maui Suffocation Killer, to Emerson Thomas Gladstone. Along with being fingered for attempted murder by surviving victims, Ruth Paquin, Jose Menendez, Marissa Sheffield and Daphne Dockery, and additional physical, documentary and digital evidence to that effect, Gladstone faced charges of illegal firearms and drug-related offenses. It was all more than enough to convince him to plead guilty. In the process, he spared his victims' families and friends from having to relive their nightmares in court.

Kenneth was happy to be able to put this trying investigation behind him to the extent possible, knowing that the effects of such a case that had shattered so many lives would not simply disappear just like that anytime soon. The one person who gave him solace through it all was Daphne, his fiancée and best friend. After never getting the chance to see if things might have worked out between him and Cynthia Suehisa, he couldn't be more excited to make a life with Daphne, who embodied all the qualities he could have asked for in a future wife and mother of his children. In turn, he intended to give her everything he had to be a great husband and father, making his own parents proud in the Hawaiian tradition.

When he'd accompanied Daphne to Tuscaloosa a month ago, Kenneth was more than a little impressed with her upscale townhouse and its rustic furnishings, located near the University of Alabama. Had she wanted to keep it, he would have understood perfectly, only wanting her to be happy rather than homesick. But with her parents having been cremated and no real reason to stay in Alabama, Daphne had insisted that putting the place up for sale and moving to Hawaii was the best thing for her, both personally and professionally. Besides, Daphne knew she could always come back to visit her Aunt Mae and other relatives and friends whenever she liked, with his encouragement.

"Being with you is all I could ask for at this point in my life," Daphne told him persuasively once they left the bar and went back to his house alone.

"I feel the same," Kenneth said, knowing what they had hardly came along every day. He'd seen enough relationships go off the rails before ever getting a chance to blossom. He intended to make sure that never happened with them, no matter what it took.

"Then we'll make the most of each and every day," she said, holding his hands. "That's sure to keep things interesting."

"I'm all about interesting." He gave her a kiss while already thinking of ways to make that line of thought hold up. "And making the days and nights count."

Daphne chuckled. "I guess we understand each other."

"Agreed. Like reading between the lines of a good book by a certain author," he said jokingly.

"I'll go with that." Her blue-green eyes lit and Kenneth took the ball and ran with it, knowing she was a dream he never wanted to wake up from.

AT THE ALOHA LAND BOOKSTORE in Lahaina, wearing an orchid in her hair and plumeria lei around the neck, Daphne Dockery Kealoha sat on the uncomfortable wooden chair signing copies of her latest true crime bestseller, *A Maui Mass Murder.* The tragic tale of mass murder and suicide had received rave reviews and Daphne was grateful to have an editor, Gordon Yung, and publisher that she worked so well with. But she felt even more blessed to be married to a wonderful man for the past nine months, Detective Kenneth Kealoha. Relocating from Tuscaloosa, Alabama, to Lahaina, Hawaii, on the island of Maui, had been everything she hoped it would be, and more. For Daphne, having fun on land and in the water with her husband was a priority, along with the adventurous joys of romance, in spite of the demands of their busy professional lives. They had made plans to start a family after Daphne's next book tour this summer and she couldn't be more excited while trying to decide if she wanted their first child to be a boy or girl.

She gazed up at the handsome face of the last person waiting in line for an autographed book and asked in a level voice, "What would you like me to say?"

He thought about it before responding nonchalantly, "Oh, how about to Ken, the world's greatest husband and most adorable fan?"

Daphne blushed at her husband. "I think I can manage that." She thought about Marissa Sheffield, her one-time obsessed fan, who had stalked her last year before saving Daphne's life in a totally unbelievable and brazen confrontation with serial killer Emerson Thomas "Tommy" Gladstone. After her arrest, Marissa had immediately gone into therapy. Daphne footed the bill, with the criminal charges being dropped in light of her heroic efforts and successfully dealing with her mental health issues. Though Marissa was still a fan of her books, Daphne was happy to see it had toned down considerably to a normal level and from a safe distance.

As for Tommy Gladstone, Daphne was already more than halfway through her next true crime book about the infamous serial killer titled *The Maui Suffocation Killer*. Gladstone had survived his injuries from being shot twice, as had Officer Jose Menendez, who had made a miraculous recovery and was now back at work full-time. Gladstone, who was spending the rest of his life behind bars at the Halawa Correctional Facility on Oahu, had surprised Daphne by granting her an exclusive interview. In spite of still having flashbacks of her ordeal while in his clutches, she had jumped at the opportunity, wanting to get greater insight into the mind of a psychopath that would make for a better book for true crime readers and criminologists alike. Moreover, Daphne had chosen to donate a generous portion of her royalties to organizations that offered support to the families of victims of serial killers, believing it was another way to give back to society.

Daphne wrote in the book and handed it to Kenneth. He looked at it and said sweetly, "Mahalo." He grinned at her while sporting a new look with his short curly locks in a brush back, mid-fade haircut. "What do you say we get out of here, Mrs. Kealoha?"

"That's a great idea, Mr. Kealoha." Daphne beamed

and got to her feet, flipping her long hair to one side. She gave Kenneth a kiss and asked, "So, where would you like to go?"

"Oh, let me see…" He put a hand to his chin thoughtfully. "How about your place? Or mine?"

She showed her teeth. "How about *our* place?" At least for a while, though they had already begun to make plans for having a new house built in Upcountry Maui.

"That works." Kenneth smiled back, sliding an arm around her thin waist lovingly. "Let's do it."

"Thought you'd never ask," Daphne teased him as they went home.

* * * * *

COMING SOON!

We really hope you enjoyed reading this book.
If you're looking for more romance, be sure to
head to the shops when new books are
available on

Thursday 2nd March

To see which titles are coming soon, please visit

millsandboon.co.uk/nextmonth

MILLS & BOON

MILLS & BOON

THE HEART OF ROMANCE

A ROMANCE FOR EVERY READER

MODERN
Prepare to be swept off your feet by sophisticated, sexy and seductive heroes, in some of the world's most glamourous and romantic locations, where power and passion collide.

HISTORICAL
Escape with historical heroes from time gone by. Whether your passion is for wicked Regency Rakes, muscled Vikings or rugged Highlanders, awaken the romance of the past.

MEDICAL
Set your pulse racing with dedicated, delectable doctors in the high-pressure world of medicine, where emotions run high and passion, comfort and love are the best medicine.

True Love
Celebrate true love with tender stories of heartfelt romance, from the rush of falling in love to the joy a new baby can bring, and a focus on the emotional heart of a relationship.

Desire
Indulge in secrets and scandal, intense drama and plenty of sizzling hot action with powerful and passionate heroes who have it all: wealth, status, good looks…everything but the right woman.

HEROES
Experience all the excitement of a gripping thriller, with an intense romance at its heart. Resourceful, true-to-life women and strong, fearless men face danger and desire - a killer combination!

To see which titles are coming soon, please visit

millsandboon.co.uk/nextmonth

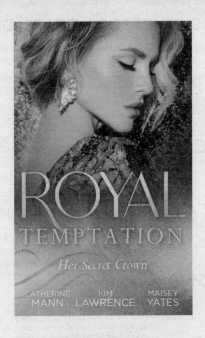

LET'S TALK
Romance

For exclusive extracts, competitions
and special offers, find us online:

f facebook.com/millsandboon

🐦 @MillsandBoon

📷 @MillsandBoonUK

Get in touch on 01413 063232

For all the latest titles coming soon, visit
millsandboon.co.uk/nextmonth

JOIN US ON SOCIAL MEDIA!

Stay up to date with our latest releases, author news and gossip, special offers and discounts, and all the behind-the-scenes action from Mills & Boon...

 @millsandboon

 @millsandboonuk

 facebook.com/millsandboon

 @millsandboonuk

It might just be true love...

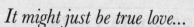

GET YOUR ROMANCE FIX!

Get the latest romance news, exclusive author interviews, story extracts and much more!

MILLS & BOON
MODERN
Power and Passion

Prepare to be swept off your feet by sophisticated, sexy and seductive heroes, in some of the world's most glamourous and romantic locations, where power and passion collide.